Shades of the Past...

Shadows of the Future

Fall, 1967

Also by DH Parsons

Life Ain't Nothin' but a Slow Jazz Dance
Summer, 1966

Not Exactly What I Was Expecting
Fall 1966 –Spring 1967

1967 San Francisco:
My Romance With the Summer of Love

The Muse:
Coming of Age in 1968

The Diary of Mary Bliss Parsons
Volume 1: The Strong Weet Society

Volume 2: The Lost Revelation

Volume 3: Beyond Infinite Healing

Eat Yoga!

Book of Din

All available on Amazon

Shades of the Past ...
Shadows of the Future

Fall
1967

DH Parsons

BLISS-PARSONS
BP
PUBLISHING

Shades of the Past ... Shadows of the Future
Fall, 1967

Copyright 2022 by DH Parsons

Illustrations by DH Parsons

Editing, layout, and design by Susan Bingaman, Bliss-Parsons Publishing, Columbia, MO

Disclaimer

This story is an impressionistic account of people and events in the life of the author as recorded by him from September, 1967 to January, 1968. The names of the participants, and certain specifics of some of the events have been altered for the preservation of anonymity and the exercise of artistic license. The work is based on journal entries and, as such, depicts the experiences and thoughts of the author of that time.

ISBN: 978-1-948553-19-3
Library of Congress Control Number: 2022907242

If you have ever wondered
Who you are,
How you came to be,
and
Where you are going,
then

This book is dedicated to you.

1
Friday

Noon on a Bench in the Quad

Double shifts at the Sunkist Lemon Factory in Corona haven't left much time or energy for much more than eating and sleeping, let alone keeping up my journal. On the other hand, the physical labor has left my mind free to sort out recent experiences and figure out how to put them into words.

The week I spent in San Francisco with my good friend, Manny, an aspiring musician, was fantastic. I met a lot of people, saw a lot of things, and enjoyed a lot of new experiences. I even fell in love more than once.

San Francisco is a big city packed into a small space, and it's filled with all kinds of people. In the summer especially, there seem to be as many tourists as there are residents, and it doesn't take long to learn to tell the difference between the two. In the last year or so, they've been joined by a third group, the hippies, and I got to know them all in that one short week. Looking over my journal entries for the trip made me realize I must have had a guardian angel with me the whole time keeping me out of trouble.

Just getting on the airplane was a radical thing for me to do, but I'm glad I did. After seven days, though, I was happy to be back where I have no fear of being mugged, no concerns about stepping in human waste, and where my friends are sober more often than not. I also don't miss breathing everyone else's smoke — tobacco and otherwise. Even my job at Sunkist is a welcome routine after a week of spontaneous and unpredictable experiences in San Francisco. I will cherish the memories of that trip for the rest of my life.

I don't mind working at Sunkist except that while the job may be regular, the hours are far from it. By definition, summer help is used to fill in when full-time employees take their vacations. I'm expected to work any job and any shift. I frequently don't know what I'm scheduled for until a day or two before I'm needed, and sometimes I work two or even three shifts back to back. Now that I'm back in school, I'll still be on call for weekends and holidays. I'll give Sunkist some credit, though. They hire a lot of college kids, and they treat us pretty well. Even though they work us hard in the summer, they respect our needs during the school term. We work mainly weekends and holidays and are rarely scheduled for a swing or graveyard shift unless we ask for it. The pay is not too bad, either. It's above minimum wage, but even so, $1.65 an hour will hardly pay my rent when I eventually move out on my own.

This is the first week of my third semester at RCC. I'm halfway through a four-semester program that will earn me an Associate of Arts degree in an undeclared major. In other words, I'll be handed a piece of parchment that means absolutely nothing. If I want to do anything other than work in a factory, I need to continue for at least two more years at a four-year college and earn a bachelor's degree in something, and maybe even two years beyond that for a master's degree. To be honest, I'm not sure what all those years in college will actually get me. It seems that many people who pursue a so-called higher education wind up teaching, but how many teachers can the system hold?

The way I see it, the universities and colleges are becoming little more than factories for teaching students to be teachers, who then go out and teach their students to be teachers. What if I don't want to be a teacher? What if I want to be a plumber? College doesn't have classes to train plumbers, electricians, or carpenters. I have heard, though, that RCC has some pretty good courses in auto mechanics, secretarial training, and nursing. Still, this country needs more trade schools and fewer institutions that turn out nothing but teachers and academics. At least English, math, and science have some potential value in the "real world," but philosophy? What kind of a job can a philosophy major get? Who the heck is going to hire a philosopher? What does a philosopher actually do? And what's with the growing popularity of political science? What do you do with that, lead protest riots against the Establishment? Run for office and become part of the Establishment? I don't know how many people I talked to in San Francisco this summer were working on or had completed their degree in political science or something similar. What are they doing besides waving signs protesting anything that represents authority and order, handing out daisies to policemen, practicing free love and eating free food in the park, and sleeping outdoors in their own excrement? Sorry, not for me.

What about art? I think I'd really like to be an artist. I haven't declared a major yet, but I've been loading up on art classes. Still, as with philosophy, the apparent end goal at RCC is to prepare art teachers and not real artists. I don't want to teach art. I want to do art. I want to have a large studio where I can drink a lot of wine, paint pictures all day and all night, and have a girlfriend who walks around topless in the studio and poses for dozens of nude paintings the world will never see — because I don't want anyone else looking at my naked girlfriend.

Art teachers never become real artists — they get stuck in the classroom for the rest of their lives. It's almost as if the universities have an agreement to do nothing but turn out teachers to perpetuate the system of getting paid for turning out more teachers at the expense of the creative spirits that could be encouraged to do amazing things with their lives. I know. I'm ranting, but it makes a lot of sense, doesn't it?

I'm an art student now, but where will I be in ten years? I want to contribute something to this wonderful, capitalistic country of ours. I don't want to march against it. Artists can do much more than teach. Many artists have become engineers, others have worked in commercial art, and some go on to design cars or even airplanes. Wherever creativity and design are needed, an artist can be used.

Beyond that, I believe that art has its own value and doesn't have to do anything.

This semester should be a good one. I don't have any painting classes, but I am taking a sculpture class and a ceramics class taught by Bill Mitchkelly. He was one of my teachers from last year, and he and I have become pretty good buddies. We've had some pretty good times together along with my friend, Jack. Jack is primarily a sculptor, but he also paints. He also likes to cook—a skill he put to good use at a couple of art parties he hosted in his big, convert-ed-warehouse apartment. I've also been to Mitchkelly's house for dinner a time or two.

One day at the end of last semester, Jack and I were sitting on the porch of the sculpture and ceramics house and talking about taking a trip down to Laguna. Mitchkelly—or Mitch to his friends—came out to sit with us. Jack and I invited him to join us for a day at the beach as we had several times before. This time, he surprised us and accepted. Mitch is diabetic, so he doesn't drink very much, but Jack and I agreed to drink enough for the three of us while we were there on the beach. The mere proximity to wine was enough to get Mitch drunk. Jack and I drank the wine, but Mitch got tipsy right along with us. We sat there on the beach, drinking wine, puffing on our pipes, writing poetry, and doodling in our sketchbooks. Mitch, who is usually not given to flights of fancy, came up with some spectacular plans for a life-sized sculpture of a nude Marilyn Monroe set on a wheeled base so it could roll around in his studio while he worked. We had a blast that day.

The three of us spent the next two hours figuring out how to stick a motor inside Marilyn to activate the wheels. After considering and dismissing several creative suggestions about inserting the motor, we decided it was impossible. Instead, we proposed a plan to construct a giant, hollow plaster head of Marilyn that would fit over a lawnmower engine. Yes, it would be noisy, impossible to steer, and fill the room with noxious fumes. But it would be Marilyn Monroe wandering all around the studio. Jack and I celebrated our brilliance with more Red Mountain, and Mitch joined us in spirit. After some contemplation, though, we scraped the whole idea as the contraption would wreak havoc on the content of Mitch's studio.

In addition to the two art classes, I'm also taking the advanced astronomy course. I took the beginning course last fall and really enjoyed it, so I'm looking forward to this one. Unlike the other teachers I've had here, who tend to be casual and are usually on a first-name basis with their students, the astronomy instructor is a more formal academic. He always wears a suit and tie even in hot weather and addresses the students as "Mr. Jones" or "Miss Smith." He introduced himself on the first day of class by saying, "My name is Robert, not Bob, Drake, but you may call me Dr. Drake." He may seem a bit stodgy, but he obviously knows his stuff and always keeps it interesting. Some of the students are a little intimidated by him and just sit quietly and take notes, but not me. I asked a lot of questions in class last year and continue to do so this year. He always listens carefully and begins his responses with "I'm glad you asked, Mr. Parsons," or "That's an excellent question, Mr. Parsons." I believe he's taken a bit of a liking to me.

American History with Fred Garcia, Sociology with Stan Anders, and Psychology with Jill Ocean fill up the rest of my schedule.

Psychology—now that's going to be a challenging class. Not because of the subject matter, but because I'll have a hard time concentrating on the lessons and not daydreaming about Jill Ocean. Yes, that's her real name. I asked her about it, and she told me that her family was from one of the Scandinavian countries. Their original name was totally different and wholly unpronounceable but meant something like "many waters" or "deep blue sea." When her grandparents came to America, it was changed to Ocean. At least that's what her parents told her when she was young. She looks like the Scandinavian goddess, Freya. She is tall and has long, straight, white-blonde hair that hangs halfway down her long, equally straight back. She wears simple dresses that stop just above her knees. Their single solid shades of blues, greens, and purples highlight her fair Scandinavian coloring. Her face is almost too beautiful to look at—perfect ivory white skin with a blush of pink on her cheeks and a deeper rose on her lips. It's the eyes, though. I could get lost in those eyes. They are huge, and the color shifts constantly from green to gray to blue like the ocean she was named for. Her eyebrows are nearly white and almost invisible—she's definitely a natural blonde.

Needless to say, I'll be spending much of my time in the sculpture house, as the regulars in the Art Department call it. I'll keep up with the other classes, but my focus will be on learning how to "do stuff with clay and metal," as Mitch told us on the first day. As I'll be going there right after psychology class, I'll undoubtedly be inspired.

It's a lovely day here in the Quad. It was a hot summer this year, and all of nature reflects that. The big old trees are still in their late-summer dress, and their leaves are green but dusty and dry. Still, the trees are beautiful, and they cast a deep shade on the bench where I'm sitting. It will keep me comfortable for some time while I watch the girls wiggle by in their mini-dresses. Ordinarily, I'd be sitting down in The Pit, the outdoor dining area at the bottom of the giant concrete steps next to the main building. The Pit is an open-air extension of the basement, but a portion of it is tucked under the main building. The building above The Pit extends out over it for about twenty feet, creating an alcove sheltered from wind, rain, and sun. I like to sit at a specific table in one corner at the very back. It has become my spot, and it's especially pleasant on rainy days when I can sit there and enjoy the rain without getting wet. I'm usually too preoccupied to think about earthquakes and what I'm sitting under.

I'm up here in the Quad because someone else is sitting down in The Pit at my table. Apparently, he doesn't know it's my table, although Mitch has told me that the other guy seems to think it's his table. In all fairness, though, I'm sure he staked it out before I did. Mitch also told me that he's an artist—a real artist, not a teacher—and he's actually had some one-man shows not just here in the USA but also in Europe. So, Wow! That's pretty impressive. I feel much better about him stealing my table than, say, one of the nursing students, a mechanic, or, heaven forbid, an art teacher.

Mitch said, "This guy will never be a teacher. He lives art. It's inseparable from who he believes himself to be." I thought that was an odd way to put it—"who he believes himself to be," not "who he is."

The artist's name is Frank Reed. I've seen Reed walking around campus now and then, but we've never had a class together. We have different courses this semester too, so it may not happen this year either. I'd like to meet him eventually, but I must admit that I find him a little intimidating from my position as a young art student. I doubt that a guy like that would waste even five minutes on a nobody like me.

In the meantime, I'll sit here and enjoy the hot late-summer air on my face while I try to sketch an impression of this beautiful Quadrangle into my new sketchpad and hope that I don't have a message from Sunkist waiting for me at home calling me wanting me to work this weekend. It's Friday night, and I'd love to hook up with some art people and maybe have a bit of a get-together tonight or tomorrow night. A call from the factory would eliminate that possibility—again.

Whoa! What the heck was that? It sounded like something downtown just exploded. The college is just a block from downtown Riverside, and it sure sounded like something big just blew up. I hope it wasn't the Fox Theater.

"DH!"

It's Fr. Bob Erstad, a soon-to-be Catholic priest who befriended me last year. What the heck is he doing here? I thought he graduated.

"Did you hear that?" he said, grinning. "Wow, man, I almost peed my pants!"

"It sounded like something downtown just blew up," I said.

"Naw, it was a sonic boom," Fr. Bob replied. "A jet out of March Air Base, I suppose. I heard one last week too."

"Are you sure?" I wasn't convinced. I was still looking for a pillar of smoke to appear above the trees.

"Yep, know it for a fact. I looked up and saw the shiny metal jet whipping by. That puppy was travellin'."

"I guess I should have known. I've heard those booms before out where I live. I just wasn't expecting to hear one here in town. They're louder here, too. Closer to the airbase, I suppose." I shifted my gaze from the treetops to smile at Fr. Bob. "What are you doing here, Padre? I thought you graduated?"

Fr. Bob is studying for the Catholic priesthood at the seminary in La Sierra. He's been taking some art classes here at RCC to round out his education, but he should have finished in June.

"I did," he said. "I got my wings, too," he grinned and pointed proudly at the little white strip of cloth just under his neck.

"Congratulations. So, you're a real Padre now."

"Any time you want to confess those nasty little sins of yours, I'm all ears."

Almost everything Fr. Bob says comes out as a joke or a witty sarcasm. His humor is sharp and double-edged, and I often have to think twice about things he says.

"What are they gonna do with you now?" I asked. "Are they going to send you off to a parish somewhere to get your feet wet? Will you be an assistant under an older priest, or will you be on your own?"

"I haven't got an assignment yet. I wish I could stay in Riverside, but there aren't any openings around here. There are a few spots out in the desert, though. Maybe I'll get one of those."

"That's too bad. Riverside will miss you when you leave."

"Everyone in town will weep bitter tears," he said melodramatically. He wiped a fake tear from his eye and then asked me in a normal voice, "Why are you sitting up here in the Quad? Somebody got your table?"

"Frank Reed," I said flatly.

"Ah," he said, nodding in understanding. "I should have guessed. He's not really a bad guy, but he can be a bit intimidating at first. I kinda like him."

"You actually know him?"

"I told you. I know everybody."

"I remember you talking about him, but I don't remember you telling me you actually knew him."

"Yep. I was in a painting class with him. The guy's incredible."

"A realist?"

"Most of what he does is expressionistic with a heavy dose of abstract thrown in. You know — distorted trees, animals, people, and such. I've seen some of his realist work, though, and it's really good. The guy can paint."

"Really," I said.

"He's been around the block. I don't think he's much older than thirty, but he's shown his work all over the world. He just got back from Spain not too long ago. Took his whole family with him."

"He has a family?"

"A wife and two sons. His wife's a babe."

"You aren't supposed to talk like that, mister Priest man," I said.

"I don't suppose I'm supposed to look at that either." He lifted his chin in the direction he had been looking.

I followed his gaze to see a girl crossing the Quad. She was blonde and gorgeous, and the path she was on took her past the bench where we were sitting. We watched in silence as she approached, passed before us, and receded from view. She studiously avoided making eye contact with us, but she seemed to acquire an extra bounce to her already jaunty step as she walked by. The added swing of her hips gave the hem of her short yellow go-go dress an energetic lift that flashed alternating glimpses of her butt cheeks.

Bob shook his head ruefully and said, "It is gonna be sooo hard bein' a real priest."

"Yep. I'm afraid your lusting days are over," I said. "By the way, what did you say you were doing here today?"

"I didn't," he said. "I'm here because I want to have lunch with Mitch and maybe OK Harry if he's around. Just shoot the bull a little. Maybe see if they want to get together tonight for a little confab, or whatever."

"I was thinking that same thing."

"You still workin' at the lemon plant?" Bob asked.

"Yep."

"Then you better not drink too much. Not a good idea to run all that heavy machinery with a hangover."

"I don't really do the heavy machinery, just the little stuff. Hopefully, I won't get a call tonight."

"If they call, just say you're sick."

"Now you're telling me to lie to my employers. Some priest you're gonna make," I teased.

"If you drink enough wine, you just might be sick. Then it wouldn't be lying," he said.

"Well, at least there won't be any lusting if we have a party. I don't really know any girls yet this semester, so it'll probably be an all-guy thing," I said.

"I know a couple of nuns ...."

"Geez, Bob, you're never gonna make it. I give you six months, and then you'll be knockin' on the door at Sunkist for a job."

"I'm allergic to lemons. Come on, man, don't you know any girls? We don't have to lust over them. It's just nice to have them around to look at. What's an art party without the babes?"

"I'm not a priest. I can lust all I want," I said smugly.

"Don't rub it in."

"There are a few girls in my sculpture class," I said. "It never hurts to ask."

"I bet Harry knows a bunch. He's an ex-marine and you can bet your life he's got an eye for the wicked flesh. I'll run it by him when we do lunch."

"You don't even know if he'll do lunch yet," I said.

"Are you kiddin'? I'm buyin'. Harry never turns down a free meal."

"He ought to be paying for your lunch, Padre. He has a job. You're a poor priest without a priest-dom."

"Priest-dom—I like that. Don't worry, I got some cash. My Aunt Tillie left me a bundle when she passed away a couple of years ago. I'm supposed to turn that all over to the church now, but I haven't told them about it yet. I may just hang on to it for a while."

"You're really starting out on the wrong foot, aren't you? Breaking all the rules before you say your first Mass."

"I'll give them the money eventually, just not today." He grinned and stood up. "I'm outta here. Go round up some girls, and I'll call you later. We can set a time for the confab. You gonna be by your phone?"

"I should be in an hour or so."

"Cool. Later, gator." He slapped me on the side of the head and walked off.

2
A Week Later

The Party at Home on the Patio

My parents are away on a camping trip, so I offered to host the get-together here tonight. They know I entertain when they're gone, and they don't mind. I wouldn't think of betraying that trust. Mother has even started to stock the pantry and fridge with extra snacks and supplies.

The house was deserted today, so even if Sunkist had called me, there was no one here to answer the phone, and it's too late for them to call now. Looks like I'm free for the weekend.

It's just a small gathering. There's Fr. Bob and me, of course, along with the art teachers OK Harry and Bill Mitchkelly, and my sculptor friend, Jack. Everyone showed up about an hour ago, and now we're all sitting out on the patio chit-chatting. The girls I asked from my sculpture class are here, along with a couple more that Harry invited, and a nun. Yes, Fr. Bob brought a real nun.

Sister Teresa is not draped head to toe in the complete black and white outfit usually worn inside her convent. Instead, she's dressed in what she calls her street clothes: a black skirt that falls just below her knees, a white, short-sleeved shirt, black shoes, and a silver pin on her collar representing the order she belongs to. The Padre was wearing a big grin when he walked in with her because he knew he'd got me good. I'm not too worried because these guys are usually pretty considerate with their language and behavior. Still, with the influence of art, philosophy, and a good deal of wine, you never know. I've always had a fondness for nuns. I hope we don't embarrass ourselves in front of this one.

As I mentioned, there are several other girls here tonight—actually, "women" would be more fitting as they are all well into their twenties and beyond. Jenn and Thelma are the two I invited from my sculpture class. The younger of the two, Jenn, has dark brunette hair that does not quite reach her shoulders. It would be much longer if it weren't for the big, bouncy curls that seem to have a life of their own. Her eyes are bright blue, and her nose is not one of those skinny beauty queen noses, but a lovely full one that would be fun to kiss. An oval face, soft round cheeks, and a heart-shaped mouth with red-tinted lips shaped into a broad smile showing blindingly white teeth complete the portrait. Jenn is one of what I call the elite pottery students. I've often seen her throwing pots on one of the kick wheels in the Ceramics House while we beginners are busy constructing chunky vessels from slabs and coils of clay on the other side of the room. I couldn't help but notice her, and not just because of her exceptional skills with clay. Every time she kicks the wheel to spin her bowl, some of the energy travels up her leg, through her torso, and into her well-shaped breasts, which are confined only by a single layer of t-shirt material. The diverted energy is transformed into a mesmerizing side-to-side movement under the thin, accommodating fabric of her low-cut shirt. Needless to say, the quality of my own poor pots tends to suffer on the days Jenn is working compared to the days she is not.

Tonight, Jenn is wearing a light green t-shirt, well-worn Levi's, and no shoes. She really is one of the most beautiful women I've ever seen. She reminds me of someone, but I can't quite think of who. I'm sure it'll come to me.

Thelma, the other woman from my sculpture class, is a bit older than Jenn, but she has that timeless look that makes it difficult to tell just how old she is. She's an attractive blonde with one of those bodies the women's lingerie ads describe as "full-figured." Tonight, she's wearing a dress that, on anyone else, would be pretty modest. It's not particularly low-cut, and it covers her knees, but it's made out of some sort of tan fabric that clings to her curves almost as if it were painted on. When she walks, the motion of her lovely round butt beneath the skin of her dress makes it look like it's trying to escape. Thelma's large breasts are a perfect counterbalance for her ample derriere. She's wearing a light blue, short-sleeved shirt over her dress like a jacket. The buttons are undone, though, so it does nothing to obstruct the view of her enticing cleavage. Do I sound like a teenager here, or what?

Marie, one of Harry's guests, appears to be in her late thirties. Like Thelma, she's wearing a light blue, short-sleeved shirt unbuttoned over her dress, but that's where the similarity ends. Her pink dress is very short, like a go-go dress. I'm surprised that she's wearing brown sandals instead of white boots. Where Thelma's body has curves, Marie is all angles. Thelma's blond hair falls to her shoulders in soft waves; Marie's dark brown hair hangs straight down her back. While Thelma looks ageless, Marie's dress, hair, and make-up combine to make her look like someone trying to look younger than her years.

Harry's second guest is a young girl named Janie. Janie is a rather pretty girl with a long, blonde ponytail. The most obvious thing about her is that she's pregnant—about eight months or even a little more, as far as I can tell. Her belly is quite large, and she works hard to keep her balance. Fr. Bob—always kind and considerate—was the first to greet her as she came out to the patio. He gently took her arm, guided her to one of the more comfortable lawn chairs, and steadied it for her as she settled into the seat, spreading her legs to accommodate her belly and resting her hands lightly on it. Her dress is a lightweight cotton material with a paisley pattern that reminds me of the tie I bought in San Francisco last summer. The bottom part of the dress is quite full and extends to somewhere near her ankles. The "waist" is above her belly, and the top part of the dress, which barely contains her swollen breasts, is held in place by thin straps. Her breasts are massive, and the dark, wet spots over her nipples draw further attention. I guess that's a common problem for pregnant women.

"I'm sorry," she says as she pulls a couple of soaked cloth pads out of her dress and replaces them with dry ones yet again. "My doctor says the baby could come any time now. The sooner, the better as far as I'm concerned. I don't really feel like going out much these days, but OK talked me into it. He said it would do me good."

So, that's the lineup for tonight. Everyone brought something, so there are chips and dips and other munchies along with several jugs of Red Mountain wine on the table at the edge of the patio. Right now, we're all just sitting around sipping wine and engaging in what passes for small talk in this group. I suggested that we go around the circle and have everyone tell a bit about themselves to better get to know one another. Fr. Bob asked us to wait a few minutes so that he could "go do what needs to be done," so we're just passing the time until he gets back. Here he comes now.

"Ah, much better. So, which one of you sinners is going to go first?" The Padre beamed at each of us in turn.

"Why don't you go first, Padre, since you're already on the stage, so to speak," I said. "Tell everybody who and what you are."

"Okay," he said, sitting down again. "I'd think it is obvious what I am," he continued, pointing at his little white priest collar. "But for those who don't know, I'm a Buddhist monk, and I spent most of the past five years on top of a hill in Tibet spinning prayer wheels." He grinned as his response produced the desired snickers and groans.

"Where are you stationed, Father Bob?" Is that the correct term?" Thelma asked, bringing him back to the topic at hand.

"Works for me," The Padre grinned. "But I have no idea. I just got the collar a few weeks ago, but I don't have an assignment yet."

"Are you an artist too, like these other fellows here?" Thelma asked.

"I love art. Dabble in it whenever I can."

"Do you paint?"

"That's about all I can do. They won't let me do sculpture at the seminary—there's really no space for it. Sculpting is a pretty messy business if you do it the way it should be done. Ain't that right, Mitch?"

"It can be," Mitch agreed. "If you're doing pottery or clay sculpture of any kind, the process gets sloppy fast," he added.

Mitch is in his forties. His black, salt-and-pepper hair is wavy and curls around his collar in the back. He's skinny and diabetic, so he generally avoids alcohol. I have seen him drink wine at art parties, but it's usually mixed with a lot of water, and he sips it slowly like he's doing tonight.

Father Bob continued, "I'm afraid if I started sloppin' clay all over the place, they'd kick me out of the priesthood, and if I ever do get kicked out of the priesthood, I want it to be for something a bit more spectacular than that."

Even Sister Teresa laughed at that.

"That's really all there is for me right now," Father Bob said. "I paint, and I do the priest thing. Other than that, I like to talk, discuss, argue, and be generally obnoxious. Ask me again after I get a year or so of priesting under my belt."

"I'm looking forward to it," I said quietly.

The Padre turned to Sister Teresa and said, "Sister, why don't you go next."

"You're a hard act to follow, Father," she said. "I'm afraid I don't have much to add to the conversation. As you all can see, I'm in the religion business, like Father, but I do nun things. There are several other nuns besides myself attached to the seminary—mostly as teachers in the elementary school, but we do other things, as well. I teach third and fourth grades, but I also help tend the gardens—really more of a hobby than a chore. Whenever there is a social gathering, open house, or some such thing, we nuns arrange it and make sure it comes off smoothly."

"You washed my car last week," Father Bob smiled.

"Yes, we did. It was not required, but it was a good excuse to have fun on a lovely day."

"They did a good job, too," Father Bob informed the rest of us.

"Pardon me, Sister," Harry interjected. "Do you mind if I ask how long you have been a nun? You look quite young."

Sr. Teresa smiled at him and said, "I don't mind at all. I've been a nun for almost twenty years, and I was thirty-eight last Monday."

Almost everyone registered some level of surprise as we all believed her to be much younger. She looks like a teenager.

"You do look young," I said. "I took you for about twenty at the most."

"Well, thank you. All women past a certain age like hearing they look younger — even nuns."

"Many of the nuns I have known look younger than their years," Fr. Bob said. "A nun's life isn't an easy one. Much of what they are called to do involves a lot of stress and hard labor. I think their spiritual life and commitment to God give them that ageless quality."

That seemed to leave Sr. Teresa speechless and a little embarrassed. Jenn filled in the awkward gap by asking, "Do you do art, Sister?"

"A little, but most of what I do is what one would call crafts. I'm always trying out ideas for projects my students can do. Keeping third and fourth graders engaged mentally and physically is a real challenge."

"Well, I like you both," Thelma said. "Father Bob, you're probably the goofiest priest I've ever met. I have a lot of respect for you, though, and for what you do — or in your case, what you plan to do. I couldn't give up my life and live the kind of life either of you lives. And you, Sister Teresa — you're such a cute little thing. Isn't it tough giving up certainly worldly things ... like men ... and dating ... and ... you know ...?"

Fr. Bob leaned toward Sr. Teresa and said in a loud stage whisper, "She means sex, Sister."

"Our order takes good care of us, so we don't have many of what you might call worldly needs," she said after giving The Padre a big eye roll. "It's not like we live a cloistered life. Some still do, you know. We have contact with the public. We go shopping and see a movie now and then. We even have a television in our recreation room. Heavens, I'm here tonight with the permission of my Mother Superior. As for the other ..." She dropped her head and pretended to look at her hands. "Well, I'd be lying if I said I did not have the occasional fantasy or daydream."

Jack looked up from the ever-present piece of sculptor's wax he had been kneading in his right hand. He studied Sr. Teresa intently before going back to the little wax figure he was working on.

"So, who wants to go next?" I asked quickly to move past the awkward moment. "Everybody here knows Mitch and Harry, so I guess they don't have to say anything, but Thelma, Jenn, and Jack—"

"I'll pass," Jack said. "Everybody knows me too. What you see is what you get."

Jack is a man of few words. I've known him for about a year and attended a few parties with him. He's always the guy sitting on the edge of the action, watching rather than doing, listening rather than talking. I respect that, but it does tend to make some people uncomfortable.

"I'll go next," Thelma said. "I'm a few years older than Sr. Teresa, but, unlike her, I'm afraid it shows. I like art, especially ceramics, and I think I'm pretty good at it." She looked at Mitch as if seeking his agreement.

Mitch nodded his head. "She is. She's one of my best students," he confirmed.

"I'm holding down my day job, though. I'm an accountant at the Harris store in the mall. I'm not married, I have no kids—it's just me, short and sweet."

"You mean your explanation was short and sweet, or you're personally short and sweet?" Jack asked with a glint of humor in his ice-blue eyes.

"Both," Thelma replied cheerily. Then she looked directly at Jack, and her voice took on a huskier tone when she said, "We can discuss it later if you'd like."

Fr. Bob looked from one to the other and said, "Just remember, you two, there's a priest here ... *and* a nun."

I cleared my throat and asked Jenn, who is sitting next to Thelma, "How about you? I've seen you in the Ceramics House, so I know you're into art."

Jenn smiled and said, "Yes, I've seen you seeing me there."

"Uh oh ..." I stuttered.

"Well, like Thelma and Sr. Teresa, I'm old enough to have had some experience in life. I love art, and I do a lot of ceramics, but I mainly like to paint and draw."

"When are you gonna take one of my classes?" Harry asked her. I'm sure he'd love to have Jenn in his class. She is physically attractive, but more than that, something about her tells me she really has had some experiences in her life. I have a feeling she has more than a few stories she could tell.

"I tried to get in this semester, but all your classes were full," Jenn told Harry.

"Sorry about that. If you're around next semester, let me know, and I'll make sure to get you in."

Jenn smiled at Harry and said, "Thank you. I'd appreciate that."

"So, Jenn," Fr. Bob said, "art can be a pretty expensive hobby. What do you do to pay the bills?"

"I'm a cop." She paused just long enough for us to respond with various expressions of interest and surprise. "I'm a detective," she continued. "I investigate burglaries and homicides." That statement really caught our interest.

"I'm impressed," I said. "Do you carry a gun?"

"I do."

"Even now? Here at our party?"

"Yep. It's under my shirt in the back. I never know when I'll be called to go after a bad guy."

"Wow. I've never had a cop at one of my parties before."

"As long as you're all law-abiding citizens, you don't have anything to worry about." She looked at me and winked.

"Uh-oh," I said, glancing guiltily at the mug of wine in my hand.

I'm still a year shy of being "legal."

"Don't worry," Jenn said. "I don't tattle on my friends. Just don't do anything stupid—like drive."

"Well then, I'm glad I'm your friend," I said.

She smiled enigmatically and said, "I'm sure you will be."

I thought it wise to move along before things got more complicated with Jenn, so I looked at Marie and said, "And that brings us to Marie. Harry talked you into coming tonight, didn't he?"

"He did," she said. "I turned down two other invites for this."

"Why did you do that?" Jack asked. "Surely, just about anything would have been more exciting than this."

"Harry said this would be a small gathering with good conversation," Marie said. "I'm not into excitement. I'm into things like this—sitting out under the stars on a warm night, sipping wine, and talking about silly things with friends."

Fr. Bob raised his mug of wine and said, "I'll drink to that." Then he drank down a large portion of the mug's contents.

"I'm just a country girl at heart," Marie continued. "I was born in a little town in Kansas named Howard, so Riverside is big enough for me."

"I was born in Kansas," I said. "And Howard is my middle name."

She smiled and said, "Small world. What town?"

"Winfield."

"That's not too far from Howard down in the southeast corner."

"Yep. It's also not too far from Parsons and another tiny town called Dennis."

"What an interesting coincidence," Marie said. "It's always nice to meet a fellow Jayhawker."

"Are jayhawks real birds?" Fr. Bob asked.

"No," I answered. "They're a mythical bird that combines the noisy, quarrelsome, thieving qualities of blue jays with those of the sparrow hawk, a courageous and cunning hunter."

"The origin of the actual word is difficult to pin down, but Jayhawkers go back to before the Civil War," Marie explained.

"When people think about Civil War Battles, most imagine vast armies of Blue and Gray going head-to-head in places like Gettysburg or Bull Run. In reality, the war started almost a decade before along the Kansas-Missouri border between bands of marauders backed by pro-slavery and anti-slavery supporters. These rough gangs fought to determine whether Kansas would enter the Union as a free state or a slave state. The free-state fighters became known as Jayhawkers, and the pro-slavery fighters were called Bushwhackers. Even with such lofty goals, they both employed the same brutal guerrilla tactics — and heaven help the innocent bystanders who got in their way. Anyway, since the Union won and the Confederacy lost, the image of the Jayhawk was elevated to represent bravery, cunning, tenacity, and dedication to independence and freedom at all costs.

"That's fascinating, Marie," Fr. Bob said. "I guess I should have paid more attention in history class."

"I was a history major before I went to law school and did my senior thesis on what they call the Border Wars. The Civil War is far more complex than most people realize, and you can still feel its effects on the social structure of many of the small towns in southeast Kansas and southern Missouri.

"So, you're a lawyer, Marie?" Mitch asked.

"Yes, I'm a prosecutor out of the DA's office." Marie looked at the detective and said, "I just realized that I've had you in the witness chair a time or two, Jenn. It's funny how you don't recognize someone when you see them where you don't expect them."

Jenn laughed and said, "That's for sure. I just now figured out who you are, too. You've grilled me thoroughly on several occasions. You're good."

I happened to look over at Jack. He seemed to have forgotten his little wax figure and was paying close attention to the conversation. I don't think I've ever seen him this interested in the people around him before.

Marie stood up and walked over to the refreshment table.

She refilled her mug and said, "Would anyone else like more wine while I'm up?"

OK Harry and Fr. Bob answered by raising their mugs and saying, "Yes, please," like kids when asked if they want more ice cream.

While Marie was busy pouring wine, Sr. Teresa turned to me and said, "So, DH, what about you? What are you all about? Are you a Catholic?"

Everyone looked at me expectantly. Mitch and Fr. Bob both grinned as they knew that as much as I like asking others about themselves, I'm not that comfortable when the tables are turned.

"Always looking for newbies, aren't you, Sister?" The Padre said to her.

"I was just curious," she answered.

"Nuns get a bonus in their paychecks every time they snag a soul for the Church," Fr. Bob explained to the group. The Sister punched him lightly in his shoulder.

"No, Sister Teresa, I'm not a Catholic. I grew up a Southern Baptist boy. My grandparents are very devout. Granddad's a deacon in the church that he built with his own hands."

"Really? Well, that's something then."

"Yep, he's been building and fixing things all his life. He even built a little bedroom for me in the garage over there." I tilted my head to indicate the structure attached to the house by the breezeway.

"He calls it The Hole," Jack said.

"The what?" Jenn asked.

"He calls his room The Hole," Mitch repeated. "We've all been in there. It's quite a place."

"Oh, come on, you guys." This is all getting a bit too personal.

"Well, we have." Mitch protested.

"What's so special about it?" Janie spoke for the first time since we started the round-table talk.

"Well," Mitch began. He leaned back and looked up into the darkening sky as if he might find inspiration. "It's not the room that's so special. It's all the memories it holds."

"I'm not sure I know what you mean," Janie said.

"Yes. Explain, please," Marie said, looking at me intently. "I want details."

I wouldn't want to be in court facing her from the witness stand. I cleared my throat and began, "For a long time, my brother and I shared an upstairs bedroom in the house."

"A very nice house, too," Thelma said. "What do your parents do?"

"My dad's an aerospace engineer—"

"A rocket scientist," Harry said gleefully.

I rolled my eyes at him and continued. "And my mother's the head secretary at Sunkist Lemon Factory in Corona." Turning my attention back to Marie, I said, "Anyway, I wanted my own room, so Grandad used about a quarter of the big garage to make a bedroom and a sort of studio. That's where I live."

"And that's where his friends go for wise counsel when they're depressed," Jack added.

"And that's where I spend most of my time studying art history and philosophy, pondering the meaning of life, and occasionally listening to jazz."

"Really?" Janie responded with genuine interest. "I love jazz."

"Really. I've been hooked on jazz for quite a while, but I appreciate it even more after my trip to San Francisco last summer."

"Do they have a lot of jazz up there?" Thelma asked.

"I've heard they do, and I was hoping to get to a live performance. All I ever heard, though, was loud hippie rock music—Janis Joplin, The Doors, the Airplane. That's all anybody ever played. I was only there for a week, but I had all of their songs memorized by the time I left. I was glad to get back to my jazz records."

"Who's your favorite?" Janie asked.

"I like a lot of them—Brubeck, Getz, Jonah Jones. Lately, I've been listening to some singers like Julie London, June Christy, and Peggy Lee. I've really come to like a young British girl, Helen Shapiro. She started out singing rock and roll, but recently she's been getting kind of jazzy."

Janie smiled and nodded approvingly. "I like all of those," she said, "but I'm not familiar with Helen Shapiro. Maybe you can play one of her records for me before the night is over."

I smiled back at her and said, "I'd love to."

"So, Janie," Jenn, the detective, began, "what's your story? You're the only one left."

The joy that Janie had on her face when we were talking about jazz turned quickly to what looked to be sadness.

"I don't have much to give to you all, really," she began, "my life's not exactly a bed of roses at the moment."

"Do you need to talk to a priest?" Fr. Bob asked with kind concern.

She smiled at him sadly and said, "Thank you, Father, but I've already talked to a few." She drew a deep breath before she spoke again. "As you see, I'm expecting a child. My husband was a captain in the Marines. He's not here because he was killed in Viet Nam just a few weeks ago."

No one spoke a word. What could we say?

"I'm so sorry, Janie," Fr. Bob said. "I meant what I said. If you feel the need to talk, I'm available — for a while at least."

"Thank you, Father. I may take you up on that. Even though I just met you, I feel that you probably have a lot more to offer than just the usual platitudes."

"Can I ask how your husband was killed?" Harry, an ex-marine himself, spoke quietly,

"He was a chopper pilot, and he was running a rescue and recovery mission when his chopper was shot down. Everyone on board was killed, even the wounded they'd just picked up."

"Oh my ..." Mitchkelly murmured. I was not surprised to see tears in his eyes when I glanced at him.

Even Jenn, a hardened cop who has, no doubt, seen and been through a lot, was wiping her eyes.

"So," Father asked softly, "how *are* you doing? I mean, is anyone helping you out? Are you getting counsel or any type of aid?"

"I'm doing okay. It was hard at first, but I'm not the kind to sit around and dwell on things. I'm resigned to accepting that this is the way it is and that I need to go on with life. I've got a little bit of money, for now, that should hold me until all the paperwork goes through so that I can collect the benefits I have coming as a captain's widow. As for counsel, I do have those priests to talk to. I don't really care for them, though. I like you better, Father. Those other guys are so serious all the time, and I usually come out feeling worse than when I went in to see them."

"I know what you mean. I've encountered more than a few of those in my time, too.

"Your widow's pension will help, but it's not much when you have a child to raise," Marie said. "You'll need to get some kind of job after your baby's born. Do you have any work experience?"

"I got married right out of high school. I'm only nineteen, but I've done odd jobs all my life, so I'm no stranger to work." She smiled shyly at Jenn before she continued. "I thought I'd like to be a cop. I had planned to enroll at RCC while my husband was away and take some classes to prepare me to enter the police academy."

"Really?" Jenn said.

"Yes. Really," Janie replied. "Except I got pregnant on our honeymoon, so I guess that dream is history."

"Maybe not," Jenn said. "You're not gonna want to be a patrol officer with a new baby in the house, but there are lots of other jobs in law enforcement that are every bit as important and challenging but are safer and have better hours. I'll give you my card, and we can keep in touch. I'll help you along."

"That would be wonderful. Thank you, Jenn," Janie said.

"I know a lot of people in the legal system," Marie added, "I can help, too. You'd be surprised how many options there are."

"This is fantastic." Janie was genuinely smiling for the first time this evening, and the tears welling up in her eyes were tears of happiness. "I had no idea that tonight would turn out like this. I didn't feel like coming at first, but Mr. Harry talked me into it. He said it would do me good to get out of the house for a while.

He was right. I haven't felt this optimistic in months. I'm really glad I came."

"Well, we are all happy you came," I told her. I wanted to change the subject before the party dissolved into total maudlin mush. "I don't know how to top all of the love and goodwill we just experienced, but since our little round-table discovery talk is over, we should decide on something constructive to fill the rest of the evening."

"What's wrong with just sitting here drinking wine and chatting?" Harry asked.

"Not a thing," I replied. "I just thought that since this is supposed to be an art party, we should be doing some art."

"We are achieving the fine art of creative conversation and building friendships," Mitch said.

"Well, that's good enough for me, then."

We sat there under the stars for the next three hours, drinking wine and talking about this and that and everything else. It was one of the most enjoyable evenings I've ever had. When everyone was getting ready to leave, we promised ourselves that we'd do it regularly, either here when I have the place to myself or at one of the other's homes.

"We got us a club!" Father Bob said. "We need to have club meetings at least once a month."

The party broke up at about one in the morning, and everyone drove off, but not before Fr. Bob bestowed a blessing for a safe trip on them all.

Actually, they all drove away except one, Janie. She asked if she could stay just a little longer to hear a Helen Shapiro record. She said she needed to unwind a bit before she went home to sleep.

After seeing the others off, Janie and I returned to the backyard.

"Do you mind if I sit on the ground, DH?" she asked. "This chair is getting uncomfortable. I can't move around, and the baby is all squashed up into my lungs, so I can't breathe right. I'd love to sit cross-legged or even lie back and look at the stars."

"That's a good idea," I said. "Wait here."

I went to The Hole, my bedroom in the garage. I opened the window overlooking the backyard, set my stereo speakers on the sill, and put on a stack of records — jazz, of course. I grabbed a spare blanket and went back outside. "Follow me," I said, and I led her to my favorite spot at the back of our property.

We made ourselves comfortable on the slope leading down to the grotto behind our house. The voice of Helen Shapiro is drifting down from The Hole. I had the volume adjusted just high enough for us to hear it without bothering the neighbors. The nearest ones are pretty far away, so I'd have to have it really cranked up for them to hear it at all.

"I really like this Helen Shapiro," Janie said.

"Me too, but it's hard to find her records here in America."

"How did you get them?"

"I got lucky. A friend of mine got them from a friend of his. He's not into her kind of music, so he gave them to me."

"I can't imagine anyone not liking her."

"I suppose she's an acquired taste. Her voice is kind of deep and husky, and her songs are different, too. She started out as a pop singer, which I don't normally care for. It's a change, though, and while you could still call it pop, it's got more jazz and blues in it. I really like it."

"It's nice," Janie said. "It's familiar enough to be comfortable but different enough to be interesting." She stretched her legs out and leaned back, resting her weight on her forearms. "The stars are nice, too."

"Yes, they are," I said. We sat without talking while Helen Shapiro finished her song and June Christy took the stage.

"So, how did you like the party tonight?" I asked. "What did you think of the other guests?"

"It was fun," Janie said. "As for the guests, that was the oddest group of people I've ever seen, all together in one place at the same time. It certainly makes for interesting conversation, though."

"It sure does," I agreed. "A couple of art teachers, a priest, a nun, a cop, a lawyer, an accountant, a student or two—"

"And don't forget the pregnant young widow with no job and no real talent to speak of," Janie added.

"Come on," I said. "I'm sure you have a talent or aptitude for something."

"Not really. I married a Marine right after I graduated from high school. I had planned to go to school while he was deployed, but then ..." Janie spread her hands and smiled wryly as she looked at her belly. "When this happens, it pretty well takes control of who you are, regardless of what your dreams might be."

"What were your dreams before 'that' happened?"

"Like I said earlier, I wanted to be a cop or something along those lines."

"That's not what I meant. That's just a goal for a job. I'm talking about your *dreams*. Didn't you have some big dreams and desires for your life besides just being a cop?"

"Not really. Just to be married, have a kid or two, live in a nice house, and invent creative ways to please my husband every night." This time, her smile was wistful.

"Well, it looks like you pleased him at least once," I smiled, looking down at her pregnant tummy.

"Yep, and that was it."

"What?"

"We got married the day before he left for Nam. That night was the only time we had sex. The little critter in my belly is the result of a one-night stand. My husband literally loved me and left me ... and never came back."

"Wow. I'm so sorry. At least you had that one night. That's a good thing, isn't it?"

"I'm not so sure." Her smile is gone now.

"Why?"

"Two reasons. My husband knew when he left that the chances were high that he wouldn't be coming back. He also knew how hard it would be for me to support myself and a child. I suppose I'm as much to blame as he is, but I was so young, and I trusted him. Besides, who thinks of these things on their wedding night? I love—loved—him dearly, but I can't help but feel angry with him, and that makes me feel guilty." Janie appeared to be struggling to sit up, so I took her arm and helped her into a more upright position.

"You said there are two reasons."

"The second reason is purely selfish. I'm only nineteen. Basically, I'm a horny teenager that no man in the world would want to go to bed with now. Men don't find pregnant girls very attractive, and I can't say as I blame them—all this leaking and pissing and grunting when I get up and down. They won't want to come near me after the child is born, either. Nothing like a baby to scare a man away. What man wants to support a woman with a child that's not his own?"

"Wow. I hear what you're saying, but I'm not sure I agree with it."

"Which part?"

"The part about being unattractive. I think you're very pretty."

"You're just saying that."

"No, I'm not. You have a killer smile, and as far as your body is concerned ..."

"Uncomfortable pause. See what I mean? I'm fat and sloppy, and my tits are gushing all over my dress."

"I wasn't pausing because I was thinking that you are fat and sloppy. I was pausing because I was trying to find the words to tell you that wouldn't offend you."

"Go ahead. It takes a lot to offend me, and I've heard it all. Don't mince words."

I took a deep breath and fired out my words like bullets from a machine gun. "I find you very alluring. Erotic—especially your tits. They're huge and filled with milk. I really don't think you can get more feminine than that. Can I see them?" I took another deep breath and finished. "There, I didn't mince words."

It took her a moment to respond. "You mean you want to see my titties?"

"Yes."

"You're so sweet." She smiled and leaned toward me to touch my face with her hand. "This is a one-piece dress, you know, and I'm not wearing anything underneath. I can't show you my titties if I don't take the dress off. When I take the dress off, I'll be totally naked."

"You're not wearing panties?"

"No."

"Well, if you're not comfortable …."

She began before I could finish what I was saying. I thought she would just drop the straps, but she grabbed the bottom of the dress and pulled it out from under her and up over her belly and her huge breasts. Within moments she was sitting there in front of me, totally naked. I was spellbound.

"You're telling me this isn't absolutely beautiful?" I said, putting my palm on her tummy.

"You're an artist," she said. "Does that mean you'd paint something like this?".

"I'd love to paint you. In many poses."

"Touch my breasts."

I did as she asked. They were firm and too big to cup with one hand.

"They're sticky," I told her.

"That's my milk. Would you like to taste it?"

3
Saturday

10 AM

We sat on the edge of the cliff overlooking the grotto below us with Riverside in the distance, talking and drinking wine. I drank mine straight—I can still feel it sloshing around in my head—but Janie's was mostly water with just enough wine to give it some flavor. Needless to say, Janie needed to pee frequently. After the first long trip up to the bathroom in the house, she found a convenient spot a few feet from where we sat to relieve herself over the cliff's edge. I told her that if she spent a week with me, the empty grotto would become a lake. We could name it Lake Janie and stock it with fish.

We started out talking about a lot of things but soon settled into a discussion about art and artists. It turns out that Janie knows quite a bit about art. She particularly likes the Impressionists and knows all about the movement, the painters, their subject matter, and even the details of the artists' lives and where they lived. She explained that reading—especially books about art history—helps keep her mind off her problems. I told her we should take a trip to the art museum in LA together sometime.

We finally decided to call it a night sometime around 3:30 AM. We stopped to look at my paintings stacked up against the walls on our way through the garage to The Hole.

"My parents are kind enough to park their cars outside when they're home so that I can use the garage as my studio," I explained as I arranged them so Janie could see them.

She didn't just look at them. She studied each painting carefully before moving to the next one and then worked her way back to the first painting. She turned to me and said, "These are really good. I'm impressed."

"You're just saying that to be nice," I said.

"You mean like you were just being nice earlier when you told me I was beautiful?" she quipped.

"No! I really meant that," I said. I did, too, and the bright lights in the garage confirmed my judgment. Her skin was the color of milk, and her breasts were even bigger than I thought they were. Her dark pink nipples stood up and out like little soldiers guarding something precious. It was her face, though, that I found most captivating. The only illumination on the patio the evening before came from the house through the French windows. Everything was soft and indistinct in the dim light. The studio lights in the garage revealed a face composed of features that are rather plain when taken individually: eyes set just a little too close; a nose just a little too long and straight; a mouth just a little too wide. There are other flaws, too: a tiny zit on her chin and one on her forehead and her slightly crooked top teeth. Somehow those ordinary and blemished components come together nicely, and she is really quite pretty.

We finally got to sleep around 4 AM. The bed in The Hole is only a twin size, and Janie and the baby in her belly left little room for me. I wrapped up in the spare blanket and slept on the floor. I've been awake for several hours as the hard floor is not the best place for a lie-in. Janie is still asleep in my bed, and I'm sitting at my little desk, bringing my journal up to date.

I suppose Janie was right when she said men shy away from pregnant women or women with a new child. New relationships between men and women are complicated enough without adding in a third party and extra responsibilities. I can't imagine Janie looking at me as her knight in shining armor. I know I'm not ready for that, and I'm certainly not going to lead her on. We had a great evening, but it wasn't a promise of anything for the future. It was simply a fun time that came at the right moment for both of us.

I have no idea what we'll do after Janie wakes up. We'll need to get something to eat and being that it's Saturday we might want to go somewhere and do something. We could drive into LA and spend the day at the art museum. That would also give us some time to talk about "us." I need to get a better idea of her expectations and clarify that we're not in this for the long haul. I wouldn't mind spending more time with her, though. She's a nice person, bright, and likes art—definitely worth getting to know better as a friend. Beyond that—well, who knows?

"Are you writing in your journal?"

She's awake.

"I quit writing early last night, so I needed to update it before I forgot everything."

"That thing is like a drug to you. I bet you'd go through withdrawals if you couldn't write," she teased.

"I wouldn't go that far, although sometimes it seems that something is compelling me to write. But don't worry—I don't get too graphic."

Janie stood up and stretched, then she stepped across the room and stood next to me, leaning over a bit as if trying to read over my shoulder. "That's good," she said, "because we got pretty graphic last night. Did you have a good time exploring every inch of me?"

"I did, but it was pretty dark," I said, turning to face her. "I'd like to explore you again by daylight. You really are a beautiful woman."

"You're sweet, but how you find all of this beautiful …" She slid her hands over her tummy and up under her heavy breasts, lifting them off her chest and squeezing. The movement and pressure caused another flow of milk, which dripped off her nipples and splashed onto me and the page I had been writing on.

"Oops! I'm sorry. I hope I didn't ruin your journal."

"That's okay. It's meant to have things like that happen to it. One day, years from now, I'll open this up, see those stains on these pages, and I'll remember all of this."

She smiled at that idea and stepped back to sit on the edge of the bed. "So, what are we doing today?" she asked. "Do you want me to go home?"

"No way! I was just thinking that the first thing we should do is get something to eat."

"What? Didn't you get enough to eat last night?" she asked playfully. "You made quite a meal out of me."

"A banquet," I replied, "and I wouldn't mind a little more of that later. Right now, though, I'm thinking more along the line of sausage and eggs."

Janie plumped up the pillow and placed it behind her so she could lean her back against the wall and stretch her legs out on the bed while she pondered the options for breakfast. Her naked, pregnant form stretched out on the bed made it hard to concentrate. That smile of hers made it nearly impossible.

"So, shall we make breakfast here?" I asked after clearing my throat. "Seeing you lying there like a Greek goddess gave me an idea."

"Let me guess," she said. "You think we should learn how to speak Greek."

"Close, but no. How would you like to drive to the museum? I'm pretty sure there's a Greco-Roman exhibit going on. We could spend the day there, then come back here and sit outside under the full moon, inspired by what we see at the museum."

"You mean LA? I'd love that! And I really don't need any breakfast if you don't. Why don't we just head out and catch a bite at the museum café? I love their hot dogs."

"Great. It's a plan."

Janie stood up and started looking for her dress. When she found it, she held it up, looked at it, and frowned. It was badly wrinkled, and there were dark stains where her nipples had leaked. "I can't wear this to the museum," she said. "It's a mess."

"You can wear a pair of my pants. You won't be able to get them up over your belly, but I'll bet we can make it work. I've also got some shirts that are about two sizes too big for me but would fit you like a maternity blouse. I'll put your dress in the washer and let it wash while we're gone."

"You think of everything. You're not just an artist but a true gentleman as well." Janie put her hands under her breasts and hoisted them up. "I really don't want to put a clean shirt on over these sticky things." She looked at me and grinned playfully. "Can you clean these off for me?"

I found a pair of Levi's, a short-sleeved light blue shirt, and a sleeveless undershirt for Janie. Getting the pants to fit right was a challenge, but Janie did something clever with a giant rubber band and a necktie that succeeded in keeping them in place. The shirt was roomy enough for her belly, and the snug-fitting undershirt gave her a place to tuck in the cloth pads she uses to soak up the fluid from her leaky breasts. When she was done, she stepped back and turned around to show off her outfit.

12:30 PM at the LA County Museum of Art

Since we hadn't eaten before we left home, we decided to make the museum café our first stop. The hot dogs really are good here. We each bought two and shared a large side of fries. We found a table by the window, and Janie is sitting across from me, making little obscene sucking gestures with her mouth while she eats them, and I'm looking around to see if anyone is watching. The place isn't too crowded, and no one is paying us any attention.

"You really are a mess, aren't you?" I said.

"I warned you," she said, then took another large bite. "Am I embarrassing you?" she asked around a mouthful of hot dog.

"Nope, not at all," I replied with equal delicacy. I finished my hot dog and chased it down with one last French fry. "Are you about ready to head inside and look at some art?"

"You bet," she said.

After a few moments and a couple of handfuls of napkins to remove all traces of ketchup, mustard, and grease from our fingers and faces, we headed for the exhibit galleries.

◎ ◎ ◎

We made our way to the central space in the museum and paused for a moment to get our bearings. I was considering which way we should go when Janie grabbed my hand. "What's this over here!" she exclaimed while dragging me across the room.

Janie stopped, and I was finally able to see that we were standing in the first room of the connected galleries that housed the display of works by the Impressionists. "Look at this," she said, her voice hushed and almost reverent. "I see a couple of Monets and Degas. What else is here?"

"That looks like a Pissarro over here, and I see a Manet over in the next room," I said.

"You're right," she said. "This is wonderful. I'm so glad we came."

"Most of these are different from the ones I saw last time I was here. I wonder if they're on loan from a private collection."

"I think they keep extra paintings in the basement, and they change them up from time to time," Janie said.

"Could be," I said as I slowly turned to take in the paintings. One of the Degas caught my eye. "Wow, look at the Degas over there," I said as I stepped toward it. "I need a closer look."

"You just like it 'cause it's a naked lady," Janie teased as she stepped up beside me.

"Partly," I said. "You got a problem with that?"

"Not at all. Underneath these borrowed clothes, I'm a naked lady."

"I'll tell you—Degas knew how to paint a natural woman. Look at that," I wanted to touch the painting, but I didn't dare.

Leaving the Bath is a pastel drawing of a nude woman standing on a carpet. She is bent over, giving the viewer a perfect view of all her charms.

"Wow ... He didn't leave much to the imagination." Then she turned to me and, smiling mischievously, asked, "Will you paint me like that?"

"I'll paint you in any pose you take."

We returned our attention to the painting in front of us and studied it in silence for a few moments. Janie spoke first. "You are right about this painting. She looks so natural, so … every day."

"His paintings are like that, especially the bathers. They're like snapshots of ordinary people doing ordinary things. He really knew how to capture the succulence of a woman."

"Succulence? Is that a word?"

"It is now."

"Since his women are all fat, and you like them, I guess that means I have a chance with you, huh?"

"They're not fat. They're normal. And you're not fat. You're pregnant. Even if you were fat, I'd still like you because I do like women with a little flesh on them."

"Maybe I should have eaten more hot dogs."

"You know, this picture really is amazing. It all looks random up close but back up a few feet, and it comes together like magic. By the time Degas did this in 1895, he was nearly blind. He had switched from paint to pastels several years earlier because they were easier to use, and he had to work around his blind spot to get in the whole picture. What a master."

Janie moved over to stand in front of me. She took my hands and wrapped my arms around the top of her tummy.

"Umm … this is nice," she cooed.

"Your hair smells good," I said.

"I'm surprised it doesn't stink. You made me sweat buckets last night."

"It might be stinky to some, but to me, it just smells like you. It smells the way the women in Degas's pictures must have smelled."

"What a lovely compliment … I think. Are there any Renoirs in here?" she asked.

"On the wall behind us by the big Monet."

Renoir's painting, *A Young Girl with Daisies,* is also one of my favorites. It is of a young girl, a teenager perhaps, seated and holding some daisies. She's wearing a brown skirt and a loose-fitting white blouse. The blouse is so loose that it's falling off her shoulders and exposing the top half of her plump breasts. It is in defiance of the law of gravity that her breasts are not naked in their entirety.

Janie stared at the painting for a few moments before offering a critique. "Nice tits," she said.

"Yes, they do look inviting," I agreed.

"And she has red hair," Janie continued. "I've always wished I had red hair."

"I had red hair when I was born. It turned blonde pretty quickly, though."

"A California beach boy," Janie said as she ran her fingers through my hair. "Do you spend time at the beach just looking at the girls in their bikinis, or do you surf the waves?"

"Neither. For one thing, I can't swim. And for another, I usually go at night and sit on the beach writing poetry and drinking wine."

"All alone? How romantic."

Actually, it is romantic in an artistic sort of way to sit alone at night on the beach, but I think she was being sarcastic. "Most of the time," I replied. "Sometimes I bring my buddy Manny with me if he's not too busy with his rock band."

"You can't write romantic poetry with some guy hanging around. You need a woman. Someone like her," she said, indicating the woman in the Renoir painting.

I reached up and ran my hand through Janie's hair. "I already have a someone much better than her."

Janie turned, put her arms around me, and kissed me right there in front of the museum guards and visitors and the redheaded girl with the daisies. I swear I saw the girl in the painting turn her head just a little to look at us and smile. Really. Then it hit me—she looks a heck of a lot like Annabelle, the ghost who kissed me in the haunted house last Halloween.

Janie pulled back and looked at me curiously. "What's the matter? Did I do something wrong?"

"No, I just had a bizarre thought."

"You look like you've seen a ghost."

"I think I have."

"What?"

"It's a long story," I said. I wasn't sure if I wanted to tell Janie about it.

"Well, judging by the look on your face, I think I'd like to hear it."

"Maybe later tonight when we've had some wine," I told her. "I'll fill you in then.

"So, do you want me drunk before you tell me, or do you need to be drunk before you can?"

"Maybe a little of both." I smiled at her, but my mind was pre-occupied with my sudden insight.

"I gotta pee. I saw a ladies' room on the way in here."

Janie took my hand and led me through the Impressionism gallery and back into the main lobby. We found the restroom in a hallway behind the reception desk, and she told me to wait by the door while she went. She had her hand on the door to push it open when she turned to me and said, " We can wander around the museum a bit more when I'm done here, but I'm not going to forget about your ghost story. I want to hear that when we get back to your place."

"I'll tell you. I promise."

"And all those tittie paintings made me horny. We're gonna have to do something about that, too."

It's going to be a long night.

Back Home on the Edge of the Grotto

We spent the next hour exploring more of the museum. They rotate the exhibits regularly, so every visit is different. I could have stayed much longer, but Janie's feet were swollen and starting to hurt. We had a good time anyway and promised ourselves that we would come back after her baby was born.

We got back to Riverside at about 6:30. We stopped to pick up burgers and fries when we left the freeway, then headed for home. On the way out to the grotto to watch the city lights come on and the sky change from blue to violet to black, I stopped in The Hole and got a blanket for us to sit on. While there, I also put a stack of jazz albums on my stereo by the window. The music drifting down from the house, the scenery, and the wine push all mundane life concerns from our thoughts.

The weather is stuck in the dry heat of late summer and early fall, so it's still pretty warm, and we're both sweating. That's okay, though. I've always been a summer boy, and I like it hot. There are swamp coolers in the main rooms of the house, but I just have an electric fan out in The Hole. The slight breeze it creates feels good, but I turn it on mainly for the sound. The whirring noise helps me sleep.

"What are you writing about?" Janie asked around a mouth full of cheeseburger.

"The weather."

"You're kidding," she laughed. "We had all that fun at the museum, and I'm sitting here now wearing nothing but a pair of your underpants, and all you can think about is the weather?"

"Good point. I think I'm the luckiest guy alive." The mention of her near-nakedness reminded me. "You want your dress?" I asked. "It's clean now."

"It's still sitting in the washing machine. I can't wear it till it dries." She punched my arm lightly and asked again, "So, what are you writing?"

"I was just commenting on the heat and how we're sitting here sweating and waiting for the moon to rise."

"It will be lovely when it does. I may not even go to sleep tonight. I think I'll just stay awake and stare at the moon."

"Sounds good to me. What if I fall asleep?"

"You can use me as a pillow," she said. "But not before you tell me why you went white looking at the Degas girl in the museum."

"Oh ... I forgot about that." I hadn't.

"No, you didn't."

"I'll tell you, don't worry. I'm not hiding anything. I just don't think you're going to believe me."

"Why wouldn't I believe you?"

"Because it's a very strange story involving a ghost."

"Really? I like ghost stories."

"But it isn't a ghost story. It's a real story, and every time I think I've come to the end of it, something new gets added."

"That sounds weird."

"It is."

"Why don't you go into the kitchen and get yourself some more wine. You can refill my mug, too, but make it mostly water again. I haven't had much in the way of alcohol since I found out I was pregnant, so this little bit is more than enough for me."

I had just entered the kitchen after moving Janie's dress from the washer to the dryer when the phone rang.

"Where you been? I've been tryin' to get you all day."

"Manny?"

"Yeah, buddy, it's me. No kiddin', where you been? You'd better not be out getting into trouble without me."

Manny's the one who talked me into going to San Francisco with him last summer. He has a band that practices in the garage of the house where he lives with his mother and sister. We've been friends for a long time, and I have a standing invitation to come and listen to them practice. Manny takes his music seriously and holds his band to high standards. They really are pretty good.

"You'll hate me for this," I said.

"I already hate you, so get on with it."

"I went to LACMA."

"What! And you didn't take me! That's not the first time you've done that. Now I do hate you."

"It was a date, Manny. I couldn't take you."

"A date? You mean with a girl?"

"Of course, I mean with a girl. A pretty girl, too, I might add."

"What's her name? Do I know her? Does she go to RCC?"

"Her name is Janie, and no and no. She isn't a student."

"You're not dating an older woman, are you, DH? Should my

mother be worried about this?" His sarcasm was hard to miss. Manny's mother, Hester, is a gorgeous forty-something woman who wears short skirts, tight shirts, and tiny bikinis and who seems to delight in teasing me with "innocent" glimpses of her boobs and ass and flirtatious looks and comments. Manny hates it.

"Your mother has nothing to worry about," I said. "Janie's only nineteen."

"And she's not a student? What does she do in her spare time?"

"It's a long story."

"I got all night."

"Well, I don't. She's here right now, and we're sitting out in back, drinking wine, and chatting."

Janie chose that moment to come through the door.

"I thought I heard the phone. Who is it?" she asked.

"My friend, Manny."

"The guy you're always bragging about?"

"You've been bragging about me, DH? Heck, I guess I can't hate you anymore. What's goin' on over there? Can I come over?"

"We were going to have a nice intimate evening together, Manny," I said, winking at Janie.

"I don't care if he comes," she said, "as long as he doesn't spend the night. I have plans for us later." She kissed me right there in front of the phone and everything.

"Did she just kiss you?" Manny asked. "I heard that."

"How are you going to get here, Manny? I don't want to have to pick you up."

"I'll drive myself."

"You don't know how to drive, and you don't own a car," I said.

"That's what I'm callin' about. Mom's been teaching me to drive for the past few days, and I've been driving her car. She told me I could drive it over there tonight if I wanted."

"Did you get a license?"

"No, not yet."

"You can't drive without a license. What if you get stopped by the cops?"

"I'm young and foolish. What would they do?"

"It's up to you, man. I think it's stupid, but if you want to chance it—" I heard a click from the other end of the line.

"I take it he's coming?" Janie asked.

"He'll be here soon. You'd better put some clothes on.

"Bummer. It feels so good hanging out like this." She wiggled her breasts.

"You don't want to hang out in front of Manny. I don't think he can take it. I've got some shorts and a shirt in The Hole that should cover you up and still be comfortable."

"What about that story you were going to tell me? I still want to hear it."

"I'll tell you when Manny gets here."

About twenty minutes later, Manny drove up in his mother's car. I was surprised and pleased to see Pet step out from the passenger side. Pet is the gorgeous and talented lead singer for his band, The Riders. Apparently, the band was just leaving when he called me. Pet overheard the conversation and asked if she could come along. Manny, who would do anything to get into Pet's pants—no success, so far—agreed.

As I said, Pet is very talented. Not only can she sing, but she also has a killer body and knows how to get attention before she even opens her mouth. She does this by flirting with the guys in the audience while flipping her long, straight blonde hair from side to side and strutting back and forth along the front of the stage. Everything she wears, whether it covers her from neck to ankle or is the shortest of skirts or briefest of tops, somehow reveals her spectacular form in all of its glory.

I think Manny's been sharing observations from our San Francisco trip because tonight's outfit looks like many we saw there, both on the street and on the stage. She's wearing very short, very tight white shorts and white go-go boots. Her green tube top barely contains her large breasts, but that's okay because she is also wearing a vest that gives the illusion of more complete coverage. The top of the vest is a brief assembly of colorful crocheted squares that reminds me of the blanket my Nana made for me. A row of knotted and beaded fringe hangs from the bottom edge almost to her knees. I didn't see anyone in San Francisco look nearly as good as Pet did in that outfit.

I suggested that Pet might want to take her white boots off and leave them in the breezeway before we went out back so that they wouldn't get dirty. I also switched out the jazz on the stereo for some Beatles — Manny's not a big fan of jazz. I picked up a jug of water for Janie and a jug of wine for the rest of us, found mugs for Manny and Pet, and we headed across the lawn to join Janie.

When Manny caught sight of her, he put his hand on my arm and held me back. The expression on his face was close to panic when he leaned close and whispered, "She's pregnant ... Are you ...? Did you ...?"

"No, I'm not the father," I assured him. "The Marine she was married to was killed in Viet Nam about a month ago. Long story."

Manny and Pet both responded with, "Oh ... wow," and "So sorry."

◎ ◎ ◎

So, here we sit, the four of us, like a police lineup on the edge of the cliff, dangling our bare feet over the side. It's dark, and the moon is rising over the hills on the other side of Riverside.

The introductions are over, and the usual remarks about the weather and the beauty of the night have been made. Manny and Pet are uncharacteristically quiet — not sure how to proceed given the awkwardness of Janie's situation.

Janie solves the problem by opening the conversation. "DH tells me that you two are in a band."

"Yes, The Riders," Manny replied, "I'm the drummer, and Pet sings the leads."

"You're more than just the drummer, Manster," Pet said, exhaling smoke from her long menthol cigarette. "You *are* the band."

"She's right, Manny," I said. "You're the leader, and without you, there wouldn't be a band. How many times has it broken up, leaving you as the lone survivor, the guy who rounds up a new band from scratch to take its place?"

"That's because Manny's always the only one who takes it seriously. He fires the misfits," Pet said.

"You're right," Manny said. "And I always hire you back because you take it seriously, too."

"Where do you perform?" Janie asked.

Manny chuckled. "Anywhere we can," he said. "No kidding. We'll play any place that will have us. There's a lot of competition here in Riverside, so we take what we can get."

"We sure do," Pet agreed. "There are hundreds of garage bands around here, and all of them are looking for weekend gigs. The competition gets even crazier if they're paid events."

"There may be hundreds of bands here," I said, "but yours is the best."

"I like to think that. We work pretty hard at it," Manny said.

"Manny told me you and DH went to LACMA today," Pet said. "How was it?"

"It was great," Janie said. "Especially the hot dogs in the café." Janie winked at me. "We spent a lot of time in the Impressionist gallery. It seemed like all of my favorites were on display this time. Then we walked around the other galleries to see what else might be new."

"DH must really like you, Janie," Manny said. "He loves being alone with famous paintings, and he loves the art museum. He doesn't take just anybody there. Don't get him started on his Van Gogh lecture, though."

"Oh?" Janie asked.

"He knows everything there is to know about Van Gogh," Manny continued, "and he loves telling every bit of it to anyone who'll listen."

"Well, he didn't lecture me on Van Gogh, but I did learn some things about Degas I'd never heard before."

Pet asked, "What do you do, Janie? I mean, do you have a job?"

"Not much right now. I'm just getting over some personal stuff, trying to get my head back to normal. Besides, this isn't exactly the best time for me to go job hunting." She drew attention to her condition with a glance and a wave of her hand.

I didn't know if Janie wanted to tell them about her husband or not. Even though I'd already told them, she didn't know that, and I knew it would be awkward if I didn't mention it. I also noticed the tears forming in Pet's eyes.

"Janie's husband was a Marine. He was killed in Viet Nam a few weeks ago."

Pet reached over and squeezed Janie's hand. "I'm so sorry, Janie," she said.

"That's terrible," Manny said. "Damned war. Were you guys married long?"

Janie replied with her well-practiced line, "One night before he shipped out."

"One night? And now it's just you and the little one there?" Pet asked, nodding at Janie's tummy.

"You know," I said, "if there's one point where I agree with those hippies up in San Francisco, it's this war thing. It sucks. I went to school with a lot of guys who were sent over there and never came back. There are thousands of stories just like yours, Janie. It's terrible."

"It is," Janie said. "But what's done is done. The only thing left to do now is to live with it."

"What about your family?" Pet asked. "Do you have friends who can hang with you?"

"I do now," Janie said, smiling at me.

"She met a lot of our friends yesterday, and they all said they'd help her," I told Pet. "Not just the usual 'let me know if you need help' way, either, but with some real solutions."

"Geez, she didn't meet the art crowd, did she?" Manny asked.

"She did," I said.

"Look out, Janie," Manny said. "They're all nuts."

"Shut up, Manfred," Pet said, slapping Manny on the back of the head. "You're just jealous because they're all so talented."

"And I'm not?" Manny asked, feigning to be hurt.

"A different kind of talent, Manny," I said.

"Well, we'll help too, Janie," Manny said. "You just name it, and if we can do it, we will. Hey! We've got a gig comin' up in a couple of weeks. We'll do it for you. We can give you the proceeds."

"That ought to buy you lunch, anyway," Pet said.

"You guys are so sweet," Janie said. "I told myself I wouldn't cry about this anymore, but here I go again."

"Well, I know how to take your mind off it," I said. "It's storytime."

"Good grief," Manny sighed. "Which one do we have to suffer through tonight?"

"Annabelle."

"Well, at least that's a good one," Manny said.

"Have I heard this one?" Pet asked.

"I don't think so. I haven't told too many people. Just Manny, and maybe one or two more."

"Don't get jealous, Pet. He tells me everything," Manny said. "Pass me the wine jug before you get started."

We all topped off our mugs as the jug made its way down the line. Even Janie added a splash to her water.

When we were all settled, I began. "It's a perfect night for this story, with the full moon and all."

"Is this gonna be a spooky story?" Pet asked. "I scare easily."

"It all depends," I said. "I don't think it's spooky. It's actually kind of sweet, in a way."

Manny nodded thoughtfully and said, "Sort of."

"Last Halloween, my friend Greta and I agreed to spend the night in a haunted house together," I continued.

"Oh?" Janie looked at me with mock disapproval.

"Nothing like that, Janie. We were there to see if we could contact a ghost that supposedly haunts the place. In fact, we were told there was more than one ghost, but we only encountered one."

"How did you land a gig like that?" Pet asked.

"Greta's family owns the place. It's an old farmhouse over in La Sierra, and it hasn't been lived in for years. Her aunt thought it would be good for us to stay there to keep the trick-or-treater criminals from breaking the windows and damaging the property."

"Greta — That's not a name you hear much around here," Manny said. "Where's she from? The Alps?"

"She's from Germany. Her parents helped a lot of people escape the Holocaust. They made it safely through the war, but a few years later, a secret group of Nazi supporters learned who they were and what they did and were going to kill them. Greta was just one month old when her folks snuck out of Germany to avoid assassination. They came here to America, changed their name a couple of times, and eventually landed in Riverside."

"Wow," Manny said. "You never told me that part."

"It gets even more interesting," I said. "Greta's parents were killed in a car crash under questionable circumstances not long after moving here. A childless couple adopted Greta and changed her name yet again. She didn't know anything about her family history until just a few months before the night I'm going to tell you about."

"That's a pretty amazing story in itself," Pet said. "I can't imagine what you're going to tell us next."

"Yes. Well, back to the ghost story," I said, then described the events of that night almost a year ago when I first met the ghost of the young girl, Annabelle, who had died tragically many years before. My audience listened with rapt attention and did not interrupt except for the occasional exclamation of "Oh," or "Wow," or "No, really?" Even Manny, who had heard most of the story before, seemed spellbound. By the time I got to the part about meeting the ghost, all three of my listeners were sitting up straight, wide eyes sparkling in the moonlight, hanging on my every word.

I came to the part where Greta and I returned to the upstairs bedroom and sat on the bed opposite the one that had been Annabelle's.

"Then we heard what sounded like someone sitting down on Annabelle's bed. I said, 'Annabelle, is that you?' I didn't expect an answer, but I knew I had to try to communicate with this girl."

"And?" Pet impatiently asked when I paused to take a sip of my wine.

"And then we heard another noise like someone getting up from the bed. Then the floor creaked like someone was walking from Annabelle's bed toward the one Greta and I sat on. Greta moved to put as much distance between the two of us and still stay on the bed. She was just a little bit scared."

Janie shivered even though the night was still warm. "I would be too," she said.

"The footsteps came closer until they stopped just in front of me. I had been straining in the dim light of the room to see anything. Now I saw a face take form inches from my own. It started as a filmy, transparent, watery shape at the limits of visibility, but it gained substance with every second, as if the ghost was drawing energy from me.

"I asked Greta if she saw anything, and she said she could see a face in profile. I soon saw that it was the face of a teenage girl. I knew it was Annabelle because I had studied her photo on the dresser by her bed. Her features were unmistakable. I could even see the freckles on her nose. Her face hovered just inches from mine, and she smiled right at me. I looked into her eyes as she moved closer and closer to me.

"Suddenly, Annabelle's face merged with mine. I felt her warm energy. I felt her warmth. I felt her lips merge with my lips, and then—I don't know if I should tell you the rest."

"You're kidding," Pet protested. "You've gone too far to stop now."

"Yeah," Janie chimed in. "We're big girls. We can take it."

"Well ... okay then. I wrote all this in my journal right after it happened, but I haven't told this part to anyone—not even you, Manny.

I just don't want you to get any wrong ideas about this." I took a deep breath and dove in. "Annabelle kissed me. And it wasn't just a peck on the cheek or a light touch of her lips on mine, either. It was a full-on French kiss with her tongue caressing my tongue inside my mouth. When she finished, she moved away slowly, looking deep into my eyes as if studying me. The last thing I saw of her before she disappeared was her melancholy smile. The encounter left me filled with unfamiliar and unidentified emotions and tears in my eyes."

Everyone sat in stunned silence. I felt as if the whole world was holding its breath.

Finally, Janie let out a whoosh of air. "I honestly don't know how to react to all that," Janie said.

"That's about the spookiest ghost story I've ever heard," Pet said. "There is such a thing as a succubus, you know—a chick who comes to a guy in the night and humps him while she sucks the life out of him."

"That's not what Annabelle did," I insisted. "She was gentle. It was a very ... tender moment."

"You may not have filled me in on that last part," Manny said, "but I do know it doesn't end there. Tell 'em rest of the story, DH."

"Really? There's more?" Janie gave me an accusing look. I can tell this bothers her now as much as it had Greta when it happened, but I can't help that.

Manny poked my arm with his finger and said, "Tell them about the dreams."

"We've got dreams, too?" Pet asked.

"Ever since that night, I've had vivid dreams of Annabelle and me. I won't go into detail, but they seem very real."

"Oh great," Janie said. "I don't know what to say. I don't think I should be jealous of a ghost, but—"

"That's what Greta said, too," I told her.

"If you still have dreams about her, well, that's another story."

"Don't worry, Janie," Manny assured her. "He isn't going to

be running off with a ghost any time soon. I'm not sure that's even possible."

"It's not," Pet said confidently. Then she looked at me and frowned. "Is it?"

"I don't know what to think," I said. "I only know what I encountered that night and in my dreams and how it makes me feel. It's not like I'm lusting after Annabelle. It's more like—

"Like you're missing her?" Manny said.

I looked at Manny and was surprised by the understanding and sympathy I saw in his eyes. "Yeah. Sort of."

4
Monday

In The Pit catching up on last night

We sat on the edge of the grotto for another couple of hours after I finished my story about Annabelle. Needless to say, our conversation centered mainly on music, art, and other simple things rather than things that lie in the realm of the unknown. Manny and Pet took off around 1 AM, and Janie and I stayed out on the lawn. It didn't take long for Janie to fall asleep with her head on my lap, and a few minutes later, I laid down and followed her into the land of dreams.

When the sun woke us up, we went inside and made breakfast. Janie left right after we finished eating. She told me she needed to go home because she didn't like leaving her house unattended for so long — she had been here since Friday, and it was now Sunday morning. I think the real reason she left so quickly is that the ghost story disturbed her more than she let on last night. I think she needed to get away and decide whether she was jealous, or I'm crazy, or maybe both.

It's probably just as well Janie took off. For one thing, I still needed to do the assigned reading for my astronomy class this morning. Also, I don't want Janie to get too attached to me. We swore we wouldn't go there, but I don't want to take any chances. After the ghost story, though, that may not be a problem. She might want to dump me altogether. Oh well, that's the breaks.

The last year and a half or so have brought a lot of changes, adventures, people, and ideas into my life. One of the reasons I started this journal was to help me keep track of it all. I've also become aware of tensions and problems brewing in the world at large and in the US. It's hard enough for me to keep up with my own life right now, but am I selfish to be concerned only about myself in times such as these? Most of this world is unpleasant, and a great deal of that unpleasantness is pure evil, and there's not much any individual can do about it. I'm not evil, and I believe my efforts are best spent trying to work out the complications of my own life so that I can define who and what I want to be. Maybe then I can make some slight difference in this world.

For now, the complications are personal and focused. The most troublesome and persistent seems to be women—has been since high school. They come into my life so effortlessly, make their mark on me for better or worse, and go away. They just up and leave. The pattern has been recorded and repeated many times in this journal, so I won't dwell on it here. But geez, Louise, all the women I've dated have had problems, not just the ordinary, day-to-day kind. Their issues were serious and compelled me to go along for the ride, so to speak. And in the end, every one of them was forced by their difficulty to leave me high and dry. No, not *forced*, because they had a choice in the matter. Maybe *coerced* is a better word for it. I believe now that Janie is getting ready to bail on me pretty soon, too. Perhaps she already has. I wouldn't blame her. She has the welfare of her child to consider, after all. I could offer her friendship, but I am in no position to give her the kind of support she needs. Also, the Annabelle story is pretty bizarre. If Janie doesn't believe in the supernatural, or if the supernatural scares her, then I'm probably not someone she wants to be around.

I do believe in the supernatural. I can't explain it, but I believe in it. And I know what happened on Halloween night. Annabelle was REAL, she did kiss me, and she did smile at me as she poofed away into who knows where. And, by the way, all of my dreams with Annabelle are REAL too. They are the most vivid dreams I've ever had. The colors are brilliant and pure. The objects and people are as lifelike as if they were standing right there in front of me. They are literally a part of me.

That all may change soon, however. In the last dream I had,

Annabelle whispered that I would forget the dreams and that they wouldn't stay with me long. She said, "One day soon, your dreams of me will fade. You will forget you ever had them. You will … forget about me."

I woke up from that dream with tears in my eyes, but I haven't forgotten yet. I remember the last dream three nights ago as if it had just happened, but now that I think about it, I can't remember my first dreams about Annabelle. I can't remember a thing. That means the forgetting part has begun. How long will I remember this last dream of her, and will there be any more dreams after I forget them all?

I'm going to record all the details of my last Annabelle dream right now so that I'll have my journal to refer to. What if I don't even remember writing about it, though? I might find this journal entry one day and ask, "What the heck is that all about? Why did I write this down? Who is Annabelle?"

I hope I never forget her. I want to remember her, and I want to have more dreams about her. Am I falling in love with a ghost? Could that be why I have so many ill-begun relationships with girls in this realm of existence? Could it be that I am already in a relationship with a ghost? Maybe these dreams aren't dreams at all. Maybe I actually leave this realm and travel into her domain. Maybe I go to sleep, and my spirit leaves my body and joins with the spirit of Annabelle in some distant Heavenly dimension or some other-dimensional world that we don't see with our ordinary eyes. Is it time travel? Could I be traveling through time? Maybe I'm speeding across the endless miles of outer space at speeds that defy the laws of physics as we think we know them here on Earth?

What the heck am I writing? I have no idea. But I'm gonna try as best as I can to relate my last dream of Annabelle. I'm not sure where to start, though, because the dreams don't really have a beginning or an end. They just happen. They just are.

My Dream of Annabelle

Three nights ago, I went to sleep, and within minutes I was into her dream. She met me there like she would if I had knocked on a door. She opened it and said, "Hello."

That's what she did, only she wasn't inside a house or a building. She was outside, standing at the edge of a beautiful forest. She saw me, got that wide, gleaming grin on her face, and said, "Hello."

That single word, hello, sounded so sweet, like the tinkling of a small porcelain bell. One little magical tinkle, like a faerie's voice might sound. "Hello!"

In the dream, Annabelle was wearing a skirt and a long-sleeved shirt. The shirt was white, and the skirt was plaid like a Scottish tartan with lots of red, some blue, and some green. Her hair was tied back in a ponytail that fell halfway down her back. I can see her in my mind, plain as day. She was so beautiful. She appeared to be a teenager, maybe fourteen or fifteen years old.

Annabelle raised her hands and motioned me to walk toward her. I believe that I never did anything of my own accord in these dreams. Annabelle directed everything, and I didn't hesitate to obey her. I approached her slowly. I got close enough to feel her breath flow gently out of her nose and against the skin of my face. I was so close that when I took a breath, it was her breath that went into me. I felt the heat of it going into my nose and down my throat. It was wonderful. It was as if she were inoculating me with some sacred Faerie sustenance that made the world around me look brighter, revealing every detail with incredible precision. Then, Annabelle wrapped her arms around me and kissed me. When she ended the kiss, she took hold of my shoulders and turned me around. "Look," she said. "This is our home."

Perhaps a mile away, there was a flower-covered hill with a beautiful building at the very top like a palace. In my dream state, I knew that the building was a house made entirely of glass. I tried to speak to Annabelle, but I couldn't. I wanted to say, "We live in that palace? It's beautiful."

Annabelle could read my thoughts, though. She said, "Yes, that is our house. We own this world." She paused as if she were listening to another voice, then continued, "And all other worlds. Goodbye for now."

She began to dissolve into a glittering, multicolored shower of tiny droplets of light and left her final words hanging in the air, "You will see me again, but not for a while. I love you."

This is a poor telling of my dream, but I hope it is enough to trigger my memory of the entire experience when I go back to read it in some future time.

Back to Earth

I'm sitting at "my" table down in The Pit watching the girls go up and down the steps. Access to The Pit from the Quad is not by way of ordinary stairs. The steps that span the width of the sunken area from one wall to the other are a short step up but a long stride from front to back. A person with very long legs can easily take them at one stride per step, and a short-legged person can comfortably fit two strides on one step. Most people, though, fall somewhere in between.

The way a person takes those steps—their stride, speed, and rhythm—says a lot about them. Some people run up and down like they are on the stairs of their own home—one foot per step without even looking. Others proceed slowly and cautiously, stepping down with one foot and forward with the other in a rhythmic limp, never taking their eyes off their feet. Many people take the steps at an angle or zigzag if there's a crowd. That way, they can proceed comfortably with their normal stride for two or three steps before moving to the next level. You'd think that the runners would collide with the limpers and the zigzaggers, and they would all land in a pile at the bottom, but I've never seen it happen.

I wonder how all of this relates to personality. Are the runners type-A people? Are they first in their classes with straight A's? Are they always on time for everything? I'm rarely first in my class, and

I certainly don't make straight A's, but I am punctual. I can usually take one step per level for about three steps, then I have to adjust my gait and take an extra step on a level or two before going back to one step each. I never run up or down the steps, but I never dawdle either. I guess I'm a type-B kinda guy. I need to run this by Bill Hunter. I'm sure he has a theory that covers it.

It's almost time to head over to astronomy class. Dr. Drake makes that vast and complex subject easy to follow even though — or maybe because — he is a perfectionist and a precisionist. He fills his chalkboard with lists, diagrams, and drawings as he talks. They are easy to reproduce in my class notes, even though they are extensive and detailed.

For the class on the Andromeda galaxy last week, he lectured from an intricate chalk diagram of the galaxy relative to the stars and other objects visible from Earth. He pointed out things that no one but a trained astronomer would see in that section of the sky. He added connecting and boundary lines and arrows to mark significant areas and objects as he spoke. At the end of the lesson, he showed us the slide he had used to draw his diagram. We had all seen the picture before. This time though, we saw an orderly three-dimensional arrangement of celestial objects and understood their nature and the spatial relationships between them instead of a random scattering of white dots and hazy areas on a flat black background.

Somehow, despite his somewhat old-fashioned formality, Dr. Drake's love of his subject and love of teaching is infectious. Under his guidance, my passing interest in astronomy is developing into a genuine interest in deep space and all the possibilities it holds.

10:25 AM After Class

Today's class was interesting even before it started. Dr. Drake had created a solar system model out of what appeared to be styrofoam and suspended it from the ceiling to dangle down over our heads. It was pretty impressive. The sun, all the planets, and every tiny moon of every planet were represented, each painted with its identifying colors and characteristic markings, including the canals of Mars, the Great Spot of Jupiter, and even the rings of Saturn. The distances between the planets were not to scale — that would have required extending the model out into the Quad — but it was good enough to convey the relationship of one body to another. He spent the entire class moving between the model and the chalkboard, describing how our solar system works, how it's put together, why it stays together, and why large asteroids rarely ever hit the Earth. It was fascinating, and I, as usual, was the one asking most of the questions. I hope my frequent interruptions don't irritate him, although Dr. Drake should be used to me by now since I had been in his class last year.

I guess I'll head back to The Pit, grab some lunch, and think about what I'll be doing the rest of the day. Wait a minute. Dr. Drake is headed my way and looks like he wants to talk to me.

He greeted me with a smile. "Mr. Parsons," he said.

"Dr. Drake," I said, returning his smile.

"You haven't changed a bit."

What an odd thing for him to say. "I haven't? What do you mean?"

"I mean, the lecture is over, and you're still writing. That must mean you're still keeping that journal of yours."

"You remember that?" That's what I get for asking so many questions in class. "I promise you, though, the only thing I wrote during class was notes on your lecture, which was quite fascinating, I might add."

"I'm sure that's true. You were far too busy asking questions."

"Sorry, I don't mean to be a blabbermouth. I need to clarify stuff as we go along, or I won't retain it. I guess I'm just a bit slow."

"That doesn't make you slow, young man. That makes you smart."

"It does?"

"The slow ones are the ones that don't get it, don't know they don't get it, and don't pass the test. You got a B in my last class, right?"

"Yes, I did. You have a good memory, Dr. Drake."

"Well, I expect an A out of you this time around," he said sternly. "And I believe it's time you stopped calling me Dr. Drake. You should call me by my first name, Rob."

"Not Bob?"

"Heavens no. How they got Bob out of Robert, I'll never know. My friends call me Rob."

Rob extended his hand, and we shook.

"Perhaps we can have lunch together sometime," Rob said. "I'd like to know more about the young man, DH, who seems to think it's important to write down everything in the universe." He made a sweeping motion with his hand above his head.

"I'd like that, Rob," I said, and I really would.

"What do you think of my solar system model?" he asked.

"I love it. You put a lot of work into that."

"Not as much as I put into hanging it from this ceiling." He pointed upward.

I looked up past the planets and moons. The ceiling in the old classroom was high and offered few points where anything could be attached to it. Even so, Rob had created an intricate web of nearly invisible fishing line from which to suspend his solar system. I studied it for a moment before I said, "It's the eighth Wonder of the World."

He grinned at that. "I wouldn't go that far," he said, "but it was a task."

"How long did it take you to make that thing?"

"I've been working on the planets and moons off and on for about a month, but it took me all weekend to get it hung."

"You sacrificed a weekend of your personal time to make a model for your students?"

He smiled up at his work. "Not a sacrifice," he said. "A privilege."

Later in Manny's Garage

After astronomy class, I made my way down to The Pit. My plan was to grab a burrito at the snack bar to eat while I caught up on my thoughts. I got to the top of the steps, looked down at my table in the back corner, and changed my plan. The spot was already occupied by none other than Frank Reed, the worldly, semi-successful artist character I have yet to actually meet. He wasn't just sitting at *my* table. He was sitting in *my* seat at *my* table. Frank wasn't just sitting there, either. He was holding court. He sat alone on his side of the table with his back against the wall, occupying the spot as if he were a king on his throne surrounded by loyal subjects. Five or six girls sat on the bench on the other side of the table, and maybe as many as twenty others of both sexes stood around them.

Frank was putting on quite a show. I couldn't make out his words, but I heard the rich resonance of his voice and saw his hands wave extravagantly to make a point or to illustrate a story. His audience looked like excited penguins as they responded with bobbing heads and sounds of agreement, approval, and admiration.

The clear and unmistakable sound of Frank's laughter reached me at the top of The Pit from time to time. It started deep in his chest, gathered strength as it traveled up his throat, and exited from his mouth with a force that seemed to defy the laws of physics. *The Laugh* was a machine gun-like spewing of great bursts of energy, and his audience responded to every fusillade with their own giggles and twitters. He wasn't just pontificating. He was entertaining. He was Bob Hope, Milton Berle, Groucho Marx, and Johnny Carson. The man—the artist—possessed a sort of magical aura that engulfed and entranced everyone within a dozen yards of where he sat. I would not have been surprised to see a shower of red rose petals drift down from the sky and land all around him.

Suddenly, Reed looked up, and our eyes met. I'm not sure how long I had been watching—probably only a minute or two. His smile froze, and he got that look he always gets when we see each other in passing. It's like he was thinking, *Where have I seen that guy before? I know that guy.*

The moment passed, and I continued on my way down to the snack bar. I purchased a burrito, but instead of sitting in The Pit, I ate it on my way back to my car and went home.

◎ ◎ ◎

So, why am I sitting in the back of Manny's garage? As soon as I got home from school, my phone rang. It was Manny, and he was pretty excited about a new song he'd written for his band. He wanted me to come over and listen to it.

"I've got plenty of wine, and Mom made a ton of food. It's like a church potluck," he said.

That was all I needed to hear. If they had plenty of wine, that must mean Pet was there since she's the only one in the band old enough to buy it, although Manny's mom, Hester, buys wine for us all the time. She's cooking major food for the band now, too? I wondered what she cooked—and why. I couldn't help but think, Hester is food. Every time she walks into the room, I devour her with my eyes. Of course, that's pretty much all I can do. Even though she flirts with me all the time, there's still at least a twenty-year gap between our ages.

For the record, Hester had made fried chicken, potato salad, coleslaw, and a couple of apple pies. A lot of it was already eaten by the time I got here, but there was more than enough left for me to fill up on, which is what I'm doing now back here in the shadows. I have a full plate and a big mug of wine on the table beside me. The band played Manny's new song for me when I first got here, and it was, indeed, really good. They're practicing some Beatles stuff now because that's what everyone wants to hear.

Pet is exceptionally alluring today in a light-yellow tube top, a short white skirt, and long blonde hair flowing down her back almost to her butt. Her shiny, hot pink lipstick glistens in the light and makes her lips look wet. That's kind of fun. Other than the lipstick and eyeliner, she doesn't wear any makeup—she doesn't have to. The skin of her face is creamy and flawless, with nothing to hide. On stage, the excitement and physical exertion of her performance add a natural glow to her cheeks that no makeup can mimic. Manny's lucky to have her in his band. The guys are good enough as musicians, but they're nothing special when it comes to looks or personality. Until he finds some sort of direction for his music — and can drop the Beatles songs — Pet is the main attraction at their gigs. Pet really can sing, and when she's on stage, she throws everything — and I mean *everything* — into her performance. There are guys who follow the band just to get a glimpse of her tits or crotch, so they watch every move she makes. They're her groupies, but if they pay for the ticket to get in, Manny's all for it. I doubt I'd like it if it were my band and Pet was a close friend like that. I wouldn't want those moronic vermin staring at her like that. It just doesn't seem right.

Speaking of staring, Hester hasn't made an appearance yet. Don't get the idea that I'm one of those moronic vermin I just mentioned simply because I like to look at Hester. She does that flirty thing to me on purpose, and it's impossible not to look. The way she dresses and then parades around in front of me like she does is actually embarrassing. It would be different if I were her age and we were wooing, but that ain't the case. I assume — hope — that one day, Hester will find some guy she's really attracted to, and then she'll stop working on me. Until that day, I'll remain content with the way she is, and I'll eat all the chicken she makes with great gusto. This stuff is excellent.

Manny is yelling at me from up on the stage. "Hey, DH. What did you think?"

"I think you need to play fewer Beatles and more Manny." The lead guitarist, who is totally smitten by all things Beatles, responded to my honest opinion with a semi-audible grumble. Manny chose to ignore him and came over to talk to me.

"I know," he said as he sat down in the chair beside me. "We do a lot of Beatles, but I don't have enough Manny things to play yet. Besides, that's what the band is comfortable doing right now. If we did something out of the ordinary, I don't think they could handle it. Well, Pet could. She can handle anything."

"Pet's the grownup in the room," I said, then reconsidered. "Well, maybe not grown up. Experienced might be a better word."

"I don't know, DH. I'm tired of the puny gigs we've been getting. We need to land something big soon, or I'm gonna tear my hair out."

At least he didn't say he was gonna dissolve the band again.

"Look, Manny, you just need a break. Something's gotta give one of these days. Have you ever thought about getting out of Riverside?"

"You mean move away?"

"Not you, just your gigs. Look for places in LA to do your thing. LA is much more with it than Riverside. There are clubs there that have introduced bands to the world that were nothing when they walked in the door and famous the minute they walked out."

"I know, but you gotta have a connection to get in those places."

"Probably," I agreed.

"So, how do I get a connection?"

"I don't know, but I have an idea."

"What's that?"

"Why don't we drive into LA next weekend, maybe Friday night, and hit a couple of the clubs. Maybe we'll meet somebody that knows somebody."

"Hey, I like that, but it's gonna be hard for a couple of ugly nobodies like us from the boondocks to meet anybody."

"Why don't we take Pet with us? We can spruce her up, put her in a sexy outfit, and she can be our magnet."

"A sexy outfit? You mean like the one she's wearing now?"

"That would work, but maybe even sexier. Let me talk to her."

"Do it." Manny got up and walked back to the stage and talked to Pet for a moment before sending her over to me.

"Hey DH! What's shakin'?" She smiled as she sat down in the

chair Manny had vacated.

"The San Andreas Fault," I said, returning her smile.

"Manny says you got somethin' important to talk to me about. You finally gonna propose to me?" She grabbed my left hand with both of hers and held it to her chest.

"I thought about it, but I know you wouldn't take me up on it."

"I might." She leaned over and kissed me on the cheek.

"I have a plan to help the band," I said seriously.

"Really?" She sat back and gave me her full attention.

"The Riders need a break, and the only way they're gonna get one is to find somebody with some kind of a connection who will listen to their stuff. That somebody could then get them a better gig someplace in LA."

"Cool idea. So, what's the plan? How we gonna pull that off?"

"Simple, I want you and Manny to come with me to LA this weekend and check out some clubs. Maybe we can luck into meeting somebody who knows somebody."

She thought about that for a minute, then gave me a calculating look and said, "Let me guess. You want me to go along as bait, don't you?"

"Well …" I began sheepishly, "Nobody's gonna give a couple of ugly guys like Manny and me a second glance. On the other hand, you're pretty hard to ignore. If people come and talk to you, we'll be waiting."

"I get it. You want the tits and ass routine. I can do that," Pet reached into her tube top, pulled her left breast out, shook it in my face, and then stuck it back in.

"That's not quite what I had in mind," I said after catching my breath. "But I do want you to attract some high rollers. You never know. There may be a big-time scout at one of those clubs, and all we need to do is talk to him for just a minute."

"When do we leave?"

"How about Friday around noon? We can hit one or two clubs, find a place to crash for the night, and maybe hit a couple more on Saturday if we need to."

"Where we gonna crash?" Pet asked.

"I don't know. We can always head to the beach and sleep out on the sand. I know a little cove the cops always miss when they check the beaches after curfew."

Pet leaned close to me again and ran her finger lightly down my cheek. "Does Manny have to come with us?" she purred.

I swallowed hard, then asked, "Why?"

"Because I'd love to lay out on the beach with you all night," she murmured, "I'm afraid we wouldn't get much sleeping done, though."

Pet licked my ear and stood up. It seemed that her hips swayed more than absolutely necessary as she walked back to the stage, and when one hand dropped down and flipped up the hem of her short skirt, I was given a brief but clear view of her naked bottom. I, too, wish that Manny didn't have to come with us.

Oh, well. I'm sure it's for the best.

5
Friday Night

At the Troubadour in West LA

We arrived in LA in the afternoon, several hours before any clubs opened. We stopped at Tiny Naylor's on Wilshire Boulevard for a bite to eat, then headed down to Santa Monica, where we walked along the beach between the pier and Venice Beach. We watched the sunset over the Pacific, then headed back up Santa Monica Boulevard to the Troubadour. Manny and I divided our attention between ogling the girls and finalizing our game plan, and Pet worked at keeping us focused on the reason we took this little trip.

Manny and I were a little concerned that they may not let us in because of our ages, but apparently, they only check ids once you're inside and try to order booze. However, admission to the club seemed to be based on some other more subjective criteria. I don't think Manny and I could have gotten in on our own, but Pet worked her magic on the door attendant. He was so dazzled by her obvious assets that he didn't notice the two of us slipping in behind her.

Inside, the small stage is well lit with various colored lights, but the rest of the club is relatively dark. There's a reddish tint throughout the place that gives the club a decadent, almost forbidden atmosphere. If I didn't know exactly where we were, I could easily believe we were in Shanghai, Tokyo, or wherever red lights mean sleaze and sometimes danger.

By contrast, Pet shines tonight in her very short white dress. The fabric is just thin enough to suggest that she is wearing nothing underneath it. Add to that her gleaming yellow hair, bright blue eyes, and perfect face, and she practically glows in the dusky atmosphere of the club, drawing looks like a flame draws moths.

69

My understanding is that the Troubadour is known for folk, folk/rock, and sometimes even rock music. The group on stage now is none of the above. They're okay, I guess, but I'm not going to be rushing out to buy their records any time soon. The guys in the group seem kind of effeminate. They all have long wavy hair, high nasal voices, and tight pants. Maybe the tight pants account for the high voices. They're okay, I guess. They can carry a tune, and their songs are kind of catchy, like the one in that ride at Disneyland. The women seem to like them despite their goofy looks and bad teeth. I don't get it.

Since we were here to check out the people rather than the band, it did not take us long to find seats at a table where we could do that. We've been here for about half an hour, and Manny's been scanning the room for likely scouts, but the crowd blurs into one big, loud people blob with all the noise and bad lighting. Pet's good looks have been drawing appreciative glances from both men and women, but no one has approached her or invited her to join them. She's been sitting close to me since we got here, teasing me and stealing kisses now and then. I think Manny noticed, but he doesn't really care. He's absorbed in listening to the music and looking out for important people. I guess my idea wasn't such a good one after all. We're having fun, but we could have done that back in Riverside.

"That drummer's pretty good," Manny said, leaning in close to make himself heard.

"He's pretty loud," I replied, unsure if he heard me.

Pet must have, though, because she shouted, "Everything in here is loud."

"This place is too small for this kind of music," I yelled.

"I think we need to go somewhere else," Pet said, speaking right into my ear so she wouldn't have to shout. "Let's go back to the beach and find a soft spot on the sand. I think I've heard and seen enough."

"We might as well." Manny looked depressed now. "There ain't nothin' here for me anyway. I don't see anybody that looks even halfway like a music scout. They're all a bunch of silly drunks."

"They're just groovin' to the music," Pet said.

"Maybe. But they look silly doin' it."

The people in the audience are mainly young adults. The women are all swaying and bobbing their heads like they're oh-so into the music, and the men are all bobbing and swaying because they're oh-so into the women and are trying to impress them. I have to admit the women are attractive at first glance, but most of them have a drink in one hand, a cigarette in the other, and they are all trying hard to look really cool. All I can think about is how bad their breath would be if I were to kiss any of them.

◎ ◎ ◎

Pet's breath is sweet tonight. She told me earlier today that she's trying to quit smoking. That was followed by a long discussion about how cigarettes not only make a person's breath smell bad, but they make their clothes stink, too. I said to her, "The one thing I can never understand is how women can spend tons of money on expensive perfume, put it on their necks, and then light up a cigarette, which completely destroys the scent of the perfume. It makes them smell like a bus station bathroom."

Pet laughed at my comment and said, "I haven't had a cigarette all day, and I don't like wearing perfume. Come a little closer." Then she pulled my head over to her and held my nose to her neck.

◎ ◎ ◎

Here in the club, the music just stopped, and the loud chatter and laughter of the audience have filled the void. I don't know why, but the tinkling of all the bottles and glasses is unnerving to me tonight. It goes right to my brain like the sound of fingernails on a chalkboard.

"I like what Pet just suggested," I said.

"Which part?" Manny asked.

"The part about leaving this place."

"You mean you want to go back to the beach?" Manny asked.

"I don't care where we go as long as it's quiet."

Manny said, "Fine with me," then got up from his seat and stretched. "Let's blow this joint. The music sucks anyway. Who in the world told those fruity zombies they could sing?"

On the Beach

Since we were done with LA clubs for the night, we decided that we would head down the coast to Laguna, which we all love and believe is the best beach around. We found a nice soft piece of sand next to a rocky outcrop that makes it kind of private. It's a warm, clear night, and the stars are exceptionally bright. We stopped on the way down, and Pet bought a gallon of Red Mountain, which we keep out of sight behind the rocks in case a cop strolls by and decides to enforce the ten o'clock curfew. People used to sit here all night, but I guess some homeless dope heads started camping out on the beach and spoiled that for everybody else.

Yes, I'm sitting up here on the dry sand writing in this journal instead of frolicking down there in the gentle waves. Manny and Pet left their shoes up here with me, and they are both wading in the ripples. Manny's been pretty quiet since leaving the Troubadour, so Pet is keeping her distance. She's out in the water up to her knees, and Manny is standing at the waterline but not actually in the water. He likes the beach, but the ocean's not really his thing.

◎ ◎ ◎

Our experience at the club kind of put me off music. Instead, I'm thinking about the yoga class I teach and the martial arts class I just started taking. I've been doing yoga for years now, and it's done me a lot of good. It's kept me limber and has been a big help with my breathing. I got into it mainly because I'm asthmatic and my options for physical exercise are pretty limited. I picked up the martial arts class—kung fu, to be specific—because yoga has become pretty routine, and I wanted something a little more physically and intellectually challenging.

I've taken classes in another martial art form, Okinawan karate, and have earned several belts to mark my advancement. I've only attended three kung fu classes, but I can already see the differences between them. Karate is more physically aggressive. The movements are quick and direct, with the energy directed outwardly at the opponent. In kung fu, the motions are fluid and circular. The student is taught to use his physical and spiritual powers to avoid, deflect, and neutralize aggression. The lessons include more than training in defensive movement. Master Chan, our instructor, also provides instruction on self-control and the energetic and spiritual nature of all things in this world. When I mentioned that I had asthma, Master Chan explained that my asthma results from the improper flow of chi, or life force, through my body. He said his instruction would teach me how to open up my body and allow my chi to flow freely. If true, the classes will be worth the effort just for that.

Pet's waving her arms and yelling something at me. "DH! Come down here with us."

"I'm fine right here," I answered. "I'm deep in thought."

"You need to put your journal away and have some fun," she said.

"Writing in my journal *is* fun."

Pet threw up her hands and turned back toward the ocean. I think I heard a "Whatever" float up with the breeze above the sound of the waves.

I have to admit, it is a bit dark for writing out here. There's just enough light from the nearly full moon for me to see where my pen is on the whiteness of the journal pages. I'll have to wait until I get home to read what I've written because it's too dark to make out the individual words. I hope I can read what I've written.

◎ ◎ ◎

I guess Pet and Manny have had enough of the water as they're both headed back up this way.

"Are your feet getting cold?" I asked Pet as she plopped down beside me.

"No, the water's pretty warm tonight. Where'd you hide that jug of wine?"

"Here it is," I said. "Here's your canteen, too, Manny." He took it and walked away to sit by himself.

When Pet bought the wine, she neglected to get any cups. I remembered that I had a couple of canteens in the car from my last camping trip, so I offered them up as a substitute. Manny grabbed one right away and filled it up, saying that he didn't like the idea of sharing spit. I offered the other canteen to Pet, but she turned it down. "No, thanks," she said. "I don't mind sharing spit if you don't."

I told her I didn't mind either, so Pet and I share the jug, and Manny has the canteen. The way Pet drinks wine, I'm betting our jug goes empty before Manny gets to the bottom of his canteen.

Pet took a couple of swallows, nestled up close to me, and put her arm around me.

"I want to spend the night out here tonight," she said. "Can we do that?"

"As long as we don't get caught."

"It must be at least ten o'clock by now. If the cops come around, we'll hear them, and we can duck behind these rocks."

"That might work," I said.

"I want to fall asleep with my head in your lap," Pet murmured, then nibbled on my ear.

"Don't you think Manny might be a little uncomfortable with you and me getting so cozy right next to him? Besides, I thought you and Manny were kinda together right now. He took you home from a party a while back, so I thought maybe you two had hit it off."

"Are you kidding? All Manny ever does is talk music, and the drunker he gets, the more he talks. He's never even kissed me."

"Really?"

"Really. I don't think I want to kiss him anyway. He's got that squirrelly little mustache, and that's a real turn-off."

"I thought girls liked men with mustaches."

"I suppose it might be okay if it were a real mustache, but all Manny has is a few scraggly hairs lined up under his nose. He looks like a teenager trying to grow a mustache."

"Oh well," I sighed.

"So, what are you writing about?"

"Kung fu."

"Kung fu?"

"It's a martial art, kinda like karate. I'm taking classes."

"What for?"

"I thought it might be good for my asthma."

"Getting beat up is good for asthma?" Pet teased.

"Kung fu isn't meant to be about aggression. It's almost more like a dance. It's hard for me to explain as I've only been at it for a few weeks."

"A dance, huh?"

"My understanding is that kung fu was devised centuries ago by Buddhist monks who were allowed to defend themselves but were forbidden to cause harm or take a life. When the movements are done slowly, they are like a dance. They have the effect of confusing an adversary and causing him to underestimate his intended victim. When push comes to shove—pardon the pun—the defender puts energy and speed into the movements and successfully defends against the attacker, incapacitating him or driving him away. Any actual damage to the attacker is most often the result of the attacker's own uncontrolled aggression and lack of foresight.

"So far, Master Chan has been teaching us two or three movements at a time. We practice them over and over again, moving slowly and focusing on the flow of our body's energy, or chi as Master calls it, until we can do it perfectly and without thinking. The exercise is very exacting, but it's also calming and puts the mind in a peaceful state."

"Kinda like screwing?" Pet said, licking my cheek.

"Nothing like screwing," I said. "It's a philosophy. A gentle and logical way to interpret and deal with the things life brings you."

"Is it a religion?"

"No. As I said, it is a system of thought and action devised by Buddhist monks to defend themselves without violating their teachings. Many of the concepts are based on Buddhist philosophy, but a person doesn't have to be a Buddhist to practice kung fu."

"I've looked into Buddhism a bit," Pet said. "I kind of like some of what I've learned."

"You've mentioned that before. Just for the record, though, I won't be converting to Buddhism any time soon. I like some of the Buddhist thought, but it all falls apart when you make a religion out of it."

"How's that?"

"Because the people don't really follow the teachings. They don't put them into practice in their lives. They just like to masquerade as Buddhists because that seems to be the thing to do at the moment."

"I agree. I know a couple of Buddhists. They're not Chinese. They were born here in the US and got into it as adults. They're always quoting stuff from the Buddhist manual or whatever it's called. They're a couple of the nastiest people I've ever known. They talk about everyone behind their backs, and they're always telling me how they hate this or that or the other. Buddhism is supposed to be about peace and love, isn't it?"

"It's supposed to be," I said.

"Well, they're anything but," Pet said. Then she added rather sadly, "I guess you could say the same thing about many people in most any religion these days, though."

"I think you're right," I agreed. "Like I said, though, I'm not into kung fu for the Buddhism. I'm after whatever wisdom I might find in it. And it's something I am physically capable of doing."

"I thought you were already doing karate. Isn't that what that was supposed to be all about?"

"Yes, but karate isn't much more than an aggressive, physical exercise. Kung fu is different. There's an intellectual element to it and something else that I wouldn't exactly call spiritual but seems to extend beyond the obvious physical world."

"Well, I hope it helps your asthma," Pet hugged me closer.

"Thanks, I hope so, too. In fairness to Buddhists everywhere, the only ones I really know are the ones in my kung fu class. Master Chan seems very sincere in his beliefs—I'm not sure what those beliefs are yet, but he's teaching me some of them. The two Chinese guys are pretty solid in their faith, too. They're always talking about it, but not in a preachy way, mainly about how their Buddhism affects their daily life. One of them, Liko, is very much into his beliefs. He doesn't talk much, but you can see that he looks at this world differently."

"Liko? What an odd name," Pet said.

"We had a conversation about names and their meanings the other day after class. Liko said his name means 'protected by Buddha,' and Wang said his means 'royalty' or "greatness.'"

"Cool."

"They laughed when I told them that my name means 'follower of Dionysus,' the Greek god of wine."

"Well, that certainly fits," she said. She took a swallow from the jug and passed it to me.

I took a sip and said, "They really laughed when I told them that my mother's best friend suggested that she name me after the little Irish tenor from the Jack Benny Show."

"I'll bet they did," Pet said when she stopped laughing. "And you can't carry a tune in a basket."

"That's why Manny makes me sit in the back of the garage when you guys practice." Returning to the topic of names, I said, "The other Asian student, Jiao, told us that her name means 'dainty' and 'lovely.'"

"And is she?"

"She is certainly dainty. She's only about five feet tall, but what meat she has on her bones is all muscle. She's been practicing martial arts for quite some time."

"But is she lovely?"

"Yes, she is pretty in a delicate, almost childlike way." I'm not sure what Pet thought as she didn't say anything after that.

We sat on the sand without speaking, watched the luminescent waves, and listened to their rhythmic roar and hiss as they broke and slid up the beach. The dry sand where we sat was still warm from the day's heat, and Manny lay back with his hands behind his head. He might have been deep in thought or just contemplating the sound of the waves. He might have fallen asleep. I love that sound. I wish I had a house here on the beach. I'd leave my windows open every night and let the sound lull me to sleep.

◎ ◎ ◎

Eventually, Manny stood up, stretched, and brushed the sand off his clothes. "Don't you think we ought to head back to River City soon?" he said as he walked over to us.

"Do we have to?" Pet cooed.

"Do you need to get back home?" I asked. "Is your mom okay with you being out all night?"

"She's okay with it. I just thought a soft, warm bed would be nice. I'm not much for sleeping on the beach."

"You seemed to be doing a pretty good job of it," Pet teased. "I think it would be fun."

"For you two, maybe." The Troubadour had been a disappointment to Manny, and now he seemed disgruntled by the way Pet had cozied up to me.

"Don't be silly, Manny," Pet said. "DH and I were just talking."

"Yeah, right," Manny grumbled.

"And so, what if we weren't just talking? What business is that of yours?" Pet snapped back.

"It's no business of mine, and I don't care what you were doing.

I was just saying that you two would have a lot more fun sleeping together than I would if I were to just sleep by myself. Is that so hard to understand?"

"I think it's a good idea to head back," I said soothingly. "Manny's right, Pet. A soft bed would be better than this sand."

"Whatever," she huffed. "I'll carry the jug. Let's go."

6
Saturday at the Mall

Catching up

We were tired when Manny, Pet, and I got back to Riverside after our less than successful visit to the Troubadour and the beach but were too wound up for sleeping.

"I've got too much going on in my head now. No way I can go to sleep any time soon," Manny said as we got off the freeway in Riverside.

"I'm really sorry the experiment was a bust, Manny. I had hoped you would at least get some ideas or leads about reaching a wider audience," I said.

"Don't worry about it," he replied. "It was worth a shot."

"You look so discouraged, Manny," Pet said.

"I *am* discouraged but not because we couldn't find a connection at the Troubadour."

"Then what's the problem?" I asked.

"I'm discouraged because the music we heard there was so bad. It completely sucked. I'm discouraged because the whole direction music is taking these days is really shitty."

"What? You didn't like the Goober Brothers?" Pet said, dripping sarcasm.

"It's not that they were *bad*," Manny said. "They were boring, which in my opinion is worse. Sure, they sang and played well enough and hit all the right notes at the right time. They had the right look, too—you know, the clothes, the hair, and the cool moves—but they had no depth, no feeling. They were just three guys dressed up and acting like musicians. Real music has a heart and a soul. It has edges."

That was a long speech for Manny. I don't remember when I

last heard him string so many words together or speak them with such emotion. Our little field trip really got him worked up. I took a moment to consider my words before I responded. "Manny, I've been hanging out with you for quite a while now. I can't begin to count the number of practice sessions I've sat in on or how many other band members you've "fired" in that time. I can tell you that you've got real talent and have come a long way as a musician. The songs you write have all the heart, soul, and edges you were talking about, and when Pet belts them out, they just get better. In the art world, the best artists—the True artists—have something called the Art Spirit. It drives them to create and makes their work stand out from all the others. I'd say it works on musicians, too, and you have it in spades."

Pet was serious now and had set all joking aside. "He's right, Manny. Why else do you think I've stuck with you since the beginning? I'm hitching my wagon to a star, and you're that star."

We were nearly home before Manny broke the silence. "Wow. Thanks, guys. You've given me a lot to think about."

"Why don't you come back to my place for a while? My parents aren't home, and it's a warm night. We could sit out on the patio, drink some wine, and play some good music. I think I can even find something to snack on in the kitchen."

◎ ◎ ◎

We spent the next couple of hours chatting out on the patio. Eventually, we all decided that we had wound down enough to try to go to sleep. We kept things simple by going inside and stretching out on the family room floor. I think Pet still had some energy to burn off because she curled up close to me and kept trying to get me to "play" with her. I pretended to be asleep. She finally left me alone, and I really was asleep pretty soon.

We woke up around nine this morning, and since no one felt like cooking and cleaning up after, we went to the Royal Scot for breakfast. We didn't talk much. I think we were all still mulling over the events and conversations of yesterday—especially Manny.

"I really should be getting home soon," Manny said as he finished his last bite of egg and toast. "I promised Mom I'd get some things done around the house for her."

We paid our bill and left a generous tip before returning to my car. I dropped Manny off at his house, then headed toward Pet's house. Before we had gone very far, she asked, "Do I have to go home now?"

"I don't know," I said. "Do you?"

"I still have clean underwear in my drawer, and there are no dirty dishes in the sink, so I'm free. What are you gonna do, DH?"

"I thought about heading over to the bookstore in the mall. I need something new to read."

"Can I go with you?"

◎ ◎ ◎

I found a couple of books to add to my growing art history and philosophy library, and Pet found a copy of a brand-new magazine—The Mossy Rock, The Slick Pebble, or something like that. It's supposed to be all about the latest trends in rock music. Now we're sitting on a bench under a tree, each of us sipping on an Orange Julius. Pet's head is buried in her magazine, and I'm bringing my journal up to date.

"Manny's going to want to see this magazine," Pet said as she turned another page. "It's packed with all kinds of stuff you don't see anywhere else. I hope they can stick to stories about music and musicians and not get bogged down in politics."

She closed her magazine and turned her attention to me and my journal. "I can't imagine what you're writing about," Pet said. "We pretty much covered everything last night."

"But that's what I'm writing about, my dear," I said, grinning at her. "I'm just getting it all down in my journal before I forget."

"All of it? Does that include what we did on the beach?" She grinned and waggled her eyebrows in Groucho Marx fashion.

"You mean the part about you nibbling on my ear or the part about Buddhism?"

She paused, realizing that I was serious. "Both," she said, finally.

"I think I spent a few more words on Buddhism than I did on ear nibbling. It seemed a bit more important."

"You might be right," she said, "Can I ask you a question?"

"Sure, ask away."

"You and I have talked about a lot of really cool stuff in the time we've known each other, but I'm still puzzled about what you really believe."

"What do you mean?"

"The spiritual stuff. You're a really spiritual guy, so you must have some sort of religion you follow. We've talked about Buddhism, Catholicism, Taoism, Christianity, Judaism, you name it. You've expressed your opinion on all those religions and philosophies and how incomplete and inadequate they are, but I've never heard you talk about what you believe. I can't figure out what it might be because you don't seem to like any of them."

"It's not that I don't *like* any of them—I just don't *believe* any of them. At least I don't believe what they are pretending to be."

"Pretending?"

"Sure, what else could they be doing? Even the Bible says that no human on Earth has a clue as to what makes God tick, so if they say they do, they must be pretending."

"I know. We've talked about that, too, but that's not my question. Given all we've discussed before, in every bit of all our combined hot air, you have never once told me what it is you *do* believe. You must have some kind of personal faith."

"I've touched on it, Pet, but honestly, without making up my own religion and being guilty of the same nonsense as all the others, I don't really know how to answer you."

"Give it a try. Just pretend for a minute that you're gonna make up your own religion, one that you believe is closer to the truth than any other religion on Earth. What would it look like?"

"Wow, that's a tall order. If I could go back through all of my journal entries, I could probably come up with a list of things that I'd include in a personal religion plan, but off the top of my head like this—"

"DH, hey! And pretty blonde lady, hey!"

I know that voice. I look around and, sure enough, it's Fr. Bob and his sidekick, Sister Teresa, bearing down on us.

"Padre! Wow. As usual, your timing is impeccable."

"Always happy to oblige." Fr. Bob executed a theatrical bow and said, "How may I be of service?"

"Pet and I were about to engage in a serious discussion about religion and spirituality," I said. "But first, let me introduce you. Pet, these are my buddies, Fr. Bob Erstad and Sister Teresa ..." I paused and looked at her. "I don't think I've ever heard your last name Sister."

"We don't use last names," she said. "When we take our vows, we drop our worldly names and develop our lives around new, spiritual names."

"It's nice to meet you, Pet," Fr. Bob held out his hand for Pet to shake, "I'm betting Pet isn't your name either."

"You would win that bet, Father," Pet said, shaking his hand.

"So, Fr. Bob, what brings you out on this fine Saturday," I asked.

"We're just roaming around, casting out demons along the way," he said. "Sister here is much better at doing that than I am. Her mind is much purer than mine."

"It has to be if I'm to keep you on the straight and narrow, Father." Turning to Pet, Sister said, "It's very nice to meet you, Pet."

Pet took the hand Sister offered her and said, "I don't think I've ever shaken hands with a nun before," Just for a moment, I saw an innocent ten-year-old girl looking through the eyes of mature and worldly Pet.

Sister smiled warmly and said, "I don't think I've ever shaken hands with a rock star before."

"What?" Pet looked at me with raised eyebrows demanding

an explanation.

"I think I may have mentioned you and Manny to Father Bob and Sister Teresa once or twice," I said.

"Yes, he did, Miss Pet," Fr. Bob said. "He's bragged about you a lot."

"Really?" Pet's look this time was a demand to know what I had said—or maybe a warning that I had better not have said too much. I know I must have mentioned her talent as a singer, but I don't think I ever said anything too personal, like how I thought she was a sex goddess ... or did I? I returned Pet's look with a sheepish grin.

Fr. Bob shifted his discerning gaze from me to Pet and back again. His light-hearted demeanor returned, and he said, "A more important question than what we are doing here is what are you two doing here? Sister and I have the protection of all the holy aura stuff that envelopes us everywhere we go, but you not-so-holy ones are takin' a big chance by exposing yourselves to the temptations of the shopping mall."

"The only temptations I'm likely to fall for around here are found in the philosophy and art sections of the bookstore." I laid my hand on the shopping bag from the Little Professor. "As you can see, Father, I have sinned."

Father Bob waved his hand over me in a vague sign of the cross and said, "A minor sin and one that is easily forgiven."

"I really am happy to see you here," I said. "Pet and I were just embarking on a serious discussion of religion. Have a seat and join us." I indicated the bench that formed a right angle with the one Pet and I occupied.

"Religion, huh? Fr. Bob said as he and Sister sat down and got comfortable. "That's all you ever talk about—except for ghosts and art."

Eyes wide, Pet leaned close to Fr. Bob and said in a hushed and earnest voice, "You know about his ghost girlfriend?"

"Of course I do, young lady. I am his confessor. He tells me everything."

Sister Teresa said nothing, but I did notice the eye roll.

Pet sat back and continued in a more normal tone, "I was trying to pin DH down on what he really believes about God and religion."

"Good luck," Fr. Bob said. "I've spent hours trying to get him to do that. He's got a lot to say about what he doesn't believe but very little about what he does."

"Come on, guys, don't gang up on me," I protested. "I'm just being honest. It's all a mystery to me, so I'm not about to come out and profess something I don't understand like everyone else seems to do."

Pet looked at me and frowned. "That's a cop-out."

"Yeah, what Pet said." Fr. Bob leaned back, crossed his arms over his chest, and nodded emphatically.

"If I may ..." Sister intervened in her sweet and reasonable way. "I believe we arrived just as Pet asked you what your own religion would look like should you make one up. I'd like to hear your answer, too."

"How long were you two standing there behind me, anyway?"

"They were there for a couple of minutes," Pet said. "I thought it was odd, but since he's wearing that black shirt with the funny collar and she's wearing that nun outfit, I figured they were officially religious. They kind of unnerved me at first, and I didn't want to say anything to them."

Fr. Bob pointed his finger at Pet and said with mock solemnity, "Yes, always be careful when confronting a priest, young lady. They hold the power of Heaven and Hell in their very hands."

Sister punched him lightly in the arm and scolded him. "I think they're attempting a *serious* conversation here, Father,"

"What can be more serious than Heaven and Hell?" Fr. Bob protested.

Pet seems to be thoroughly confused by this exchange.

"See, Pet? That's what I mean," I said. "These crazy Catholics think they hold the keys to heaven and hell, even though the Bible never says so."

"Not in so many words," Fr. Bob responds. "The New Testament does say that Jesus gave Peter the Keys to the Kingdom. Jesus told Peter, 'Whatever you bind on Earth shall be bound in Heaven; and whatever you loose on Earth shall be loosed in Heaven.' Since Peter was the first Pope, those words certainly imply that Jesus gave the keys to the Catholic Church."

I defended my opinion. "Those words certainly can be taken that way if you're a Catholic, but I'll bet any Baptist has a different take on them. There are thousands of words in the Bible, Padre, and depending on who you are and what religion you belong to, they can be read to mean just about anything anyone wants them to mean. How many words does it take to clarify the few simple truths that Jesus taught while He was here among us? Why is the Bible hundreds of pages long? And why are all the commentaries even longer? Take the Catholic catechism, for instance. Why is it so long? Why can't church leaders just take Jesus's words and put them in a little pamphlet? It seems to me that everything a person needs to know is contained in the teachings of Jesus, and not in all the other stuff that was added later."

"Here we go," Pet muttered, rolling her eyes.

"You are right, DH. All the truth a person needs is in the Bible and in the words of Jesus especially. Reading those words with an open mind and an open heart will plant the seed of faith. The Bible presents the Truth as experienced by a multitude of people across the span of thousands of years. The catechisms and commentaries are efforts to unify the Truth of these stories and make it plain to people wanting to learn more about what they have faith in and are looking for examples of how to live their faith."

"But that's my point," I said. "People use the excuse of 'clarifying the truth' or sharing some special revelation to invent religions. They hold up their own beliefs and opinions as absolutes that their followers *must* believe and follow if they're not to be condemned as lacking in faith and judged to be 'unworthy.' That's a problem."

Fr. Bob nodded and sighed deeply. "Well, you know that I agree with most of what you just said. You also have to agree that there must be some absolutes to follow if civilized society is to survive. If everyone were allowed to live according to their own individual interpretation of truth, or if right and wrong were determined according to a sliding scale, this world would be a more dangerous place. The Catholic Church has been collecting and analyzing the writings of the Prophets, Apostles, Saints, and Martyrs for two thousand years. A relatively small portion has been grouped together in what we now call the Holy Bible. A vast number have been approved as suitable for instruction. Those additional writings offer clarification and inspiration to humans who want to understand the teachings of Jesus and want to live according to God's will. I suppose they're not strictly necessary, but they do make things easier to comprehend for many people."

"I can't argue with you on that, Padre," I said.

Fr. Bob smiled broadly and said, "Then why don't we just leave it there. Sometimes, religions may be a pain in the butt, but they are the only checks we have on an out-of-balance society that seems bent on evil, hatred, and self-destruction. It is important, though, that people give careful consideration to who or what they choose to follow and why."

"I definitely agree with you on that, Fr. Bob."

"DH still hasn't told us what his religion would look like if he could invent his own," Pet said.

"Yes, DH, I'm kind of curious about that myself," Sister Teresa said.

All three of them looked at me expectantly, so I really had no choice. "Okay. At the risk of being presumptuous, I'll give it a shot just to shut you guys up."

I took a moment to gather my thoughts, then began. "First of all, I would have only one rule or commandment that would encompass every situation encountered by humans, and if everyone followed it, there would never be any problems. That commandment is to 'do unto others as you would have them do unto you.' In other words, the Golden Rule. It's that simple. If everyone followed that rule, there would be no need for more rules or commandments as that one covers all situations. If free will is really that important, then people should not be burdened with a plethora of commands that arbitrarily limit or threaten free will. The plain and simple words of the Golden Rule give every person the tool to determine their own boundaries for living in a civilized culture. Further guidance is found when those words are stated in reverse—do NOT do to others what you would not have done to you.

"Yes, this culture needs some boundaries that should never be crossed, but those boundaries ought to be obvious. In fact, I believe they are inherent within every human heart, mind, and soul. Take murder and theft, for instance. Most people have a natural aversion or even revulsion to them. If you take the Bible literally word for word, then any form of murder or stealing is subject to severe punishment. Those acts are certainly not allowable under the Golden Rule. Who wants to be stolen from? Who wants to be killed? Even so, theft and murder happen. Those acts can never be condoned and are often motivated by envy, greed, or just plain evil. Still, people often find themselves in situations where they feel their survival depends on theft or murder. They steal food because they or their family are starving. They kill someone to defend their own life. These situations are opportunities for others to follow the Golden Rule by practicing compassion, charity, and forgiveness."

"But human nature is such that your simple logic would be crushed on this planet in a minute," Bob said.

"Only because that is how humanity has been taught for centuries," I replied. "Had egotistical humans not instituted their multitude of rules in the first place, people would have learned to respect each other, and my one rule would be all that is necessary. If a person were starving and needed to eat, then a hundred people living by the Golden Rule would be right there for him, and he wouldn't need to steal.

Religions have presented people with hundreds of often-conflicting systems of rules and regulations, and they've confused and complicated just about everything Jesus said in the Bible. Over time, people have become dependent on laws that regulate every detail of their lives. Like drugs, people not only need them, but they demand them."

I paused to catch my breath and let out a single, ironic laugh. I shook my head and continued, "Even as I say all that, I can hear in my own head just how simple-minded and maybe even stupid it sounds. But I'm young, so I may change my mind a hundred times before I settle on what I believe."

"Is that all your religion would be? Just that one rule?" Pet asked.

"My religion is not so much what it *would* be as what it would *not* be. It would not have buildings—people would worship God in the outdoors. It would not have rituals and ceremonies. And, sorry to tell you, Padre, it would not have a clergy because it wouldn't need one."

Fr. Bob threw up his hands and said, "There goes my pension."

"How do you worship God without ceremony and ritual?" Sister asked. "What sets your worship of God apart from anything else you do? Shouldn't the act of worship be something special and distinct from any other daily activity?"

"The essence of worship is prayer, and the most perfect form of prayer is silence. People following my religion would find places close to nature—under the stars, at the seaside, in the desert, or even in their back yard or on their front porch. Once there, they would simply sit quietly in God's creation, feel the beauty of it in their hearts, and be totally silent. At most, they could say, 'Thank you, God, for giving me this wonderful beauty to enjoy,' and that would be it."

"Sounds good to me," Pet agreed.

"But it would never work," Fr. Bob said.

"Only because those in charge of religious institutions have convinced humanity that it can't get along without them," I explained. "Dumping them all for mere truth would put a lot of powerful, rich people out of their jobs."

"A lot of other people would be out of work, too, if the world adopted your religion, DH," Sister said, "including me."

"Would they really, Sister?" I asked. "Would you not still be the same person you are on the inside, with or without the habit you wear? You would still help people by teaching, healing, and comforting them. And with everyone living by the Golden Rule, you would still have as much support for that purpose as you do now, if not more."

Fr. Bob said, "There's just one more thing I'd like to know before we close off this conversation."

"I'm all ears, Padre," I said.

"When you've sorted out all your philosophical and spiritual ramblings, is there any chance you would ever consider becoming a Catholic?"

"I don't rule anything out. For the time being, I'm just exploring ideas, and I don't want to toss anything out completely. Honestly, though, if I were to follow any religion right now, it would be the Catholic faith, mainly because of the Saints. They were driven to live their lives in the way Jesus taught as perfectly as they could, often suffering and even dying because of their determination. That's how the saints became saints. They didn't just sit inside the church building praying their rosaries and crying, 'Why me, Lord?' They asked real questions and learned to listen silently for real answers. They didn't look for God in a church building. They saw Him in all of Creation and in all of His Creatures, especially Saint Francis — he even preached to the birds. Their example gives us the freedom and encouragement to explore many things of a spiritual and even supernatural nature. If a Baptist did that, they'd probably be tossed out."

"I've known some narrow-minded Catholics in my time," Sister said. "Some Catholics seem to be more receptive to such things than others."

"True," Fr. Bob said. "I knew a man who had a near-death

experience similar to yours, DH. He gave a talk about it at the church one evening, and a handful of people walked out on him."

Sister nodded and said, "One of the sisters in the convent told me of a man who talked about seeing ghosts. The bishop called him in and told him not to talk about such things."

"That's exactly what I mean," I said. "For cryin' out loud, the saints saw ghosts and had supernatural experiences, and they got canonized. Why is the Church so critical now?"

"I suppose it has to do with the difficulty of validation," Fr. Bob said. "People, Catholics among them, believe a lot of silly things these days. Events presented to support canonization or even as worthy of serious thought need proof. Many people talk about seeing ghosts or having visions or other supernatural experiences. Those claims make their way through the Church hierarchy and are examined and discarded until what is left can only be explained as miraculous. Very few make the grade. People tell these stories because they are looking for attention or want to elevate their stature in the Church. After all, the Fatima kids are famous, but old Mabel and Jake in the third pew from the back aren't. There are a lot of Mabel and Jakes in the Church telling stories all the time. They want to be famous too, and that's why the Church demands proof of the supernatural. There would be chaos if it didn't."

"I suppose you are right on that," I agreed. "It would be nice, though, to talk about these things openly as possibilities rather than as true or false."

"Well, I'm glad to know that you don't completely dismiss the Church." Fr. Bob smiled warmly. "Maybe I'll see you at Mass one day,"

"Who knows. For now, though, I believe the most beautiful cathedrals are the national parks, the holiest priests are the wild animals of the forests, and the truest worshipers are the wind and the sunshine. I don't worship nature. I worship God. I don't limit Him to any definition or image made up by humans. I don't limit Him to human abilities. I give God the freedom to do as He wills with all things, and I praise Him for the wondrous miracle of nature that He made. That is my religion."

"Now you sound like St. Francis," Sister Teresa smiled.

I smiled back at Sister. "Well then, maybe Francis was an even greater saint than the Church imagines him to be."

7
Two Weeks Later

In The Pit

We are several weeks into this semester now, and I can see why psychology is a mandatory class for graduation. You would think that the study of what makes humans tick would be interesting, but this introductory-level class is so dull that no one would take it if it were an elective. The best thing about it is the instructor, Miss Jill Ocean. She is truly gorgeous. Frankly, though, I'd rather be painting her than listening to her. Today's topic was particularly dull, and the page in my notebook is covered with drawings instead of notes. I'm afraid my grade will suffer if this class doesn't get more interesting soon.

After class, I managed to snag my table in The Pit before the enigmatic Frank Reed claimed it this afternoon. I saw him briefly a few minutes ago when I glanced up from my journal. He stood at the top of the stairs, saw me sitting here, then turned and left. I wonder if he knows that I know that this is his table. He looked right at me before he walked away and gave me that slightly puzzled look he always does when we see each other. I thought about leaving so he could come down and occupy what I have come to think of as his throne, but he turned away before I had a chance. It's odd that no one ever sits here except Frank or me. If one of us is not sitting here, the table is always open. It's as though the entire college knows that Frank Reed sits here, and I am the only one who dares to encroach on his space.

I'm sure I'll get to meet him eventually, but I'm not so sure I'll be very comfortable when I do. It'll be like meeting the Pope. What do you do when you meet the Pope? Do you bow? Kiss his ring? I'm not gonna kiss anybody's ring. I suppose I'll shake Frank's hand if he offers it, but he might not do that. Some high and mighty people don't like to be touched. Like Howard Hughes—I've heard he's afraid of getting germs from other people. Maybe Frank will be like Howard. Oh well, I'll cross that bridge when I come to it.

My classes are finished for the day, so I thought I'd sit here, sip some iced tea, and write in my journal. I'm not sure what to write about—I haven't done much more than attend class, study, and paint and draw these last two weeks. My classes are all going well. I'm keeping up with them anyway, with the possible exception of sociology. Like psychology, it's a requirement for my AA degree. Also, like psychology, it's boring. Again, you would think that a class about the development, structure, and function of human society would be interesting. Somehow, though, the Powers that Be have managed to reduce the introduction to this potentially rich and fascinating study into deadly-dull and irrelevant nonsense. At least the presence of Miss Ocean gives me something pleasant and diverting to look at in psychology class.

To her credit, Miss Ocean takes the time to organize the lessons and back up her commentary with verifiable references. On the other hand, Dr. Anders puts no logic or order in his sociology lectures—if you can call them that—at all. He just shows up in class and begins a rambling dissertation filled with rants and complaints about current events and the evils of The Establishment. He doesn't teach anything. Instead, he imparts his own personal opinions with no verifiable facts or references. Most of his views deride conventional values like faith, traditional family structure, strong work ethics, and personal responsibility. Based on the body language of the other students in the class, I'd say that most of them aren't buying it, but beyond some head-shaking and eye-rolling, no one's challenging him, either. I can't really blame them. It's easy and safe to sit quietly in class, repeat the lines that will make the teacher happy, take the grade, and move on.

I know that's what I should do, too, but sometimes I just can't help myself. One day, I felt brave and spoke up. "Where did you get that info? I watch the news and read the papers. What you're saying is pretty much the opposite of what I see and hear."

Anders gave me his condescending smirk and said, "You're going to the wrong sources. You have to know where to look and who to talk to."

Of course, there are a couple of students who agree with everything he says. These groupies — I call them bobbleheads — give Anders their rapt attention and show their approval by nodding their heads continuously while he speaks. The bobbleheads are representative of the few hippies we have here at RCC. I met some and observed many hippies during my trip to San Francisco last summer and came away with mixed feelings about them. They may have been sincere going into the movement, but the justifications for their lifestyle and beliefs quickly turned into excuses for not finding work and for engaging in anti-social habits and behaviors.

In spite of — or maybe because of — my disillusionment with my "general ed" classes, I'm more focused than ever on art. I love my ceramics and sculpture classes, and Bill Mitchkelly is a terrific teacher. In all honesty, though, I'd rather be drawing and painting.

Ceramics and sculpture are messy, and each project takes so long to complete. There are too many steps and processes to get through before anything is finished. I can pick up a brush and turn out a finished painting in an hour, or I can work on it for days. It's an ongoing, emotional, stream of consciousness kind of thing, dependent on my mood rather than the laws of chemistry and physics like so much of ceramics and sculpture are. I don't have to worry about a vase sagging under its own weight or a mold breaking because the temperatures were wrong for casting. I can attack a canvas with wild movements and bright, pure colors, and the satisfaction is immediate.

I see Jack coming down the steps. I haven't talked to him in a while. He looks like he's looking for me.

Jack has, indeed, located me and is headed toward my table in the back of The Pit. "Hey," he said while still a good twenty feet away.

I greeted him with a smile and said, "Hey back," as he reached the table and sat down across from me.

"What's up?" he asked.

"Just sitting here and catching up on my writing."

"Ah ... the old journal."

"Yep, the old journal."

"How would you like to have something really cool to write about in there?"

"Whattaya mean?"

"I'm drivin' down to Mexicali tomorrow to pick up some meat. I'm runnin' out of fillet. Wanna come with me?"

"You mean Mexicali in Mexico?"

"I'm pretty sure that's where it is," Jack said sarcastically.

"That would be interesting. I've never been there before. Is it hard to get across the border?"

"Heck no. Been there many times. That's where I go buy all my meat. They've got fillet mignon down there for the price of hamburger. I bring it back up here and grind it myself."

"How do you plan to get there? You don't have a car, and I'm not riding all the way down there on the back of your bike."

"We'll take the truck."

"What truck?"

"The factory truck. The one I use to deliver mattresses."

"You mean your boss will let you drive his truck to Mexico and back?"

"I drive it all over town all the time."

"Yeah, but Mexico?"

"The boss is out of town for the weekend. We'll only stay one night, and he'll never know."

"Isn't that like car theft?"

"Heck no. I'm just gonna borrow it for a short run to Mexicali, and I'll replace the gas."

"It's, like, 200 miles down there," I said.

"175."

"Well ... I don't know."

"I'll go alone if you got somethin' better to do, but you'll be missin' out. We can do some clubs down there, and you oughta see the sisters in the family I'm gonna stay with."

"Are they pretty?"

"Pretty ain't the word. They're gorgeous!"

"And they're all underage, right?"

"No! They're all in their twenties — silky black hair flowin' down their backs, pretty faces, big jugs. One of them has the hots for me, but the other two are single and like to have fun. You can have your pick."

"I don't know. I'm kind of a boring guy, and I don't really care for clubs."

"Look, DH, these are sweet Mexican girls from a nice family. Not a bunch of hookers or whatever. You'll get along. They live on a beautiful little ranch with lots of trees and paths that light up at night. Really nice for strollin' around with a girl by your side. They're daddy's rich, too. They have servants, and the food, wine, and beer never stop flowin'."

"Sounds like heaven," I said cautiously. "What's the catch? How do you know these people?"

"No catch. I've known 'em for a long time. The girls' brother went to UCR and worked part-time at the mattress factory just for something to do. We got to be pretty tight buddies. He got his degree last year and moved back to Mexicali so he can help his dad in his business."

"What's his dad do?"

"I'm not really sure what his title is. He works in the government somewhere — some kind of engineering. That's what Paco's degree is in, too."

"Well, I tell you what, my friend. This whole thing sounds a bit crazy, but I'm in the mood for crazy. The only part I really worry about is the truck thing. What kind is it?"

"It's a great old truck. A '52 Ford. Sounds like the devil, but it gets from Here to There every time. It'll do seventy goin' downhill without shaking too much."

"Shaking?"

"Yeah, it starts vibrating when it gets past sixty. I don't know what's wrong with it. Probably just a wheel weight or two."

"Great. Driving to Mexico in a borrowed truck that shakes at highway speed. What could possibly go wrong?"

8
A Trip to Mexicali

Four Hours Down the Road

We drove south on Highway 395 through Perris and down to Escondido. After Jack filled up the truck with gas yet again, we went around the corner to a little hole-in-the-wall Mexican café where the two cute senoritas in short, tight skirts and heavy makeup waiting on tables greeted him like an old friend. One of them put her arm through Jack's and led him toward a table. The other one smiled at me, took my arm, and followed. After an exchange in neither Spanish nor English, we placed our orders punctuated with winks, smiles, and gestures transcending the language barrier. The girls brought us big glasses of ice tea and then returned for our food—a chili relleno and a couple of tacos for me and a large bowl of menudo for Jack. They also brought us a giant bowl of refried beans, which they insisted was *en la casa*, and a bowl of salsa. I tasted the salsa. It nearly brought me to tears, so I gave it a pass. Jack shook his head and smiled at me as he liberally dowsed his menudo with the fiery concoction. We both ate the beans. I always thought that refried beans were pretty much the same everywhere—bland and boring—but these were really tasty. We ate every bit and cleaned the bowl with pieces of the tortillas that came with Jack's menudo. We still had over a hundred miles to go. I hoped we wouldn't come to regret the beans and salsa.

The two waitresses remained attentive and kept up their flirtation throughout our meal. When we made preparations to leave, they seemed sorry to see us go. The one more fluent in English told us that she had family in Mexicali and we should look them up for a good time.

"You know what a 'good time' is, don't you?" Jack asked as we pulled back onto the highway. "Sex and drugs," he said flatly.

For me, anyway, drugs are definitely out of the question, and the sex is probably not a good idea, either.

We headed east from Escondido on Highway 78, drove through Ramona and Julian, over the mountains, and down into the desert toward the Salton Sea. It's been one long haul through the hot, barren desert. It's surprising how simply crossing from one side of the mountains to the other can make such a difference in the temperature. It was a comfortable eighty degrees in Escondido, but it's got to be pushing a hundred degrees where we are now.

According to the map, our next opportunity for gas is in a town called Westmorland. I hope we make it. From where I'm sitting, the needle on the gauge looks like it's sitting on empty.

"What kind of mileage does this old truck get, Jack?"

"How many times have we stopped for gas?" he replied.

"Three, so far."

"What does that tell you?"

"It gets pretty crappy mileage."

"Bingo."

"Can we make it to Westmoreland?"

"Hope so."

Fuel is not the only thing I'm worried about. This old bucket of bolts is not just vibrating. It's shuddering. The glass of the open window next to me is rattling down inside the door like it will bust into pieces any minute. We'll be lucky if we make it to Mexicali, and I have serious doubts about making it all the way back to Riverside tomorrow.

"You should be more worried about the Mexican police arresting us for driving a stolen truck," he said when I expressed my concerns. Then he took his eyes off the road momentarily and grinned at me.

We made it, but I have no idea how.

At Paco's House Two Hours Later

The streets in Mexicali are confusing, and Jack managed to get lost even though he's visited his friend, Paco, several times before. We parked Bertha—that's what we named the truck—and went into a little market and asked to use the phone. The market owner told us in broken English that he didn't have one and pointed the way to another store down the street that did. The owner at the second store wouldn't let us use his phone either, but he did agree to make the call for us. He dialed the number we gave him and was soon engaged in a rapid-fire conversation that I don't think I could have followed, even if it had been in English. Whatever they were talking about, it involved a lot of laughter. Jack finally lost patience with the owner and practically yelled at him, "Just find out how to get from here to there!"

The owner smiled at Jack and patted the air with his hand to tell him to calm down. Finally, after a couple more rounds of talking, listening, and laughing, he hung up. Still chuckling, he led us to a rough bench by the front door. He told us to wait there, then returned to dusting his shelves or whatever he was doing before we interrupted him.

We waited with a growing sense of unease. We were, after all, sitting in a strange neighborhood in a foreign city where we knew only one person and did not speak much of the language. About ten minutes passed when we put our heads together to quietly discuss our options. The bell over the door jingled, and we braced ourselves for action.

"*Hola*, Jack!" It was Paco. "*Qué pasa?*" It turned out that we were not far from Paco's house, and he thought it would be easier to come and guide us than to give us directions. Paco tried to tip the owner for helping us out, but he just smiled and waved him off. Jack and I shook hands with him, thanked him for his assistance, and followed Paco out the door.

Jack wasn't kidding when he told me Paco's family had money. The house doesn't look like much from the outside. In fact, most of the homes in Mexicali are pretty plain on the outside. Jack says it makes it harder for any would-be robbers to decide which houses are worth the effort. A brick wall separates the small front yard from the street. A thick jungle of desert plants and trees—cactus, thorny trees, oleanders—disguises the house's actual size and shape. A gravel path through a dense stand of prickly pear cactus leads from the front gate to a plain wooden door on that side of the house.

The main entrance, though, is on the side facing a gated private drive. Big, carved wooden double doors open into a large entry paved with marble floors. There are skylights in the roof, allowing filtered light to shine on the mega-sized potted plants that line the walls. About fifteen feet beyond the front doors, the entry narrowed and continued straight along the length of the house, but an opening on the right revealed a sunken living room. We descended the steps into an enormous room filled with ornate furniture. Beautiful handmade rugs cover most of the marble floor, and old oil paintings cover the walls. A stone fireplace with a thick, natural wood mantel occupies most of one wall. Heavy posts and a wide beam matching the fireplace mantel define an opening at the far end of the living room. That room is shadowed, but I think it's a dining room as I can make out a table and chairs. There is also just enough light filtering in from the living room to sparkle on something hanging over the table. A chandelier, maybe? Shadowy squares on the part of the wall that I can see look like they might be more paintings. I'm looking forward to seeing that room with the lights on.

"Have a seat and make yourselves comfortable," Paco said as he guided us to one of the big, cushy sofas. "My father knows you're here, so he should be along to meet you in a few minutes."

So, here we sit. Paco and Jack have been engaging in small talk, but I've been too busy examining the room and what little I can see beyond it to pay attention. I've already counted three women of various ages dressed in maid outfits bustling here and there and carrying this and that. I think the house must be much larger and more important than it appears from the outside to justify having that many maids.

◎ ◎ ◎

Paco has just returned accompanied by a striking-looking older man. "Hey, guys," he said, smiling broadly. "This is my Dad, Cesar Diego Maria Escondo Flores."

Señor Flores is a big guy. He's at least six feet tall, barrel-chested, flat-bellied, and the sleeves of his white *guayabera* fit snuggly around his thick biceps. He looks a lot like the actor from *The F.B.I*, only bigger and better built.

"Dad, I believe you know my friend, Jack," Paco said as we stood to greet him.

Señor Flores smiled and extended his right hand. "Yes, I do know this young man. Welcome back to Casa Flores."

Jack shook the offered hand and replied, "Thank you for having me, sir."

"And this is DH, Jack's friend from Riverside," Paco said, waving me forward.

I stepped up and extended my hand. "I'm pleased to meet you, Señor Flores."

"Enough with the señor and sir. Call me Cesar. Please, be seated," he said, waving us back to the couch. He turned his attention to the maid standing quietly by the entrance to the dining room. "Katia, please inform the cook that we have guests and will be needing some refreshment." The little maid nodded her head and scurried off on her errand.

Cesar crossed the room to a large, glass-fronted oak cabinet filled with various liquor and the appropriate glassware for enjoying all of it. He opened a door and removed one of the bottles and a few glasses that looked like crystal balloons. "Would you care for some brandy?" He began pouring before we could answer. "The French make the best brandy in the world," he said as he handed us the goblets containing a scant inch of fragrant, amber liquid. "Just as the best painters in the world are French," he continued.

"Dad collects art — especially French art," Paco explained.

"Really?" I said. "My favorite painters are the Impressionists. Most of them were French."

Cesar looked at me with new interest. "You are an art lover?"

"I am. I'm studying art at the college in Riverside."

"You are? I am most impressed. I must show you my collection of Impressionist paintings."

I had just taken my first sip of the brandy and nearly choked, not because of the brandy but because of what Caesar said.

"You collect Impressionist paintings? Like, from the famous guys, Monet, Degas, and the others?" I said when I was able to speak.

He smiled at my amazement, his eyes twinkling. "I have a great many throughout the house. I will show you around soon."

I turned to Jack and said, "You didn't tell me about the paintings."

"You never asked," he replied. Typical Jack.

"I believe there are one or two Impressionist paintings in nearly every room except this one," Cesar said.

"This room and the dining room contain only art by Mexican artists," Paco explained. "Dad entertains many important people — government officials, businessmen, and others with influence. He thinks this all makes a good impression on them."

I looked around the room and realized that there was far more art than just the paintings on the walls. The cabinets, shelves, niches, and tabletops were filled with sculptures and pottery — some of it finely crafted and some very primitive. I saw, too, that even the colorful rugs on the floor were hand-woven works of art. All unique and beautiful. I turned to face Cesar again and smiled. "Well, it's made a good impression on me."

"And you are an important guest," Caesar said expansively. "I can see that you are a lover of art, unlike most government officials."

"Thank you. I do love art, but I'm not sure that makes me more important than a government official."

"Oh, it does," Paco said wryly. "Dad doesn't think much of bureaucrats."

"But that is the subject for some other time." Cesar waved his hand like he was brushing away a fly. "For now, we sip brandy and talk of things that really matter, like art, music, and women."

"Hear, hear," Jack said, raising his brandy glass.

We sat and chatted for another half hour, then I noticed the lights in the dining room turn on. The maid who had taken Cesar's order to the kitchen had returned accompanied by two older women wearing aprons. All three of them carried large trays loaded with food and serving utensils. They placed the trays on a large sideboard and arranged the food on the table, along with a stack of plates and some forks and napkins. The women worked quickly, and as they left the room, one of them rang a small bell to indicate that all was ready.

Caesar stood and said, "It is my custom to take a small snack at this time of day. Please, join me." He extended an arm toward the dining room. "Let us fill our plates, then return to the living room where we can sit in comfort and continue our conversation."

It hadn't been that long since Jack and I had eaten in Escondido, but the aroma of the food soon had our juices flowing again. It not only smelled good, but it was also beautiful to look at, as well.

"This is wonderful. I hope your staff didn't go to all this trouble just for us," I said.

"Not at all," Paco said. "People come and go here all the time. Our cook is a master at planning and preparation. She can pull together an intimate dinner for two, a banquet for twenty, or a buffet for a hundred at the drop of a hat, any time, day or night.

The table held an array of items that could be assembled in various ways for easy eating. There were several different kinds of meat, grilled or roasted, shredded or cubed; a veritable palette of fruits and vegetables; piles of corn and flour tortillas, warm and fresh, both soft and crisp. Bowls of beans and rice and a platter of steaming tamales rounded out the menu. All of the cooked food was well-seasoned but not too spicy. Bowls of salsa and dishes of chopped or sliced peppers were lined up according to their heat, from just a little extra kick to full-on blow torch. I took a little from one end of the line while Jack nearly emptied the dishes at the other.

While we filled our plates, a couple of muscular young men wheeled in a low cart bearing a wooden half-barrel filled with crushed ice. Numerous amber glass bottles poked their necks up through the ice.

"Drink up, my friends," Cesar shouted. "Do not be shy. The cerveza never runs out here in our home."

"Is your dad like this all the time, Paco?" I asked. "He's fantastic."

Paco laughed as he spooned some beans onto his plate. "Yes, he is. Sometimes we have to reel him in like a big fish. He loves to entertain, and I guarantee that if you and Jack and I go out somewhere tonight, there will be food ready when we come back home."

"What if we come home at three in the morning?" I asked.

Paco added some rice to his beans. "It makes no difference. There will be food and beer waiting for us on this very table."

Jack chuckled softly, "If we come home at three in the morning, we'll probably be too drunk to enjoy it."

"Speak for yourself," I said.

We returned to the living room with our food and picked up our chat where we had left off. During our conversation, much of which was about art, Jack mentioned to Cesar that I was a pretty good painter. I don't know where he got that idea because I've only painted a few paintings so far, and they really aren't that good. Nonetheless, Cesar was curious.

"And what do you paint?" he asked. "Are you an impressionist?"

"I'm not sure what I am. I'm pretty new at it. I've tried to paint in an impressionistic style, but I've not been very successful yet. Mostly I just push paint around on the canvas and hope it looks like something when I get finished."

Cesar leaned toward me and spoke earnestly, almost passionately.

"No, my friend. You must take your time and allow *El Duende* to take you over from the inside. *El Duende* will help you paint."

"I've heard of that," I said. "Isn't *El Duende* the same thing as the German *Kunstwallen*, the Spirit of Art?"

"Yes! That is exactly what it means. Well, not exactly. It is difficult to define *El Duende*. The Spanish poet Federico Garcia Lorca probably explained it best. He said that it climbs up inside you from the soles of your feet. He called it a power that can animate the artist himself, take him over, and compel him to bring forth the emotions that burn within him. How do you translate an emotion? How can one explain beauty?"

"I believe in it," I told him. "I don't think there's any other rational explanation for what drives a man to be an artist. When you think about it, why in the world would anyone want to spend his entire life smearing colored grease onto endless yards of cloth for little or no monetary reward? Especially when a camera can take a picture better than most artists can paint these days. There must be some sort of Spirit inside a man that drives him to paint. It's a form of possession."

"Do you feel this Spirit, young DH? This possession?" Cesar looked at me as if he could find the answer somewhere behind my eyes.

"I think I do ... yes. I do. That has to be it. I have no other explanation for it. I should study something else like astronomy or English literature. I should take up a trade like plumbing. But no, I want to paint—an occupation that'll probably bring me to the poor house before it's all over."

"Or the asylum," Jack said.

"'Tis true," Caesar shook his head. "Many artists are driven mad by their emotions. *El Duende* is not always a kind Spirit, I'm afraid."

"A lot of them drink themselves to death," Jack said. He raised his brandy glass in a salute and swallowed what remained in it. He studied the empty glass for a moment, then turned to Cesar. "You got any more of this?" he asked.

"I remember you now," Caesar said as he retrieved the brandy bottle. "You are the one who likes to drink much,"

Caesar refilled Jack's glass. He turned to take the bottle back to the liquor cabinet but stopped. Instead, he smiled and set the bottle on the table next to Jack. "Keep it, and there is plenty more where that came from."

"Thanks," Jack smiled and then changed the subject. "We gonna sit around here all day drinkin'?"

"What would you like to do," Paco asked.

"Why don't we find a bar with lively music and some girls," Jack said.

"El Toro Azul," Paco said.

"Somethin' about a bull?" Jack queried.

"The Blue Bull. It's a local bar. They play good music, and there are usually girls."

"They have good beer?" Jack asked.

"Corona," Paco shrugged his shoulders. "It's what we drink here in Mexicali. And wine. And tequila."

"You said girls. Lots of girls?"

"Enough," Paco answered. "How many can you handle?"

Speaking of girls, two lovely ones just entered the room. I'm assuming they must be Paco's sisters because they certainly did not have the demeanor or dress of the maids.

Cesar welcomed them with a wide smile. "Come in, my daughters. I want you to meet Paco's friends from California."

The girls smiled and said, "Hola." They spoke softly but were more coy than shy. Jack hadn't lied when he told me they were gorgeous. The taller one has brown hair streaked with blonde, and the shorter one has raven-black hair. The taller one's nose is long and straight, what might be called aristocratic, and the shorter one is smaller, nicely curved, and turned up at the end. The shorter one's eyes are dark brown—almost black—while the taller one has lighter brown eyes with a hint of green.

The shorter girl looked directly at Jack. She smiled at him, and a dimple appeared on her cheek. Jack held her gaze briefly, then cleared his throat and looked away. So that's the one that's hot for him. That's okay. The taller one's more my style—a bit sassy looking, dressed like a cowgirl—I could spend some time with her.

Paco stood up to formally introduce his sisters. "DH, please meet my sisters. Elena and Clara," he said, indicating the tall one and the short one in turn.

So, Jack's girl is Clara, and the streaky-blonde cowgirl is Elena. The girls appear to be quite different both in looks and style. Clara is wearing a short, light blue skirt with a long-sleeved white shirt, and Elena is dressed in tight jeans, a blue shirt, cowboy boots decorated with fancy stitching, and a white cowboy hat.

"I'm happy to meet you both," I told them, but my gaze was riveted on Elena. I can't help staring at her.

"So, what have my girls been doing this day?" Cesar asked them.

"Shopping! What else?" Elena said, holding up a large bag. Clara held up the one in her hand, too.

"And what's in those bags?" Paco teased his sister by reaching for her bag, but Elena pulled it away from him.

"Just stuff," she said. "I got a couple of pairs of pants and some shirts, and Clara bought some shoes and a cute little dress."

Clara held up her bag and smiled, "They're for the fiesta at the church tomorrow."

"I forgot about that," Paco said. "That will be a fun time."

"What's the occasion?" I asked.

"Our old Padre is retiring, and we are welcoming a new one," Cesar said. "The fiesta is to celebrate them both."

"There will be lots of food and drink and dancing," Paco said.

"Mariachi?" Jack asked.

"Of course!" Cesar said. "What is a fiesta without mariachi music and dancing? You are both more than welcome to come."

"Thank you," I said. "I've never been to a real fiesta before. It does sound like fun."

"Do you know how to dance?" Cesar asked.

"I'm afraid not." I smiled and glanced at Elena.

"Then we must teach you," Cesar said exuberantly. "My lovely daughter, Elena, would be happy to. Wouldn't you, Elena?"

Elena looked me over as if she might be appraising a horse. Then she smiled at me and said, "I'll give it a try."

"Why don't you young men settle into your rooms," Cesar continued. "You can rest a little before you go out for the evening. El Toro Azul does not open until seven."

"Rooms?" I looked at Jack. "I thought we would just sleep on the floor somewhere."

"Not in Casa Flores," Cesar protested. "You may stay here for as long as you wish. Make yourselves comfortable, and please, feel free to roam around and come and go as you wish. Paco will show you where your rooms are located. There is a swimming pool out back, paths for strolling in the gardens, and, of course, *la cocina* is always open."

"*La cocina?*" Again, I looked at Jack.

"The kitchen," Jack said. "This is the best restaurant in town, and they've got a cook on staff all through the night. Like Paco said, if we come back at three in the morning, the cook will whip up anything we want."

"You're kidding."

"Not kidding," Jack replied. "Tamales, tacos, beans, and rice. He makes the best menudo in the world."

"Menudo? Isn't that the stuff you had back in Escondido? What the heck is that anyway?"

"Don't ask. You'll just have to try some and see what you think."

Everyone laughed at Jack's last statement. I didn't know why, but it was a friendly laugh, so I just went along with it. Then we all got up. Cesar shook my hand again and told Paco to show us the way. I thanked Caesar and then turned to the daughters. I smiled and said, "Nice meeting you."

They both smiled back and said, "You too."

As we headed down the long hallway to the bedrooms, I couldn't resist turning back to get one last look at Elena. She was standing in front of one of the doors we had passed and was getting ready to enter. She looked down the hall just as I looked back. She saw me looking, smiled, then turned and entered her room.

At El Toro Azul, about 9 PM

In some ways, this bar could be anywhere. It's dimly lit. A band is playing loud music on the stage at one end of the room. The beer is endless, and there's a bowl of salty peanuts on every table to make you want to drink more. The place is packed with people, all laughing and talking at the same time. There are plenty of girls looking for guys, guys looking for girls, and girls and guys who have found each other. I can tell I'm in Mexico, though, because the band is playing Mexican music, all the conversation is in Spanish, and I think Jack and I are the only blondes in the place.

"You were right, Paco," I said. "This place is full of girls. I wonder if the ones wearing all that heavy makeup have any idea how much prettier they'd be with far less or none at all."

"You'll want to steer clear of the clowns," Paco warned.

"Clowns?"

"The ones with the heavy makeup. I call them clowns. Many of them are prostitutes, and all of them are trouble. You want to look for the ones with very little makeup. They are a much better class. They are more likely to speak English and be able to carry on an intelligent conversation. They are also much less likely to give you a nasty little gift to take back to California."

"He means you don't want to catch any diseases," Jack said condescendingly.

"I never did think it was a good idea to pick up girls in bars," I protested. I turned to Paco and explained, "Jack has been trying to get me to do that for weeks now, and I've turned him down. It just doesn't seem like a bar is the best place to find a girl for a long-term relationship."

"And what do you know about long-term relationships?"

Jack smiled.

Paco looked at Jack, who was looking smug, then at me. I was somewhere between embarrassed and defensive. "Jack's talking about all of the girls I've dated who, for one reason or another, have dumped me before a relationship could get going," I explained.

"Is it something you are doing?" Paco asked.

"No, it's just fate. I meet a girl, things are going great, then something happens in her personal universe that makes it necessary for her to leave the town."

"That's too bad, DH," Paco said. "Of course, it will be difficult for you to find a long-term girl here in Mexicali. Being separated by hundreds of miles is not a recipe for a successful friendship."

"I know," I said. "That's not what I'm here for. I'm just here to have a good time and take back some cool memories."

"That is an excellent attitude," Paco said, slapping his hand on my shoulder.

"That's the way he is, Paco," Jack said, shaking his head. "He can be pretty boring at times."

"Thanks, Jack," I said, tossing a peanut at him.

We had been enjoying a few minutes of relative silence while the band took a break. Five musicians have returned to the stage amidst a sea of empty Corona bottles and are cranking up again. The band started the evening with eight members. One of them passed out and was replaced by someone less drunk. Another one passed out and was not replaced. A third musician started to wobble, but the bartender got a chair under him before he fell. This last one did not return after the break. The band played the whole time and did not miss a beat. It was amazing.

"What do you call the kind of music these guys are playing, Paco?" I had to speak right into his ear so that he could hear me.

"You like it? I call what we're hearing right now Mexican jazz. It's really just a mix-up of Mexican styles."

"I don't know much about Mexican music beyond what I hear in the Mexican restaurants at home."

"They are all pretty similar. The songs are all about love or heroics, and the style depends on the instruments and the rhythm. If there are more guitars than brass, it's *ranchera*. If the group is heavy on the brass, then it's *banda*. If they've got an accordion and maybe a tuba, and the music sounds like a polka, then it's *norteño*. If they're singing sappy love songs about their *corazón*, it's *mariachi*, and they could be playing it with any instrument."

"Well, whatever they're playing, I like it. I'd get up and dance if I knew how to dance to this stuff."

"They don't dance much in this bar. The band is just the background for people getting drunk and flirting or fighting with each other."

"I don't think that band's gonna be playin' much longer," Jack said, nodding his head toward the stage.

One of the band members has passed out, and a couple of guys are dragging him over to the side of the stage. They laid him next to the wall, and a third person brought the musician's half-empty Corona and set it on the floor beside his head. The crowd applauded, and the fellow strutted off the stage, waving his hands in the air like he had just won a championship prizefight.

"That's another one down. Four more to go," Paco said.

"Whattaya mean?" I asked.

"We need to talk to them at the next break. Most of them will be on the floor by two in the morning."

"On the floor? You mean they'll all pass out?"

"They will, and we need to get to them first," Paco said.

"What are you talkin' about?" Jack asked. "Why do we need to talk to them?"

Paco grinned and said, "I'm going to hire their services. I want them to come with us to help me serenade my Maria."

"You kiddin' me?" Jack barely contained his laughter. "In a couple of hours, they won't be able to walk, let alone sing."

"That is why we must get to them at the next break," Paco insisted. "Before they are incapable of negotiating the terms."

"What terms?" I asked.

"*Dinero*. How much *dinero* I will pay them to ride in my station wagon across this lovely town to Maria's house, where they will get out and sing some romantic *mariachi* to Maria. They will sing a song, then I will give her a dozen roses and propose marriage to her."

"Wow," I said, looking over at Jack. "How cool is that, Jack?"

"I got a bad feeling about this," Jack said, shaking his head.

"It will be fun, amigo!" Paco said.

"Yeah," Jack muttered. "What could go wrong?"

Back at Casa Flores

Everything went wrong. At the break, Paco asked the guys in the band if they would help serenade Maria. They replied unanimously with an enthusiastic "Si." They were so enthusiastic that they wanted to go right away before doing their next set.

Miguel, the trumpet player, said, "Serenading a woman is much more important than playing for drunks in a bar." *Who is calling whom drunk?* "Besides, it shouldn't take too long. We will come back later, and they will never know we were gone."

As it turned out, only two of them, Miguel, the trumpet player, and Francisco, the singer/guitar player, were able to make the trip. The other guys were even drunker than those two and couldn't get themselves off the stage and out the door. Paco was not the least bit discouraged, and the five of us plus a trumpet and a guitar, piled into the station wagon and sped off to the other side of Mexicali to serenade the fair Maria.

"Maria will be so surprised," Paco said as we whipped around a corner. "She will not be able to resist my proposal."

"What if she isn't home?" I asked, bracing myself for another sharp turn.

"She is always home at night," Paco replied. "Her mama is very strict."

"But it's so late," I said. "It's almost midnight. What will the neighbors think about a trumpet blaring so late at night?"

"We will not get there until after midnight, my friend, and then it will no longer be late. It will be early!" Paco and the musicians rolled with laughter. Jack and I gave each other looks that expressed our shared doubts about this little adventure.

Paco drove like a maniac through the streets of Mexicali. Everyone but me laughed and talked, smoked cigarettes, and passed around bottles of Corona beer from the ice chest in the back of the station wagon. I held on for dear life and tried to remember to breathe while Paco narrowly missed various obstacles and ignored stop signs.

"Aieee!" Francisco yelled out from the back seat. "*Un policia nos esta persiguiendo!*"

"What?" I asked.

"We got a cop behind us," Jack said coolly.

"Damn," Paco said, not bothering to slow down. "I wonder which one it is."

"Which one?" That was not what I would expect someone to say in this situation.

"We only have two this late at night. I know them both, and they will be pissed if they catch us drinking like this."

"You only have two cops?" Jack asked.

"We have no trouble here. Two is all we need."

"What difference does it make which one is chasing us?" I asked.

"We have two policemen, two motorcycles, and two guns. The two policemen always sit on their motorcycles at the same street corner and look important. Nobody wants to mess with two armed policemen on two fast bikes like that. But what some of us know is that only one motorcycle works, and only one gun works. One of the policemen has the working gun, and the other has the working motorcycle, and they trade off, so you never know who's got what until they start chasing you. I assume that the one chasing us now does not have the gun that fires bullets. We will soon loose him."

I didn't think we could go any faster, but Paco put his foot down hard on the gas, accelerated through a couple of turns, ran a half-dozen more stop signs, and knocked over a few trashcans. Paco was right. We soon lost the cop. Francisco, who was watching out the back window, said it looked like the cop ran out of gas. When Paco saw in his rear-view mirror that the cop had come to a stop, he eased up on the speed, and we continued on to Maria's house.

"How did you know he had the gun that didn't work, Paco?" I asked.

"He did not shoot, and had he shot, he would not have hit us."

"How do you know that?" I asked.

"Because I know him. He is probably drunk, too."

We finally arrived at Maria's home in a residential area of Mexicali. I can't describe the house or neighborhood because it was very dark and we weren't there for very long.

Paco pulled up in front, got out of the car, and walked to the middle of the yard, where he stood looking at the house. Miguel and Francisco grabbed their instruments and joined Paco.

Jack settled back in his seat and said, "I'm stayin' here. I'm tellin' ya, this isn't going to end well."

I decided to ignore Jack's warning and got out of the car. I exercised some caution, though, as I chose to stand about halfway between Paco and the station wagon. If things did go wrong, I wouldn't have as far to run.

Paco gave the signal, and the musicians did what they were hired for. Francisco strummed his guitar and sang as loud as he could, and Miguel joined in on his trumpet. They sounded pretty good, considering how drunk they were.

A floodlight came on at the end of the first line and brilliantly illuminated the yard.

At the end of the second line, the front door opened partway, and a large vase full of flowers hurtled across the yard, barely missed Paco's head, and smashed into pieces in the street. Francisco and Miguel continued the serenade unfazed while lights came on in the houses up and down the block.

Finally, the lights came on in Maria's house. The front door opened, and a very short, rotund older woman—Maria's mother—stepped onto the porch. She carried a shotgun, and a torrent of what I assumed to be curses, threats, and warnings in Spanish flowed from her.

Movement at one of the windows revealed a young woman peeking out at us. It had to be Maria. She and Paco saw each other at the same time. Maria smiled and waved at him. He blew her a kiss, then took to his heels, yelling, "*Vámonos! Vámonos!*"

I ran back to the car immediately, but the musicians seemed oblivious to the rising chaos until Maria's mother and her shotgun were nearly upon them. Miguel made a clean getaway, but Francisco slipped and fell as he tried to escape. The older woman stopped a few feet from him, and we all watched with horror as she raised her shotgun, took aim, then raised it higher and shot into the air. BLAM! Everyone in the normally quiet and peaceful neighborhood who had so far slept through the noise and commotion was awake.

Maria's mother slowly lowered her shotgun and took aim at Francisco. "*Aiee, Mamacita! No! No!*" Francisco screamed. He pushed himself up off the ground and ran for the station wagon, clutching his guitar.

BLAM! That was a close one.

Francisco threw himself into the station wagon's open back, and Paco sped away with Francisco's feet still dangling out the back end. We heard one final BLAM as we turned the corner.

What a night. I have no idea what time it is. A few times during the adventure, I was afraid I might not make it through the night alive. I'm relieved to be back in my assigned guestroom at Casa Flores, all in one piece.

Paco is crazy. What was he thinking? What made him think he could get away with waking up the whole neighborhood at midnight anyway? Obviously, Maria and her mama found out about his plans. Mama was far too ready with her shotgun for it to have been a surprise. Paco probably bragged about it to his friends, and one of them snitched on him. Even before the first shotgun blast, lights were coming on, and people were coming outside. They yelled, shook their fists, and made rude gestures as we sped away. Some of them even chased us on foot. I hate to think how things might have ended if any of them had gotten into a car and followed us.

Anyway, the excitement is over, and I'm relaxing on this big, comfortable bed, waiting for my adrenaline levels to return to normal so I can go to sleep. This guestroom is more like a suite in a luxury hotel than a bedroom. There is a spacious bathroom through a door on one side of the room. An alcove next to it contains a small kitchenette. The arched opening between the sleeping area and the sitting area can be closed off with doors that slide out of the wall—I think they're called pocket doors. The sitting area is furnished like a living room with a small sofa, a couple of comfy chairs, a coffee table, side tables, and lamps. Another alcove across from the kitchenette is set up with a desk and chair. The room is decorated with beautiful examples of Mexican art—paintings, masks, tapestries on the walls, pottery and sculpture on shelves and tables, and hand-woven rugs on the floor. There is also a beautiful shrine to La Virgen de Guadalupe in a niche on one wall. I get the impression that the Flores family is in the habit of hosting some high-powered guests. If I weren't so exhausted, I'd feel intimidated.

9
Sunday

Still in Mexicali

A lot has happened since the adventures of last night. Or should I say this morning?

I slept till noon when I was awakened by one of the maids who introduced herself as Luz. Actually, I think I was awakened by the delicious aroma of the food on the large tray she carried rather than her soft knock on my door. I sat up in bed and adjusted the pillows behind me while she set the tray on the sideboard across the room. I settled back to admire the view as she bent over to reach into a lower compartment. She came up with a small tray. She unfolded the legs of the tray and set it on top. She opened a drawer, pulled out a placemat and silverware, and arranged them on the tray. Finally, she pulled out a plate and filled it with food from the big tray. She brought the laden tray to the bed and carefully positioned it over my lap. She stepped back, smiled sweetly, and said, "*Desayuno*, Señor DH. Breakfast."

"*Gracias*, Luz," I said, using one of the few words I can reliably remember from my high school Spanish classes.

She smiled and watched until she was satisfied that I could feed myself. Then she went over to the windows and pulled open the drapes to let the sunlight stream into the room. The windows are large and provide a broad view of the lush garden filled with oleanders, palms, and cacti. The scene is only partially obstructed by the decorative but practical wrought iron grills securely bolted over the windows.

Luz busied herself with tidying up the room. The place looked spotless to me, but she found surfaces to dust and small items to rearrange. She picked up the clothes I had left in a pile on a chair when I undressed for bed last night and hung them in the closet or folded them and put them in one of the dresser drawers. Satisfied with her work, she returned to the bedside and smiled. She pointed to a spot just above my right shoulder. I looked and saw a red velvet cord hanging from the ceiling. She mimed tugging on the rope and said, "*Tira de la cuerda si necesitas algo más.*" I looked at her blankly. She thought for a moment, then repeated in broken English and more gestures, "You need more ... pull rope ... I come."

"Ah," I said, nodding my understanding. I thought of several things I might need the lovely Luz for, but I quickly put those aside. I smiled at her and said, "*Gracias*, Luz. I did not expect such lavish treatment. It's a lovely surprise."

She shook her head and smiled sadly. "*Perdón.* I speak little English."

I returned her smile and said, "Well, I don't speak much Spanish, so we're even."

Luz gave me one last, bright smile, curtsied, and left the room, closing the door softly behind her. I leaned back against the pillow, and one thought after another ran through my head, like:

I hadn't heard her knock. What if I'd been standing there naked when she walked in?

And *Cesar has all kinds of security everywhere. I think I saw cameras outside and in the living and dining room.*

And *I wonder if they have hidden cameras in the guest rooms?*

And *Do they keep an eye on everyone everywhere, all the time? That's kind of creepy.*

It's hard to shut my mind up sometimes. I know I'm a little paranoid, but I can't help it. I've had enough experiences with real-life spies to recognize that the fantastic exploits of *Man from Uncle*, *Secret Agent*, and James Bond have at least a tenuous link to reality. I have actually met and hung out with a CIA agent who worked undercover as a student at RCC—that's a story for another time and place. Nevertheless, that relationship taught me to observe people and their surroundings in detail and practice what is called situational awareness, that is, the ability to know what is going on around you and be prepared to react effectively as circumstances change. Even without all that, though, I would have realized that there is far more to Cesar Flores than meets the eye. Who knows if the guestrooms of Casa Flores are being watched? I don't see any cameras in here, but I sure don't want to be caught snooping around looking for them.

While all of that was going through my brain, the rest of my body was enjoying the delicious breakfast—something Luz called *machaca* that reminded me of my grandmother's pot roast only with Mexican seasonings. It shared the plate with potatoes cubed like hash browns but cooked in a seasoned broth, fried eggs with runny yolks, and a pile of soft, warm flour tortillas. After that, I dressed, made myself presentable, and went in search of Jack and Paco to see what they had planned for the rest of the day.

The Fiesta

The fiesta turned out to be a pleasant affair. It was your basic church potluck, Mexican style. There was plenty of food and drink, adult chit-chat and laughter, and squeals and giggles from children running around playing kickball, tag, and hide-and-seek. Fifteen or twenty people brought musical instruments—guitars of various sizes, trumpets and trombones, even a couple of accordions. They gathered in the back of the church grounds to tune up and practice some music to play later for people to dance to. They sounded pretty good from where I sat.

I met and spent some time with both priests during the afternoon and evening. Paco had told me that the older one, Fr. Juan, is nearly seventy, but he sure doesn't look it. He is slim and looks fit. His jet-black hair is only lightly brushed with silver at his temples, and the only wrinkles on his face are laugh lines at the corners of his eyes.

"I have a car if I need to travel far or take a parishioner to the doctor or some such thing," he told me. "Most of the time, though, I make my rounds on foot or on a bicycle, which is a good thing.

Almost every visit I make includes an offer of food, and I cannot say no without offending. The walking and cycling work off the extra calories, so I do not get fat."

"What will you do when you leave here, Fr. Juan?" I asked. "You don't strike me as someone who is content to just ride off into the sunset."

He chuckled softly and said, "You are right. It is time for me to move on from this place, but I will not be retiring. I will be joining the faculty of a new seminary for the education and training of priests. I was forced to go north of the border to receive my religious education, so I am very pleased to be a part of an institution that will make this training available closer to home."

His words confused me. "You were forced to go north? Why was that?"

"The people of Mexico have been Catholic for centuries, but the government of this country has made it difficult to practice the Faith. For most of this century, the Church was effectively outlawed. The worst of the oppression led to a bloody rebellion, *La Cristiada*, in 1926 that lasted until 1929. The government had seized church property and closed all the monasteries, convents, and religious schools. If anyone wanted to enter the priesthood, they had to leave the country. Many seminaries in the U.S. accepted students forced out of Mexican schools, and at least one was built in the U.S. specifically to prepare Mexicans for the priesthood in Mexico. That is where I received my training. Many of those laws are still in place but not strictly enforced. Small seminaries have been quietly opening up all over the country in the last decade or so. It is my welcome duty to help raise up a new generation of priests. My prayer is that they will usher in a new era of faith and trust in this country."

"I had no idea," I said. "We learned a little bit in school about Mexican independence from Spain and the Mexican Revolution, but I never heard of this conflict between the Church and the government."

"*La Cristiada* is considered by some to be the last battle of the Revolution," said Fr. Miguel, who had joined us a few minutes before. "The Constitution of 1917 contained some pretty devastating regulation of the Church which was not uniformly enforced until the mid-20s. What started out as resistance soon became active rebellion. Even though an agreement was reached in 1929, the bloodshed did not end right away. Eventually, some of the worst anti-Church laws were repealed, but the foundation of those laws still remains in our Constitution."

"*Si*," Fr. Juan said. "Since the mid-40s, life has become easier for us. While we clerics must still be careful how we express our faith in public, we no longer have to hide it. We are also able to build schools where young men like Fr. Miguel here can receive their training without having to go to a foreign country."

"Ah, Fr. Juan, there you are." I turned to see that the voice belonged to Elena. "The *abuelas* are beginning to think you have gone already."

Fr. Juan chuckled as he stood up. "Elena is right, DH. As much as I am enjoying our conversation, I really must make sure I say a proper farewell to my parishioners. Remember, Fr. Miguel, your job will be much easier if you keep the *abuelas* happy."

"That's one thing Catholics and Baptists have in common—the grandmothers," I said. "I love them all, and I can't imagine what it would be like without them, but if they are offended in any way, they can make things difficult. My psychology professor described it as 'passive-aggressive behavior.'"

Fr. Miguel and I continued to converse on the differences and similarities between the Catholic and Baptist faiths for a bit longer. Elena, who had taken Fr. Juan's seat when he left, did not say much but paid close attention. Her facial expressions telegraphed her understanding and opinion of what was being said.

The conversation paused after about thirty minutes of brisk exchange. Fr. Miguel leaned back in his chair and looked thoughtfully at me, then Elena. As he looked back and forth between us, the corner of his mouth turned up in a lopsided smile, and his eyes took on a knowing and amused look.

"Well," he said as he stood up and stretched, "I think I had better be following Fr. Juan's example and circulate among the parishioners. I certainly don't want to start out on the wrong foot with the *abuelas*." Fr. Miguel looked at Elena and me one more time, then smiled and went off to mingle.

Elena and I looked at each other. She smiled, and I hoped that my face was not as red as the back of my neck felt.

◎ ◎ ◎

Before we left Casa Flores for the fiesta, Paco and Jack told me that they didn't want to stay very long and intended to leave early to find a bar. I'm not really into bars, and I did want to have the whole fiesta experience. It was decided that Paco and Jack would go together in Paco's new Ford pickup, and I would ride with Elena in her blue Corvette convertible. That way, we could all do what we wanted. I was a little nervous about being alone with Elena, but she quickly put me at ease.

We did not go directly to the church. Instead, Elena took me on the Grand Tour of Mexicali. I noticed that there were certain areas she seemed to go out of her way to avoid. When I asked her about it, she simply said, "Those are not good places for me to go." I also noticed that someone was following us wherever we went, whether in the car or on foot.

When I first met Elena yesterday, I thought that even though she was very pretty, she was also very much a tomboy. She disguised any femininity by wearing clothing typical of a ranch hand, and her speech and mannerisms seemed to indicate that she was "just one of the guys." Boy, was I wrong.

While I'm sure she can wrangle with the best of them any day, Elena had her feminine side on full display tonight. She was still dressed in denim and leather, but the denim was a very short skirt decorated with an intricate pattern of silver-colored studs.

The leather was a hand-tooled belt with a silver buckle. She wore a white, western-style shirt with colorful embroidery and pearl snaps, but it was shaped and fitted to her female form like a second skin. To finish off her look, she traded her worn and dusty everyday cowboy boots for an expensive, hand-tooled pair that were patterned and colored to match her belt.

It's not just Elena's clothes that are different, either. She dropped the ranch hand vocabulary and cowboy posturing. Her speech softened, and her voice took on a more musical quality. Her body relaxed, and her movements became more graceful. I found myself wondering more than once why this beautiful young woman would take so much time with a guy like me. I know that she did it at least in part as a favor to her father and brother, but she really seemed to enjoy her duties as my minder. Go figure.

About dusk, just after Fr. Miguel left us, Paco and Jack came by to tell us that they were taking off to find a bar.

"Have a good time, you two," Paco said.

"You, too," Elena and I said together.

Jack added, "Be sure to stick with Elena, DH, so she can translate for you and keep you out of trouble."

"After last night, I think you two are in more danger of getting into trouble than we are," I said.

We all laughed, and Jack headed off with Paco to find their own adventure.

Elena and I sat and talked and sipped wine while the night got darker. The colored lights strung up around the stage, the dance floor, and the trees came on. The crowd got drunker and noisier, and the music ramped up to brain-concussion level. It was accompanied by whoops and hollers and the sound of boots stamping on the wooden dance floor. Elena and I found ourselves shouting at each other.

"This is the part I hate!" Elena yelled at me.

"What do you mean?" I shouted back.

"The noise. We can't have a conversation without yelling. I'm not into all this noise."

Once again, I was amazed that she wanted to have a conversation with me. "I don't like the noise either. Maybe we could find a quieter place to sit."

"We could just go back home. I can show you the gardens. They're beautiful at night. And we have plenty of wine, much better than this stuff." She grimaced and poured what was left in her cup onto the ground.

We made our way back to the parking area, and Elena drove us back to Casa Flores. Sitting next to the gorgeous blonde in her turquoise blue Corvette with the top down, I couldn't help but feel like I was in a James Bond movie. That fantasy was probably fueled, at least in part, by the glimpse of a small black pistol I got when she pulled her keys out of her purse.

◎ ◎ ◎

Back at Casa Flores, Elena took my hand and guided me along a gravel walk that wound maze-like through the gardens surrounding the house. The giant cacti and thick vines arched over the path in some places, making living tunnels. After many twists and turns, an opening like a door appeared in the wall of plants alongside the walkway. Elena stepped through and pulled me in after her.

I looked around and discovered that we were standing in a kind of alcove or grotto a little larger than The Hole—my bedroom at home. It was surrounded by an impenetrable wall of vines covered with thorns and brilliant, magenta-colored flowers and the roof of the grotto was open to the sky. A chaise lounge big enough for two people to lay side by side to look at the stars occupied the center of the space.

The sudden appearance of a soft white light startled me. I turned toward the source and saw Elena looking into an open refrigerator tucked into the wall of vegetation.

"A refrigerator? Out here?" I asked.

"Yes. It's painted to look like the cactus and bougainvillea so that even in the daytime, you can't tell it's here unless you stumble upon it. The kitchen staff rotates the contents, so the food is always fresh."

The refrigerator was filled with wine, cheese, a couple of meat platters, an assortment of fruit, and other things I couldn't identify from where I was standing.

"I take it there's an electric outlet somewhere behind the frig."

"Yes. The entire property is wired. There are outlets and lights all over." Elena said.

"How cool is that?"

"Very cool," Elena said. She pulled a bottle of wine from the refrigerator, closed the door, then opened a small cabinet, also camouflaged and lit from within. She extracted a couple of wine glasses and a corkscrew. "Are you hungry?" she asked as she handed me a glass of chilled wine.

"Not yet. Where I come from, it's considered bad manners not to take at least one small portion of every food at a church potluck. There were so many dishes at the fiesta that one bite from all of them was pretty filling."

"Well, if you do get hungry, just help yourself. If you want something that isn't in the frig, just push that little button on the side. There's a speaker, and you can tell a maid to bring you whatever you want."

"What do you do if you have to go to the bathroom?" I asked.

"You need to piss?" she asked bluntly.

"Not yet, but I probably will soon."

"The nearest bathroom is in the house. Out here, we usually just go behind a bush. When you get ready, let me know. I'll probably have to go too, and I can show you where to do it. I wouldn't want you to run into any cactus."

This was not exactly the conversation I thought I'd be having with this beautiful woman. Also, there is something about her speech and mannerisms. She's not exactly your typical Mexican señorita.

"Come on." She took my free hand and pulled me over to the chaise lounge. "Let's lie here and look at the stars. It's a lot quieter, isn't it?"

"Yes, it is," I said as we lay down together, our bodies touching. "This is very nice. I'm not big on loud noises either."

"Is that why you didn't head to the bar with Paco and Jack?"

"Partly. I don't care much for the atmosphere or the people you find in bars."

"I don't either," Elena said. "Guys go to bars to pick up girls, and girls go to pick up guys. That seems a bit sleazy to me."

I took a swallow of my wine and then said, "Can I ask you a personal question, Elena?"

"Sure."

"I couldn't help but notice that you look different from your sister, Clara. You talk differently, too. Are you more like your other sister?"

"That's more of an observation than a question, isn't it?" she asked. "It's a good one, though. The reason that Clara and I look so different is that I'm adopted. I doubt you'll ever meet our other sister, Maria Teresa. She's a nun in a convent near Mexico City."

"Wow ... I mean, that's quite a story."

"You think I made it up?"

I answered quickly, eager to correct any offense. "No, I think you're a fortunate girl. You've got a great dad."

"Yes, I am, and I do. He is a wonderful man, and he has been the best father in the world. I am honored to be his adopted daughter."

"Do you know anything about your biological family?"

"I do. I came here as an exchange student in high school, and I never returned home."

"Really?"

"I was a straight-A student in high school and actually ahead in my requirements for graduation. My parents fought all the time. My mother was a drunk, and my father was seeing another woman and never came home. They eventually got a divorce, but there was lots of angst and anger, and life was hell. I heard about this exchange program when I was a sophomore. Because of my grades and advanced standing, I was accepted right away. Mom signed the papers without even reading them, and I came down to live with the Flores family and go to school. When my year was up, Caesar asked me if I wanted to stay on with them. I jumped at the chance. My parents didn't give a damn about me. I didn't get a letter or a visit from either of them that whole first year I was down here. Cesar went up to see my family to make it all happen. He is pretty persuasive, but to be honest, I think he paid them off. I got my diploma, turned eighteen, and decided that this was my home. Cesar adopted me, and I am a citizen of Mexico.

"That's an amazing story. What do Paco and Clara think about having another sibling at this stage? Are they at all jealous or think that you're just after their father's money?"

"Oh, heavens no. We really are family. Cesar has plenty to go around, and his business is quite diverse. He has brought in each of us to work in areas that best suit our interests and talents. Clara is quite creative and artistically talented. Among other duties, she is the curator of the marvelous art collection you see in the house. She also coordinates many of the charities the family supports. And Paco, despite his recent love-crazed, erratic behavior, has an excellent head for business and diplomacy. He is in line to take his father's place."

"You're right. I never would have guessed that about Paco." So, where is your place in the family?"

"I have discovered a love for ranching. Cesar has put me in the position of learning the ropes and eventually taking over that branch of the family business."

"What a story," I said with amazement. "You seem to have taken pretty well to life here in Mexico. No joining a convent for you, huh?"

"Never. I'm not very religious. I hope that doesn't bother you."

"Heavens, no, I'm not all that religious either. I just like to consider the possibilities of different ways of thinking."

"My parents weren't religious, so I didn't go to church except now and then when a friend would invite me. I don't think I ever went to the same church twice. Cesar and this family are Catholic, of course. I think it's as much about culture and lifestyle here as it is about faith and religion. I go to Mass once in a while, but I don't put much stock in it. I just try to live the best life I can and hope that's okay with the good Lord above."

I turned my head so that I could see Elena's face. She was smiling and gazing up at the sky. The light of the half-moon made her eyes glitter, and her skin look like marble. I could not look away, and I had no words worth saying.

Elena turned toward me, cocking her head a little to look at me — to study me almost like a scientist studies a specimen.

Suddenly embarrassed, I looked away. "I'm sorry ... I ... uh ... guess I kind of zoned out on the silence and the ... uh ... the beauty." Crap. Did I say that out loud?

"You know," she said softly, "it's nice having someone from the States here to visit with." She paused for a moment, then continued in almost a whisper. "I'm enjoying your company."

"I'm enjoying yours, too," I replied. Had anyone told me that I would one day be sitting in a foreign country, touching thighs with a blond, gun-toting goddess while drinking wine in the moonlight, I would have called them a liar

"When are you and Jack going back to California?" I could tell from her voice that she had returned her gaze to the moon.

"*Mañana*," I smiled.

"Do you have to go back so soon?"

"Jack and I have classes and other things that need attention."

"I can't see Jack being too concerned about school or much of anything else. Except for maybe art."

"He's a free spirit, alright." I grinned.

"I'm sure Cesar would let you stay longer if you want. If you were to spend a week, I could give you a more complete tour of Mexicali and the surrounding area. There are some places I cannot take you, of course, but we could hit all of the beauty spots."

"Why are some sections of the town off-limits to you, Elena?"

"All I can tell you is that the work that I do requires that I remain unseen by some who live here in Mexicali."

"You mean you have to remain anonymous?" The romantic, irrational part of me wanted to say, *Count me in. Tell me everything.* The logical and cautious part won out, and I actually said, "I won't ask you anymore about it. As for staying longer, I would love to, but my parents are expecting me back. They would not object if I called and said I was staying longer, but I know they would not be happy about it. I do have a great deal of freedom, but blowing off school and other responsibilities would cost me the trust I have earned with my parents."

"So, you have parents that actually love you," she said.

"Yes, I do. I'm so sorry you didn't have that."

"It was tough growing up, but since the Flores family took me in as their own, it has been wonderful. Even though I was eighteen when I decided to stay here in Mexico, Caesar insisted on adopting me legally. That's how much love he has shown for me. What more could I ask?"

"He sounds like a great guy."

"You seem like a great guy too, DH. Isn't there anything I can do to change your mind and get you to stay a little longer?"

"I really wish there was because right now, you're making it very hard for me to want to leave tomorrow."

"What if I do this?" Elena rolled over so that her face was directly above mine and kissed me sweetly. Then she rolled back on the lounge, and we remained like that for about an hour, staring up at the stars.

I really don't want to leave tomorrow. I want to hang around here with Elena for a few more days and get to know her better. She obviously lives a life filled with some kind of intrigue. I would love for her to share that with me, but I know it isn't possible. In fact, I will probably never see her again.

10
Thursday

Six Weeks Later in The Hole

It's the last day of November. Except for Thanksgiving Day spent with my family, this month has been uneventful. There is one thing, though, that I have put off writing about, and I need to do it now before I lose my resolve and while I still retain the memories.

Halloween was a month ago. This year I did nothing to commemorate what had always been one of my favorite holidays — no parties, no costumes, no trick-or-treating, no pumpkins and scarecrows. It was also the first anniversary of my first encounter with the ghost girl, Annabelle, and I was a little on edge that night.

I've dreamed of Annabelle about once a month since that first meeting. In one of my first dreams, she told me that I would forget them quickly, and that has been the case. I've been trying to record the dreams immediately upon waking to keep from losing them altogether. In one of my last dreams, she told me that there would come a time when I would not remember them at all. She said that I would have one final dream of her that would seem like reality, but upon waking, it would disappear, and I would have no recollection of it at all. I wouldn't even have time to write any of it down. Part of me wants that to happen soon, but a part also enjoys the dreams. I had one last night that I must record now, as I can feel the memory fading away even as I try to recall it.

As usual, I was asleep on my back when I dreamed that I opened my eyes and saw Annabelle's face just inches from my own. During that dream, I finally got to see what she really looks like. Even though I knew I was sleeping in the dark, I saw her as if I were wide awake in a brightly lit room.

Annabelle's appearance in my dream matched her image in the

photo that I saw last year on the nightstand by her bed in the haunted house. This dream confirmed my observations and impressions of her from that photo and from other dreams. Her skin is the soft, delicate, rosy white of a porcelain doll, and her cheeks are flushed as if she has just been out in the wind. The end of her nose is round, and in the dream, she let me touch it. It was soft and warm and dusted with freckles. Her large eyes are a clear, light blue. Her mouth is perfectly proportioned to the rest of her face, and her soft, dark pink lips glisten as if they are wet. Her light, red-brown hair is long, but she wears it in a ponytail that seems almost to have a life of its own. It swings and bounces in response to her slightest move. She is, without a doubt, the cutest girl I've ever seen. I can't imagine how God could make any improvement.

I thought Elena was lovely. I could hardly take my eyes off her while I was with her. Heck, that's what I think about every girl I date. Annabelle, though, has a different kind of beauty and my reactions to her are different from any I've had for any other girl I've known. When I look at Annabelle, I do more than just see her—I actually feel her. My entire body is aware of the softness of her skin, the warmth of her breath, and the sweetness of her hair, and last night, it was as if I fully merged with her—actually *became* her. You heard me right—I *became* her. How bizarre is that? I have never experienced anything like that with any girl. It is clearly something supernatural.

I have felt emotional about girls, and I have felt pretty darned good about touching girls and having fun with them, but this is different. In my dreams, Annabelle's flesh is my flesh. Her breath is my breath. I don't understand any of it, but I don't need to because I have a feeling it's beyond human understanding.

In the dream that was more than just a dream, Annabelle laid the length of her body on top of mine. There was no weight to her as we simply merged together so that her weight became my own. She stayed like that for quite some time, her mouth just inches from my own, breathing her breath into me. I laid still beneath her and took it all in as if it was the very essence of life and my own life depended on it. After a while, Annabelle moved her face closer to me and kissed me—at least that's what it felt like. Her kiss went on for what seemed like hours. It couldn't have been that long because dreams are never that long, but my body responded in ways that any man's body would respond to a kiss like that.

It was more than a simple kiss. It was the declaration of the reality of each of us and a physical manifestation of what we mean to each other. It was almost like we were inside a womb together—huddled and cuddled inside a warm, liquid, energetic womb.

The moment of our merging expanded to an infinity of time with no beginning and no end. Eventually, though, we separated into our individual selves, and I looked up to see Annabelle's face above mine as it had been at the beginning of the dream. She smiled sadly and told me that my dreams of her would soon stop entirely, and I would not remember any of them ever again.

But don't worry, she said. *I will take on a physical form for a time and visit you soon. When I do, I will seem familiar to you. You will recognize me as someone special, but you will not remember me from your dreams, nor will you know my name.*

So, Annabelle is to remain a mystery, but I will want to be with her, listen to her, and even learn from her. That is certainly something to look forward to—if it is possible to look forward to something that will have been forgotten. She also told me that even though those future meetings and interactions will alter my life in ways I cannot imagine, they will not be remembered.

◎ ◎ ◎

Bill Hunter once queried, "What is realty, the dream, or the waking? Which is really real?" What are dreams, anyway, and what do they have to do with reality?

The last thing Annabelle said that night got my full attention. She said, *"All of this was planned long before you were born into this life. It has a valued purpose and a deep meaning, but in the end, there will be consequences, for better or for worse. The final decisions will all be made by you."*

I closed my eyes when Anabelle finished speaking. When I opened them again, it was daylight, and I knew I was awake.

I've pondered this dream—if that is what it was—and I don't know what to do.

Time will tell.

11
Friday

At THE Table in The Pit

I just got out of my American history class, and I'm sitting at my favorite table here in The Pit. I've always been turned on by some histories like ancient Egyptian and Greek, England, Scotland, Vikings, Druids—that sort of thing. Still, I've never been big on American history. That's probably because I've heard versions of it every year since I started school, and it's always been the same old stories told in the same old way with all the same old names and dates to memorize. They never sparked my imagination or triggered my curiosity. Dr. Garcia, though, really knows how to make it all come alive. His lessons on the early colonies really resonated with me, especially how he told about the witch hunts. He didn't spend much time on the subject, but I reacted to those particular stories almost as if they were from my own personal memories.

We've spent the last couple of class sessions leading up to the Civil War, and Dr. Garcia has been masterful at sorting through the complex issues facing the country at that time. If I had had Dr. Garcia back in high school, I might have considered majoring in history like my brother is doing.

Today Dr. Garcia moved forward from the causes of the war to some of the actual battles, and he did it in his typical dramatic way—he talked about ghosts. The Civil War was brutal, and the cost in lives lost was enormous. Reports of ghosts arose almost as soon as the battles were over and continue to this day. Dr. Garcia brought the war to life for us—pardon the pun—by relating some of these stories. He accompanied his talk with a slide show of the battlefields as they are today and historical images made at the time of the battles or shortly after.

Along with the historical and current photo of each site, Dr. Garcia showed us a third picture of each location in which there appeared to be ghostly figures of Civil War soldiers. The highlight of his presentation was a short film showing a group of soldiers moving out of a clump of trees near Gettysburg. Their forms had a milky translucence that you could see through. Even so, there was enough detail to suggest that they were Confederate soldiers.

I sat through the presentation with a growing sense of recognition and something that was not quite unease. When I saw the ghostly platoon walk out of the woods, I felt the hair on the back of my neck stand up, and I knew exactly what it was—Anabelle. The phantom soldiers had the same filmy, watery look that Anabelle had when I first saw her in the haunted house last year.

After class, I approached Dr. Garcia at his desk, where he was busy shuffling papers and putting away his lesson materials. After a little mental hemming and hawing, I asked him if he, personally, believed in ghosts.

He smiled and replied, "Is the Pope Catholic?" Then he rolled his eyes heavenward and said, "Forgive me, Father. I do not mean to offend," before crossing himself and returning to his task.

"I gather you're Catholic," I said. "Do Catholics believe in ghosts?

"You've never heard of the Father, Son, and the Holy Ghost?" he said, somewhat glibly.

"Of course, but I've been a Baptist all my life. I'm not sure how Catholics feel about haunted houses and ghosts and stuff."

"I'm not belittling any of that. I'm actually a very good Catholic, and I positively know that ghosts and haunted things are not outside the realms of Catholic belief. What's your point, anyway?"

His last remark made me afraid that I might have annoyed him, but I blundered on. "My point is that I've had an ... experience ..." I looked down at my feet, hoping I had gotten all the words right.

I must have expressed myself adequately because Dr. Garcia put down his papers and looked directly at me. "What kind of experience?"

With a sense of relief, I told him all about my first encounter with Annabelle on Halloween last year and about my dreams since then, including the latest vivid one of Annabelle lying on top of me in bed.

When I finished my story, Dr. Garcia sat down at his desk and silently motioned for me to pull up one of the classroom chairs and sit. He leaned back, looked at me, and said, "Wow, DH … It is DH, right?"

"Yes."

"That has to be one of the strangest things I've heard all day." He chuckled and shook his head. "Hell, maybe in all my life."

I nodded in agreement. "It's pretty strange, alright. I hardly believe it myself, but it's all true. I swear it."

"I believe you, DH, but I'm not sure what to tell you. You could get a priest to perform an exorcism." He paused and grinned before continuing. "Or you could marry the girl. She sounds pretty nice to me."

"Right," I shook my head.

"All kidding aside, your experiences could be classified as occult. The Catholic Church would likely recommend an exorcism in your situation. However"—he looked down and fiddled with his watchband, which hung loose on his wrist— "the problem is that most exorcisms involve someone who is clearly tormented by a spirit in some terrible way. Do you feel tormented, DH?"

"Not really. I'm mostly distracted from other things in my life that need my attention. These events—they're too vivid to be called dreams—are generally pleasant and interesting. I think I'm worried about whether I should be worried about them."

"Exorcism can be a long, drawn-out ordeal, and it doesn't always work. Honestly, though, I don't think you need that. Your ghost sounds like a friendly one who just wants to get to know you." He shook his head and laughed. "I really don't know what to tell you." He grew serious again. "This Annabelle said you would eventually stop having the dreams, and you won't even remember them?"

"That's what she said."

"Then I think, if I were you, I wouldn't worry too much about it. If I were in your shoes under a naked girl ghost, I think I'd just lie there and enjoy the ride" — He cleared his throat — "so to speak."

"You don't think it's some sort of evil possession then?" I asked.

"From what you say, there doesn't appear to be any evil attached to it. She sounds pretty nice to me." He paused for a moment. "Now, if I were a priest, I might tell you something like go to Mass more often, say some Hail Marys, pray that the friendly little girl ghost leaves you soon, and all that. But since she said she's going to leave you soon of her own accord, I don't think there's any need for you to rock the boat. Best let her do it on her own. If she's got the kind of supernatural power to do that visitation stuff, I don't think you want to mess with her too much. If you're not careful, she's liable to zap you out of this dimension and into the next. You'd better be nice to her." He grinned. "Besides, she isn't finished with you yet. It seems she has some things she wants or needs to tell you, and she'll be visiting you again soon ... maybe even in human form. That's what she said, right?"

"Yes, she did. Only I won't know who she is when I see her. I'll only sense that there's something special about her."

"Well then, as an old friend once told me, 'Ride with the tide, and go with the flow.' Know what I'm talkin' about?" He gave me an encouraging smile.

"I do. Thanks." Then I smiled and said, "I'd keep you posted on how this all turns out, but I'm not sure if I'll know it when it happens.

I thanked Dr. Garcia for his time and understanding. He went back to packing up his lesson material, and I made my way down here to The Pit.

◎ ◎ ◎

The conversation with Dr. Garcia eased my mind about Annabelle. I feel better about it all now — like maybe I'm not destined for hell because I've got a ghost hanging around with me. Fr. Bob had also told me not to worry about it. He said that ghosts are just our loved ones trying to keep in touch with us and that if the Church sees nothing wrong with what all the dead saints do, they shouldn't see anything wrong with loved ones chatting with us from the other side occasionally. He said it's communication, not haunting, which is pretty much what Dr. Garcia told me. Still, it's good to have a second opinion — from the Catholics, at least. I wonder what the Baptists think.

I've been trying to draw some pictures of Annabelle here in my journal. If she's gonna stop the dreams and make me forget about her, I'd like to have an image of her to look at once in a while. But if I forget about her, will I even know who the drawings represent when I look at them? I'd better label them all just in case.

I'm just getting started on my first sketch when I hear a rich, deep voice rise above the general babble of The Pit. It sounds something like, "Whatcha got there, Bud?"

Since I'm engrossed in my drawing, I simply grunt in response to the voice. It could be Fr. Bob, or Jack, or any number of people. The voice may not even have been speaking to me — at this point, I really don't care.

A minute or two passes, and I hear the voice again, much closer. "That's not a bad drawing," it said. "Could use a little work, though. That left eye looks like it belongs on the Frankenstein monster."

I turned my head and looked up to see who my critic might be. A tall male figure stood on the other side of the table, positioned so that his head was directly in front of the sun. All I could make out was a silhouette with a brilliant halo, which I soon realized was sunlight shining through his unruly curls. I raised my hand to shade my eyes. The halo resolved into a mop of wild, curly hair over a face that I recognized.

"I'm Frank Reed," the voice announced as Frank leaned over the table and offered his hand to me.

I was dumbfounded and wondered vaguely why I did not hear the sound of trumpets and choirs of angels. My arm seemed to move of its own accord as it extended, and my hand opened up to grasp his. Here he is, looming over me, THE Frank Reed. This is the guy I pass on campus nearly every day. He's the guy who looks at me with a question he never asks. He's the guy held up by art teachers and art students alike as an art god here on Earth. He is also the guy whose seat and table I occupy.

"Hi," I heard myself say.

His face broke into a huge grin, and he let loose with one of those great *LAUGHS* I have heard from him many times when he's holding court with his admirers down here in The Pit. Until now, though, I've always been at some distance — never in such close quarters. The ground shook.

He grabbed hold of my limp hand and began to shake it firmly and vigorously. "What the hell's the matter with you, Bud?" he asked as he seated himself across the table from me. "You look like you've seen a ghost."

Ghosts. Again.

"You okay, Bud?"

"Uh ... sure. Yeah. I'm fine. Nice to meet you, Mr. Reed."

"It's Frank. Call me Frank." There's that Laugh again. "I'm only mister to my patrons ... and maybe the IRS."

My God, he has patrons? He actually has people who regularly buy his work? That's what a patron is, isn't it?

"I'm DH." My voice wasn't much stronger than my handshake had been.

"DH, huh? Like the writer?"

"Yeah ... I guess. DH Lawrence, right?" I responded.

"That's the one." Frank shifted his position on the bench to lean back against the concrete wall. He pulled out his pipe and started loading it. "DH Lawrence," he mused. "Pompous son of a bitch but one hell of a writer."

He got the pipe going, and a cloud of pungent smoke rose into the air above the table and filled the space around us. The smell of it was odd but not unpleasant.

Frank didn't say anything for a couple of minutes. He puffed his pipe and rubbed his shoulders against the wall behind him like he was settling into an armchair. I almost didn't hear him say, "Never sat on this side of the table before. Kinda hard to get used to."

Then it hit me. Every time I saw him at this table, he had been sitting on this side, where I am now. Good grief, I have HIS spot. Is he trying to send me a subliminal message?

Then Frank looked at me and pointed at my journal with the stem of his pipe. "What the hell are you doing? You makin' a grocery list or somthin'?" *The Laugh.*

"I'm writing in my journal," I told him.

"A journal, huh? Looks more like a sketchpad. What's that drawing of?"

"It's a long story." I started to close the book, but he reached over and laid the palm of his hand on it to prevent me.

"Whoa there, Bud. I didn't mean to disturb you while you're writing down what needs to be said."

I looked up at him and saw that his smile was warm and genuine, not the satirical grin usually on display. "It's nothing really …."

"The hell it is," he said firmly. "It's important to you, or you wouldn't be writing it. Don't tell me it's nothing."

"I was just writing down some stuff that Dr. Garcia and I talked about earlier. I didn't want to forget some of the things he said."

"Old Garcia, yeah, he's a pretty good guy. Every once in a while, he comes out with something smart," *The Laugh.* "What were you and the old boy chit-chattin' about, Bud?" He actually said chit-chattin'.

"That's a long story."

"I got all day." He made a show of settling into his seat on the hard, narrow bench and making himself comfortable against the concrete wall—if that's possible.

I can't believe it. Not only am I finally sitting down with this iconic figure, carrying on a conversation, but Frank also seems interested in what I have to say. He has all day? For me?

So, for the second time that day, I told the story about Annabelle, the dreams, the visits — everything. He puffed on his pipe and listened without interrupting except to nod his head now and then or to interject a 'Really,' or an 'Honestly' or a simple 'Uh-huh,' just to let me know he was paying attention. I finished my tale and looked at him expectantly.

"Are you writing down every word we say?" Not exactly the reaction I was looking for.

"Ah ... No ..." His remark had caught me off guard. "I just make notes and fill in the details later."

"You are serious about that journal, aren't you, Bud?" *The Laugh*. "If that's what you do with every conversation you have, you must have hundreds of those black books filled up by now."

"I just started doing this a couple of years ago."

"Excuse me. You must have *dozens* of those books by now." Once again, *The Laugh* has people here in The Pit looking around for the source of the explosive discharge. It was soon identified and dismissed as Frank Reed just being himself and everyone went back to what they were doing before being startled into the awareness of Frank's presence.

He got serious and returned to his initial inquiry. "So, the chick in the drawing is the ghost, Annabelle?"

"It's supposed to be," I muttered, somewhat embarrassed to have my poor sketch examined by the resident celebrity artist.

"Well, it is, or it isn't?" he chided gently. "You're the artist, Bud."

"Yes," I said with greater conviction. "It is Annabelle."

He slid the book out from under my hand and spun it around so he could examine the pages right side up. He looked at the drawing, nodded his head, and smiled. "She's a cutie, and you ain't a half-bad *arteest*." He smiled and slid the book back to me. "A little rough around the edges, but there's lots of promise in those hands of yours."

Wow. The great Frank Reed just told me that I have a lot of promise! What could I say?

"Thanks," I said, feeling slightly stunned. "I have a lot to learn. I haven't been drawing very long."

"There's no learning to it. You either have the Art Spirit, or you don't. If you have it, you need to use it—all the time. You can't learn art. You have to live it." He leaned back against the wall again and puffed his pipe while I digested his words.

Again, I wish I had met Frank earlier. I could have approached him at any time in the hallway or down here in The Pit, but I didn't. The truth is, he scared the hell out of me. But now that I've met him, I've discovered that Frank Reed is actually a very nice guy.

"That's how I feel about it … Frank," I said, finally working up the confidence to use his first name. "I visit the LA museum as often as I can just to sit in front of the paintings and study the details—the lights, the shadows, every single brushstroke. I wonder how the artist decided to put that one single stroke in the one single place on the entire canvas where it belonged so that one single stroke could turn the whole collection of brushstrokes from a simple picture into a masterful painting bursting with emotion. I wonder about what was in the artist's head while he was painting on the canvas. What he was thinking? What did he feel? Hell, what did he have for lunch that day? I don't know what I'm talking about, and I'm havin' a tough time sayin' it."

Frank looked over at me and smiled sympathetically. "You got it bad, Bud. I think you just might be crazy enough to be a *real arteest*."

"Do you think I ought to declare art as my major here at RCC?" I asked.

"Uh … Yeah! Like yesterday!" *The Laugh*. "I've been hangin' around this college for a couple of years now and I ain't never run across someone like you. You need to paint, Bud!"

"But going to classes or just painting doesn't make it happen. How does one really become an artist? I mean, what do I have to do to wake up the Art Spirit inside of me?"

"Like I said, you just live it. Live art. Every moment of every day. Live it."

"But how do I do that?"

"Simple. You hang around with me! It'll rub off of me and on to you." Frank punctuated his statement with the most explosive *Laugh* yet.

Really? You have got to be kidding. Two hours ago, I was afraid to pass Frank in the hall. Now he's inviting me to hang around with him. Life is full of surprises.

"I got the rest of the day off. You got a car?" Frank asked.

"I have a little VW."

"So, you don't have a real car," *The Laugh*. "Just kidding. Come on." He stood up and moved toward the steps leading out of The Pit. He glanced over his shoulder to see if I was following him. "Where you parked?" he asked.

"Out behind the art houses,"

"So am I. I've got a motorcycle. You can follow me."

"Follow you where?" I asked, hurrying to keep up with him.

"To my studio, Bud!"

You have got to be kidding!

In Frank's Studio

We arrived at Frank's house — he calls it his castle — about fifteen minutes ago. As soon as we walked in, Frank told me to make myself comfortable, said something about wine, then disappeared into what I presume is the kitchen. I'm sitting on a mattress in the corner of a room that seems to be the living room, awaiting his return.

Frank's house is a secluded farm-style house of indeterminate age located somewhere on the outskirts of Riverside. I really have no idea where we are as Frank went so fast on his bike that I had to concentrate on keeping him in view and had no time to really see where we were going. I'll be lucky to find my way home after a few glasses of wine. I know I won't be able to find my way back here on my own.

The front door opens directly into a small, sparsely furnished living room. The mattress I'm sitting on is in one corner, a little coffee table is in the middle of the room, and one of those canvas sling chairs is next to the front door in the other corner directly across from the mattress. An archway marks the transition from this space to another larger space that Frank appears to have adapted to serve as his main studio area. Another archway leads to what looks like a dining room—I can see a table in the middle of the room with chairs arranged around it. A light shines into the dining room through an open door on one side. It's probably the kitchen, as I can hear Frank opening and closing cupboards and a refrigerator.

At this minute, though, Frank's studio holds my main interest. The center of the room is occupied by a sturdy wooden table about eight feet long. A long, narrow cabinet like a buffet or a low dresser sits against the wall under the window. Dozens of small sculptures—some wire and some clay—and an assortment of pottery, stacks of sketch pads in various sizes, and an array of tools used to make art are arranged on the large table. The top of the cabinet along the wall holds countless tubes of oil paint and an assortment of jars filled with paintbrushes of all sizes, turpentine for cleaning the brushes, and cans and bottles of linseed oil and other liquids used to mix and manipulate paint. What is truly amazing, though, is that despite the amount of stuff on the tables, it is all neatly arranged and organized. On top of that, the studio is entirely dust-free. I can't find a speck of dust anywhere.

The easel standing in the corner near the end of the cabinet by the window is not one of those flimsy, collapsible tripods. Frank's easel is a professional model that almost touches the ceiling. It sits on a wheeled platform and is substantial enough to support the most generously sized canvases. It is currently occupied by a three-by-three-foot work in progress. The subject is a young girl. She is wearing a dark blue shirt that hangs open to expose her torso from her breasts to her naval. I love it—not just the naked boobs part, but the whole thing. The colors are bright and clean, and the girl's face is captivating—quite beautiful, in fact. That painting is as good as any I've seen in the LA Museum.

◎ ◎ ◎

It's quiet here in the house. The only noise I've heard is Frank rattling around in the kitchen. He told me earlier that his wife, Maxine, works in the security department at the university, so she must be off doing her job. He also mentioned that the kids were spending the night somewhere, so they're not home, either.

Aha. Here he comes now.

Frank is carrying two large, handmade ceramic mugs, one in each hand. "Here ya go, Bud. Drink up! This is one of the best wines you'll ever taste. It's been on a plane all the way from Spain to the good old US of A." He added with a wink and a confidential tone, "I have friends in the Spanish government."

"You mean it isn't Red Mountain?" I asked as I accepted the offering from him.

"What the hell's that?" He really didn't know what I was talking about.

"That's the stuff everyone I know drinks when we get together."

"Never heard of it, and if I haven't heard of it, it ain't worth ca-ca." *The Laugh* exploded from him as he sat down in the sling chair.

"It's worth a buck twenty-nine a gallon," I said.

"You're kidding! My shoelaces cost more than that." Frank waved his foot, calling attention to his bright red leather shoes with lemon yellow shoestrings.

"Wow." They are impressive shoes and laces.

"So, what do you think of my Castle?" He flung an arm out to invite my inspection of his domain.

"It's nice. I wish I had a place like this."

"It's a bit small, but most of it's studio. We don't really do much lounging around like a normal American family, so we don't need to waste space on that kind of thing."

"You don't own a TV?"

"There's a small one in the bedroom, but it's hardly ever on. There's nothing much worth watching, and besides, who's got time for it? "

"There's a good documentary now and then."

"Name one."

"I saw a pretty good one the other day about Germany."

"Ah, good ol' Germany, the country that invaded my home country during the war. They have produced some pretty good artists, though."

"What's your home country?"

"Norway. *Alt for Norge*, as the king's motto says. All for Norway. Not too creative, but the sentiment is sound." *The Laugh*. "Hell, I'm the king of this Castle filled with masterpieces. Maybe I should get a motto."

"So, Germany has some good painters?"

"You bet your butt they do, Bud. Emile Nolde, Ernst Kirchner, Max Ernst, Otto Dix, George Grosz, Frank Auerbach, Gerhad Richter, Max Beckmann, to name a few. There are hundreds of decent German painters."

"I have a lot to learn. I can't even pronounce the names."

"It just takes time, patience, and lots of reading. Stick with me, Bud, and I'll get you headed in the right direction."

"Well, I appreciate that, Frank. I need all the help I can get."

He pointed his finger and "fired" it at me to emphasize what he said next. "Never forget that you have that Art Spirit inside you, whether you like it or not, and the Art Spirit will *force* you to learn. If you're a real *arteest*, then, damn it, you're an *arteest*. You can't stop the process."

I let Frank's last statement soak in before I proceeded. "You were saying that the Nazis occupied Norway during the war?"

"Yep. The German army just waltzed right in even though Norway had declared neutrality in 1939. John Steinbeck wrote a book about it— *The Moon is Down*—if you're interested."

"I had no idea," I said. "That Hitler was a real nut case. We're lucky he didn't win the war and take over the world."

"He was a mess, alright. I sometimes wonder how things might have turned out if he'd been allowed to live out his real dream and skip the mad dictator bit."

"What kind of dream did he have besides wiping out the Jews? I'd call that more of a nightmare."

"That was terrible and unspeakable. Before all that, though, all Hitler wanted to do was paint pictures. He had the makings of a fairly good artist."

"You're kidding."

"I'm serious. He painted some decent stuff before becoming a murderous politician. He turned out hundreds, if not thousands, of drawings and paintings—mostly watercolors. I've seen a few of the ones that weren't destroyed. They beat the crap out of a lot of what passes for art these days. He was dirt poor and lacked any training but was incredibly prolific."

"I had no idea."

"I've got a theory about old Adolf."

"You do?" I have a feeling Frank has a theory about most everything.

"Hitler's big dream was to get accepted to the Academy of Fine Arts in Vienna, but he failed the entrance exam. He tried twice, they rejected him both times, and that really pissed him off. He hated Vienna from that day forward. You know he was actually born in Austria, not Germany, don't you?"

"I thought he was German."

"Nope. He was born in Austria in 1889 and moved to Germany in 1913."

"I wonder why he became so anti-Jew."

"Some people say the old boys running the Art Academy that refused his entrance were Jews, and that's what did it. Hitler thought his work was more than good enough to be accepted, and when the Jewish guys tossed him out, he never got over it. His natural paranoia took over, and he fell under the influence of some of the notable anti-Semites in Austria. His fertile imagination latched onto their teachings. Pretty soon, he was convinced that all of his problems and those of Austria and the rest of the world were the fault of the Jews. Hell, Hitler was likely part Jewish himself. See why my theory's a good one?"

"Yes. Had Hitler been admitted to the Academy, he probably would never have gone the way he did. He would have been happy, and his paintings would now be hanging in every museum in the world."

Frank smiled and nodded his approval of his prize pupil. "Could be, but he became a prick instead. The irony is that most of the people who supported his artistic endeavors back in Vienna before he applied to art school were Jewish."

"That is ironic."

"So, that's your first lesson. Art—or the lack of it—has consequences." Frank pulled himself out of his sling chair and grinned at me. "Now I think it's time you learned about the tools a guy needs to have at hand if he wants to become the *arteest* he's meant to be. Grab your wine, and we'll head into the studio. I'm gonna teach you some stuff you'll never learn in Harry's classes."

Five Hours Later in The Hole

Frank gave me the Grand Tour of his studio and lectured me on the materials required to paint paintings of any great worth. I already had a basic understanding of the bare-bones necessities, but Frank filled me in on brand names and the range of price and quality. I've been buying the cheapest of everything, so all of this was an eye-opener. Frank must have sensed my concern about the expense of being an artist. He made it clear that price does not always equal quality and that I would soon learn where I could cut corners and where I shouldn't.

"Another thing, Bud, you're gonna have to buy an easel. Holding a canvas board on your lap while you're tryin' to paint just ain't gonna cut it." Frank opened a door and started rummaging around in the closet it concealed. "And while we're at it," he continued, "I forbid you to ever buy another canvas board."

He emerged from the closet with a roll of canvas under one arm and a bundle of wooden slats, or stretcher bars, under the other. He leaned the canvas roll and stretcher bars against the back wall, then slid open a drawer in the cabinet under the window and pulled out a mallet, some clamps, and a heavy-duty staple gun. Before long, we had three stretched and primed canvases. Frank made the first, smallest one himself, describing every step in detail. I helped him with the largest one next, then Frank supervised while I made the medium-size one myself.

When we finished, I realized that it was getting late and I needed to get home. We said our goodbyes, and I headed out to my car. When I got there, I was surprised to discover that Frank had followed me with the three canvases we had just stretched tucked under one arm.

"Why don't you take these with you and give them a good home," he said. I could think of nothing to say, so I stood back and watched as Frank managed to fit them into the back seat of the VW.

Frank returned to the house, and I leaned into the car to reposition the canvases a bit. I pulled my head out and looked up to see Frank coming back. He was smiling and carried a large canvas bag. He held the bag out toward me and said, "Don't forget your doggie bag."

Puzzled, I took it from him and looked inside. It was filled with tubes of oil paint — one each of red, yellow, blue, white, and burnt sienna — an assortment of new brushes, some bottles of drying medium and linseed oil, and some other things deemed essential to the well-equipped painting studio. When did he do this? I never had a clue about what he was up to.

"Frank ... I can't accept this ... This stuff must have cost a bundle."

"Nonsense, Bud. What are friends for?"

"But we just met this afternoon."

"What is time, anyway? Days, hours, weeks, years?" He grinned. "Now, go home and do some real painting. I want to see a masterpiece in a few days."

I'm home now, sitting on my bed in The Hole, wondering if I should call it a night and turn in or break out the supplies Frank gave me and paint through the night. Nah, that would be stupid. If I rush through those three new canvases, I'll probably just make a mess of them. I'll wait and get started tomorrow. My parents will be away for a few days, so I'll have the garage to myself and lots of peace and quiet to work on the masterpieces Frank wants to see. If I go to sleep now, I'll wake up with a clear head and some fresh ideas.

Maybe I'll dream of something to paint.

Maybe I'll dream of Annabelle.

12
Two Weeks Later

It's hard to believe that it's the middle of December already, and Christmas vacation begins on Monday. My plans for the next two weeks are pretty loose, but I have promised myself a sort of art pilgrimage. I hope to make several trips into the LA area for visits to the LA County Museum of Art, the Norton Simon in Pasadena, and the Getty over by Santa Monica. Frank mentioned some galleries and studios in and around the city that I should visit. He told me that museums are great for history and inspiration, but the studios and galleries will show me what's going on in the art world now and what the trends are for the future. I need to map their locations and work them into my visits to the three museums.

Frank and I have become pretty good buddies since we finally got together a couple of weeks ago. We actually say "Hi" when we see each other on campus, and we've met up at "our" table in The Pit several times. I managed to find my way back to his house a couple of times and met his lovely wife, Maxine, and he's been to The Hole a time or two as well.

I had explained my living arrangements at my parents' house to Frank, but I don't think he got it. Whenever I mentioned it in conversation, he would come back with a joke, usually about me living like a hermit in a cave high up on a mountain. Frank invariably punctuated these quips with *The Laugh*. All of Frank's preconceptions went out the window with his first visit.

Frank arrived on his motorcycle while my dad was out mowing the front lawn. He cut the engine and ran his finger through his hair in a vain attempt to bring some order to the wild, curly mop before dismounting the bike. He straightened his Levi jacket with a quick tug, then pulled his pipe out of a pocket and lit it up.

Dad turned off the mower when he saw Frank come up the driveway, and I joined him in the yard. Dad leaned toward me and said, "You're right. He does look like Mark Twain."

The business of lighting his pipe taken care of, Frank turned his attention to his surroundings. When he saw Dad and me standing on the lawn, he smiled and strode toward us, right hand extended in greeting.

"You must be the proud papa of DH here," Frank said as he and Dad shook hands. "You got a good kid there."

"Well ..." Dad hesitated, looked at me, then smiled and said wryly, "We're workin' on the proud part."

"Dad's right, Frank," I said. "I haven't done anything yet to make anybody proud. I haven't even figured out what it is I'm meant to do."

"Don't worry about that, Bud," Frank said. "Some people are just late bloomers. I'd say you're off to a good start, though." He turned to my dad and said, "DH tells me you're a rocket scientist. That's a tough act to follow."

"Not really a scientist, more of an engineer," Dad explained, "and I certainly don't expect him to follow in my footsteps. He seems to be making his own path in life, as you, no doubt, have made yours, Mr. Reed."

"More like a highway. It may have started out as a path, but now it's a six-lane freeway with all the obstacles that come with it," Frank answered and followed up with *The Laugh*.

I had told Dad about the earthquake-inducing *Laugh*, but this was the first time he had heard it for himself. Dad, the master of the deadpan, looked at me and said, "I'd say that was about a 4.0." Then he smiled at Frank and said, "I'd better get this lawn finished while I still have some light. It was nice meeting you, Mr. Reed."

Frank shook Dad's offered hand and said sincerely, "You too, sir. It's an honor."

Dad started up the mower, and I led Frank through the breezeway and into the garage, stopping at the door to The Hole.

Frank paused to take in the surroundings. Finally, he said, "You gotta be kiddin', Bud. This is worse than a cell. This is a third-world country. This little wooden box in the corner is your room?"

"Don't worry. it's bigger on the inside."

Frank looked at me and grinned. "Like the Tardis?"

"You watch Dr. Who?"

"Dr. Who is one of the few things worth turning on the television for," he said. "They replaced the old doctor a while back. The new guy reminds me of one of the Three Stooges. I'm not sure how he's going to work out."

"Yeah, I don't care for him either. Still, it's fun to watch."

With Frank fully prepared for the experience, I unlocked the door, slowly swung it open, and motioned for Frank to enter with a dramatic flourish. He gave me a sideways look with a raised eyebrow, then cautiously stepped into The Hole with me right behind him.

Frank said nothing while turning in place three or four times to take it all in. Finally, he declared, "Well … it ain't the Taj Mahal." *The Laugh.*

I grinned. "That's what I tell myself. It's just a room."

"But it's your room," he said, "and all kidding aside, it's just fine. Whatever suits your needs at this stage of your life is great. You'll go through many rooms before you finally settle in."

"I figured that out already," I told him. "You want some wine?"

He looked at me with surprise. "Your parents let you drink out here?"

"They don't really know I keep wine here."

He smiled wryly and said, "You wanna bet? Parents know everything. Your dad seems like a pretty cool guy — not to mention smart — so I'll bet he knows all about it but just hasn't said anything."

"Could be."

"Have a seat," I said, indicating the little office chair sitting under the desk my grandfather had attached to the wall. I stepped over to the closet, opened the door, and pulled out a gallon of Red Mountain and a couple of clean mugs I keep for occasions like this.

"I'm glad you've got a chair for me to sit on," Frank said. "I was a little uneasy about sitting next to you on the bed while we sip our wine. I really ain't that kind of guy."

"Don't worry, Frank, I ain't that kinda guy either."

Frank and I sat in The Hole and talked about this and that for about an hour, then I took him out back and showed him the patio, the yard, and the grotto where I often spend a lot of time doing nothing. Frank told me he could see himself sitting on the edge at night, staring out at the lights in the valley and drinking wine, "A guy could really get into this place," he said.

"I come out here all the time—almost every night—even when it rains. The valley out there is beautiful."

Frank nodded in agreement. "I can see that. You ever thought about having an art party out here? I mean, in the summertime?"

"I actually have had a couple of small parties out here. They were pretty neat."

"Great place to bring a girl!" *The Laugh*. "Pure romance on a moonlit night."

I promised Frank I would consider having a big art party come next summer—which will be on top of us before we know it. He told me he'd put it on his calendar and build his entire schedule for the next year around it.

"Sure you will, Frank."

"No kiddin'!" he protested. "Just watch. You give that party, and I'll be here even if I'm in Europe doin' a show and have to fly back for it."

I believe he would.

13
Christmas Vacation

The last class before Christmas vacation was yesterday, and I'm free for two weeks. I'm hoping to spend this time immersing myself in art since that seems to be my life's direction. Meeting Frank was a significant turning point for me. My association with him has sparked a desire to be fully engulfed in art. I can't get enough of it. If I'm not reading about it or taking a class on it, I'm doing my best to produce it. I'm beginning to understand Jack a little better, too. I never see him without a piece of sculptor's wax in his hand. His hands are always busy doing something artistic all the time. My journal has been my constant companion for several years, and lately, sketches take up as much room as my writing. I've started carrying around bits of the sculptor's wax Frank gave me like Jack does. I've also taken to carrying a small spiral notebook in my pocket to write or doodle in if I forget to bring my journal with me. I'm always arting. Sometimes I even carry a paintbrush in my pocket just so I can reach down and feel it from time to time to remind myself of what I'm becoming. Silly stuff, I know, but it all helps me wrap my mind around the goals I'm drafting for my life.

I'm driving to LA Monday morning to spend some time at LACMA, wandering around and studying the paintings. I'm not sure what I want to look at, but the museum is enormous and has art from every period of history from all over the world and in every style imaginable. I'm sure I'll find something to suit my mood and stimulate my imagination.

There's another aspect of this trip I'm looking forward to. After class yesterday, I stopped at the health food store for a cottage cheese and date sandwich. *Hey, don't knock it till you've tried it.*

"Stop and put your hands on top of your head." The voice came from behind me just as I was about to get into my car.

Alarmed and confused, I froze in my tracks. The voice sounded like it meant business, whatever that business might be, so I did as I was told. I was then instructed to "Turn around slowly."

Again, I obeyed. I turned, careful not to make any movements that could be misunderstood, and located the source of the voice. It was Jenn, the lady detective who had attended a party at my house a couple of months ago.

"You should see the look on your face, DH," she said once she had her laughter under control.

"Jenn!" I said. "You really had me going. What are you doing out here?"

"The chief needed some good detecting, so he sent me out to do it. I was just on my way back to the station to check in. What are you up to?"

I explained that classes had just let out for the Christmas break, and I was thinking about my plans for the next two weeks.

"That sounds like fun," she said when I mentioned going to the museum Monday. "I've got the day off. Can I come along?"

Her response took me by surprise, and before I could think about it, I heard myself say, "Sure. It would be nice having someone else along."

"Great," she said. "Why don't I pick you up at your place? I have some papers that need to be delivered to the LAPD. Since it's official business, I can use one of the department's unmarked cars and make the drop-off. We won't even have to pay for the gas."

"Really? I get to ride in a cop car?"

"Yep, and I won't even make you ride in the back seat."

"You mean behind the grill?"

"You aren't gonna jump me if I let you ride in the front, are you?"

"Hmm ... maybe not on the first date."

"Hmm ..."

So, I'm going to the art museum next week with a woman I hardly know who just happens to be a cop — and a gorgeous one, at that.

Monday Morning

I heard the crunch of the tires on the gravel drive and went out to meet Jenn before she got out of her car. She opened the passenger door, told me to get in, and we hit the road. After the initial greetings, the first few miles of the trip passed in awkward—for me at least—silence. There was nothing uneasy about Jenn, though. She seemed entirely serene. Her lovely mouth curved in a half-smile as she slipped sidelong glances at me while she drove. As my grandmother would say, she looked like the cat who ate the cream.

Jenn got tired of waiting for me to speak and opened with, "Do you go to the museum often?"

That seemed to do the trick. Once I got started, I could hardly stop. "Actually, I've only been there a couple of times—maybe three—but I really love the place. It's like Oz. Stepping through the doors is like entering another world. There's so much energy, so much emotion ..."

"You get all that out of a museum?" Jenn laughed.

"Just think about all of the paintings and sculptures in there, all done by different artists living their own individual, unique lives at the centers of their own universes. So many of them never received any notice for work or sold very few or even none of their paintings. Just think of the emotion, frustration, and love they poured into every piece of art in that building. The tension, the aggravation, the drunken nights, the lost loves ..."

Jenn smiled. "I hear ya. They're not just pretty pictures," she said. "Artists really are a different breed—mostly loners from what I've seen."

"I kind of think that too. If a person is a real, dedicated artist, he's probably pretty much married to his work. He lives for it, and he probably doesn't get much out of it beyond fulfilling a personal need or desire." I smiled.

"Are you sure you want to be an artist?" she asked.

"Mostly ... mostly sure. I'm just a little torn now. I can't decide between writer or artist, but several people have told me that I can do both, which seems logical. Right now, though, I really can't get enough of art."

11 AM at LACMA

Jenn and I are relaxing on a bench in a room filled with works from the Italian Renaissance. She remembered my attachment to my journal from the party last fall, so she isn't sitting there watching me write and wondering what the heck I'm doing. She is pondering a medium-sized painting of a Madonna and Child surrounded by four angels playing musical instruments. I'm not sure who painted it. We're too far away to read the little sign beside it, and I'm too lazy to go up and look. It's a lovely work depicting the Virgin Mary wearing a black and gold robe and the baby Jesus lying on His back with a golden halo behind his bright blonde hair. What the heck's with that anyway? Jesus was a Jew from Judea, and those folks have black hair. Maybe some have brown hair, but I've never seen a bright yellow-headed Judean Jew. Anyway, the angels are wearing pink robes with blue capes, and the entire background is painted gold. It's gorgeous, and Jenn seems almost mesmerized by it.

I nudged her and said, "That's a lot of gold, isn't it?"

"It sure is. I wonder if the artist used ground-up gold in his paint. It sure is shiny."

"He may have," I said. "Although it could be gold leaf. I'd need to get closer to be sure."

"Whichever it is, that painting looks like it needs to be locked up in Fort Knox," Jenn said.

"I think this museum is as secure as Fort Knox. Maybe more so. Just think of all the money that one single painting you're looking at is worth, and multiply that by the hundreds of paintings in this museum."

"It's more than I have in the bank," Jenn said wryly.

"It's somethin' all right."

"It is ironic, though, that so much money and effort were lavished on these artworks intended to show devotion to Jesus, Mary, and the saints," Jenn said. "When it comes to money and possessions, Jesus had none and lived a very simple life. Didn't He teach that we should use our wealth to help others? Feed and clothe the poor, heal the sick—that sort of thing? Most of the saints did just that. That's why they were made saints. What good are these fabulous paintings and statues to the Kingdom of God that Jesus talks about?"

"That's a good question," I said, "especially when many of these Renaissance paintings were commissioned by merchants and bankers to show off their wealth and power. That's one reason the people in these paintings look so European. The artists often flattered their patrons by painting them as major figures in the biblical scenes."

"You can't hardly blame them," Jenn said. "The life of an artist has never been easy or secure. I guess they were only doing what was necessary to keep a roof over their head."

Nodding in agreement, I continued. "The Church at that time was different, too. Some of the popes and other leaders were as concerned about worldly political status and power as they were about Heavenly power, if not more so. They commissioned the cathedrals and monuments and decorated them with fabulous sculptures and paintings. They claimed that they were glorifying God, but I think they did it to glorify themselves at the expense of the common people. They sold indulgences—tickets to Heaven—to support their pet projects when they needed more money. People paid because they were afraid not to."

Jenn shook her head. "It seems a shame that the creation of these beautiful and glorious things was motivated by ordinary ego gratification."

"That's only true in a limited sense. Many of the artists who fulfilled these commissions did their best to express the spiritual nature of their subject. Most people in those days were illiterate. The paintings illustrated hundreds of stories from the Bible that those people could not read for themselves. What difference does it make if the characters looked like the rich banker or merchant when no one knew what the original people looked like anyway?

Who remembers which cardinal hired Michelangelo to sculpt the Pieta or which Pope decided to build St. Peter's Basilica? People are aware that when they look at them—experience them—they are deeply affected and moved to think of things much larger and more important than their own puny selves. I know the Catholic Church has had its ups and downs, but I'm glad it's been able to preserve so many of these beautiful things."

Jenn said nothing for a few minutes, then, "Wow. I never really thought about it that way. My family was never involved in church or religion when I was young, but I always knew that I was meant to help people—help the people who are hurt and can't help themselves and stop the people who are doing the hurting. I've been a detective for a while, and I think even less of religion now than before. I've seen some pretty brutal stuff in my job."

"I'll bet you have."

"I know none of it is God's fault because people have the choice to do the things they do. It's the fault of human beings, and women are just as ruthless as men. Sometimes more so."

"I can just imagine ... well ... no, I can't. I'm not old enough to have seen any real brutality. The worst thing I ever saw was a small plane crash a couple of blocks from my house. I went down to check it out. There were guys—cops, firemen, rescue workers—walking around the scene, picking up body parts and putting them into big plastic bags. I'll never forget that. I wish I hadn't seen it."

"Then don't become a cop. Accidents aren't so bad because they're just that, accidents. It's the stuff humans do on purpose to other humans that gives you nightmares."

"Do you get nightmares about it?" I asked.

"I'm used to it now, so it doesn't affect me like that anymore. I'm not so sure that's a good thing, though. Sometimes I wonder if there is a God up there—and I want to believe there is—then why doesn't He rain down a ton of bricks on the heads of the demons committing these heinous crimes? I know, free will and all that, but where's the justice?"

"The Bible teaches that justice will come in the afterlife."

"If there is an afterlife."

"Boy, you're a bundle of optimism, aren't you?" I said.

"Sorry." She took my hand in hers. "I don't mean to be a crappy date."

"You're not. I was just kidding." I squeezed her hand gently.

After a moment, Jenn sat up straight and looked around. "You know, I'm kinda hungry. They've got a café somewhere in this place, don't they?"

"Yes, they do. It's just burgers and fries, hot dogs, and stuff like that," I said.

She grinned at me. "Are you kidding? That's my favorite on-the-go cop food."

"Sounds good to me."

Jenn stood up, and we headed off to the museum café, still holding hands.

LACMA Café

Jenn is in the restroom, so I'm taking the opportunity to describe her in more detail.

This morning on the way to the museum, I complimented Jenn on her short, curly hair. Since the current fashion is for girls to have their hair long and straight, Jenn's short, bouncy curls really stand out. I find it much more interesting.

"Policewomen really only have two choices — long and pinned up, or short," she said. "My natural curls make the first option too much trouble, so I went with the second. The real advantage is that it always looks about the same whether it's combed or not. I have more important things to do than keep my hair out of my face or worry about how it looks."

Jenn's short, dark curls are the perfect frame for her lovely face. Her face has a soft, silky appearance — not leathery like some women who get too much sun. Her skin color is best described as ivory, but her cheeks are pink and have a golden glow from spending time outdoors. I haven't had the opportunity to touch her face yet, but I hope I do soon.

I've got it! That actress in *The Thin Man*—the movie about the wealthy married couple, Nora and Nick Charles, who are detectives. They fuss all the time and drink too many martinis but have lots of fun solving crimes. I just saw it a couple of weeks ago and fell in love with Nora. Now, I'm here on a semi-date with her. I've been trying to figure out who Jenn reminds me of, and that's it. My star carries a real gun, though, and she can protect me if we get mugged at the museum.

Anyway, that's who she looks like. I mean, not exactly, but pretty darned close.

Here she comes.

"Did you order for me, too?" she said, eyeing the mound of food on the cafeteria tray as she pulled out the chair next to me and sat down.

"I did. Two cheeseburgers, a large order of fries, and a large coke."

"What did you get?"

"Same as you. I figure that if you eat like that all the time and look as good as you do, then maybe the same diet might do something for me."

She had been squeezing ketchup from small plastic pouches onto her fries and was licking the excess off her fingers. She paused to say, "You think I look good?"

"I do. I think you're one of the prettiest girls I've ever seen."

"Come on. Nobody thinks female cops are pretty—especially female detectives. The men cops don't even like us," she said, then bit into one of her cheeseburgers.

"You're kidding."

She shook her head and swallowed. "I'm not. Detectives are supposed to be men. Most people think that the only job a lady cop can do is hand out parking tickets or work dispatch. Even the most open-minded men on the force worry that they'll have to protect a female cop rather than take care of the business at hand. People don't know what to think if we don't look like Jack Webb or Broderick Crawford."

"Anybody who thinks you look like either one of those guys has a screw loose. You're stunning! I just realized that you remind me of that actress in *The Thin Man*."

"Myrna Loy? I loved that movie."

"Yeah, that's her name! You're a ringer for her."

"You're not the first person to tell me that. I'm actually related to her. My last name is Williams—Jennifer Adele Williams. Myrna Loy was born Myrna Adele Williams. Her grandfather was Welsh—that's where we got our curly dark hair—and her grandmother was Scots. Myrna and I are cousins."

"Incredible. Well, you're absolutely gorgeous. Myrna Loy must get her looks from you."

"Well, gorgeous or not, I have a tough time getting a date. I was shocked when you said I could come to the museum with you."

"I have a hard time believing you can't get a date."

"It's against department policy to date someone else on the force. As for civilians, as soon as I mention that I'm a detective, guys find some excuse to leave and not come back."

"Wow. You being a detective is one more reason for me to hang around with you. I think it's pretty cool."

"Well, I think it's pretty cool that you think it's pretty cool. Come here." Jenn pulled me over and kissed me.

Her action took me by surprise. I noticed at first that some of the other diners glanced at us and smiled before looking away. Then I focused on the kiss. She tasted like salt, and ketchup, and cheeseburger.

Jenn brought the kiss to an end and put just enough room between the two of us so she could speak. "Well, how was that? You ever been kissed by a cop before? Do I have too much spit?"

"I've never been kissed by a cop before," I answered, "and you have just the right amount of spit."

"I shouldn't have done that, though."

"Why?"

"I have cheeseburger breath."

"So do I."

"I liked that kiss," she said, placing her hand on mine. She looked down at nothing in particular. She wasn't frowning, but she wasn't smiling, either. She looked ... pensive? ... Wistful?

"What's the matter? You don't look very happy."

"I don't know. I'm just a little shy when it comes to relationships with guys. They usually don't turn out too well for me."

"I know the feeling. I have the same problem with girls. They never seem to stick around for long."

She looked up at me sympathetically and asked, "Why is that?"

"It's not that we don't get along, or they suddenly decide they don't like me. They all just seem to have a compelling reason to leave town. It's kind of bizarre."

"Mine just get tired of dating a cop, usually right after a night of ... um... intimate activity is interrupted by a phone call, and I have to get out of bed, get dressed, and run to a crime scene."

"Wow ... dating you must be like being in a movie."

"Yeah, a bit. Does that bother you?"

"Are you kidding? I think it would be a kick in the pants," I said, grinning at her.

"Hmm ... maybe you'd better be careful what you wish for."

Jenn and I finished our lunch and then spent another couple of hours wandering around the museum, taking in as many exhibits as possible. We had a lot of fun — probably more than we should have. What started out as humorous comments about the art, the artist, and art critics accompanied by episodes of giggles and laughter that drew the attention of the museum guards culminated in a game of hide-and-seek in the Greco-Roman gallery.

The game started off innocently enough. I made some comments about a statue of a Greek goddess we were looking at. I expected some reaction to what I said, but none came. I looked at the spot where Jenn had been standing next to me, but she was gone. I looked around the gallery but could not see her anywhere.

After a brief moment of panic, I realized that she was playing a game with me, and I quietly began to circle each statue to flush her out. Two can play at that game, so I used the other statues as cover while I made my way across the gallery. Pretty soon, I heard a little giggle coming from behind a marble man with a curly beard on the other side of the gallery. I found her crouching behind the statue and concentrating on where she had last seen me. She had no idea I was right behind her until I hollered, "BOO!"

Jenn let out a loud yelp and nearly fell over as she leaped to her feet and turned to face me.

I responded with a loud, "Gotcha." Then we completely forgot where we were, and hide-and-seek turned into a lively game of tag, complete with shouts and laughter.

It didn't take long for a couple of museum guards to come running in to see what all the commotion was about. Jenn had just chased me out from behind one of the massive marble statues, and we were laughing like teenagers — no, make that a couple of ten-year-old kids — when we all but ran into them. They were big and stood shoulder to shoulder, and they were not amused. We did our best to sober up and act like adults, but it was hard to keep a straight face while they glowered at us and strongly suggested that our day at the museum was at an end. We kept our responses to a minimum because ... well, you know, what was there to say? Also, neither one of us wanted to risk breaking out in giggles.

"Yes, sir," I agreed. "You're probably right."

"We're sorry, sir," Jenn said, trying to sound contrite. "I don't know what got into us."

Apologies over, we made our way to the exit without speaking, and the guards followed discreetly to make sure we stayed out of trouble.

Once outside and out of sight, we collapsed in laughter.

"Well," I said when I finally caught my breath, "that was fun. What do you want to do now?"

Jenn looked at me. She wasn't laughing anymore, but she definitely had a twinkle in her eye when she told me, "We're heading back to Riverside. I'm taking you to my house, and you're gonna spend the night with me."

Later at Jenn's House

We arrived at Jenn's house in an area of town called Jurupa Hills at about four o'clock. The neighborhood is a typical, slightly-upscale California housing tract. The stucco exteriors and red tile roofs give a vaguely Spanish look to the otherwise ordinary-looking homes. Jenn's spacious three-bedroom house is more than big enough for a single person. The living room is situated at one end of the house so that there is a large picture window looking out toward the street and a big sliding glass door that opens onto a patio and yard in the back. The kitchen and living room are separated by a bar, making it easy for her to converse with guests while she is busy in the kitchen. I'm sitting at the counter on a barstool, bringing my journal up to date while she's pouring wine.

Jenn set a glass of wine on the counter and watched as I finished up a sentence. "Do you ever stop writing? You must have filled up at least half of that book today."

"I have more at home," I said without lifting my pen.

"Just like that one?"

"Yep. I buy them by the dozen at Aaron Brothers or Standard Brands. They're supposed to be sketchpads, but I use them mostly for writing."

"And you've been doing that for how long?"

"Oh, two or three years."

"What do you do with them? You must have shelves filled with them."

"Actually, I keep them in stacks under my bed. There's not much room in The Hole. Just a small bookshelf for my art books and text-books and a closet where I keep my clothes, wine, and other stuff."

"The Hole? Do I even want to ask about that? Do you live in a cave?"

"Ha! That's what another friend of mine said. No, it's my bed-room. I used to share a bedroom in the big house with my brother, but it got too cramped for the two of us, so my grandfather built me a small room out in the corner of my parent's garage. I guess it is kind of a cave."

"How romantic," Jenn quipped.

"Not really. It is kinda solitary, though, but it suits me," I explained.

Jenn took a sip of her wine and said, "I'm going to run into my bedroom and get more comfortable, so I can really enjoy our wine and the evening on the patio. I've got all kinds of food in the frig if we get hungry."

I spent the time waiting for her sipping my wine and surveying the items in her living room. You can tell a lot about a person by the things they collect and display in their own home. The room is furnished for comfort with a large, overstuffed sofa and two matching chairs upholstered in shades of green and brown. The rugs, lamps, and other assorted items are also primarily green and brown, giving the room a woodsy look. Her appreciation of art is evident in the display of framed posters of famous paintings, most by Impressionists like Van Gogh, Monet, and Pissarro, including the *Mona Lisa*. The central position over the couch, though, is occupied by an oversized poster from the Charlie Chan movie *Shanghai Cobra*.

The wall over the bar between the kitchen and the living room supports a collection of items documenting her law enforcement career. A diploma bearing the gold seal of the police academy, certificates of achievement and recognition, and photos of her at different stages of her law enforcement career and with an assort-ment of officials and fellow officers make up a large framed collage under glass.

A copy of *Ellery Queen's Mystery Magazine* sporting a picture of a half-naked woman who appears to be in peril and a man in a trench coat holding a gun lies on the long coffee table in front of the sofa. It's hard to tell if the man is trying to shoot the woman or save her. More magazines with various titles and similar cover art are neatly arranged in three stacks at one end of the low table. Looks like Jenn spends her spare time reading mysteries and crime fiction.

"You doin' okay in here by yourself?" Jenn asked as she came around the corner of the bar. She's wearing a short red skirt that follows the curves of her hips and nicely rounded bottom and ends about six inches above her knees in a flare that flips and sways with each step she takes. The top buttons of her white shirt are unbuttoned far enough to show off her deep cleavage, and the fabric is a kind that makes it evident that she is not wearing a bra. She's got to be the sexiest cop in town.

I smiled at her and said, "I was just admiring your posters and the stack of magazines on the table. I take it that you like mystery stories."

"I always have. I don't really understand how, but these days, they help me deal with some of the stresses of my job. Grab your glass, and we'll go out and enjoy the evening."

"It does seem to be unseasonably warm." *I have a feeling it's going to get even warmer before this evening is over.*

It's getting dark, but the backyard is lit by floodlights concealed in the landscaping. The patio runs the length of the house and extends to the edge of a swimming pool. The pool is lined with small tiles in various shades of blue, and the water is crystal clear.

The concrete deck behind the pool extends about six feet to the base of a steep incline. The slope has been terraced and landscaped with rocks, cacti, and other desert plants. The sharp shadows created by the concealed lighting give the garden an other-worldly look.

She led me to a plush, double-wide chaise lounge, where we sat down next to each other. I took in the scene for a few minutes. "It's lovely out here," I said. "That's some pool you have there."

"My father loved to swim, especially in rivers or the ocean. I think he was part fish. Putting in the pool was one of the first things he did when he and Mom moved in here. It's hard to do any real swimming in a backyard pool—even this one that's bigger than most—but it's nice to get in and flop around for a while. It's a real comfort to me. I think of my parents every time I swim."

"You keep it filled year-round?"

"Most people in Southern California do. Pools are usually heated, and it's never too cold to swim if the water's warm. I just have to remember to bring a big, thick towel out with me."

Just as she said that the patio lights went dark, and lights came on under the water. The pool glowed and sparkled like a giant sapphire.

"Wow. Did you do that?"

Jenn grinned and held up a small box with a half dozen buttons. "Remote control. I kind of like the convenience of modern technology."

"If you have the money to pay for it. That kind of system has to cost a few bucks."

"It did, but I get paid pretty well, and my parents left me a little money when they died. They left me this house too, free and clear."

"How cool is that? Not that your parents died, I mean, but that they left you the house."

"I know what you meant, silly."

"What happened, if you don't mind telling me?"

"Not at all. It was a car accident. A drunk driver drove them off the road. The car rolled down a bank, and that was that."

"Man …" I couldn't imagine anything like that happening to my own parents. I didn't know what to say.

"It's been about five years now, so the pain is less, but I miss them. I send them my love every night when I get home from work. I like to think they're 'up there' somewhere keeping an eye on me. I like to think they're proud of me." I can hear Jenn's sorrow come through as she speaks.

"I'm sure they are, Jenn." I put my hand on hers.

"What parent wouldn't be proud of their little girl growing up to be a police detective?"

"You're sweet," she said.

We were on the chaise lounge side-by-side, but Jenn snuggled in closer. She laid her head on my shoulder, and I put my arm around her. We stayed like that, each lost in our own thoughts, gazing up at the sky.

"When people die, do you really believe they go to heaven and that they stay in touch with us down here?" Jenn's voice sounded small, almost child-like.

"I do," I said.

"But how can we know that for sure?" she persisted.

"A lot of people have had supernatural experiences that convinced them there's more to life than what we are aware of."

"I've read some of those ghost stories, but I'm still skeptical," Jenn said, reclaiming her adult authority. "I am a detective, you know. I need evidence."

"Yes, I know, but I've had a couple of those experiences. I'm pretty well satisfied that it's all real."

"Seriously?" She pulled back a little and looked up at me.

So, once again, I recounted the story of the near-death experience I had when I was nine years old. I described my spirit rising from my body and hovering near the ceiling, where I watched the doctor and nurses for a while before being transported to a beautiful meadow where I met an angel. The angel told me it wasn't my time yet and sent me back. When I got back to my body in the hospital bed, I was told I'd been dead for a while. I asked about the red-headed nurse who had been sitting on the bed beside me, holding my hand. They looked at each other and told me there was no such nurse on staff there. Some years later, I learned that the day I died was the feast day of Saint Margaret of Scotland, the beautiful, red-headed patron saint of dying children and that a large part of my ancestry is Scots. Of course, the story I told Jenn was more detailed, and it seemed to impress her.

"Incredible. So, you think the meadow was a part of Heaven, the guy in the white robe was an angel, and the nurse was Saint Margaret? Wow. It does all seem to fit, doesn't it?"

"I don't know any other way of explaining it. I wasn't even a Catholic, and I was only nine, so I didn't have any of that stuff programmed in my head yet. No way I could have made all that up."

"I guess if the angel told you it wasn't your time, that meant you still had some stuff to accomplish here on Earth. Have you figured out what that is yet?"

"Ha! Sometimes I'm not even sure what day of the week it is."

"I'll take that as a no. But you said you had a couple of super-natural experiences. What was the other one?"

There was no way I was going to tell Jenn about my naked Anna-belle dreams, so I just smiled and said, "I'll have to know you better before I reveal that one. Let me just say that it's most convincing. Impossible to deny, really."

"Hmm ... you have just given the detective a tease and an excuse to try to figure it out on my own."

"Like those mystery stories you read?"

"Do you like detective stories?"

"I've read a few short stories. I've never actually read a novel yet, but I love detective stuff."

"Oh, you ought to read some Agatha Christie or Ellery Queen," Jenn said enthusiastically. Then she admitted, "Actually, I haven't read any Agatha Christie yet, but she's next on my list."

"For you, that's kind of like leaving the job and coming home to the job. I think they call that a busman's holiday."

"I suppose it is, but I just love to solve puzzles. I like to figure out who the killer is or where the jewels are buried before the author reveals it. It's just me being me." She smiled a little pensively. "When I was a little girl, my parents bought me a Super Sleuth Kit, complete with a magnifying glass, invisible ink, a Sherlock Holmes hat, and several mystery stories written for children. I'd read those stories over and over. I sucked 'em up like chocolate milkshakes and acted out the plots in my bedroom. It was all very real to me. I've got a great imagination. I still have that kit in the original box on the top shelf of my bedroom closet."

"I'd love to see that sometime,"

"Don't worry, I'm sure I'll show it to you before this night is over." She leaned over and kissed me on the cheek.

"Is that Super Sleuth Kit what got you interested in becoming a real detective?" I asked.

"I think it was a big part—that and all the Charlie Chan movies I've watched. I love those."

"Me, too," I said. "I'll bet I've seen every one of them. Old Charlie's quite a character, and Number One Son is a kick in the pants."

"So, you like detecting, too? It's not just me?"

"I do. I grew up watching Sherlock Holmes movies—Basil Rathbone is still the best. My mother likes them, too. She got me some sleuthing stuff for my birthday once, probably a lot like yours. I'll bet I had the same Sherlock hat as you. Loved it."

"Have you ever thought about becoming a real detective?" Jenn asked seriously.

"I have, but I don't think I'm suited for all the regimentation and rule-following expected by a police department. If I could be more like Sherlock and work for myself, it would be a real kick."

"You don't have to join the police. You can take courses by mail to get certified as a private detective. I know a couple of PIs here in Riverside. They work for themselves and make a pretty good living at it."

"Really? A correspondence course?"

"Really. There are many out there that are a bit shady and only want your money, but a handful are legit. I can recommend several if you're interested."

"Thanks, I'd like that."

"If you decide to do it, I can give you some insights you won't get in a course, which will help you succeed in the business. There are good private investigators, and there are bad ones. We cops don't care for the bad ones."

"If they all take the same course, how can they be so different?"

"There's more than one course out there, silly, and it's not just the course work. It's more a matter of attitude. Some PIs think they're hot stuff."

"Like wannabe cops?"

"Exactly. There are a couple of guys that we actually work with, and it's a good partnership. Sometimes a private detective can eke out information a police detective can't. We share info with the good ones all the time. We even have a psychic detective we work with on occasion."

"Really? What do you mean by that?"

"A private investigator who's also a psychic medium. We work with her more than we do with the other guys who aren't psychics."

"Wow. What does she do?"

"She helps us locate bodies, criminals, missing persons — all kinds of stuff. She's really pretty amazing and very professional. She took a mail-order course, and when she finally started her own business, she discovered that her psychic abilities gave her insights we regular cops aren't privy to. She was solving crimes we couldn't, so we developed a relationship with her."

"How cool is that? I just might be able to do a bit of that myself," I said, more to myself than to Jenn.

"Are you psychic?"

"That sort of thing kind of runs in the family. My mother's sort of psychic, and my aunt is really psychic. People think she's a bit nuts, but she's really just tuned in to things others can't see. My mother thinks I get my stuff from my aunt, but I think I got it from my near-death experience. Right after that is when I first started to notice it."

"Maybe you had it all along, and your experience simply triggered it or amplified it," Jenn said. Then she smiled and said, "Wouldn't it be neat if you took one of those courses and we got to work together?"

"Yes, it would. I could wear my old Sherlock hat ... if I can find it."

Jenn put her arm around me, looked up into my face for a little while, then said, "Can I show you my Sherlock hat now?"

"I thought you'd never ask."

14
Tuesday

The Rest of Last night

Jenn and I adjourned to her bedroom, where she immediately began stripping off her clothing — not that she had much to remove. I'd been watching her breasts move and sway beneath the fabric of her shirt all evening, but I was not prepared for their exuberant display when she released them from the confines of her shirt. They were wondrous. They stood out from her lightly-tanned body in creamy white relief and looked for all the world like two perfectly round scoops of vanilla ice cream, each with a bright pink cherry on top. Really. Then, keeping her eyes focused on mine, she unzipped her skirt and let it fall to the floor. I've seen some well-built girls before, but nothing like Jenn. Jack LaLanne would be proud. She could enter one of those body-builder contests and win.

I wanted to just dive right in, but I held back. This whole thing was going pretty fast, and I didn't want to act like a little kid being offered his first piece of candy. I also thought, *Another older woman. Why is she even doing this?* She had told me how hard it is for her to date other cops, but it's hard to believe there are not plenty of other men her own age out there. Why would she want to mess with a young guy like me?

"Aren't you just a little concerned about our age difference? Especially with you being a cop and all."

"Why? I don't know what me being a cop has to do with it, and we're not that far apart in age, are we?"

"At the party I gave a while back, didn't you say you're thirty-six?"

"Yeah, why?"

"Don't you know I'm only nineteen?"

"No way!" She was genuinely surprised. "I thought you were well into your twenties. Damn, and I was so afraid you wouldn't want to date a woman my age."

"I'm sorry. I thought it came out at the party. I thought you knew."

"No ... I didn't know."

"So, what happens now?"

Jenn sat down on the bed and stared down at her lap. I sat next to her, putting some space between us so as not to disturb her thoughts.

Finally, she raised her eyes to meet my own. "I guess ... I guess what happens next is up to you."

"Me?"

"Yes, you. I'm the one who would look bad if anyone found out, but I have feelings for you that I've never felt before, and I don't want that to stop."

"You mean you'd risk losing your job to go to bed with me?"

"I wouldn't lose my job, but it might not be good for my career. You aren't underage, so there are no laws about us having sex. What we do together is nobody's business but ours, but you know how people talk. When it comes to gossip, some of the guys in the department can be worse than little old ladies, especially when it comes to making 'the little girl' look bad."

Jenn put her arms around me, put her mouth on mine, and laid back on the bed, pulling me over on top of her. "They're going to talk about me anyway, so we may as well give them something to talk about," she said when we came up for air. Then she pulled me down again, and things progressed from there.

We finally drifted off to sleep after a couple of hours of vigorous activity when Jenn's phone rang. "Oh no, not now," she muttered into the back of my neck before she rolled over and fumbled for the phone on the bedside table.

It was the police department. A body had been found at one of the hotels down on Eighth Street, and they wanted their top detective on the job. I know that's what they told her because after listening in silence, she replied sarcastically, "So, I'm your top detective now?"

They talked a little longer, then she hung up the phone and sat up in bed. She heaved a sigh and said, "I don't believe this."

"They want you there right now?"

"They're holding the investigation till I arrive. They don't want anyone messing things up until I check it out first. I told them I'd be there as soon as I could."

"Wow, you are important. I guess I'd better dress and get out of here."

"Like hell, you will." she moved over and straddled me. "We'll get dressed right after we do this again, then you're coming with me."

"What?" *Did she say what I thought she said?*

"You heard me. I'm taking you with me. Ever been to a real crime scene?"

"Uh ... No ..."

"Can you handle seeing dead people?"

"I suppose." I squeezed her shapely white butt. "Is it a messy crime scene?"

"Not really. It's a blow to the head. The guy either fell, or someone hit him." She brought her mouth down to mine and began hungrily kissing me.

"Do we have time to do this?" I asked as soon as I was able.

"I'll make it quick," she replied.

We arrived at the hotel at about eight o'clock. Jenn made up for lost time by slapping the portable red light on top of her unmarked car and sounding the siren a few times to move traffic out of our way. I hung on for dear life as she sped across town, ignoring stop signs, lights, and speed limits.

We saw the flashing lights of police cars and an ambulance in front of the hotel from several blocks away. A uniformed cop approached us when we pulled into the parking lot. Jenn rolled down her window, flashed her ID, and the cop directed us to park on the other side of the lot next to another unmarked police car.

Jenn got out of the car and started talking to the two detectives who had come to meet her. I came around to stand near her just in time to hear Detective One say, "Bout time you got here. We've got a dead guy upstairs and half a dozen possible witnesses in the lobby. The fingerprint guy and the photographer are up there now, along with Doc. We were just waiting for you to take a closer look."

"I came as quickly as I could." Jenn looked at me with a suppressed grin.

Detective Two had been eyeing me suspiciously since I got out of the car, and now, he spoke up. "Who's this guy?"

"This is DH, a friend of mine. He's researching police procedures for a book he's writing. He won't be a problem. He's just here to observe."

Research for a book? I guess that's as good an excuse as any for me to be here at a crime scene.

"A book, huh? Well, just as long as he stays outta the way."

"I'll keep an eye on him," Jenn assured him. "He can hang with me while we go through this," Jenn assured him. "DH, this is Tom, and Scotty's the one with the red beard," she said, indicating Detectives Two and One in that order.

I shook hands with both detectives as we were introduced. Tom's crushing grip felt more like a challenge than a greeting, while Scotty's welcoming grasp accompanied a friendly smile.

I returned the smile and said, "I take it they call you Scotty because of the beard."

"Bairn and raised in a little town in the Scottish Highlands," he said in the thick accent of the region. "Started out as a cop there in Sco'land, but there were nair any crime ta speak of, so I moved ta tha States and gae hooked up with these 'air loafers." He punctuated his remark with a hearty slap on Tom's shoulder.

Jenn gave Scotty a warm smile. "Yeah, he's a pretty good cop. I just can't understand what the hell he's sayin' half the time." That brought a big grin to Scotty's face.

Over the course of the investigation, I discovered that while Scotty enjoyed playing up his character as a Scotsman, the thick accent all but disappeared when he got down to work. He was, indeed, a good cop and let nothing interfere with clear communication.

"All right," Tom said impatiently, "if you guys are finished with the small talk, we got a crime scene to go over."

We approached the lobby door, where Tom made a show of holding it open for Jenn. "Ladies first," he said while executing a half-bow with a sweeping arm gesture. Jenn's glare as she walked past him made it clear that she was not amused. I tried to make myself invisible and followed the three detectives into the lobby and toward the elevators.

There were several more uniformed cops standing around in the lobby. Jenn stopped to speak to one of them, who seemed to be keeping an eye on a group of people assembled in the corner. All but one were seated on the various chairs and couches arranged there. The policeman explained that the people sitting down were hotel guests who may have seen or heard something. The group included one woman in a maid's uniform who seemed quite distraught. I found out later that it was her reaction to finding the body that brought the others running. The standing man turned out to be the night manager, and he, too, appeared to be quite agitated.

"Don't worry," Jenn told the manager. "We'll get to the bottom of this soon enough." She then addressed the guests. "Thank you for your patience. I'd like you to all wait here just a little longer while we go upstairs to check things out. We'll have some questions for you then and, possibly, some answers. For now, though, please don't talk to each other."

We continued to the elevator and rode it up to the third floor. The crime scene was easy to find as two more uniformed cops stood in front of an open door halfway down the hall.

I trailed along behind the others with a growing sense of unease. I had no idea how I would react to seeing a real live dead person. I only hoped I wouldn't embarrass myself—or Jenn, for that matter.

The two policemen stood aside and allowed us to enter the room. The three detectives pulled on rubber gloves and stepped to the center of the room while I put my hands in my pockets and stood next to the wall where I had a good view of everything. The fingerprint guy and the photographer paused in their work just long enough to acknowledge our presence.

The room was large, with a bed flanked by night tables at one end and a sitting area with an armchair, sofa, and coffee table at the other. The chair was tipped over, and the table sat at an odd angle to the couch. A mostly-empty whiskey bottle lay on its side on the table, along with a couple of glasses. A heavy, square glass ashtray lay overturned on the carpet, and its contents were strewn across the table and rug. The room smelled strongly of old smoke, stale cigarette butts, and whiskey. I noticed that the drawers in the dresser and side tables had been pulled out, and the closet door stood open.

The body was stretched out on its back on the floor near one end of the coffee table. The man, who appeared to be in his fifties, was wearing pajamas with a western print—cowboys and horses—more like something a kid would wear. In fact, I had a pair like that when I was ten, except mine were Roy Rogers. This guy was wearing Gene Autry. I wonder where he found pj's like that in his size. At any rate, he looked pretty dead. His face was waxy white, and a soggy, dark patch on the carpet around his head.

"What have we got here, Doc?" Tom asked the man kneeling beside the corpse.

"A blow to the head. Either someone hit him with that ashtray, or he fell against the corner of the table. You'll need to look for hair and blood on both."

Doc stood up, not without a small grunt and a little effort. He turned out to be a slender man of about sixty years and less than average height. His silver hair was thick and wavy. He had a beak-like nose and small, dark eyes under bushy eyebrows that looked like they didn't miss much. His khaki pants were baggy, his blue shirt was rumpled, and his navy-blue windbreaker was old and well-worn. I think he must read the same fashion magazines as my friend, Bill Hunter.

"Any idea how long he's been dead?" Jenn asked.

"I can't really say until I get him on the table, but it looks like somewhere between three to five hours." He dropped his instruments into a black medical bag, snapped the bag shut, and headed for the door. Before he left, he turned and said, "I'll send the guys up with a gurney and have them take him to the morgue. I'll let you know as soon as I have anything."

"Thanks, Doc," Jenn said. She came over to where I was standing and asked, "So, what do you think of all this? You doin' okay with the body and all?"

"So far, so good. What happens next—or are we done here?"

"This is where the fun begins. We'll scour the room for evidence as soon as they remove the body. The photographer has already taken pictures of everything in plain sight, but he'll hang around to document anything else we might find. The crime scene specialist has dusted for fingerprints, but he'll be going over everything with a fine-tooth comb for hair, fibers, that sort of thing. Tom, Scotty, and I will be looking for other kinds of clues—things that are here that shouldn't be, things that aren't here that should be. Most of the time, we don't know what we're looking for until we see it."

"Or don't see it," I added with a smile.

She grinned back at me and said, "You're starting to catch on."

I remained standing but settled my back against the wall to more comfortably observe the activity. The crime scene specialist used a magnifying glass to examine the carpet, upholstery, and all the nooks and crannies. He had dozens of plastic bags filled with bits and pieces of potential evidence, including the ashtray, whiskey glasses, cigarette butts, and things nearly invisible to the naked eye. The detectives were systematic in their search, too, but more broadly focused. They examined the bathroom and closet and looked under the furniture. The drawers in the dresser and side tables had been pulled open before we arrived, and the contents were in disarray. The detectives removed the drawers and examined everything inside and out. The photographer took pictures as directed, and the crime scene specialist dusted for fingerprints anywhere that had been previously overlooked.

After nearly two hours, the team was still busy, but they moved more slowly and less enthusiastically. Jenn came over and stood next to me and asked, "So, what do you think? Is this detecting business living up to your expectations? It's like this most of the time—just sifting through all the bits and pieces looking for any kind of a lead. It can be pretty tedious."

"Actually," I said, "It's rather interesting, especially seeing how you all work together without hardly saying a word. It's almost as if you can read each other's minds."

"We've got a good team here despite the ... um ... quirky personalities. We've been working together long enough to know each other's strengths. We've learned that what one of us doesn't see, another one will."

"I can see that. Have you found anything yet, or at least figured out what you are looking for?"

Jenn took a moment to think before she answered. "Well, one thing we're sure of is that this was no accident."

"Really? How's that?"

"First of all, if the victim had fallen and hit his head on the coffee table, there would have been traces of hair and blood, as Doc suggested. Also, we only found a faint smear of blood and no fingerprints on the ashtray. What do you make of that?"

She sounded like one of my professors trying to get me to come up with a solution to a problem she already had the answer for. I played along. "I'd say that someone hit the poor guy on the head with the ashtray, then did a bad job cleaning it up. He managed to wipe out his fingerprints but missed a bit of blood. I'd say our victim was murdered. That's not all you've got, though, is it?" I smiled at her, and she smiled back, looking both pleased and a little surprised.

"Very good," she said, nodding her head. "Other than the body, what else did you notice when we entered the room?"

I closed my eyes and tried to envision the scene. "Well, for one thing, all the drawers and the closet door were open. That chair over there was overturned, too. I thought maybe one of the cops might have done some poking around on his own before we got here."

"No," Jenn said. "They know better than to do that. Their job is to secure the scene and nothing more."

"So, what does it mean then?"

"It means that whoever killed the victim spent a little time searching for something and trying to hide his tracks."

I frowned and thought some more. "From the way things looked, I don't think he searched very hard."

"I agree," Jenn said. "I thought that whatever he was after might still be here, but we've looked everywhere. I guess we'll just have to take all this stuff we've collected back to the lab and see if we can figure out who else was here in this room."

Jenn started to go back to the others when an odd sensation flashed over me. "Wait a minute, Jenn," I said.

She stopped and turned to look at me. "What is it, DH?"

"Do me a favor and look under the sofa."

She looked at me like I was crazy. "We've all looked under that sofa. Some of us two or three times."

"I know, but humor me. This time, don't just look under it. Look in it. Turn it over, pull the bottom off, and look up between the springs and the cushion."

She stared at me, but I didn't flinch. Her expression softened. She nodded her head and returned to the others. "Hey, guys ..."

They grumbled and groaned about it, but they got to it. Tom and Scotty got the sofa bottom-side up, and Jenn pulled off the thin cloth to expose the space inside. The crime scene specialist stood ready with his tools to collect evidence, and the photographer documented the operation. I stepped away from my wall for the first time to get a closer look. I just had a feeling ...

Everyone held their breath while Jenn used her flashlight to illuminate every nook and cranny of the sofa's innards. "Well, well. What have we here?" she said. She leaned in and gave a little grunt as she reached even further and came back up, grasping a manila envelope triumphantly between two fingers.

"Wuid ye look a' that!" The depth of Scotty's accent betrayed his excitement.

Tom responded with a more world-weary, "Well, I'll be."

Jenn gave me a look that said, *How the heck did you know?*

I asked, "Aren't you going to look inside?"

Jenn answered by undoing the clasp and gently shaking the envelope until the ends of several strips of photographic negatives emerged. She used her tweezers to carefully grasp one pull it out. She held it up to the light and gave a low whistle.

"Well, boys, it looks like we may have our motive."

Tom, Scotty, and I leaned in and peered over her shoulder, but none of us could make out much more than bodies captured in what is euphemistically called compromising positions. Some of the negatives looked like they would reveal recognizable faces when they were enlarged and printed.

"Yep," Tom said. "Looks like someone's tryin' a bit of blackmail."

Jenn slipped the film strip back into the envelope, resealed it, and handed it to the crime scene officer with instructions to label it, log it, and hand it over to the photographer for priority processing. Then she looked at me and asked pointedly, "Are we done here, DH?"

"If you say so," I replied.

"Okay, then. Let's go talk to the people in the lobby."

Jenn and I stood aside to let everyone file out of the room ahead of us. Tom scowled at me as he passed, but Jenn shook her head and gave me a sympathetic smile.

The people in the lobby all looked up expectantly when we got off the elevator. It seemed that curiosity had won out over impatience, but it was a close thing. The manager had calmed down a bit, and the housekeeper had regained her composure. There was evidence that coffee and snacks from the vending machines had helped pass the time.

I found myself looking at one person in particular. As I studied him, I realized that he was not quite like the others. While he had looked toward us at first, his eyes now darted around the room from the front door, back door, stairway, and then back to us. He remained seated, but his body shifted slightly, putting weight on the balls of his feet. I could tell that he was putting great effort into keeping his expression calm. Then it hit me. This guy wasn't looking for answers. He was looking for an opportunity.

I put my hand on Jenn's shoulder to get her attention and direct her focus. "He did it."

"Which one?"

"That one over there," I said, turning her head toward him so he wouldn't see me pointing at him.

"You think so?"

"Yep. The guy in the Gene Autry pj's was blackmailing him. This guy told him he wasn't gonna pay. One thing led to another. This guy picks up the ashtray and whacks Pajama Man over the head. He starts to search for the negatives, but something scares him away. He's been waiting down here for everyone to leave so he can go back up and finish his search. He's never been involved in anything like this before, so he's nervous. Now he's just lookin' for a way out of this mess."

Jenn listened to me stone-faced. When I finished, she frowned at me and said, "Granted, you got lucky with the envelope in the sofa, but I've never heard even our best psychic consultant come up with this much detail. Are you sure this story isn't just a product of your artistic/literary imagination?"

"No, this is different. I can tell."

"Well, you know I'm inclined to believe you," she said. "But I can't arrest someone on a hunch. I wish I could."

"Don't worry. He's going to confess."

"Really?"

"Yes, really. You're going to talk to everyone here, aren't you?"

Jenn crossed her arms over her chest and nodded her head.

"Well, you'd better question him first. Otherwise, he'll try to get away."

Jenn just looked at me like she wanted to say something, but she couldn't, and it suddenly hit me that if the guy didn't confess before the night was through, my psychic credibility with her would be zilch.

It turns out that I did not have to worry about my budding reputation. The nervous man chose that moment to turn and look in our direction. He and I locked eyes. Jenn turned to see what I was looking at, and that was when the guy took off across the lobby. He knocked over one cop on his way to the door, and the other cops followed in hot pursuit.

Jenn took off after him, too, and I followed along. Jenn's command to "Grab the bastard" wasn't necessary. The other officers and detectives were already in motion, taking off to corner the fugitive from different directions.

Sure enough, a couple of cops chased him into an alley while another group of cops ran around the corner to block the exit. When the guy saw the guns pointed at him, he stopped running and put his hands up. The officers chasing him caught up to him. One of them patted him down thoroughly and then cuffed him while another read him his rights. After that, they marched him back to the hotel, put him into a squad car, and took him off to the station. The rest of us got into our cars and followed along.

"Now comes the hard part," Jenn said on the drive downtown.

"What's that?" I asked.

"The paperwork."

"Well, that turned out to be a lot easier than I thought it would be," Jenn said. We were on our way back to her house a couple of hours later. "The guy — his name is Harlan Perkins, by the way — confessed to everything."

"Really?" I said.

"Yes, really. As we thought, Pajama Man had been blackmailing Harlan for a while. He hadn't planned to kill him, but when Pajama Man just laughed at him, Harlan went after him. He says he doesn't remember picking up the ashtray, only that the guy was suddenly on the floor and not moving. Harlan started looking for the negatives but lost his nerve when he heard the housekeeper enter the room next door. He made his way downstairs to wait and see what happened next. He started getting nervous when we all came back downstairs. When you and he made eye contact, he knew it was all over, and he ran."

"He should have kept his cool and stayed put," I said.

"He might have gotten away with it, but not for long. Between the negatives and the fingerprints, we would have gotten him sooner rather than later," Jenn said as we pulled into her driveway. "And without your insight up in the hotel room and in the lobby, it would have been much later."

She turned off the engine and set the brake. We sat in the dark listening to the engine tic, then Jenn turned to me and said in a voice thick with lust, "What you did back there really made me hot. The idea of you as a psychic detective turns me on." Then she pulled me close, and before I knew what was happening, we were locked into the most passionate kiss I had ever experienced, right there in her driveway.

When we finally came up for air, she said, "I want you to get that PI course ASAP. I may just find a way to get you on the payroll."

"I'll write myself a note: 4 Jenn RPD — PI Course ASAP."

Jenn grabbed me again, only this time she opened the driver's side door and pulled me out after her. Her mouth remained glued to mine while we made our way to her front door and as far as the living room, where I soon found myself on the floor with Jenn on top of me, undoing my pants.

Eventually, Jenn got up and went to the kitchen. She returned with a bottle of wine and a couple of glasses, and we moved to the couch. We cuddled between sips, but the activity and excitement of the day had exhausted us both, so nothing much came of it. In fact, after a long silence, I looked down at her snuggled up against me and saw that she was fast asleep. I gently released Jenn's fingers from the stem of the wine glass and set it safely on the coffee table, and I shifted my position on the sofa so that we would both be more comfortable. Then I saw the face of Charlie Chan and a giant green cobra staring down at me from the wall. I was wide awake again.

I don't know how long I lay there going over the events of the last twenty-four hours — the museum, Jenn, and especially the murder investigation. I loved it. It was fun. Not for the dead guy, of course, but for me, it was a kick in the pants. I think I'd like being a detective.

Jenn must have sensed my wakefulness. She reached up, spread her hand over my face, and petted it like one would a St. Bernard.

"Are you awake?" I mumbled through her fingers.

"No," she groaned.

"Well, that's too bad."

"Why?"

"Because I have to pee."

"You're kidding," she groaned again. "I don't wanna move."

"Well, it might be a good idea if you did."

She finally sat up so I could move, but her eyes remained closed. By the time I returned from the bathroom, she was more awake.

"Now that you mention it, I have to pee, too."

I went over to the big glass patio door and looked out at the stars. It was one of those warm, dry nights we often get in Riverside in December, and the stars seemed close enough to touch.

Jenn must have been reading my mind because she returned with an armful of blankets. Without saying a word, she slid the door open, stepped out, and I followed her into the night. We spread one of the blankets on the soft sand at the end of the pool. Then we stripped off our clothes, laid down next to each other, and covered ourselves with the second blanket. We were a tidy little blanket sandwich under the bright December sky, and it wasn't long before we were both asleep with the nearly full moon watching over us and the desert breeze whispering through the dry fronds of the palm trees around us.

15
Christmas Day

I haven't seen Jenn since Tuesday. She told me that she would be working extra shifts until after New Year to give some of the other cops time to be with their families. I've spent most of my time this week reading about art and philosophy and sketching out some ideas for paintings. I had ambitious plans to visit museums, galleries, and studios in LA, but my heart just hasn't been in it.

As usual, Christmas Day has been pleasant with family, lots of gifts, and good food. Grandad and Nana, who live in the little house at the end of our driveway, came up early this morning. We all gathered around the Christmas tree in our living room to open our presents. Afterward, Mom and Nana put the finishing touches on our traditional Christmas feast of turkey with all the trimmings, including Nana's famous pumpkin pies. Grandad, Dad, Jim, and I did as we were told—set the table, fetch and carry, stay out of the way, that sort of thing.

The weather has continued to be mild, so my parents invited some friends to come and share the afternoon and evening. I mentioned before that Dad is an aerospace engineer, so many of his friends are involved in various aspects of the growing space program, and the IQ of every one of them is off the charts. Mother is the secretary for the big boss at the Sunkist Lemon Products Plant in Corona, so her friends tend to be professional, successful, and well-educated. The conversations at these get-togethers can be fascinating, and today was no exception. Nana and Grandad went back to their little house, and my brother Jim took off for a party at the home of one of his college buddies. I actually enjoy my parents' friends and look forward to listening in on the conversations of these well-rounded adults, so I stuck around.

The guests began arriving around three o'clock and many brought offerings of food and drink. Mother whipped up an impressive array of finger food from the leftovers of our dinner and the stock of staples she keeps for these impromptu occasions. Dad dipped into his stash for an offering of hard and soft drinks, including a keg of beer chilling in a tub of ice out on the patio. This is promising to be quite a shindig.

Some of the guests dropped in just long enough to offer their Season's Greetings and have a drink before leaving to call on other friends. Just as many, though, stayed until well into the evening. Among those in for the long haul were two of my mother's co-workers from Sunkist and their husbands, one of Dad's fellow engineers/ rocket scientists and his wife, and another one without his wife—I think he said she was spending the day with her elderly, ailing parents—and an astronomer.

Carl, the astronomer, is a professor at one of the big universities Back East. I'm not sure how he and Dad met, but Carl's role as an astrophysicist and Dad's job in aerospace must have brought them together. Whatever the circumstances, they hit it off and have been good friends for a long time. Carl comes to the southwest frequently to consult with the Jet Propulsion Lab or one of the big observatories and usually stops in to see us when he does. I always look forward to his visits and stick around when he and Dad get into a discussion. Carl is good at explaining incredibly complex ideas clearly and without condescension. I usually don't say much when he and Dad talk, but sometimes I get him all to myself. He never seems to tire of my endless questions but happily answers as many as I ask. He even appears to give serious consideration to some of the wild ideas I come up with from time to time. He got tired of me addressing him as sir a few years ago and suggested I call him Uncle Carl.

The party has been going on for a couple of hours, and it's getting dark now. The drop-ins have come and gone, and those remaining have settled into two groups—women in the living room with their drinks and cigarettes and the men with theirs out on the patio. I've been drifting back and forth between them, sipping a little beer and staying unnoticed like the proverbial fly on the wall.

The men have been engaged in a lively discussion of life on other planets. While no one has disagreed that rudimentary life forms like bacteria or single-celled plants and animals will likely be found on Mars and Venus and on similar planets beyond our solar system, Uncle Carl proposed that more complex organisms might be found in places thought to be incompatible with life. We all listened with rapt attention while Carl evoked images of balloon-like creatures drifting among the clouds of Jupiter's dense atmosphere, somewhat like jellyfish deep in the oceans of Earth. He told the story in his unique style, and while it elicited a few chuckles, nobody actually denied its possibility.

The conversation among the women in the living room has been as varied as the men's, although more earth-bound. They've spent the time catching up on family events—a child's graduation, a daughter's wedding, or the birth of a grandchild. One of the women described the trip she and her husband took to Europe last summer. That prompted a long conversation about plans and dreams for travels next summer. The last time I went in to refill my snack plate, Mother and her Sunkist co-workers were talking about work. I took my time at the buffet table so I could listen in.

One of the women, the head of the personnel department, lamented the difficulties of finding reliable help to cover the summer vacation schedules of the regular factory employees. I froze when she mentioned my name, but she went on to say, "He turned out to be one of the best summer workers we've had." I'm glad I had my back to the group because I could feel my face go beet red.

"He's a pretty good boy," Mom replied. "I'm sure he'll be back next summer."

I don't know where the conversation went from there because I took my plate of food and snuck out by way of the kitchen and breezeway.

It's quiet out here at the edge of the grotto. All I can hear of the party is the soft murmur of conversation and an occasional outburst of laughter tied together with the sound of Johnny Cash from the stereo. The night is brisk but not cold, and between the quarter moon above me and the light from the patio behind me, I can see well enough to write. I feel like writing some poetry, so I stopped by The Hole on my way out here and exchanged my cup of beer for a mug of Red Mountain burgundy, as wine is more suited to my mood than beer.

There are two big cottonwood trees and a couple of bushes near the edge of the grotto. The little thicket is one of my favorite places when I don't want to be disturbed. It's in the corner of our property, and the bushes hide the view from the house, so people usually don't look in that direction. The side overlooking the grotto is open and comfortable, protected from prying eyes, sun, wind, and all but the heaviest rain. I especially enjoy coming out here at night just to gaze at the twinkling lights of the city or to watch the parade of stars, moon, and planets above the horizon. It's always peaceful here. Even tonight, with the party going on behind me, it's relatively quiet here in my little cave. At least they've switched from Johnny Cash to soft jazz.

"Can I join you?"

Startled, I look up to see Jackie Harris, the wife of Bill Harris, one of Dad's co-workers. She's the woman who kissed me at the New Year's Eve party last year. I wonder what she's looking for out here. "Mrs. Harris? Is that you?"

"Can I sit down?"

"If you want to, but it's all dirt and rocks down here," I told her, noticing that she wasn't exactly dressed for sitting on the ground.

"Doesn't bother me." She tucked her skirt up under her butt and sat down next to me. "What are you drinking?" she asked.

"Iced tea," I lied.

"No, you're not." She helped herself to a big swallow from my mug. "Yum, wine. I'm not much of a beer drinker, but I've had a couple this evening. The buzz it gives helps me get through parties like this."

"I saw you arrive, but I didn't see you later with the rocket guys or with the other women. I thought you might have left early."

"So, you were looking for me?"

"Um ... just making an observation."

"I'm tired of all that space talk—I hear it all the time—and I can only take so much of the hen chatter. I saw you walk out here, and I thought I'd come see if you had other things we can talk about."

"I'm only nineteen. I don't think I can compete with star stuff, to borrow a phrase from Uncle Carl."

"I'd be willing to bet that I'd rather listen to anything you might talk about. I understand you're still at RCC. What are you taking this semester?"

"Sculpture, ceramics, American history, sociology, psychology, and ... um ... astronomy."

"No!" She laughed. "The dreaded a-word!"

Even in the moonlight, I can see that Jackie is beautiful in a conventional, beauty queen sort of way. Her large teeth are perfectly white and straight, her eyes large and placed precisely where they should be. Her nose is a little on the round side but still the perfect size dictated by current fashion. Her dark brown hair is perfectly cut to frame her face and fall just to her perfect shoulders. She'd look exactly perfect walking across the stage in one of those long flowing dresses at the Miss America pageant. Perfect. I prefer girls with a few flaws, like a crooked tooth, one eye smaller than the other, a rounder nose, maybe even a scar running down one cheek. Jackie is hot, though. No doubt about it. Everything about her body is perfect, too, and I'll never forget when she pressed herself up to me and thrust her tongue into my mouth at last year's party. Her tongue was hot — very hot, and it shocked the heck out of me. Here was this older, married woman — she's at least forty — giving me a kiss that should be given to her lover, not the young son of her husband's colleague. I will never forget that. In fact, I've often found my mind returning to that memory.

"What in the world are you doing?" she asked.

"Writing in my journal."

"You keep a journal? What do you find to write about?"

"Lots of things. I hope to use my journal entries as inspiration for books I'll write someday."

"You see? Already I find you far more interesting than rocket science."

Jackie leaned closer and tried to pull the journal over to where she could see it better. "So, what are you writing about now? I can't quite make it out in this light."

"You," I said, tugging gently to bring the book back under my control.

"You're kidding. What could you possibly find to say about me?"

"I was just describing how pretty you look in the moonlight. How perfect your face is ... your hair ..."

"Oh, my gawd." She sat up straight and looked at me. "I don't know what to say. I mean ... I love it. My husband hasn't said things like that to me since ... hmm ... maybe never."

"I'm sorry." What was I thinking? "I didn't mean to ... I'm an artist. At least I'm trying to be an artist and ..."

"Why are you apologizing? I'm flattered."

I could smell her perfume. It was sweet but subtle, like something very expensive from Europe, not Montgomery Wards.

"And you're putting that all down in your journal?"

"Yes."

"I hope you don't let anyone else read it. You're only nineteen. A woman like me, at my age, having a flirtatious evening with a nineteen-year-old would raise more than a few eyebrows."

"No one ever reads this, nor would they really want to. I'm sure it would bore them to death."

"You needn't worry about us becoming too attached," she sighed.

"Why's that?"

"We're moving next week."

"Really?"

"My husband got transferred to Texas. I'll be history after tonight.

She put her hand to my face and caressed my cheek. I could see her lovely smile and a sort of longing, a sadness almost, in her eyes.

"You smell really good," I told her.

"It's just my shampoo."

"You know, ever since the New Year's Eve party last year, I've racked my brain over who it is you remind me of. I've got it now."

"So, you still remember that party?" she asked hesitantly, moving away from me a bit.

"Of course, I do. I don't ever want to forget that," I replied honestly.

Her eyes searched mine. Was she trying to read my mind? Finally, she asked, "So, who do I remind you of?"

"Lara, the character in *Dr. Zhivago*. You resemble her — or rather, Julie Christie, the actress who played the part — except your hair is darker."

"Really? Wow ... that's quite a compliment. She's beautiful."

"Yes, she is. So are you."

She looked deeply into my eyes again, then, "Are you sure no one will ever read that journal?"

"Positive. At least not for many years. Why?"

"Because of this." She put one hand on each side of my head and drew me to her, then kissed me deeper and longer than she had last year. "Did you like that?" she asked when she pulled away. "Was it better than the first time I kissed you?"

"You mean you actually remember kissing me that night?"

"Of course, I remember. I was drunk, but I knew exactly what I was doing."

"What does an older woman like you see in a young guy like me? I just thought you did it because you were a little tipsy and into the moment, so to speak. You know, New Year's Eve and all."

"That might have been the case, to begin with, but after I kissed you and walked away, you were all I could think about the rest of the night. I went home kicking myself that I didn't try to do more with you."

"Really? There isn't much more we could have done that night. Your kiss pretty well knocked me for a loop."

"Oh, we could have done much more," she said softly, then she kissed me again while she took my hand and guided it up under her skirt.

"Do you want to do more with me?" she whispered. "I can give you something else to write about tonight if you swear to me that no one will read this for many years."

"I swear ... but ... I'm not sure this is a good idea."

Jackie turned her back to me and bent forward. She pulled her skirt up around her hips and said, "Take your time."

◎ ◎ ◎

So, there I was again. Another older woman and a married one, at that. What the heck do they see in me? And she's leaving, too, like so many others I became interested in over the last couple of years.

Then there's Jenn. I really like her, but she's thirty-six years old with her career as a detective to consider. She's probably already come to her senses about getting into a relationship with someone my age. I doubt I'll ever hear from her again.

I wonder if I'll ever meet someone closer to my age who will stick around long enough to develop a genuine bond?

16
The Next Day

This morning, I took a walk across the backyard and down to the bottom of the grotto, where I am right now.

I've spent a lot of time in this sheltered nook—my own private Pit—since my parents first bought this property out in the country. I played with cars and marbles here as a little kid. My schoolmates and I played army down here. We had sword fights with sticks. I've searched for buried treasure while pretending to be a pirate and acted out many other childhood fantasies at the bottom of the grotto. Other kids had little sandboxes in their backyards, but I was blessed to have my own full-acre private sandlot in mine. I'm not a little kid now, of course. I'm nineteen, part of the kid is still in me, and I can be pretty immature sometimes. Still, I know I've matured in other ways. For one thing, I know I don't think like other guys my age. Apparently, my thought processes are very different than other nineteen-year-olds—at least that's what some of my friends and teachers tell me.

Professor Mancini described me as a seventy-year-old man in a nineteen-year-old body. He said, "The man is struggling, fighting to free himself from the kid." Of course, I can't take him too seriously since he's a philosophy teacher who doesn't think like other people, either.

Frank Reed, one of the most level-headed thinkers I know, even if he is an artist, said to me, "You're only nineteen? You gotta be kidding. I thought you were about fifty. What nineteen-year-old kid reads the boring crap you read?" Then he laughed his *LAUGH* and added, "*The Egyptian Book of the Dead?* Camus? Kerouac? And all those saint dudes and dudettes? You ain't normal, Bud. That stuff would even put me to sleep!" Then *The LAUGH,* again.

Even Bill Hunter said, "Don't you think you ought to slow down a little, DH?"

When I asked what he meant, he said, "Your mind. It's traveling through this universe at a million miles a minute. You're going to burn out too soon if you aren't careful."

They may have a point. When I set out this morning, I took two things with me: my journal, of course, and a copy of *The Confessions of St. Augustine*. I'm not a Catholic, but I've been reading through *The Confessions* to get a glimpse into the mind of a man who lived hundreds of years ago and underwent a conversion experience so powerful that he was compelled to write it all down and share it with the world.

My journal pales in comparison to Augustine's. The things I write about — art, philosophy, girls, etc. — are trivial next to his deep, personal insights, spiritual thoughts, and conviction. Of course, we're writing about different things and living in different times. He was also much older than I am when he started — forty-something, I think — so he was more mature and had more life and knowledge to reflect on. Even though he lived into his seventies, people tended to die earlier back then. Maybe he felt like he only had time to write down the really important, deep stuff before he died. Whatever the reason, the result is intense, profound, and penetrating. At least that's what I'm finding.

Nobody writes like that anymore. It's so ... so grown up. Books written today by people twice Augustine's age sound adolescent in comparison. And who shares their sins today? Who even cares? I'm not sure anybody really knows what sin is in this world that allows people to do just about anything they want, regardless of what it is — short of murder, maybe ... maybe.

I'm not trying to get all holier-than-thou. I'm just letting my mind wander the way I always do. I suppose one day, years from now, I'll open up my own journal, read a few pages, and find out what a jumbled mess I made of it all. I'll find my own "confessions" on these pages, only much more naive, more childish than those of poor Augustine. I'll find that all the struggles I went through were more to maintain my sanity than my sanctity. My confessions will be about girls and poetry and all of the silly things I did along the way to try to understand this chaotic and apparently meaningless culture and what my place is in it.

Oh yeah ... and about all of the paintings I should have done in the time I wasted sitting here at the bottom of the grotto thinking about meaningless things.

17
New Year's Eve

There was a lot of activity at the sculpture house the last week before Christmas vacation. Many of the students — including me — worked feverishly to complete projects before the break. A few of us gathered on the front porch for a short break, and the conversation naturally turned to plans for Christmas and New Year's Eve. Bill Mitchkelly joined us there and listened while he went through the ceremony of lighting his pipe.

"Why don't we have a party right here?" he said when he finally got his pipe going.

We all expressed our approval of the idea but never got to the planning stage. A couple of days after Christmas, though, Mitch called and asked me to help spread the word that the party was on.

"Six o'clock," he said. "Bring food and invite your friends."

So, here it is, about eight o'clock on New Year's Eve. I'm sitting on the couch in the corner of the main room of the Sculpture House, doing what I do best in these situations — watching everyone else and recording my thoughts in my journal.

In my almost three semesters here at RCC, I've discovered that gatherings like this bring together an odd, if not unlikely, assortment of individuals, and tonight is no exception. Among the regulars are Mitch, of course, and OK Harry, the painting instructor; Bill Hunter, my English professor and an honorary member of the Art Department; and Lois, a part-time art student and frequent model for life drawing and sculpture classes. Lois and I shared an intimate moment out by the big kilns one evening last year. It was brief and didn't go beyond what some might call heavy petting, but for me, it was unforgettable. I was looking forward to spending more time with her, but she seems to be avoiding me this evening.

Manny is around here somewhere, too. I saw him a few minutes ago chatting with one of the girls. He must have stepped out for a smoke—he doesn't seem to be able to go for long without one. He goes through close to two packs a day, which can't be good.

I was glad to see Professor Mancini. Except for chance meetings in the hallways, I hadn't spoken with him since I was in his philosophy class last year. Annette Wong is also in attendance. She and I were also part of the Magnificent Seven, a group of students from that same philosophy class.

My odd but lovable friend, Father Bob Erstad, arrived a while ago with Sister Teresa. I've begun thinking of her as Fr. Bob's sidekick as I rarely see one without the other these days. I think the fellows in charge of the seminary where he was recently ordained as a priest send her along with Fr. Bob when he goes out to keep him out of trouble until he gets assigned to a parish of his own.

I was surprised to see Frank show up. He spent a little time with me earlier this evening but didn't stay long. He said he had another party to go to that involved rubbing elbows with rich folks and talking them into buying his paintings.

"I'd love to stay," Frank said on his way out, "but, hey, money's money!" He followed up with his famous *Laugh* as he exited the party. Before he left, he told me he planned to do a big bronze cast soon, and he wanted me to help him out with it. I'm not sure what that will entail, but I feel honored that he asked.

There is also an assortment of other art students that I know by sight but not well enough to comment on—lots of girls trying to look artistic and lots of guys trying to look like artists.

Mancini has drawn a small crowd on the other side of the room. He's describing the trip he took up into the Himalayas a couple of years ago. He is a master storyteller and can hold an audience spellbound and paint word pictures that make the guys from National Geographic look like amateurs. Of course, his resemblance to Victor Mature doesn't hurt. I notice that most of his audience is female.

Mitchkelly, Hunter, and Harry are sitting in another corner of the room near the food table. Their conversation appears to be lively, but they are too far away, and the room is too noisy for me to overhear. Mitchkelly and Harry are focused on the discussion, but Hunter is also keeping an eye on the refreshments — rearranging the food to fill in gaps as things get eaten; replenishing plates, forks, and napkins; generally keeping things tidy. He is that one at all gatherings who makes sure that everyone has what they need. It's a natural extension of his kind heart and good nature.

Father Bob and Sister Teresa have been all over the place interacting with everyone and liberally dispensing New Year's blessings, which have been graciously received in the spirit they were given. Those two are an interesting pair. Fr. Bob is very outgoing and direct with people. He gets right up close and takes people by surprise with his pointed remarks and dry, sarcastic humor. People open up to him before they know what's happening, and soon, they're laughing and wondering what in the world they were so unhappy about.

Sister Teresa, on the other hand, is very quiet and reserved. She has a knack for steering people away from conflict or toward truth without hardly saying a word. It only seems to take a particular look, a smile or a frown, a shake or a nod of her head for her to guide others to resolution or revelation. And did I mention that she is beautiful? Well, she is, and the shorter skirt, better fit, and abbreviated veil of the modernized habit she wears do little to hide that fact.

That just about covers everyone who is here. Someone who is not here, though, is Jenn. When I talked to her this morning, she said she'd be here unless she got called to cover a case. I guess crime doesn't stop for holidays. That's too bad. I was looking forward to spending more time with her. The night of the murder investigation and what came after was special. I felt a kind of closeness to her that I've never felt with any other girl. Have I said that before? I don't think so. Anyway, we definitely clicked in a way that almost seems like there might be more to come. If the record of my previous attempts with other girls is any indication, though, a lasting relationship with Jenn is far from a sure thing. For one thing, Jenn herself warned me that because of the demands of her career and her experience with men in the past, anything long-term is highly unlikely. But still ... I do really like her.

With that in mind, I'll keep the door open as far as Jenn is concerned, but I'm not gonna hang around and wait for things to materialize between us. If a girl who seems interested in me comes along, I'm not going to be afraid to explore the possibilities. That's also why I don't feel guilty about what Jackie Harris and I did the other night.

What does bother me about all this is the nagging feeling in my gut that suggests there's a lot more to life than just dating girls and drinking wine—as if I didn't already know that. The question is, should I worry much about wasting time on the world at my age? Should I spend more time on higher pursuits like religion, the ultimate goals of eternal life, heaven and hell, and all that? For now, the only church I would consider giving half a chance to is the Catholic Church, and that has little to do with sin or heaven and hell. I am drawn to the mysticism, formality, and symbolism of the Mass and the awareness of the proximity of the spiritual plane to our physical existence. Try talking about the supernatural with a Baptist preacher and see where it gets you.

On the other hand, I can have an honest conversation about such things with almost any Catholic priest I know. Just the other day, Fr. Bob, Sister Teresa, and I had a lively discussion about the many mystics among those people recognized as saints by the Church. They not only experienced the supernatural in the forms of dreams and visions, but they also befriended angels, ghosts, and even animals. I'm convinced that many of the Catholic saints were, in reality, nature mystics, including Jesus. I read the Bible and am familiar with His sermons. Most of them involve nature either directly or as examples. The Old and New Testaments both reference the super-natural to either warn against evil or describe gifts and encounters that may be sought. So, how is it that I've never heard a sermon about nature or ghosts in a Baptist church? The Baptists believe in the Holy Ghost, I'll give them that, but if you were to suggest to a Baptist that talking to a Catholic saint—by definition, also a ghost—is a good idea, guess where that would get you. The Bible is filled with ghostly encounters and manifestations, so why not recognize the supernatural in a sermon or two?

"Good evening," says a voice from behind me. I feel the weight of someone settling on the sofa beside me and look to see who it is.

"Annette, how ya been?" Mancini must have invited her. I first met Annette at a small gathering of philosophy students at his house last year. The seven of us in attendance that night named ourselves The Magnificent Seven and swore to meet once a month to talk philosophy, drink wine, and whatever. We managed to convene a couple of times before we all seemed to have more important things to do.

"I'm very well," she said. "How have you been? It's been a whole year since I last saw you." Her smile was warm, and she seemed truly glad to see me.

"I'm doing fine. I'm just having fun watching everybody else have fun." I returned her smile. I was just as glad to see her.

"So, are you still a philosophy major?"

"No, actually, I never really was. I was torn between philosophy and art that first semester, but by the middle of the second semester, art was the clear winner."

Annette laughed. "I'm so glad to hear that. I wouldn't wish the life of a philosopher on anyone. Look how Mancini turned out."

We both laughed. Actually, Mancini turned out pretty well. At least he seems to be happy.

"So, what have you been doing with your life," I asked.

"Well, I spent most of the last summer in Hong Kong."

"You did?"

"Yes. My parents decided they wanted to visit the family, and I went along with them."

"You have family in Hong Kong? I thought you were from somewhere around Shanghai."

"You're right. Hangzhou, to be exact. My parents are classified as intellectuals by the current Chinese government. Father was afraid that if we flew into the People's Republic, we'd never fly out. We have family in Hong Kong, so we went there."

"Sounds like a wise decision. So, how's Hong Kong?"

"It's like any other big city. It has some very nice parts and some dangerous parts."

"Sounds like LA."

"The Hong Kong branch of my family has done well for itself, so they live in one of the better neighborhoods. My uncles and cousins took us to all the best places, and we had a wonderful time. I had an especially good time when my cousins broke loose from the uncles and took me to their favorite spots."

"I remember you saying that you didn't speak much Chinese. How did that go for you?"

"I understand it better than I speak it," Annette explained. "My cousins speak English quite well, so it wasn't much of a problem. I did practice my Chinese with them, though. They were only laughing at me two or three times a day by the time we left. I'm trying to speak it more with my parents and any other Chinese speaker I encounter. I have a feeling that the ability will be a valuable asset in the not-too-distant future."

"You may be right," I said thoughtfully. "The most exotic place I've ever visited was China Town in San Francisco, and I'm sure there's no comparison. I wouldn't mind visiting Hong Kong someday. It's definitely exotic, even a bit glamorous, and with just enough danger to keep you on your toes."

Annette smiled and nodded her head. "I think that about sums it up," she said.

I hadn't really gotten to know Annette last year. We only shared the one class, and our paths didn't cross outside of class. I remember thinking she was cute—pretty, actually—but I also got the impression that she wasn't interested in guys—if you know what I mean. Now that I think of it, she didn't really seem concerned with building a relationship with anyone, male or female. She seemed more interested in ideas than in people. I certainly hadn't taken time then to appreciate her exotic beauty, which is unmistakable tonight. Her face, framed by her short black hair and graced with flawless, delicately colored skin, seems softer tonight—more relaxed, maybe. Her form-fitting, dark pink sweater worn with tight, faded denim jeans matches the color of her lips and shows off her perfectly round breasts, their smooth curves accentuated by the bumps of her nipples. Her whole demeanor makes me think my first impression might have been wrong.

Wanting the conversation to continue, I said the first thing that came to mind. "So, you're still a student here?"

"Yes. The spring semester will be my last one here, and I'll be transferring to the university in the fall. I'm going for a Ph.D. in chemistry, and I've been accepted into a program that will cut a couple of years off the process."

"Wow. That sounds like a lot of work."

"It will be, but it'll pay off in the long run."

"I suppose it will."

Annette looked around the room, and a shadow of irritation briefly crossed her face. She leaned in close to me and cupped her hand over one ear. "Do you think we could go outside on the front porch for a while? It's getting really noisy in here. I can barely hear you, and I feel like I have to shout just to have a conversation."

It has gotten noisy. Everyone talking and laughing is bad enough, but someone brought a record player and is playing something loud and jarring that sounds nothing like music. I heard someone call it electronic music. I have no idea what that means, but I don't care for it. Jazz would be better.

"You're right," I said. "Let's go."

"What a relief," Annette said when we finally shut the door against the pressure of the party. "I hate noise. I grew up in a house filled with Buddhists, who made it a point not to make noise."

"Really? I visited a Zen Buddhist monastery last year. That was an interesting experience." I didn't mention that I did very little Zen stuff while there. I mostly drank wine and made out with my girlfriend — the one who ended up becoming a Catholic nun.

"Was it the one up on Mt. Baldy?" When I indicated that it was, Annette went on to explain. "Their teachings and practices come mainly from Japan. The Buddhism followed by my family is a little different and includes some principles of Taoism, another Chinese religion or philosophy."

"I've heard of that. I took kung fu classes for a while a few years ago, and Master introduced us to it."

"Really?" She looked at me as if adding that bit of information to a scorecard.

"Really," I said. "It's a lot different from Catholicism."

"Very much so, but with as many rules and rituals."

"I guess all religions are pretty much the same that way."

"The biggest difference is that Buddhist teachings do not require belief or disbelief in a supreme god or deity," Annette explained. "That's left up to the individual. Many Buddhists are actually atheists."

"I have a hard time not believing in God," I said. "I don't mind dumping the rules and rituals, but dumping God altogether takes things a little too far."

"You get used to it," she smiled.

"I suppose it relieves a person of all the guilt and fear of going to hell for sins and wrongdoings." Funny, I was just thinking about that the other day.

"Buddhists don't believe in sin. We believe that people should be good just for being good and that no judgment should be placed on any person's behavior. Many believe in karmic retribution for harming others, but no sin will keep you out of heaven or send you to hell. For that matter, Buddhists don't believe in heaven or hell, either."

"So, a person can do just about anything he or she wants to do without fear of paying an eternal price?"

"Yes, but good Buddhists would never intentionally do harm. We believe that everyone will experience suffering of some sort anyway, but not because a god keeps track of a person's wrongdoings."

"That line of thought leaves all the doors open," I told her. "It implies that there really is no good or bad and that actions simply lead to sterile reactions, without consequences or rewards. Life is just some sort of science project with 'stuff happening' totally out of your control. Like growing bacteria in a Petri dish."

"But some things are in your control. The bacteria will grow slowly if you put the Petri dish in a cool spot. In a warm spot, it will grow more quickly. The perfect temperature for growing bacteria is between 70° and 110° Fahrenheit. If it's too cold or too hot, they won't grow at all. Humans are the same. Humans are capable of doing good or bad, but it is the human's choosing that produces the final result, and that has nothing to do with any religion or god."

"It's all complicated," I said. "I think about things like that all the time, and sometimes I think that even thinking is a useless endeavor."

She smiled at me and said, "You would make a good Buddhist, DH."

I shook my head. "I don't think that's the path for me. I'm holding out for the perfect thing. Something simple. No rituals, no goofy costumes, no rules. I don't mind the stuff about right and wrong in general, but I have a hard time believing that any single group can claim to have the only Truth and hold the right to declare absolutely what is right and what is wrong. Certain foods eaten as delicacies by people of one faith are condemned as sinful or unclean by people of another. Some religions believe that interracial friendships are okay. Others do not. I imagine some people somewhere might have a cow if they saw me, a Chinese girl even talking to you, a Caucasian guy. Go figure."

"Imagine what would they do if they saw me do this." Annette smiled, put her arms around me, and before I could react, she kissed me.

"Did I surprise you?" she asked when she finally released me.

"Yes ... you did." I wasn't lying.

I've grown accustomed to girls ambushing me like that, but the thought of kissing Annette hadn't entered my head. Lois maybe, but not Annette. And it had nothing to do with her being Chinese. Heaven knows, she's lovely, but I'm too confused about life right now to be messing with any woman of any race or age. I don't want to bother with the sex game tonight—and it is a game.

"You thought I was a lesbian, didn't you?"

"Well ..."

"Just because a girl rooms with another girl, doesn't flirt with every guy who comes along, and uses a cuss word now and then doesn't make her a lesbian. I've pretty well conquered the cussing habit. Haven't said a bad word in months. Besides, I have more important things to think about than making out, like calculus and quantitative analysis."

"To be fair, all I knew about you was what you told us that night at Mancini's house. You said you shared an apartment with another girl. That, combined with some other things you said and your choice of words, well, I got the impression ... I mean, I thought ...."

"You thought I had sex with girls and hated men."

"Well ... I guess I did," I muttered sheepishly. When I finally met Annette's gaze, I was surprised to see her struggling to hold back her laughter.

"Well, I don't. I don't have sex with girls, and I love men." Then she grabbed my butt, pulled me in, and held me tightly to her. "How does that feel?" she whispered into my ear as she swayed her hips ever so slightly.

"It feels good, Annette," I whispered back. "But I'm not so sure we ought to be doing this out here on the front porch."

"I know just the place where we can."

Before I could answer her back, Annette grabbed me by the hand and pulled me down the front steps, around the side of the Ceramics House, and back to the storage garage near the kilns.

"I don't think this door is ever locked," she told me as she tried the doorknob.

Sure enough, the door swung inward. We walked through and shut it behind us. The light filtering in through the small, dusty window was barely enough to see by, and it got darker as we worked our way further in. "There's another small room in the back." Annette's voice came from out of the shadows. "I was getting more clay one day, and I saw Mitchkelly come out from behind those shelves. If we're lucky, that door won't be locked either."

"Annette ... I really don't think ... I'm not really ..."

"Just be quiet."

The door wasn't locked. We went in, closed the door, and stumbled around in the dark, trying to find a light switch. I reached up when I felt something brush my face and found a string dangling from the ceiling. I pulled it, and a bare, dusty light bulb produced just enough light for me to see Annette pulling off her sweater. She grabbed the back of my head with one hand and tugged it down until my mouth crashed into her hard, elongated nipples. She used her other hand to pull off her jeans, revealing a jet-black triangle between her smooth white thighs that sparkled in the dim light. The relentless pressure of Annette's hands on my head directed me straight toward her intended target.

18
New Year's Day

What Happened Last Night

I'm sitting in my favorite booth in the corner by the window in the Royal Scot, reviewing the events of last night. My journal is open in front of me, and my pen is in my hand, but I'm at a loss for words — a rare occurrence in my journal keeping. I'll give it my best shot, though.

First of all, Annette is no shrinking violet. I've had a number of encounters of a sexual nature with women since I began keeping this diary, but I've always managed to steer clear of graphic or offensive language. I prefer to choose words that suggest romance and possibly hint at the erotic. There was nothing romantic about our session last night, though. Nothing subtle. Annette was like a bucking horse thrashing around and bumping into walls. I haven't looked yet, but I'm betting I have bruises all over my body. The experience was not pleasant, and I thought it would never end. Just when I thought she'd had enough, she'd start up again.

We heard people walking past the garage at about 1 AM on their way to the small parking lot behind the kilns. The party had just broken up, and they were laughing and talking about what a great time they had, how they were sorry the party was over, how all good things must come to an end, and blah blah blah. I hugged Annette tightly to me during those moments so the noise of her flopping around wouldn't betray our presence in the garage. I had to kiss her rather forcefully to silence the sounds escaping from her lips. It was a nightmare.

It was almost 2 AM by the time Annette's energies were finally spent and we left our hideout and headed for our cars to go home. I walked her to her car since we were parked near each other, but

I did so as quickly as I could. I was not inclined to talk—after all, what could I say? Annette, though, had other ideas. She dropped all pretense of romantic interest and stated flatly that she wasn't really looking for a long-term relationship. She just wanted to hook up with an American guy and get married so her citizenship application would move forward more quickly. A pregnancy would just about guarantee it.

Annette's actions had nothing to do with affection or any natural attraction she might feel for me but were intended to trap me into marrying her. I was stunned by her words and angry at being used that way. Her "confession" was cold and precise and offered no apology. She honestly believed that she had done nothing wrong and carried no guilt as she had done nothing contrary to her Buddhist beliefs which she had explained in detail earlier in the evening.

"It's really no big deal," Annette explained as I listened, dumbfounded. "I think we have to stay married for a certain amount of time, but we can get a divorce after that. I'd like to be free to travel, and I'm sure you'll want to do your own thing, too."

We were still walking to her car, so she didn't notice my look of revulsion.

"If it turns out you got me pregnant tonight, you can have the baby if you want," she continued. "If not, I'll put it up for adoption. I don't really want to be bothered with carting a baby around everywhere."

I was beginning to feel like I'd been raped, and the way she talked about babies turned my revulsion to horror. I was relieved when we finally reached her car. She unlocked the door, but instead of getting in, she turned to me and asked, "Would you like to kiss me goodnight?"

Keeping my voice as flat as possible, I said, "No. That's not gonna happen." I went on to tell her that I wasn't too happy about being tricked that way, and she should have just come out and told me her plans before she started throwing me around that storeroom like she did. "Besides," I added, "I'm only seventeen. Too young to make a marriage commitment for any reason." Okay, so I lied. It was worth it to see the look on her face.

She sputtered a bit before saying she was sorry if I felt she had led me on. She knew what she had been doing, so the so-called apology wasn't worth much.

"Don't worry about it," I said. "I really had liked you — out there on the front porch. It's too bad things went the way they did."

She must have sensed that I just wanted to get rid of her because she got into her car without saying another word. Before she drove away, I wished her a good life and told her I hoped she found some guy who would marry her so they could ride off into the sunset together — or separately, if that's what she wanted. I also said I never wanted to see her again and that if I did, I would turn her over to the police.

I drove home and went to bed. I fell asleep as soon as my head hit the pillow and woke up when the phone rang an hour or so ago. It was Jenn. She wanted me to meet her here at The Scot for coffee. She said she had some good news to share with me. I can't imagine what it might be.

10 AM at The Scot

Jenn just arrived wearing a big smile and looking prettier than ever. She gave me a cheery "Good morning" as she sat down next to me. The waitress brought a fresh pot of coffee and a cup for Jenn. We told her that all we were having was coffee, so she filled Jenn's mug and refreshed mine, then retreated to the counter to keep an eye on things.

Jenn leaned over and planted a kiss on my cheek. "How are you, DH?" she asked.

"Good. I'm good. I guess you've been busy lately," I said.

"I have. I was planning to go to the party last night, but I got a call just as I stepped out of the shower."

"Oh no," I said in mock horror. "The dreaded call!"

"Yep. There was some trouble at the Safeway just before closing.

Whoever reported the incident made it sound like the store had been invaded by a gang and that a bunch of people were being held hostage. The Chief decided to send out everything we've got and surround the store. Turns out it was just three guys who'd started partying early and were out looking for free beer, and the only people left in the store were the manager and one clerk. The guys were pretty drunk, and one of them pulled a knife, but the manager talked him down. They walked out with their hands up and sheepish grins on their faces about a half-hour after we got there.

"I'm sorry I missed it," I said.

"Don't be. The whole thing didn't amount to much, but by the time we finished the paperwork, the evening was shot." She paused then asked, "By the way, how was the party?"

"It was okay. It was noisy. Lots of people, loud music that I really hated, lots of wine. Did I mention it was noisy? I had an okay time, though." No way would I tell her about Annette and our little wrestling match in the storeroom. Jenn would want to arrest her for assault and battery. "Maybe you can catch the next one. There's usually a party somewhere in the Art Department every few weeks or so."

"Well ..." She gave me a look that told me her news was momentous. It also told me that I might not be as happy about it as she was.

"Well, what?"

Jenn allowed her face to break out into a full grin. "I've been promoted. Big time!"

"Really? That's great!"

"It sure is. This kind of thing doesn't happen to women cops very often. I'll be getting paid almost twice as much, too."

"What are you gonna be? Captain? President? Pope?"

"Not captain, but close. I'll be the head detective in charge of a fairly large squad. I'll also be in charge of the whole department when the captain's out of town—and he's out of town a lot."

"I'm really happy for you. Maybe since you're gonna be the boss now, I can come out on more of your cases."

"Well, that's the other part of the news." Here it comes, the part I was afraid of. She was still smiling, but she also looked a little apologetic.

"Don't tell me. Your captain heard about me going with you on that murder case the other night, got pissed, and now I can't come around anymore, right?"

"No, not right, Mr. Psychic. You can come along on all my cases if you want to." She's looking down into her cup to avoid looking at me. This ain't over yet.

"Then what's the problem?"

Her eyes met mine, and I could see that she didn't want to say what she had to. "The job is in another city." She continued to look at me like a cocker spaniel that thinks it has disappointed its human.

I let out a sigh and slumped against the padded back of the booth. "I knew it. I knew you were too good to be true."

"You think I'm too good to be true? That's about the sweetest thing anybody's ever told me."

"Get on with it," I said. Now I'm not looking at her. "Where ya headed, New York? Texas? Siberia?"

"No, silly!" Jenn's smile is back, and she slaps my shoulder playfully. "I won't be too far away."

"Will you please just tell me where you're going?"

"Palm Springs!"

"No way." Not as bad as I had expected, but still …

"Way! Palm Springs! Sunshine, palm trees, expensive shops, good Mexican food, and warm winters."

"I wouldn't really call that a short driving distance. It's like, seventy miles, isn't it?"

"Sixty-five, but that's only about an hour. You can come out on cases with me and spend the weekend lounging around my new pool."

"You have a new pool already?"

"No, but I will soon."

"Wow." This is a lot to take in all at once.

"It's not so bad, is it? Let's get real. I'm always swamped during the week anyway. So are you, for that matter. We'd hardly ever see each other even if I stayed here. And heck, you can move in with me when you turn twenty if you want."

"The twenty-year-old psychic guy moves in with the thirty-six-year-old boss lady. I'm sure that would go over real good down at the station. I can't even grow a beard yet."

"You're probably right, at least in the interim. But you can still come out any time. Cops aren't exactly church ladies, you know. They'll get used to you after a while. They won't give a rip if you're riding me on the side once they get to know you."

"You can always tell them I'm your son." Okay, maybe that was a little unfair, but I'm not very happy right now.

"Don't be sarcastic. It'll all work out the way it's supposed to." Her face went ten shades of sad. "I really don't want to lose you," she said quietly.

Bewilderment floated to the surface of all the emotions I was feeling. "I'm not sure what you see in me, Jenn," I said.

"Everything." She paused for a moment, searching my face, looking into my eyes. "I see everything in you. I could easily fall in love with you. I think I already have. I really don't want us not to be near each other for very long."

Jenn looked at her watch and said, "I need to get back to the station. I've stolen about as much time as I can get away with, but I really wanted to tell you in person before I left town." She gulped down the rest of her coffee.

"When does this take effect?" I asked while she gathered up her purse and slid out of the booth.

"I'll be driving out there in the morning to look for a place to live. The job starts immediately, but I'll call you as soon as I'm settled in, and you can come check it out."

"What about your house in Jurupa Hills? That's your parent's home."

"I'm going to keep it. A couple of the lady cops here in Riverside want to rent it from me. They'll keep it nice and give me some extra income."

"Well, that's a good thing."

"You're really sweet for even thinking about that."

"I can be sweet when I work at it."

Jenn leaned down and kissed me on the cheek. "Sorry, that's all I can do here in a public place. I'll make it up to you in a few days."

"I hope so," I said, showing a bit more petulance than I intended.

Jenn's smile was somewhere between sad and pleading. "Don't give up on me," she said. "We're not done. Somehow this will all work out."

She turned and walked away without looking back.

I'd like to think it will all work out with Jenn and that I can get out to Palm Springs often and be with her, work on some cases together, etc., but I have my doubts. I've been through this before—more than once. I'm afraid what's good news for her is bad news for me. But you never know. All of life is a mystery.

◎ ◎ ◎

"What's shakin', brother? Where you been? I haven't seen you in a long time, White Boy."

I recognized the voice as that of the waitress, Wichahpi, an Oglala Lakota Sioux. I met her here at The Scot last year, and we became pretty close. I hadn't seen her since early last summer because she had been taking care of family matters on one of the reservations up in North Dakota.

Surprised, I looked up and said, "Wichahpi! It's good to see you."

"What's the matter? Who was the chick? She your squeeze these days?"

"No ... well ... sort of. She kinda was, for a very short time, but she just got through tellin' me she's movin' out of town."

"Not another one!" Wichahpi frowned sympathetically. I had told her my life story, and she knew about all the girls who had left me. "Let her go. If she's leavin' you, she ain't worth bothering about."

Wichahpi and I had shared a lot between us when we hung out together last year. Her mother, Shappa, was in on most of it, as well. The details are in one of my journal entries from last year. The short story is that Shappa cut her finger and my finger, then placed our bleeding fingers together and declared me a member of the Oglala Lakota tribe.

"You are Lakota now," Shappa had said. She also explained that I was now a part of her family, thus making Shappa my adopted mother and Wichaphi my adopted sister.

"Is that all there is to it?" I asked. "That seems too easy. I don't want to be taken for just another white-skinned, wannabe Indian."

Shappa repeated, "You are Lakota." Then she added, "No one argues with Shappa." She had a knife in her hand when she said it.

Even though Wichahpi and I are now considered to be brother and sister, there's really nothing to stop us from becoming a couple, if you know what I mean. In fact, Mama Shappa hinted strongly that she would be pleased if that happened, and I know Wichahpi leans in that direction, too. Frankly, it wouldn't be all that bad of a thing to be a couple with Wichahpi. She's pretty, smart, and wise for her age. Like everything else in my life, we'll just have to wait and see.

"So, who cares about her? Not me." Wichahpi declared, bringing my thoughts back to the here and now. She slid into the booth next to me and took my free hand in both of hers. The expression on her face—indignant on my behalf—warmed me.

I smiled at her and said, "You're right. I don't care either."

But I do care. I really like Jenn, and I don't want that feeling to end. I squeezed Wichahpi's hand, and she returned my smile. Her eyes sparkled like stars in a clear night sky, and I could see how she got her name, Wichahpi, meaning Star, in the Lakota language.

"What are you gonna do now, fake red man?" she asked. "For that matter, what have you been doin'? I haven't seen you since that night at Mama's ranch."

"Life's been hectic, like a runaway freight train. I've thought about you a lot, though, and I've missed you. I can hardly keep up with life these days."

"That's because your spirit is crazy mixed up, and now that prissy white lady made you sad." She slid closer to me, lifted my hand to her lips, and kissed it.

I didn't tell her that the prissy white lady is a muscled-up police detective who carries a gun in a holster under her jacket. I simply said, "Yeah, I guess I am a little sad at that."

"Not you, dumb guy. Not your silly head. Your spirit is sad. You need to make your spirit happy. It's not good to have a sad spirit."

"I'm not sure I know what you mean."

"That's just your silly head, not your spirit. Your spirit lives deep in the inside and is your best friend. You got two yous, and your spirit is the important one. Your head is your worst enemy."

"I can almost understand that," I said. "The world deals with my head all the time, screws it up, and then I feel terrible. But it's just my mind that's all screwed up, not my spirit, right?"

She grinned at me. "Not bad, *wasichu*." Wasichu is the Lakota word for white man.

I grinned back at her. "Don't forget, I'm your brother now."

She placed the hand that had been holding mine on my thigh and said very softly, "What if I want you to be more than my brother?"

"Wouldn't that be like ... incest?"

"Incest with you would be fun," she said, her eyes bright with laughter. "You let the world screw you. Why not let Wichahpi screw you? That would make your spirit happy."

"The last time we came close to doing that, your mama put a stop to it. The next thing I knew, she was poking my thumb with a knife and adopting me into the tribe."

"Mama's okay with it now. She just wanted you to be Lakota before you jump her daughter's bones." There was that grin again.

"Here's what I think, Wichahpi." I put on my grown-up face.

"I think you and I should start hanging with each other more. Go slow for a while. Date a little …"

"What is this 'go slow' thing? That's not the way Indians do things. There is no 'go slow' with love — at least not where I come from."

"You mean I should knock you on the head, grab you by the hair, drag you into my teepee, strip you naked, jump your bones, then order you to make me breakfast?"

I was being silly, of course, but Wichahpi started laughing, "Ha! You knock me on the head, and I knock you back. You got some sense of humor, brother. But you're startin' to think more like an Indian. You need to think like a warrior, not a wasichu mouse."

"You know what I mean, little girl. Can't we just take it a little slow? Just until I figure a few things out in my head. I don't want to mess up my spirit any more than it already is."

"Sure, brother. We take it slow. No insects today."

"Incest."

"Whatever, but I can tease you more than you can take. I'm gonna do things that will get you so hot you won't want to take it slow. We gonna have to do something to release the pressure inside, you know what I mean? Maybe not do the in-and-out thing, but we can do lots of other things. And don't ever try to stop me from kissing my own brother. You do that, and I'll tell Mama. She'll be after you with a meat cleaver."

I smiled. "Well, I don't want Red Thunder comin' after me." Before I could say another word, Wichahpi was sitting on my lap and kissing me right in front of all the customers, waitresses, and the restaurant manager. Nobody seemed to care, though. Everybody knows how crazy Wichahpi is.

She pulled back and looked at me thoughtfully for a moment. Then she grinned and said, "You need some medicine."

"I do? I didn't know I was sick."

"Not that kinda sick, stupid-almost-red-man. You are the kind of sick only an Indian medicine man can fix."

"Really? And how does that work?"

"Mama's sorta-sister lives out in the desert. She's what white people call a shaman, but Indians call her Big Medicine Woman. She can make your spirit better fast."

"She lives in the desert? Where?"

"Out near Palm Springs between Desert Hot Springs and Morongo Valley. It's at the end of a dirt road that takes off from the highway about halfway up to Morongo Valley."

"Palm Springs? Great …" I'm not sure if that's a good omen or a bad one.

"Great what?"

"Nothing. Palm Springs is a long way from here."

"Only a few miles. We'll take my car and go tomorrow. We can spend a few days."

"Wait a minute. Hold your horses!"

"Aww, you remember my horses." She smiled with exaggerated sweetness and batted her eyes at me.

"I do. I never got to ride them, though."

"You never rode me either," she said, then licked my cheek.

"What about this aunt of yours?" I said, wiping my face with a napkin. "Is she one of those Palm Springs Indians? Why isn't she up in Pine Ridge on the reservation with the rest of your family?"

"She's no local Indian, but she's not Lakota either. Mama just calls her sister because she saved Mama's life once when she almost died of a stomach thing. Aunt Kimi's mother was Navajo, and her father was Salish—what white men call Flathead. You can see some of both tribes in her, but she looks more Flathead than Navajo. She's real tall too. I think that comes from the Salish.

"Anyway, when Aunt Kimimela's husband died, she went to stay with a friend, an Agua Caliente, Cahuilla Indian, out near Desert Hot Springs. The woman had no other family, so she gave the house and land to Aunt Kimi when she died. There's five acres and a house up in the hills above the valley. It's nice, and no one else ever goes up there. On a clear day, you can see all the way to the Salton Sea."

"And she's a medicine man?"

"No, silly. A medicine woman. What's the matter with you?"

"I was just speaking generally. I don't know how all this medicine stuff works."

"You will learn. I'll take you to Big Medicine Woman. Stay with her two, three days. Make your Spirit happy."

"Stay with her? Three days? I don't know about that."

"Don't worry, I'll be with you." Then she grinned and added, "We can sleep together."

"What about the going-slow thing we talked about?"

"Sure, we can go slow." She leaned in close and whispered in my ear, "It will last longer that way."

I gently pushed her back far enough to look into her eyes. "Wichahpi, I'm really not sure I want to go to your aunt's place and have her do whatever it is she might do to me. I'm not into potions and spells and things like that."

Wichahpi corrected me rather sternly. "Big Medicine Woman is no witch, brother. She uses traditional chants and prayers, not spells and potions, to bring peace to your soul."

"Prayer? You mean like Christians?"

"Prayer is prayer. The Great Mystery don't care who prays."

"Oh ..." I should really take the time to think this over, but ... "What the heck, I'll do it. Pick me up tomorrow morning, and we'll head out."

"Great!" Wichahpi smiled and clapped her hands like she was ten years old, and I had agreed to take her to Disneyland.

"One more thing, though. What do I call your aunt? I can't call her Big Medicine Woman all the time. And I certainly can't use initials like I do for my name, DH. A BMW is a car."

"Don't worry. We'll figure it out when we get there. She'll probably tell you herself what you are to call her. I don't know her real name. She never told any of us. Mama called her Kimimela because she thought she looked like a big, beautiful butterfly, and the name stuck."

"I wonder why she won't tell you her real name?"

"A lot of different kinds of Indians don't like to share their real names. It has to do with guarding their spirit—medicine people, especially. They don't give you much information for fear of diluting their magic."

"So, she's Flathead and Navajo, but she goes by a Lakota name," I mused. "Kimimela—I like that. You Indians have the neatest names. Why do we white people have such boring ones?"

"You are Indian now. You are not boring. You are *Wanbli Woniya*, Spirit of Eagle."

Wichahpi's mother gave me that name at the end of our blood-mixing ceremony. "I'd forgotten about that," I said.

"You forgot your Indian name?" Wichahpi looked at me with astonishment.

"No, I didn't forget my name. I just forgot that your mother gave it to me. I haven't used it since then."

"Why not?"

"I guess I'm a little like those Indians that don't like to share their names. I know a few other Indians, but none of them well enough to feel comfortable sharing something as private as my name. My white friends wouldn't understand, and some would even make fun of me. Besides, like I told you before, I'm a bit shy about claiming to be an Indian when I wasn't born one."

"Well, your first reasons are good ones but don't ever let Mama hear that last one. She'll show you her Red Thunder for sure.

"I'd never tell her that—it would be an insult. You know what I mean, though. It's kind of a fad for white people, especially girls, for some reason, to go around claiming to be Indians when they're not. I don't want to be lumped in with that crowd."

"Real Indians know who is real and who is fake. You watch. When you meet Big Medicine Woman, she will know you are my brother."

"How could she possibly know that unless you or your mother tell her first?" I looked at her suspiciously.

"We do not tell her. She has no phone, and we have not spoken with her for a long time."

"How are you gonna let her know we're coming for a visit? You don't just drop in on somebody for two or three days with no warning."

"She knows."

"But how does she know?"

"Big Medicine woman knows many things before they happen. Knowing we are coming and knowing you are my brother is a piece of cake."

"Okay, it'll be a test. If she comes out with it on her own and tells us I'm your brother, I promise I'll take all the Indian stuff much more seriously. If she doesn't, I'll go back to being just plain DH."

I went back to The Hole to take care of a few things. I got some clothes packed and then sat down to get myself into a mood that would be more receptive to whatever the next few days with Wichahpi and Big Medicine Woman might bring.

I never expected my Christmas break to wind up like this. I realize that I'll be missing a few days of class, but it's no big deal. I'm all caught up and even a little ahead on everything. My gut tells me that what I'm about to experience is far more important than anything I might learn while sitting in a classroom.

The last year and a half has been interesting. Not too different from high school in that my days are regulated by class schedules and such, except that I have more choices, greater personal responsibility for success or failure, and many of my instructors treat me like a friend and an adult. What is very different is that non-school things have been coming at me like bolts from the blue. Activities, events, and people, both male and female, appear out of nowhere, leave their imprint, then pass on. I feel that every encounter is changing me somehow, cracking me open and filling me up. Now, I'm about to meet this old Indian woman out in the middle of nowhere, and she, too, will become a part of my life, even if I never see her again.

But what if she isn't home when we get there? I don't care what Wichahpi said. The old woman doesn't have a phone, so nobody can call to tell her we're coming. And what if she doesn't feel like having company move in with her for two or three days?

Well, it'll be a pleasant day out with Wichahpi. Maybe we can stop somewhere for Mexican food.

19
The Next Afternoon

At the Home of Big Medicine Woman

Kimimela's house sits at the end of a gravel road at the feet — or rather, up around the ankles — of the San Bernardino Mountains. Mount San Gorgonio looms behind it while the Coachella Valley stretches out in front. Wichahpi was right. The day is bright and clear, and I can see a glint of sun reflecting off the Salton Sea on the eastern horizon. Although it's only about a mile from the highway, the structure is secluded and nearly invisible unless you know where to look. The gray concrete blocks it is made from blend in with the rocks and the piles of car- and house-sized boulders. The single electric line supported by sun-bleached poles is also lost to sight in the grandeur of the landscape.

Since Wichahpi was driving, I was busy admiring the scenery and was surprised when we rounded a curve and came to a stop.

"Why did we stop? Are we there?"

"Almost. I told you she would be expecting us."

I followed Wichahpi's gaze to where a woman sat cross-legged with her eyes closed in the middle of the road about fifteen feet in front of the car. She held a large feather up in one hand and waved it in front of her. We rolled the car windows down and discovered that the movements of the feather matched the rhythm of a wordless, tuneless, yet hauntingly beautiful song she was singing.

Wichahpi carefully parked her car in a wide spot at the side of the road that looked like it had been designed for just that purpose. We rolled up the windows, got out of the car, and walked over to Big Medicine Woman. She finished her song and then spoke to us without opening her eyes. "I have been waiting for you two." She rose to her feet with surprising grace, her long black ponytails swaying against her enormous breasts, her necklaces clattering against each other. She is an imposing figure—Amazonian, even—tall and stunning in stature and manner.

"You are late," she said, still not looking at us, and walked toward the house. Wichahpi and I followed her, and the three of us walked the last twenty-five yards in silence.

"Why has my niece not visited in years?" Kimimela said as she reached for the door. "Now she brings her new brother, Spirit of the Eagle. This is good. Come, we have much to do."

I turned to Wichahpi and mouthed silently, "How did she know?"

Wichahpi shrugged and mouthed back, "I told you," and we followed Aunt Kimi into the house.

Kimimela's tiny living room is as cozy and comfortable as it is unconventional. It's a chilly winter day outside, but the only source of heat that I can see is a small, portable, electric heater in one corner. She has given the inside walls a thick coating of clay to insulate against the extremes of heat and cold that would otherwise seep through the concrete blocks. The little heater might keep it warm enough in winter, but I can't imagine getting through July and August out here without some sort of air conditioning. Even with the adobe insulation, it's got to be like an oven in here. Kimimela has been living here for years, though, so I guess she's used to it.

The room contains no couches, chairs, or tables in the usual sense. Instead, a couple of stacks of wooden pallets lined up against the wall and topped with homemade mattresses make surprisingly comfortable platforms for sitting or reclining. More pads are rolled up and arranged to give a person something besides the bare wall to lean back against. These two pallet sofas are placed on each side of the room to face each other. The bare walls are covered with designs Kimimela had painted directly on the adobe. I recognize the complex mixture of patterns as Indian, but I can only assume they are of Navajo and Flathead origin. I have no idea what they mean, but they are nicely done and very pretty.

The floor is dirt, but it's packed hard and as smooth as concrete.

There is a large circle inscribed in the middle of the living room between the two sofas that I was warned not to walk on. I'm sure that will be explained before I leave this place. Various objects are arranged on a brown cloth in the middle of the circle, including several large feathers like the one Kimimela held in her hand, a small clay bowl filled with water, a couple of arrowheads, and several other things I can't identify. Wichahpi told me these last few items had been passed down through her family for generations. "They are big medicine. Our ancestors' sweat energy still remains in them," Wichahpi whispered. "BIG medicine."

Kimimela told us to make ourselves comfortable while she went to the kitchen to prepare tea. So, here we sit, side by side, on one of the pallet couches. Being asthmatic, I am a little concerned about the offer of tea. I leaned closer and spoke softly so Kimimela wouldn't hear. "I hope she doesn't come back with some bizarre herbal concoction that'll throw me into an asthma attack."

Wichahpi lightly punched my arm and said, "Silly boy, Aunt Kimi likes regular tea like that black stuff you get at the Royal Scot. It's easier to make."

"Your aunt is…"

"Different?"

"Yes, but I was going to say she looks very nice. Very healthy. And she's so tall. How old is she?"

Wichahpi grinned. "You mean she looks like a regular person and not like an old squaw. And yes, she is tall. A little over six feet. I'm not sure of her age, but she's a few years older than Mama—maybe forty or forty-two."

"She's very pretty," I said, although pretty is not really the right word. Maybe striking? Stunning? Arresting? She is tall with large bones that carry just the right amount of flesh in all the right places. Her face is what people think of as classically Indian—high cheekbones, big, close-set almond-shaped eyes, a long, straight nose, and a wide, pretty mouth. The few fine lines at the corners of her eyes and mouth are evidence of wisdom, understanding, and humor rather than irritability and disapproval. She is the idealized pure-blooded, gorgeous Indian woman—a real Amazon.

"You were expecting someone more like my fat little mama?"

I felt the back of my neck grow hot, and I said, "I wasn't going to say that."

"No, but don't be shy. You were thinking it. Mama *is* fat, and she has health problems. Grandmother had a hard time birthing her, and proper food was scarce on the reservation at the time. That made Mama weak. Remember, *wasichu*, that Mama and Aunt Kimi are not really sisters and that all Indians do not look alike.

"You're right. I don't know what I expected. I thought your mama might have health problems even though she tries to hide them. I'm sorry about that, but I'm happy to find that your aunt is not an eccentric old woman hiding out in the desert, killing rattlesnakes all day and running with the coyotes all night. You have to admit, though, the sight of her sitting in the dirt in the middle of the road waving that big feather certainly gave that impression."

Wichahpi laughed and did not disagree. "Sorry to disappoint you. Aunt Kimi is just a regular woman. She does kill a snake now and then, though. Don't forget, she is a Medicine Woman in both the Flathead and Navajo Nations, and you gotta admit she looks like one. Her whole life is devoted to the old ways."

Kimimela is wearing what appears to be a large, handwoven plaid blanket with one end wrapped around her and secured somehow to make a skirt covering her from her waist to ankle. The other end of the blanket is pulled up her back and draped over one shoulder in front. Her jet-black hair is braided into two long, shiny ropes that frame her face and drape over her breasts, along with several heavy strands of beads, stones, and what look like small animal bones hanging around her neck. "Yep," I agree. "She does dress the part. I'll just have to wait and see about the 'regular woman' part."

Kimimela returned from the kitchen carrying a large wooden tray with a teapot, cups, and several different things to eat. She sat the tray on the floor next to the circle and said what I assume, based on her attitude and posture, to be a prayer in one of the many Indian languages she speaks. She seated herself on the other pallet sofa opposite us when she was done.

Finally, she looked directly at Wichahpi and said, "Why have you not come before this?"

Wichahpi blushed and lowered her eyes. "I'm sorry, Aunt Kimi," she said. "I have become too involved in the world, my job, and my own problems." She looked at her aunt and continued, "I have thought about you a lot—I just haven't made the trip out here. You know I respect your holy ways, but I wish you'd consider getting a phone so Mama and I can keep better track of you."

"My track is clear enough, Wichahpi," Aunt Kimi answered. "I do not need a phone to tell you that. It should be in your own mind. You have my blood. I gave it to you once, remember?"

"I remember. I guess that's why I never worried about you all that much. I knew I would somehow feel it if you were in danger." Wichahpi turned to me. "Aunt Kimi did the same blood ceremony with me that Mama did with you. I now carry some of her Flathead and Navajo Blood in me."

Looking at me, Kimimela said to Wichahpi, "So, you have brought my new nephew to see me. He will stay with me for three days so that his spirit may find harmony with his world."

"Yes, Aunt Kimi, but may I ask you a question?"

"Of course."

"How did you know we were coming out here today, and how did you know I was bringing DH?"

"Who is DH? I see only Wanbli Woniya."

Wichahpi's glance in my direction said, once again, *I told you she's a Wise Woman.* Speaking to her aunt, she said, "You even know his new name, Aunt Kimi. How do you know such things?"

"It is not his new name. It is his old name, only you have given it to him in Lakota. He has an even older name which cannot be revealed. It is the name he has known since the beginning of time. I know these things because they are in the wind—the messages are like particles of dust that come to me from all four corners of Creation."

I was shy about speaking, but I couldn't resist. "Excuse me, Miss Kimimela. You are aware that I am not a real Indian, aren't you? I mean, I'm just a white guy who met Wichahpi a few months ago. I had dinner at her house with her mom, and she, Shappa, did this finger-stabbing thing and—"

"You do not need to tell me these things. I already know them. Shappa has joined you with her family and with all her relations everywhere. You are now my nephew. I am your aunt. What is made so is made forever. You must call me Aunt Kimi, or just Kimi."

"I feel honored ... Aunt Kimi, and I thank you for allowing us to visit you like this, but I'm not sure about staying for three days, I ..."

"You must stay as many days as needed to receive the *pejuta* you need for harmony ... to be one with peace ... *wowahwa* ... in your spirit." She paused between each phrase as if she were teaching a child, which, no doubt, I am compared to her.

"*Pejuta?*"

"I use Lakota words while Wichahpi is here with us so that she may understand my intent. The medicine ... *pejuta* ... I will give to you so that you will become one ... *wanji* ... and with all of nature and find balance."

"Wow ..." We haven't even started, and already I'm feeling overwhelmed. I turn to Wichahpi. "This ain't gonna be easy. I can't even understand the words."

Wichahpi smiles back at me and pats my hand to reassure me. "You will do just fine, brother. Aunt Kimi will be gentle with you."

Aunt Kimi smiled wryly and said, "I did not say I will be gentle with him."

So, that's it. I'm here for what Aunt Kimi calls a *hanblecheya,* or vision quest. I apologize for my spelling. I've learned a lot of new Lakota words in the last hour or so, and I'm writing them as I hear them. I can only hope that the spelling is at least in the ballpark.

We spent the next couple of hours chit-chatting, sipping tea, and nibbling the snacks Aunt Kimi had prepared. The little room was cozy despite the wind that whistled through the scrubby bushes outside, and the pallets with their pads and blankets were surprisingly comfortable. Aunt Kimi's striking Indian looks are arresting, and her voice, with its distinctive tone and modulation, is melodic like water running gently over stones in a brook. She is, quite simply, beautiful, and it was a pleasure to just sit and stare at her and listen to her speak—almost mesmerizing.

I'm not sure what we talked about all that time, but I was startled when Aunt Kimi asked me, "Why do you wish to become an artist?"

What? How did she know about that?

"Well … I'm not really sure. I just know that it's something I have to do."

"Do you wish to become famous and make much money?"

"Not really … I've never thought about that. I paint because I feel compelled to show my way of seeing things. I know God did the best job of creating what He did, and I also know I can't really *create* anything. I can only take things that have already been created and smear them around on a canvas." I paused for a moment to find the right words. "Painting isn't creation. It's representation. I don't know how I came to that conclusion. I think it hit me one night while lying in bed."

"It is a good conclusion. No human can create as the Creator created, bringing something from nothing. The nothing itself was created by the Great Mystery."

"That's what Indians call God, right?" I asked.

"It is."

"Wichahpi and I talked about that one night."

"There is only one thing that humans can understand about God, and that is that He cannot be understood. He is a mystery.

His ways of thinking and doing are different from human ways of thinking and doing. That is why we call Him *Wakan Tanka*, which is Lakota and means the Great Mystery."

"If we could think and do things like God, we would be little gods ourselves wouldn't we?" I asked.

"You are right. That humans cannot think and do things like God proves that Wakan Tanka is truly their Creator and that all of Creation belongs to Him and not to them."

"And what, in your opinion, is the position of the artist in this world, Aunt Kimi? I want to be a painter, but I don't want my paintings to just be colors and shapes to hang on the wall because it matches the sofa."

"You already know the answer to that question, dear nephew. You have thought about it a thousand times. There are two kinds of artists in this world. The artist who paints for the world and the artist who paints for God. A true artist is one who paints to display the creations of the Creator and not the false, profane images of humans. A true artist is like a medicine man. You would call him a priest, for he represents God with his own work. As you have said, no human can create in the manner of Wakan Tanka. Humans can only borrow what Wakan Tanka has already made and go forward from there. The job of an artist is to keep humans honest about the process. The artist reminds humans that God is great and mysterious, not humans. From out of that mystery, it is the Creator who creates. Humans can create nothing. Painters of landscapes do this best as they paint wonderful images of nature. Nature is Wakan Tanka's greatest painting, so when an artist paints nature, he praises God and not himself or his culture. Society has always been and always will be evil, for it makes a mockery out of God in almost everything it does. An artist should concentrate on reminding humans of their Creator and that there is more to this universe than only what their childish eyes want to see."

Aunt Kimi's words are similar to a conversation I had with my friend Lissa, the one who became a nun a while back. "You're right.

I have thought about all that many times and have pretty much come to the same conclusion. Humans think they're so important because they invented airplanes and learned to use fire. They don't see that those things are like ornaments on a Christmas tree. They look pretty, but it's the tree they hang on that's really special. It's the tree that is the real creation of God, not the ornaments that hide it. It's the tree that has life. Ornaments take away from the beauty and the simplicity of the perfect little tree."

Suddenly, I remember who I'm talking to and realize what an idiot I must seem to her. "I don't know … what I just said may sound pretty stupid, but I do understand what you just said, Aunt Kimi."

"What you said sounded wonderful to my ears," Aunt Kimi smiled. "You have much to learn, and you will learn it while you are here with me. You are also very wise for your years, and if anyone should be a painter, it should be you. I am sure Wakan Tanka will agree with me on that."

After that, Kimimela invited us into the kitchen, where we sat at a small wooden table while she filled bowls with soup from a big pot on the back of the stove. I'm not sure of all that was in it, but it was a rich, meaty broth with beans and cornmeal. Very tasty.

When we finished, Wichahpi glanced out the window and saw that it was getting dark. "Well, I guess I ought to be getting home soon," she said.

"What? I thought you were staying here with me."

"That was my plan, but I believe now that you should have the time alone with Aunt Kimi. I might foul up the medicine."

The thought of being left alone for three days with this eccentric and imposing woman who would teach me mysterious things from the traditions of three different Indian tribes was unsettling, to say the least. I looked at Wichahpi, urging her to change her mind. "But …"

Wichahpi grinned at me. "No buts about it, bro. You are here to stay, and I am outta here."

"It is best that you and I spend this time alone," Aunt Kimi said as Wichahpi closed the door behind her. "We will join in many ways so that the medicine may pass from the Creator, through me, and into you."

The two of us returned to the pallets, where we faced each other in silence from opposite sides of the living room. Time stretched while her dark eyes drilled into me. I felt like a bug under a magnifying glass. I didn't know what to say or do, which was okay because I was powerless to do anything while she probed my psyche.

Finally, Aunt Kimi broke the silence, releasing me from her scrutiny. "Do you drink wine, nephew?"

"Yes, I do." I'm not sure if I was smiling at the thought of the wine or because I could speak again.

I watched as she got up and moved— Walked? Glided? Floated? —toward the kitchen. She returned with two coffee cups and a jug of wine that I recognize as being a step or two up from Red Mountain. She handed me the jug and said, "You carry this. The night is warm. We will go out and enjoy the evening with wine and conversation."

"I'll be happy to carry it," I said.

She pointed to the rolled-up pad on the pallets where I had been sitting. "Take that bedroll there. We will need it." She picked up a similar roll from where she had been sitting. I was relieved at this because the relative warmth of the evening was strictly a matter of opinion. I thought it was rather chilly.

Aunt Kimi smiled as she went about her preparations, and what a lovely smile it was. She is feminine to her core, more so than any cheerleader or fashion model. They are only girls, whereas Kimi is a true woman and more of a woman than any I have ever known or am ever likely to know. Something about her seems almost familiar, and I've been struck with a strong sense of déjà vu several times this afternoon. I have no idea where that comes from, as I never knew any Indian women before meeting Wichahpi and Shappa.

It's a strange feeling.

I followed Aunt Kimi out the door and around the back of the house. The moon is full, so the landscape is illuminated by its white light. In fact, the desert air is so clear tonight that even the pebbles are casting sharp shadows.

The area directly behind the house appears to be a garden. Some shelves or racks up against the back of the house look like they might be used for starting seeds and holding plants until they are ready to go into the ground. Some other panels and structures look like they might provide protection from the drying wind and harsh summer sun. The garden is not very big—only about twenty by twenty feet—but I'll bet Kimimela is skilled at getting everything she needs out of it. There is a small wooden shed about ten feet beyond the garden. I took a moment to glance back at the house after we passed the garden and shed and noticed a car parked beside the side of the house. I was glad to see that as it's a long walk to the nearest grocery store.

We continued uphill beyond the garden. I could not see a pathway even with the bright moonlight, but Aunt Kimi made her way without hesitation around the boulders and between the scrubby bushes scattered across the slope. She stopped about a hundred yards from the house at the foot of a wall of rock where the mountain range dug its solid toes into the alluvial deposits of the desert.

She unrolled her blanket, laid it flat on the ground, and indicated that I should unroll mine and lay it on top of hers. The blankets were thick, more like quilts, and more than large enough for the two of us to sit or lay side by side comfortably.

"We will sit here for now, and later, when it is cooler, we can crawl between the blankets," Kimimela said.

The thought of crawling between the blankets with this magnificent Flathead/Navajo woman set my mind reeling. Just think of all the romantic history encapsulated in this woman. Even from five feet away, I can feel the energy of the centuries and the combined genes of her ancestors. I can't help being full of awe and wonder.

We sat down on the blankets, and Aunt Kimi said, "See, it is quite warm this evening."

In my opinion, it was chilly out in the open with the wind blowing. It is January, after all. Up here, though, sheltered by rocks that still radiated the sun's heat, it was comfortably warm.

"Yes, it is," I said, "considering how chilly it was out in the wind."

"This desert is a magical land. It changes with circumstances and with those who are here to experience them." She turned to look at me. She patted the empty space between us on the blanket and said, "Move closer. You are sitting too far from me. Your experience with me has begun, and we must be touching each other while it unfolds. From this moment forward, unless I tell you otherwise, you must be touching me. You must touch my flesh if possible. If not, you must clutch my robe and hold it tight. Only in this way can our energies meld so that your spirit may heal."

I moved closer, but I wasn't sure what to do next. What did she mean about touching her flesh? She's barefooted. Should I take off my shoes and touch her feet with mine?

"Take off your shoes and socks so that you may join with the earth as well as with me."

How does she know my thoughts? I took off my shoes and socks, and the fresh desert air and the warm sand felt good on my bare feet. So, what now? Should I play footsies with Aunt Kimi?

"Here, take my hand." She held out her hand, and I took it. "You can write in your book with your other one."

I felt strange sitting there with my fingers intertwined with those of a goddess-like Indian woman who is nearly a half-foot taller and more than two decades older than me. Her hand is warm and dry, and I can feel her pulse throbbing as I squeeze it tight.

"Not too tight." She smiled wryly. "I will not try to get away. It only takes a light touch to transfer energy from me to you. It is best to be gentle when touching a woman."

I loosened my grip. "Is this better?"

"That is good. Now we may begin."

"What, exactly, is it that we will be doing? I'm not even sure why I'm here ... why I came out here to be with you."

"You are here because your spirit, your *nitch'i*, is unhappy."

"I thought *woniya* was the word for spirit."

"That is the Lakota word. Now that Wichahpi has left us, I will also use Navajo and Flathead words.

"Okay ..."

"First, you must find *yourself.* There is a difference between you and your spirit — they are not the same. For your spirit to be happy, you must know who *you* are and who your *spirit* is. You cannot be happy without this knowledge."

"I don't have a clue about who I really am," I told her honestly.

"You are an Indian," she said emphatically.

"So, you really believe that a white boy like me can be changed into an Indian just by touching bloody fingers with a real Indian?"

"It is not the physical blood that matters. It is the spirit within the blood. It is spirit joining with spirit. It is not a matter of belief, but a matter of Truth."

"But what is an Indian? What's so special about them? About you? Where do Indians come from?"

"The ancient knowledge of many tribes tells us that we come from the stars, from the Seven Sisters."

"Yes, Wichahpi told me about that. The Pleiades."

"She is correct. But there are Indians all over this world. Many nations, many tribes, many clans. They all have their stories. No human knows where the first Indian walked upon the Earth. Indians and others who live here in America did not originate here. This continent was an Eden filled with plants and animals for eons while humans multiplied and spread throughout the rest of the world. Eventually, after thousands of years, a few found their way to this new and rich land. Some came on foot over the Bering Land Bridge. Others challenged the ocean gods and came in boats and ships from Asia, England, Scotland, and Scandinavia, some by accident and some by design, to find new homes on the soil of this land. Many perished, but enough survived to give rise to the nations and tribes of the Americas."

"There's a big push these days to call Indians Native Americans instead of Indians. Do you know anything about that?"

"Many Indians do not like that name, and I am among them. Anyone born in America is a Native American. You were once white, but you were always a Native American because you were born in America."

"I never thought of that before."

"I believe that being set apart that way only contributes to the divisions already present in this land," Kimi said. "It would be better to call us something else. We were not the first race or culture to settle here. Vast cultures of plants and animals have come and gone on this continent. Other humans built their homes here and disappeared long before the ancestors of those now called Indians arrived.

"I see nothing wrong with being called an Indian. We are not so pure as to merit any special favor of names. There are many different Indians here in America. Many nations and tribes live on the plains, in the forests and deserts, and along the coastlines and rivers. Each is distinct in appearance, culture, and tradition. Indians are not indigenous. We just happened to get here before the modern Europeans. And just as your blood is a mixture of blood from many different European nations, Indians are a mixture of blood from other Indian nations. Many Indians now have the blood of Europeans, Asians, and Africans flowing in their veins.

"As I said, Indians did not spontaneously arise here in America. They came from places on the other side of this world. They are no more native to America than any other people. It is foolish to manufacture false importance of one race over another."

"I'm learning something already." I smiled, and in my excitement about what Kimi had told me, I squeezed her hand a little harder than I meant to. "Oops ... sorry."

She laughed and said, "Do not worry. You squeezed my hand because you understand my words. That kind of affection produces good medicine. Good energy."

Her reaction gave me courage for what I said next. "Aunt Kimi, can I ask what you are? Do you know your ancestral lines? Wichahpi told me that you are half Navajo and half Flathead. I mean … I guess it doesn't matter. I'm just curious."

"The Flathead people live in a valley just west of the Great Divide, not far from the Canadian border. The Navajo make their home in Arizona and New Mexico. The Flathead are people of the mountains, and the Navajo are people of the desert. The essences of both dwell within me. The Spirit of the Forest and the Spirit of the Desert have served me well over this lifetime."

"The yin and the yang." I smiled appreciatively. "Do you favor one nation over the other?"

"All nations hold equal honor with all other nations. My face resembles those seen in others of the Flathead Nation. The clothes I wear are made from blankets given to me by my Flathead mother, and the blankets we sit on are Flathead blankets of some age. But I also carry within my *nitch'i* many good memories of times spent with the people of my Navajo father. The necklaces I wear are Navajo, and the drawings on the walls of my house are Navajo symbols. I have also learned much of the Lakota ways from my long friendship with Shappa and her daughter. You will learn that ways and rituals have no meaning if they are only words and motions to be memorized and repeated as if one is an actor on a stage. If they are to have value, they must be made to penetrate the heart of the *nitch'i*. Only in that way can one achieve harmony, *hozho*."

"*Hozho*—that's a new one. What language is that?"

"It is Navajo for living in harmony with all things. The universe is a vast puzzle. All things in it fit together to make up the whole, and each piece must be in its proper place. One is in harmony with the universe only when their piece is exactly where it should be. The path that leads to *Hozho* is called the Way of Beauty."

"I've had thoughts like this before, Aunt Kimi, but I've never been able to put them into beautiful sentences like you do.

What a heritage you have. I am truly honored to be with you."

"You have Lakota blood in you now, nephew, and that is a strong, honorable heritage. Before your time with me is over, you will share my blood and heritage as well."

"What do you mean?"

"Do not rush the evening, nephew. Things will unfold as the stars move along in the night sky. Much wisdom is revealed after sunset, so we will be out here each night. We will spend some of that time on top of that hill." She pointed to a hill that stood out from the foot of the mountain not far from where we sat. "There is a flat rock on top where we will sit. The view from there is lovely, but we will not be admiring the scenery. Instead, the rock will bring visions to your mind."

"Just sitting on a rock can do that?"

"It is a very special rock. It is alive. It has great wisdom."

"Rocks have wisdom?"

"You have much to learn, Nephew, but you are not here only to learn. You are here to make your spirit happy. The learning will just be what it is, as it is. Sitting on the rock will help you do both."

"When Wichahpi told me I needed to come out here, I went along just to keep her from nagging me. Now, though, I'm beginning to see. I could listen to you for days."

Kimimela looked at me closely again. What she saw must have pleased her because she smiled and nodded her head. "Now it is time for silence. It is time for your spirit to touch mine. We do this so that your spirit will recognize my spirit, will learn to know who I am, and feel comfort in that knowing."

"How does that happen?"

"My actions will direct you. You must remain silent and open your mind to what comes."

Kimimela stood up and wordlessly indicated that I should lie back flat on the blanket. I obeyed. Then she set one foot on each side of my body at hip level and lowered herself, arranging her skirt to cover us both as she slowly brought her crotch down to meet mine. It took all I had to lie still and keep quiet as ordered. I was still fully clothed, but I had no idea what Aunt Kimi wore under her blanket. Maybe nothing. She sat silent and still for a moment after making contact, then she leaned forward until our noses touched, and I was reminded of my dreams with Annabelle. Kimi's breath was warm on my cheeks and smelled sweet, like fresh-cut grass.

What happened next was both wonderful and unsettling. She lay on top of me, still and silent, her unblinking eyes staring into mine, drilling deep into the recesses where my spirit resides. I tried not to blink, but I had to. I was uncomfortable because no one had ever looked into me like that. I almost felt personally violated, but it was also like making love, only without moving. I tried desperately not to react in any way *down there* at the point of our first and closest contact, but I'm afraid I failed miserably, and only one of us remained truly motionless. I also tried to look into her eyes and touch her soul. I thought that if I could, then something magical would happen.

I have no idea if we lay like that for thirty minutes or thirty seconds. I suspect it was the former. Either way, it was a very long time, and the longer we stayed together, the easier it became to maintain a solid stare into Aunt Kimi's eyes.

At last, the moment came when it seemed that we were somehow joined—when something inside my head fused with something in hers. I was reminded again of how it was in my dream with Annabelle.

In that sacred moment—yes, I believe sacred is the right word for it—I became Kimi, and she became me. I saw tears form in her eyes. Her tears overflowed, spilled into my eyes, dripped down my face, and fell into my mouth. Unlike Annabelle's tears which had no physical reality, I could taste Kimi's tears. I swallowed them, and when I did, my mind was flooded with images of experiences beyond my knowledge, things I had not done in this life, people I never knew, and places I had never been. In none of those visions of life and love was I a white man. I was unmistakably me, but I was an Indian! This all went far beyond anything I had experienced with Annabelle. Still, there was a familiarity, and I couldn't help but wonder if there was a connection.

Aunt Kimi broke the silence and whispered, "Open your mouth."

I did as she asked, then she parted her lips and let a mouthful of her spit spill into mine. "This is strong medicine," she said. "Close your mouth but do not swallow. Hold my spit in your mouth until I tell you to swallow."

We continued in silence and stillness, looking deeply into each other's eyes. At first, I felt like I would gag and wanted to swallow. That passed quickly, though. My greatest desire was to delve deeper and strengthen the bond between us. Then a single, wonderful image popped into my mind as clearly as if it were right there in front of me. I saw Aunt Kimi's face glowing like a thousand suns. She did not appear to speak, but I heard her say, "You have reached my spirit. You are here now. You are deep within. Can you feel my love for you? Can you feel your own love for me?"

I was powerless to speak, but I formed the words in my head, "Yes, I feel your love. Yes, I feel my love for you."

The Kimi outside of my head put her lips to my ear and whispered, "Is your spirit happy now?"

I answered back with my thoughts, "It has never been happier."

Kimi whispered again, "What do you wish to do right now, Wanbli Woniya? What do you desire?"

Without thinking, I wrapped my arms around her and hugged her close to me. I moved one hand to the back of her head, gently brought her mouth to mine, and kissed her. She didn't resist in any way. We held the kiss for a long time, and this extraordinary, ageless Amazon kissed me back. Passionately.

After what seemed like many minutes, Aunt Kimi slowly pulled away from me. She looked up into the night sky, then stood up in one graceful, fluid motion. I reached for the hand she held out to me, and she pulled me to my feet. She looked at me, smiled, and said, "Step over here." The pressure of her hand on mine guided me to stand next to the blankets on the ground.

"What are we doing now?"

Aunt Kimi signaled to me to be quiet and reached down and folded the top blanket back from the bottom one. Then she unwound the blanket she was wearing and let it drop to the ground beside our "bed." I had thought the blanket was just an extra layer over other clothes she wore underneath. I was wrong. I stood there and stared. She was, indeed, an Amazon Goddess. Her breasts were large and heavy, her legs long and flawless, her thighs and hips shapely and smooth. She seemed neither young nor old but mature and ageless.

"Take off your clothes, nephew. All of them."

I did as she asked. What else could I do? Then she lay down on the blanket and pulled me down next to her. She turned onto her left side and arranged the top blanket to cover us so we would stay warm for the night. "Lay on your side behind me," she said when she had made herself comfortable. "Press your body into mine like two spoons together."

I turned onto my side and closed the gap between us, matching the curve of my body to hers. The heat of her body was almost more than I could bear. I didn't know where to put my right arm, so I laid it over her and let it drape across her breasts. I didn't grab them or do anything with them because I wasn't sure where she was taking this. I lay like that with my flesh firmly pressed into hers, my hand motionless on her breasts.

"Just relax," she whispered. "I am sharing my heat energy with you."

"I'm sure my spirit is very happy right now," I said.

20
The Next Morning

We spent the night pressed together like two spoons in the silverware drawer. I hardly slept as I was intensely aware of her body against mine and worked very hard to control myself. I was also concerned that I might move if I fell asleep and break the connection between us. On the other hand, Aunt Kimi seemed to fall asleep as soon as we were settled and did not move the entire night — not even a twitch in a dream.

I drifted off to sleep eventually, only to be awakened a short time later by loud snoring. It was me. I was stretched out flat on my back and had been snoring my head off. One of my arms stayed wedged against Kimi's back, so I never lost contact with her while I slept. I quickly turned onto my side and pressed up against her again just to be sure. I don't know if she was aware that I'd pulled away from her in the night, but I have a feeling she doesn't miss much.

Anyway, there I was, wide awake, wondering what in the world was going on. Was this some sort of test? Maybe she's a little bit kinky, and she was just teasing me with her naked body. Well, she can tease me all she wants. I wondered what she would do next. What happens when she wakes up? According to my watch, it was four AM. The sun would rise in less than an hour, and she'll wake up soon.

"Yes, it is time to get up." There she was, answering my thoughts again.

"Good morning," I replied.

Aunt Kimi stood up and stretched like a giant butterfly, then reached down and took hold of my hand. "Let's go back to the house and make some breakfast. We'll leave our things here."

"Shouldn't we get dressed?"

"Why?"

"I don't know. I just thought if someone came along ..."

She smiled and shook her head. "That is not likely, nephew." She set off down the hill, and I had no choice but to follow as she had my hand firmly in her grasp.

Back in the house, Kimi pulled me along into the kitchen. "Sit over there," she said, indicating one of the chairs at the little table where we had eaten the day before. "I will release you while I work, but we will resume contact after I make coffee and breakfast." I sat obediently and watched while she went about her preparations.

The kitchen is simple but functional. A sink occupies the center of a long counter. There is a window in front of the sink between two cabinets. The electric stove and refrigerator look like they were new sometime around 1940, and there are none of the convenient small appliances in sight—no toaster, no blender, not even a coffee pot. Even though the kitchen is old and well-worn, it is scrupulously clean. Even the earth floor is packed as hard as concrete and swept clean.

The first thing Aunt Kimi did was pull a medium-sized saucepan from one of the cupboards, filled it with cold water from the sink, and set it on a burner at the back of the stove. Next, she selected a can from a row of similar ones of various sizes lined up at one end of the long counter. She pulled the lid off, held the can up to her nose, and inhaled deeply. "Mmm smells good," she said mostly to herself. She took the can back to the stove and poured some into the saucepan. She paused, peered into the pan, added in a little more, then turned the burner on. It did indeed smell good.

Next, Kimi opened the drawer beneath the oven, reached in with one hand, pulled out a large iron skillet, and set it on one of the front burners. My mother has a large iron skillet that takes both of my hands to lift properly. Kimi's frying pan is bigger than that, and yet she lifted it smoothly and gracefully from the bottom of the stove to the burner on top as if it weighed no more than a feather.

I'm beginning to think this woman truly is an Amazon. In

addition to her impressive stature — did I mention that Kimi is several inches over six feet tall? — and her ample physique, she is clothed only in the thick black hair that naturally conceals the temptation I was so aware of all night. Her large breasts are shaped by maturity, not age. They bounce and sway with her movements as if they had a life of their own, creating slight breezes against my own naked body each time she walks by. The show put on by toned muscles moving under the soft flesh of ass and thighs is also mesmerizing. The situation is surreal. It's like a dream — strange, exciting, yet so unexpected as to be almost impossible. It's almost as if I were sitting in the front row of the Stage One Theater watching a bizarre foreign film featuring this strange choreography of muscle, flesh, movement, and gravity playing out on a screen before me. Did the events of last night even transpire? Maybe I'm still asleep.

Meanwhile, Aunt Kimi has taken a stick of butter and a bowl of pinto beans out of the refrigerator. She cut off a piece of the butter and put it into the skillet. When the butter melted and started to sizzle, she ladled a generous portion of beans into the pan and stirred it around. She took the butter and the bowl of beans back to the fridge and returned to the stove with six eggs, which she cracked open onto the beans in the skillet. She stirred the eggs and beans a bit, adjusted the burner's temperature, then walked over to a cabinet standing against the wall opposite the refrigerator. When she opened the cabinet door, I saw that it contained shelves filled with boxes, bags, cans, bottles, and jars of various edibles, some of which looked like home-canned or dried produce from her garden. She returned to her workspace with something wrapped in a clean dish towel. She removed the towel and cut off a chunk of the cornbread it had been protecting. She rewrapped the remainder and returned it to the pantry. She cut the piece into smaller pieces and laid them in the skillet next to the egg and bean concoction, stirred things up again, and covered it with a lid. "Two minutes," she said after making a final adjustment to the burner.

Sure enough, two minutes later, Kimi lifted the giant skillet from the stove and set it on the table on a piece of wooden butcher block. She took a plate and a spoon from the cupboard and placed them on the table in front of the empty chair next to me.

When she was satisfied, Kimi sat down next to me, adjusting the position of her chair and the angle of her body so that we were in contact from hip to knee. The touch of her leg to mine produced an incredible sensation that was both magical and erotic. I knew, though, that the focus of this experience was not on the erotic but on something entirely different. I just didn't know what that something was.

Kimi sighed in satisfaction. "There, we have reconnected. Tell me what you feel. How did you feel when we were not connected, and what did you feel when I brought our legs together?" she asked as she filled the plate in front of her with eggs, beans, and cornbread.

I was too busy thinking of how to answer her to wonder about what I was going to eat. "In all honesty, I didn't like it after being linked with you for so many hours before."

"Explain."

"I felt heavy. While we were connected, I felt light. When we disconnected, I felt like I'd gained fifty pounds."

"That is good. Your spirit is using the medicine."

"That has to be it ... I guess." I really didn't know what I was talking about.

"Be patient. You have just started. You are but newly born into the awareness of your being. Your spirit has long been without the history of its own ancestry, so things must be done in small steps. You must join with nature gradually, not quickly. You are like a baby bird in the nest now, crying for his mother to feed him. Your eyes are opening, but you cannot feed yourself, and your spirit knows this."

"So, now what happens? Do I just sit here and watch you eat?" Those beans smelled delicious.

Kimi smiled and shook her head. "No," she said. "You are a tender baby. If you shovel large amounts of food down your throat, your spirit will be confused. Just as a baby bird must be fed by its mother, so must I feed you this one meal. Do not think it odd. It must be done this way. It will strengthen the joining process. Afterward, you will be able to eat on your own."

"Joining process?"

"Joining requires many steps. All must be done correctly and in order to be successful. Do exactly as I say, no matter how odd it may seem to you. When all is done, our spirits will be as one, and you will understand who you are. Put your trust in me, Wanbli Woniya. We have journeyed here before."

Aunt Kimi took a spoonful of the beans and eggs, placed them in her mouth, and chewed but did not swallow. Instead, she leaned over, put her mouth over mine, and transferred the chewed food from her mouth into mine. She fed me several bites this way, then took a few bites for herself. She repeated the action until all the food on her plate was gone.

I've seen birds feed their young this way, but never a human, but Aunt Kimi is not merely human. She is an Indian, and an ancient one at that. She's as much a part of nature as any bird. Even so, had someone tried to spit chewed food into my mouth a week ago and ask me to swallow it—not one bite, but a whole plate full—I would have thought them crazy, and I probably would have run for my life. But right here, right now, with her being who she is, and with her sitting there looking the way she does without her blanket wrapped around her, I trust her, and I would have done anything she asked me to do. I'm beginning to think that might be one of the things she's trying to awaken in me—total faith and obedience without question because it's right. That's the way nature works, isn't it? Why should humans go against the natural order of things—against the very laws of nature? She talks about *joining*, but how does it work? Do her spit molecules fuse with my spit molecules to become something new? I have no idea what I'm talking about.

I know I'm not here for lessons about nature or Indian stuff. As Wichahpi told me, I'm here to make my spirit happy. I don't know where these strange activities Aunt Kimi is sharing with me came from, and I certainly don't understand them. There are two things I do know, though. First, I'm happier spending this time with Kimi than I have been in my entire life, and second, I haven't given a single thought to the mental baggage I brought out here with me. Was it only yesterday? I am focused entirely on what Kimi says and does. It will require a real effort to go home when the time comes.

Then again, Aunt Kimi may not be trying to teach me anything. She may just be working to correct the imbalance between my spirit and my conscious mind. Even so, I'm learning a lot of things, and the guy who goes home to The Hole won't be the same one who left there yesterday.

Home, where is it? What is it, exactly? I love my family and wouldn't trade them for anything in the world. I call the place where I live with them "home," but I feel pretty much at home right here with this remarkable, ageless woman. Did I really meet her less than twenty-four hours ago?

21
After Breakfast

After breakfast, we went back outside, Aunt Kimi leading me by the hand as if I were a small child. She felt the tug when I slowed down when we walked by her car, an old Ford sedan, faded by sun and blasted by wind-borne sand.

We paused for a moment, and she looked at the car—somewhat fondly, I thought. "It takes me to town once a month or so for supplies and errands. I repay the favor by starting it up every few days to keep the engine oiled and the battery charged. A car does not like to sit for weeks or months at a time. If it does, it may not start for you when you need it."

"I'm glad to know your car is dependable. It's a long walk into Desert Hot Springs or Palm Springs."

"It is," she said as we continued up the hill.

Our way was not steep, so I had plenty of breath for conversation as we walked. "Aunt Kimi, can I ask you a personal question?"

"You may be as personal as you wish."

"You're really different from Shappa and Wichahpi. For one thing, you're a whole lot more *Indian* than both of them put together, but that's not all of it."

"What would you like to know?"

"Did you ever go to school? I mean like college or university. You're so at ease with this world, and you have an impressive vocabulary. You're not someone who just decided to go out into the desert and play with nature. What's the story?"

"I went to university. I studied there for eight years."

"So, I'm on the right track. What did you study?"

"I studied science. I wanted to work in a laboratory where I could be alone and play with chemicals and compounds and all of the things of which nature is constructed."

"Like chemistry and biology?"

"In part. Instead, I found that the elements of which nature is made are not the things that make nature what it is. There is a spirit and sentience within every blade of grass that cannot be measured in a laboratory. That inner essence makes nature, *Nature*, and it can only be experienced in the wild. Since this beautiful desert is here, and I did not want it to go to waste, I made the entire desert my laboratory."

"So, you quit the university and headed out here."

"I do not believe in quitting. I earned my degrees."

"Degrees? Plural?"

"Besides a bachelor's degree, I hold a master's degree, a Ph.D. in botany, and a Ph.D. in geology."

Once again, she has caught me totally off guard. "So, should I be calling you Dr. Aunt Kimi?"

"No, I don't think so. I also think it is time you stopped calling me aunt as well. To you, I am simply Kimi or Kimimela."

"Thank you. That is how I think of you. To be frank, I was a little uncomfortable with the aunt part."

"We will part soon and be separated for a time, but I will see you again sooner than you know. I will be in your life for many years to come. The course we have set upon is important and difficult. It is only natural for us to be less formal. The change will make it easier to succeed."

"So, you will no longer call me nephew?"

"I will call you by your Lakota name, Wanbli. That is a part of who you are. You are an Eagle. Wanbli Woniya, Spirit of the Eagle. Your spirit knows that, and that is part of why your spirit has been so unhappy. Our spirits become unhappy when our minds are confused and do not know or accept our true identity. That is our goal for you. I know that my methods seem odd, but you will know fully who you are, and your spirit will be filled with joy when this time together comes to an end. You will be the Eagle you were destined to be, just as I am who I was destined to be."

"You said I could ask you anything, so I will take you at your word and ask one more question."

We had been walking during this conversation, Kimi leading and I following. Now Kimi stopped and turned to face me. "You can always trust my word, and you should never be afraid of me."

I gathered my courage, faced her squarely, and asked, "What if I fall in love with you?" I paused to gauge her reaction. "I mean ... I don't really expect that to happen. After all, you're about the same age as my mother. We are not only from different generations, but we're also from vastly different cultures. We look different. You're taller than me." I think I saw the corner of her mouth twitch with that last statement.

"Is true love determined by age, culture, or appearance?"

"No ... I guess not. But just lay it out straight for me — right here, right now. I know there's no chance in the world that a woman like you would fall in love with a young, naïve kid like me. I just need to hear you tell me that so I can quit thinking about it. Just tell me that you think you're too old for me or that I'm not your type — the usual stuff — so I can try to put it out of my head and just concentrate on what it is I'm here to do."

"Why would I tell you something that is not true?"

"What?"

"I would be most disappointed if you were not falling in love with me. And since we are being honest, I have to tell you that I have been in love with you for centuries."

Before I could react or even catch my breath, she turned away and resumed walking up the hill. If it weren't for the tug at the end of my arm, I would be standing there still. My world had been reduced to the last words she said. I will do anything she asks me to do. Anything.

22
Late Afternoon

We have been stuck together all day. I don't think we've broken our flesh bond for even one second, although it hasn't always been easy. We are both still naked, and some of the paths Kimi has chosen have been rather rugged. I can't just hang on to her blanket to maintain the energy flow between us like I did for a while yesterday. Instead, we've been holding hands constantly. Once, when my grip slipped, I grabbed one of her ponytails so I wouldn't lose contact. I was afraid it might hurt her, but she just laughed and continued to climb up the hill.

Kimi encouraged me to carry my journal with me. I thought it would be awkward since one of my hands was already occupied with holding hers, and I have no pockets. It has turned out to be no trouble at all, and I'm glad I brought it along. Kimi told me that it would be good for me to make notes about our time together. She said that I'd be sharing them with the world sometime in the future, and they would help make the world a better place. I laughed at that, but who knows?

Kimi is not just an Indian, she's a Medicine Woman, but there's even more to her beyond that—something vaguely familiar. When I am most absorbed in the here and now, focusing on the task of holding on to her or where to safely put my feet, she will break into a chant that sends chills up my back and my head reeling off into outer space. Like her, the chants are unknown yet vaguely familiar, and they pull me back to the mental state required for this quest to heal my spirit.

"It should seem familiar," she said when I mentioned this. "You have been DH for only a few years, but you have always been who you really are. You have sung these chants yourself many times."

"How can I even know the words? I only know a few words of any Indian language, and I don't recognize the words of your chant at all."

"These chants are not Indian. They are far older. They are eternal."

That's the part I have the most difficulty wrapping my head around. She tells me that my spirit is eternal, and I can buy that because nearly every religion on Earth teaches it. She also tells me that I've lived as an Indian in more than one life and that I've even been married to an Indian woman before when I was a white rancher. Now she seems to be revealing an even older existence.

"You have lived as Wanbli Woniya in two other lives." Kimi is watching me record her words as she speaks.

"But are you also suggesting that I lived another life before my life as an Indian?"

"You will have answers to many of your questions before leaving this land."

What did she mean by that? This land? Did she mean *her* land—the plot of desert where she lives? Or did she mean the Earth? Did she mean that I will know everything before I drive back to Riverside or that I will know it before I die? There's a big difference. I do know that I have never met a woman like Kimimela and that my love for her grows with every breath I take. The connection between us only begins with my hand in hers. That contact allows the binding of my poor, confused spirit with the entirety of her magnificent essence, a pure, innocent, perfect, and eternal union.

We're sitting at the top of one of the hills between Kimi's little homestead and the mountains to the west.

Kimi smiles as she gazes down at her dwelling. "My tiny home looks even smaller from up here." Her smile is like sunshine.

She glanced at my journal and said, "Thank you for those sweet words."

"They're not just words. They're the truth. They come from deep inside me, where my spirit lives. My spirit is growing happier, and the longer I am with you, the happier it gets."

"You sound like your true self when you talk like that, and that makes my spirit happy." She smiled and leaned against me. "Are you cold up here in the wind?"

It's January, and it's windy. I should feel at least a little chilly sitting here in my birthday suit, but the heat Kimi and I share through our physical contact seems to warm us both. I know she is looking on as I write, but I answer anyway. "Not at all. As you just read, I'm fine as long as you and I are connected." I smile and ask, "What's next?"

"You need to tell your journal what we have done so far today. When the night sky comes a little later, I will show you the Star Dance. We will dance it together."

"We? I'm not so hot at dancing."

"The Star Dance is not like the grotesque movements that most humans call dancing. The Star Dance is worship and is Medicine for the Spirit."

A Summary of the Day Since Breakfast

Kimimela and I have been rambling through these foothills, naked and barefoot, since breakfast. If she has a specific goal in mind, I can't tell what it is.

When I was a kid back in Oklahoma, I spent all summer outdoors and barefooted in the fields and woods behind our house. My feet were calloused and impervious to all but the most vicious thorns. That was a long time ago. My feet are tender these days, and I've felt every rock, stick, plant, and bone I stepped on today. Despite that, my feet feel pretty good this afternoon. Also, I've been out here all day, naked, and while it hasn't been hot, it has been sunny. I should have a bad sunburn by now, but I don't. I suspect that my feet and skin are protected by my contact with Kimi in the same way it's shielding me from the cold.

I can't help thinking about if any of the desert rats that live out here have telescopes and what they must think when they see the two of us wandering around here stark naked. At first, I felt shy and self-conscious, but the idea made me laugh after a few minutes. Imagine: *Whoa! What was that? Hey, Jeb, you gotta see this. Thar's a man and a giant woman walkin' round out thar stark naked!*

It didn't take long to feel like it was right being naked. Now the thought of being out here fully clothed makes about as much sense to me as walking around blindfolded. Kimi's magnificent body has become less of a distraction, too. The rhythmic rolling of the flesh and muscle of her ass and the lively bounce of her generous breasts with their large brown nipples are still enjoyable to watch but, as I said, less distracting.

Kimi is reading along as I write. She's managed to control her laughter enough to scold me. "Just stick to your assignment. It will be dark soon, and you won't be able to see what you are writing."

Okay, where was I? I followed Kimi up and down through the foothills. Each uphill leg took us higher than we had been before. I couldn't see that we were following any kind of trail, but one seemed to open up as Kimi led the way. Any soft sand and smooth surfaces were behind us by the time we reached the top of the first hill, and it didn't take long for me to learn how to set my feet down on the hard, bare rocks without cutting or bruising them.

About a third of the way up, Kimi halted and turned to look out over the valley below us. "A little elevation means much in this clear desert air," she said.

I stood beside her and followed her gaze. Kimi's little house appeared even smaller and the layout of the nearest town was easy to see, as were other signs of human activity such as roads, scattered homestead cabins, and patches of desert that had been scraped clear for some future development or abandoned dream. I squatted on my haunches and stared out over the land. "It would be much nicer if cities were not there. Manmade objects scar the purity of the desert," I said. "Why can't humans learn to build things that work with the land instead of against it?"

Kimi looked down at me and smiled rather sadly. "Spoken like a true Nature Being," she said. "I'm afraid cities are here to stay, and it will only worsen with time."

"What do you mean?"

"Many years ago, this desert was filled with local Indians and other people who loved the desert way of life. Now it is filled with people who want to make money. It won't be long before those cities are overtaken by shallow, disturbed, worldly people concerned only with themselves and their deviant pleasures. They call what they are doing to the desert reclamation, but it is really destruction. They will soon obliterate the desert that surrounds them."

I looked up at Kimi and said, "I believe that. I believe everything you say. How can I doubt anything that comes out of your beautiful, ripe mouth?"

My words brought a mixture of surprise and pleasure to her face. "Ripe?"

I took a risk and continued. "Your mouth is like a ripe, succulent fruit—sweet to taste, juicy like plums, and so inviting."

She used the hand that connected us to pull me to my feet. She faced me squarely, put the palms of her hands on my cheeks, and looked deeply into my eyes, examining my very soul. Then she brought her face down to meet mine and, for the second time since I have been with her, kissed me, gently this time and so sweetly. We stood like that with our mouths locked together, holding each other while the warm sun beat down upon our bare flesh. For a few moments, we were transported to another time, another place. For a few moments, I felt eternal. I was somehow touching, *feeling* my true spirit.

After an unmeasurable time, she gently released me from the kiss, slid one hand down my shoulder to take my hand, and led me over to a large bush.

She gently caressed the leaves along one of the stems and said, "This is why we stopped here."

"What is it?" I asked.

"It is called creosote bush. It is one of the most wonderful of all desert plants."

"Why is that?"

"There are many reasons. It grows everywhere in both the high Mojave Desert and the low Sonora Desert. The bushes provide food and shelter for many small animals, and the roots hold onto the soil in the face of wind and flood. While not fit for food, the desert Indians valued it and prepared medicine from the leaves and twigs to treat many illnesses. Would it surprise you to learn that many of these humble bushes are of great age?"

"Really? I had no idea."

"Yes. Some are older even than the giant sequoias and redwoods of the Sierra Nevada and the California coast. The loveliest thing about the creosote bush is its fragrance — not from the flowers but from the plant itself. Some scent is released by gently bruising the leaves, but the full effect comes only with rain. Rain falling on the leaves sends the aroma sailing on the wind for miles ahead of the storm, and the fragrance lingers while the warm sun draws the remaining moisture back into the air."

Kimi stroked the branch again as if it were a pet. "Bring your nose close."

I leaned down and breathed in deeply, but all I could smell was dust and maybe a tiny hint of something that reminded me a little of some of the mediums I use with my oil paints. I shook my head and looked at her. "Sorry," I said. "I don't smell much of anything."

She smiled and said, "That's because there has been no recent rain. Wait just a moment." Kimi turned around and backed into the bush until she stood with one foot on either side of a leafy branch, then squatted a little and peed all over the leaves between her legs. She stepped out of the bush, shook the excess moisture off the branch, smiled, and invited me to try again.

I stuck my nose down into the shiny, wet leaves and inhaled, carefully at first, then deeply. I took another deep breath and then looked at Kimi with open delight and amazement. I'd never smelled anything like it before.

"You like it?" she asked.

"It's incredible. It's about the most wonderful thing I've ever smelled. I expected it to smell more like a telephone pole or a railroad tie, given the bush's name, but it's entirely different. Not exactly sweet or spicy, but fresh and invigorating. It has the same effect on me as the scent of the pine trees up in the mountains."

"It is the smell of the desert, just as pine is the smell of the mountains."

"That must be why dogs pee on bushes," I grinned.

"Silly man," she smiled and hugged me. "This natural fragrance, unnoticed by most of humanity but given by God by way of this common shrub, is one of the main ingredients for healing the spirit."

"I believe you. If the whole world were filled with creosote bushes, then every time it rained and set the perfume loose, all nations everywhere would cease their endless squabbling, and everybody would get along," I said.

"I doubt it would be that easy, dearest Wanbli," Kimi said. "There are many small things in this world that come together as a powerful force for good. Unfortunately, humans of all cultures, Indians included, are ignorant of such things. What once they all had, they all have lost. It has been destroyed by alcohol, tobacco, hatred, unforgiveness, greed, and politics and buried under concrete and asphalt. There is little hope now that they will ever rediscover their ancient heritage. The good has been overpowered, and it will remain submerged under the bad."

We silently pondered that dark thought, then continued our trek. We could have reached our goal—the top of the last hill before the lower flanks of San Gorgonio itself—quickly if we had taken a direct path. Instead, our walk was more of a ramble than a hike. Kimi picked out a circuitous route, frequently stopping to point out dozens of small desert life forms and features. She greeted everything—plant, animal, and mineral—as if it were a dear friend, speaking to and honoring each as if she had known it all her life. I was charmed and fascinated watching her commune with the native Beings of her desert world.

"They are all our family, Wanbli. You know that because your spirit inside you is paying close attention to all we are doing today."

"I do sense that, Kimi, but I would never have thought to dwell on it before today."

"The Lakota have a saying that has become almost a motto for their tribe — *Mitakuye Oyasin*. It means 'All Our Relations,' or 'We Are All Related.' Not just blood family, but everyone. If we are all related ... if we are all family, we will treat each other as we would like to be treated. All tribes have their own version of this motto, but this is the code all Indians are to live by. This code covers everything, just like the Ten Commandments and the Golden Rule. It is a simple code but a complex issue that covers not just humans but animals, stones, creosote bushes, clouds, everything, because everything is alive. Everything is sentient. Everything has an eternal Spirit. It is the way of the Indian. It is the truth from Wakan Tanka, the Great Spirit, and is to be followed and lived. The two words, *Mitakuye Oyasin*, are much simpler to remember and easier to take with you than the thick manual of behavior many carry tucked under their arm. The essence of these words lives in every atom, every electron, every cell, every Being. Their meaning should guide every individual's actions."

"I had a similar discussion with some Catholic friends not too long ago about the Golden Rule," I said. "We agreed that if a person remembered no more than that simple principle and lived by it, they would have a good start on the right path." I paused to consider a puzzle. "Those words, *Mitakuye Oyasin*, I'm sure I've never heard them, but they seem familiar."

"They should. The idea has always been within you, and you have lived by this code before. One reason your Spirit has been unhappy is that you have forgotten it. Now you remember, and you will be changed because of that."

"What you have told me brings up a question. It's a little awkward, but it begs to be asked."

"You needn't be afraid to ask awkward questions."

"This idea is God's code or instruction for how Indians should live their lives, and it is bred into all Indians, right?"

"Yes."

"Then, if that is the way God wants it, why do so many Indians hate all the white people today? Yes, white people did do some terrible things to Indians, but that was in the past. Most non-Indians I know acknowledge that and feel no hatred or anger about what the Indians may have done to protect themselves or retaliate."

"That is a good point, Wanbli. Many Indians today have fallen prey to the fads and practices of the common culture, and I do not mean the white man's culture. The common culture belongs to any human, Indian or otherwise, who chooses to be infected by it. White men do not fly over the reservations in planes, dropping cartons of cigarettes, cheap whiskey, and drugs into the laps of the Indians. Indians make their own choices."

"But not all Indians are this way, right? Wichahpi and I have talked about this. There are many Indians who want to put the past behind them and just live their lives as best they can."

"Yes, there are quite a few, but they keep quiet. They are intimidated by those who enjoy creating an atmosphere of rebellion and anarchy. I am afraid the Indian Nations suffer from an incurable disease that they have brought upon themselves. They have found it easier to sit on their porches drinking whiskey, wallowing in self-pity, and complaining about what was done to their people hundreds of years ago than to get a job and make something of themselves. It is easy to blame your own bad choices on someone else. The quiet ones among them have found it easier and safer to stay quiet rather than to challenge the troublemakers. Until Indians wake up and realize this truth, they will not change. They display their Golden Rule, Mitakuye Oyasin, proudly on the walls of their homes, yet ignore it in their own lives."

"That's a shame. It's a beautiful motto and beautiful words to live by."

"The real shame is that the spiritually healthy Indians do

not rise up against the bad ones and force them to keep quiet. They don't speak out against the evil that has warped the Indian Nations — stirred up by other Indians making money and reputations out of lying to their own people. Europeans of the nineteenth century and earlier once called the Indians Nobel Savages, meaning that their lives were simple as judged by 'civilized' standards, yet, the people possessed a nobility of spirit. Today, their lives are complicated, and much of their nobility has been lost. Their spirituality is buried under lies and emotions. White Buffalo Calf Woman is weeping for our people who have become shallow and hate-filled instead of the holy people they once were."

I reached over and wiped the tears from her cheeks. "Why are you crying?"

"I weep because of the hate, anger, and self-centeredness of those who boast of their regard for the sacred things of this world while acting otherwise — not just Indians, but all humans everywhere. They enjoy the drama of the role they have chosen to play more than the love and the forgiveness they should be offering. I weep for them because they refuse to change. Wakan Tanka weeps over this as well."

"You should go on the road with that speech. It sounds pretty good. You're not the first Indian I've heard express that sentiment."

"They do not want to listen to the truth. If they heard the truth, they would have to live by it. They would have to abandon their destructive ways and produce fruit in their lives. I would be run out of their midst if I spoke like that. That is why I live here as I do, in isolation. I am free to pray and practice the old ways without being threatened by drunk young men with cigarette breath and foul words."

"I wish I could do something. You tell me I'm Indian on the inside, but I'm still white on the outside. I doubt they would listen to me either."

"That is how shallow they have become. The color of skin is all that matters to them. They call the white men racist, yet, that statement is racist. I know many Indians, both family and friends, who continue to hate the white man simply because he is white. There was once a time when many white people felt the same way about Indians, but that was long ago. Our time to hate the white man has come and gone. It is time now to live together in peace and mutual respect. God is forgotten. Just think of the wonderful things people of all races and cultures could share if they would only get together in peace and love."

"Truth is truth," I said, "regardless of how it sounds."

"You speak the truth," Kimi said, smiling.

So, up the hill we went, taking note of every little thing along the way. If Kimi was following a trail, I certainly couldn't see it.

"Kimi, stop," I said after we had been walking in silence for a while. "Look at this." I pointed to a rock on the ground in front of me. It was pretty small, but it stood out from the others. It was pink in color and seemed to have been worked into shape with some kind of tool. It had the appearance of great age. I was reluctant to touch it or pick it up even though it lay there for anyone to see.

Kimi examined the flat pebble and smiled. "It is a game piece, carved many years ago by the local Indians for their children. It is very old. See? We are not the first to come this way. Why do you not pick it up and examine it closely?"

"I was afraid that it might be the wrong thing to do. Perhaps it belongs here in the desert, and I'm not meant to touch it."

"That is good thinking, Wanbli. Your spirit is happy that you say those words. In this case, though, it would be right for you to take the stone and keep it as you need ways to bring you closer to your own ancient heritage." She reached down, picked up the stone, and handed it to me.

"Are you sure? I feel like a priest being handed a sacred relic."

"That, too, is not far from the truth, sweetheart. That is your spirit feeding you impressions you need to remember so you can draw from them in the years to come. The game piece is a holy relic because it once belonged to an ancestor who followed the ancient path. His energy is still upon it. I have a gift for you back in the house, a small leather bag—a medicine bag—for carrying items such as this that hold great medicine for your spirit.

"Thank you, Kimi ... for everything ... for the gifts of your wisdom ... and for the gift of your love."

"I do it not just for you but for us." She smiled and kissed me on the forehead. "That was a sacred kiss. No matter how hard you scrub, you will never be able to wash it off."

"You called me sweetheart a minute ago.

"Yes, I did."

◎ ◎ ◎

She took my hand in hers, and we resumed our trek to the top of the hill where we are now, back in real-time. It's been sunny and warm all day. The upper seventies, I'd say—not bad for January. The sun is setting now, though, and the temperature is beginning to drop. Nights in the desert can be frigid, and there's no guarantee that the wind won't change and keep the temperature down in the fifties tomorrow. That's not exactly frigid, but certainly not suitable for running around the hills naked.

"You are of the ancient ways. You have suffered far worse." Kimi is still reading over my shoulder.

"Have I written enough, or should I continue?" I asked.

"It is enough. There are three more things to be done before we go back to our blankets."

"Three things? It's going to be dark soon. How will we be able to see the path back down the hill?"

"I know the path. I will guide you," Kimi said as she stood up.

Of course, she does. "I hope I don't step on any thorns. Or snakes."

"You will be fine." She bent down and kissed me on the cheek. "I will not let anything happen to you."

Kimi walked the short distance to the crest of the hill.

She is standing there now like a statue — no, more like an ageless goddess — surveying her domain below.

Still gazing out over the valley, she holds her hand toward me. "Our connection is broken, Wanbli. Come here where I can touch you."

I walked over to her and took her hand. She turned to face me and pressed her flesh firmly against my own.

"Here is your third kiss, the first of the three things we must do, sweet Wanbli."

The kiss was more intense than the two that came before. This time Kimi kept her eyes closed, so I knew it was meant to be of an entirely different nature, and I returned her embrace. This one had nothing to do with making my spirit happy. It was pure lust. Kimi began to sway slowly from side to side, and since we were practically glued together, my body had no choice but to mimic her movements. She pulled my arms down so that my hands, which had been on her back, were now on her butt, where she pressed them forcibly into her flesh. I knew what she wanted, so I squeezed the muscle and flesh of her magnificent buttocks. She slid her hands down my back and returned the favor.

We stood locked together like that for a long time, neither of us willing to bring an end to what seemed to be an eternal kiss. I thought, *So, this is the Star Dance Kimi told me we would dance at the top of the hill.*

I opened my eyes briefly, and my gaze was drawn to the horizon. A brilliant star, or maybe the planet Venus, had just become visible in the darkening sky above the mountains at the southern boundary of the valley. Star or planet — aside from the moon, it was the biggest, brightest thing I have ever seen in the sky. Its light seemed to penetrate the two of us, swaying together in some ancient, erotic form of worship not seen on Earth for centuries.

"Come," Kimimela whispered into my ear. "It's time for the second thing we must do." She took my hand, and we stepped over to the very edge of the hill. "Look down, Wanbli, and tell me what you see."

The last light of day was nearly gone, but I caught the faint glow of a large, flat rock protruding from the hillside a few feet below us. "It looks like a stone bench."

"It is a vision rock," she explained. "That is where we will go to see the images that will help guide you along your path."

"Seriously?" Before the word left my mouth, I knew it was dumb to say.

"As serious as anything else we have done this day. Be careful. The rock is an overhang. If you move too far out, you might fall off."

"Are you sure it's safe? What's to keep the rock from sliding down the hill?"

"It has been there for many centuries, Wanbli. It will hold us for what we need to do. We will sit toward the very back of the rock if it makes you feel any better."

"Whatever you say, Kimi. I'll do anything you want. If we do fall, then at least we will fall together."

Kimi smiled and shook her head. "I promise we will not fall."

We climbed down and seated ourselves carefully on the flat rock. It turned out to be much bigger than it had appeared from the top of the hill. The back end of the boulder was anchored deep in the hillside, so there was no way it would come loose and send us plunging down with it.

We sat close to each other and spent a few minutes silently taking in the magnificent view of the night sky over the vast desert below us. The lights of Desert Hot Springs, Palm Springs, and Cathedral City, sparkled in the middle distance below us, and the glow rising from Indio was visible farther away. Even though I believe those towns are all scars upon the land, their lights were lovely as they seemed to mirror the stars overhead.

"Now is time for the second thing we must do," Kimi said.

"And what might that be?"

"Give me your right hand."

I extended my hand, and she took it. I watched as she lifted it to her mouth.

"Ow! What are you doing?" I pulled my hand away and looked at the blood welling from my finger. She had bitten me!

Kimi just smiled and held one of her fingers to my mouth. "Your turn," she said. "Bite hard and make it bleed."

"I can't do that!" I objected. "To hurt you in the slightest way would be like taking a hammer to Michelangelo's Pieta."

"It is sweet of you to say that, but this is something that must be done."

As reluctant as I was to hurt her, I couldn't disobey. I took her finger into my mouth and bit it harder. She didn't even wince.

"Thank you, sweetheart." She kissed me on the cheek. "Hold your finger tight against mine so our blood spirits may join and become one.

"Like I did with Shappa?" I asked as I held my bleeding finger tightly against hers.

"Yes, like that, only more."

"More?"

"Yes, much more. Just as our bodies now share our physical blood, our spirits and the spirits of all our ancestors are shared as well."

"You mean my ancestors are going into you right now?"

"Yes, all of them. The spirit of your every ancestor is joining with me, and all of mine are joining with you."

"What exactly does that mean?" I'm sure there is more to it than the simple words imply.

"It means that I am now as much Viking and Druid as you are, and you are now as much Indian as I am. Our very genes hold the memories placed within them as they were being made. You now carry my genetic memory, and I carry yours. The two of us will soon be one, unified and balanced completely and eternally."

"Is this ritual from one specific tribe, or do all of them do it? The finger-joining thing is pretty much what Shappa did with me."

Kimi smiled. "It is not from any of them."

"What do you mean?"

"The rituals I do with you while we are together are pure. They were practiced long before any Indian nation or other human society existed. The joining rituals of nearly every Indian nation are similar because they exist in the dim, ancient memories shared by all tribes. The origins and meaning of those ceremonies have been lost and forgotten. Each tribe has altered them, added to or taken away from them, claimed them as their own invention, and passed them along to each successive generation."

"We used to play a game when I was in elementary school. We called it telephone. One kid would whisper something in the next kid's ear, who would whisper it to the next, and so on. The last kid in line would speak the sentence out loud. The sentence would have lost all meaning by then, or the words would have become unintelligible nonsense. We thought it was funny, but it's a good example of how a thing can change if you don't know first-hand how it was meant to be."

"That is indeed an excellent example. People seem to believe that motions and sounds are what empower a ritual and have little regard for the intent. The form of the ritual changes subtly with each generation, but that matters little. The original meaning or purpose of the ceremony is what makes it work, and that knowledge was lost eons ago to all but a few.

"What other ceremonies and rituals have been corrupted or lost over time?" I asked.

"Humans received the idea of love from God at their Creation. That idea became a part of every culture. Now, love is what humans have made it to be, not what God intended. Through many generations, humans have diluted and altered the concept of Pure Love. What is recognized as love today bears little resemblance to the original gift. The physical displays of love are very much the same from one culture to the next, even though the notion of what is acceptable in public and what should remain private varies between cultures and subcultures. Today, love consists mainly of ritual performance and recitation of meaningless words. The original intent has been forgotten.

"All of the so-called ancient ways observed by humans these days suffer in the same way. They have all been distorted by generations of mindless repetition by practitioners concerned only about form and heedless of original intent. Every ritual today is but a shadow or even a mockery of its original form."

"Incredible."

"Every ceremonial act I guide you through is focused on its original intent. Every ritual we perform together is the very essence of purity."

Kimimela finally separated our bloody fingers. "There is one more step to completing this blood ceremony," she said as she stretched out on her back along our stone bench. "Lay back next to me here on the rock."

Easy enough. I did as she asked.

"Now, place your hand between my legs."

"Really?" I had not yet touched her there.

"Yes." She opened her legs and guided my hand to her sacred area. "Now, press here firmly with your fingers. Move them around and tell me what you feel."

"You're very wet."

"It is the time of the month for my blood flow. My blood will open the door of the lodge to your memories. Use my blood on your fingers to draw a circle on your forehead."

I did exactly as she asked.

"Now, draw a circle around each of your nipples."

Three days ago, I would have probably run away from her and down the mountain. Now, though, the action seemed familiar and right. I did it without question.

"Good. Now, reach down and collect more blood on your fingers."

Again, I did as she asked.

"Draw three more circles, first on my forehead, then one around each of my nipples."

"Perfect," she said when I was done. "Now it is time for the third thing. Do exactly as I say. Do not talk, and do not be afraid."

I nodded my assent, and she opened her legs wide. "Lay on top of me here between my legs," she said. "Press your body firmly against my body, and press your mouth to mine."

I did exactly as she asked, but she issued one more instruction before my lips sealed against hers. "We must hold our mouths together in a tight kiss. Do not separate your mouth from mine. Close your eyes. There will be no more talking."

23
What Happened Next

It's difficult to describe what happened when my lips met Kimi's. My eyes were closed, but my head filled with the image of the entire universe. Spinning planets, stars, constellations, and galaxies whirled across my vision faster and faster. Then, everything slowed and came to a halt. I found myself seated by a blazing fire next to a teepee. The evening was cool, and the fire felt good. I wasn't just sitting there doing nothing. I was sewing—repairing a piece of clothing or something that looked like clothing. The night was quiet but not silent. It was filled with the soft crackle of flames and the subdued conversations of other people around other fires near other teepees.

I was concentrating on my task, so I was unaware of the woman who approached me from behind until she put her hands on my shoulders and spoke softly into my ear. "I cannot stay here long. We should not be seen together."

I replied quietly without looking at her. "My teepee is warm, and it is empty. Slip inside while no one is looking." The woman moved in the direction of the teepee, letting the fingers of one hand brush softly across my shoulders as she did. I took a moment to assess the work I had been doing, then bundled it up and followed the woman inside.

The woman sat on a pile of furs, smiling. It felt good to be with her. Her mere presence warmed the teepee more than any fire could. I moved quickly to her and took her in my arms.

"If we are caught, it will be terrible for us," the woman whispered. "You know that I am promised to another. We will be brought before

Chief Charlot and face the judgment of the people."

"Only human words bind you to another man," I said. "You do not belong to him. You belong to me, and I belong to you. We are forever. I will face Charlot myself with my own knife if I must."

"He is Chief. He is powerful. He would kill you, and I would be sealed to the other man anyway. The man is a friend of Charlot. Your death would be in vain."

"Then you must bear our child. All will believe the baby is his, but you will celebrate my presence in the child without his knowledge."

The woman looked at me and gently stroked my face. She was beautiful, and her smile was happy and sad and proud. She removed her clothing, and I removed mine. Then we laid down together on the skins and made love for many hours.

I opened my eyes, and there was the face of Kimimela, her lips still glued to mine, her gaze penetrating deep into my soul. The vision had not lasted long—only a few minutes—but I felt like I had spent the entire night with the woman. I also knew that while I had been making love to the woman in the vision, I was making love to Kimi. It wasn't at all hard to tell.

Startled, I lifted my head, breaking the connection between our lips. "What was that?" I managed to sputter.

Kimi pulled my lips back to hers, kissed me deeply, then released me. "Was anything in the vision familiar to you, Wanbli?" she whispered.

"I ... I'm not sure," I told her. "Some of it ... I guess. But ... I was with a woman who looked exactly like you, only younger. We were in an Indian camp with lots of teepees. It felt ancient. Like over a hundred years ago. Older maybe."

"What did you do with the woman?" I could see Kimi's smile even in the darkness.

I grinned and said, "Apparently, the same thing I just did with you."

"You made sacred love."

"Yes ... yes, we made love. And it did feel sacred."

"And what did the young woman tell you?"

"She told me that she was promised to another. I'm guessing that meant marriage to another man, not me. She was worried that the chief of the tribe would find out that we were in love. She said we'd be brought before him and judged. I don't think that would have been pretty."

"You have seen clearly," Kimi said. "Now, I want to ask you an important question. Think carefully before answering, as the answer is important for making your spirit happy again."

"Okay ... I'll do my best."

"What was the woman's name?"

"Uhm, I'm not sure. She didn't say."

"I know she didn't, but it is important. Simply seeing her face in your vision will cause you to remember. Think hard, Wanbli. Look at her face. What was her name?"

"Well ... I think it was ... I think it started with ... it was an unusual name for a girl." I sounded like an idiot.

"Go on. You know the name. It is buried deep within you. It is a part of your soul."

"It started with an A. I think."

"Go on."

"It was short... Adele ... Allie ... something strange ... A rock? That's it. It was Agate. What an odd name for a girl, but I'm sure that's what it was — Agate."

Kimi's smile returned, "Yes, Agate. That is what it was and still is."

"A rock ... how strange."

"Yes, a rock."

"What do you mean, 'still is?' She'd be dead by now."

"Would she?" Kimi smiled. "I can tell you no more. I know you have many questions about what you have just seen, but you must recall these things yourself. You must also know that there is more to the eternity of the memories than just the Indian ways. One day you will remember ways that are far older and far more important to your existence."

"Great ..."

"The purpose of the vision was to secure your own belief in your Indian heritage. It was also to introduce you to your memories of Agate and all she meant to you. There is a reason for that, too."

A fresh memory of the vision came to me. I looked at Kimimela in amazement and said, "She looked just like you, Kimi."

"Yes, she does," Kimi answered in the present tense and somehow managed to gently caress me with her entire body.

"Are you telling me that you and Agate are one and the same?"

"I am telling you that you must remember things on your own."

"But ..."

"Quiet." She began kissing me again. "Stop talking and finish what you were doing with Agate."

◎ ◎ ◎

We made love throughout the night, returning to Kimi's house down the hill in the morning. Once there, she made us an excellent breakfast of eggs scrambled with beef chunks and veggies, fried potatoes, and some Indian flatbread that she had made a few days before in a skillet over an open fire in front of her house. It was all very delicious.

In the daylight, as we came back down the hill, I noticed that Kimi and I were covered in her blood, our hair was ratty and tangled, and our feet and hands were filthy. We looked like two wild savages standing on a high hill overlooking their primeval homeland.

"How do you feel?" Kimi asked.

I grinned and replied, "I can't even begin to describe how I feel."

"Is your spirit happy now?"

"I doubt it could ever be happier. I hope it stays like this."

Kimi hugged me to her and said, "You need to know that, after today, you will not see me again for two years. You will remember me and often feel my presence, but I will not be a part of your physical life."

"What? Why?" I did not like what she was saying.

"It is the way it must be. You have things you must do to prepare yourself for your own future. Your past must remain dormant for a little longer."

"But why can't I come out and visit you now and then? Like once or twice a week … or maybe seven times a week."

"You must concentrate on others, not on me. Many new humans will come into your life, some you will love, and others you will not. Some will be with you for only a short time, and then they will die. You will find other women to hold."

"After you, I don't want any more women."

"It must be so. It is a part of your growth. You must experience many things. Knowledge is important, and relationships will bring knowledge."

"Will I be an artist?"

"You can be anything you wish, but art will be a large part of your life. You will count many artists among your companions in life, starting with those you have met or will meet as a student at RCC. Before the summer is over, you will have a solid base of friends among many people. You will also have experienced love and despair. Mystery will be a part of your life as well. Someone is waiting at this moment to bring a great new mystery into your life. She will be like magic. You will know her, yet you will not know her. She will be there, but not there. Her Spirit is eternal, and she is a part of us both."

"What are you talking about? Now I'm really confused."

She smiled wistfully and said, "I have said too much already. I want to see for myself where and how you live in this life. I will take you home to your Hole when we have finished breakfast. After that, I will drive back here to my land and spend the next two years reliving my memories of the short time you and I had together in this life."

I was about to question Kimi's meaning of her last statement, but she took my hand and started leading me back down the hill. The only other words that passed between us on the way down were when she asked, "Do you wish to take a bath before you dress?"

"No," I replied. "I don't ever want to wash you off of me. I will wear you like this until it disappears naturally."

Kimi laughed. "That could take days. You will begin to stink, and your friends will leave you."

"I don't care. That is the way it must be."

"Now you are you—the real you."

"But who is that? I have all these different bloods inside me. What does that make me?"

"You are a mix, just like me. You are part Lakota, part Navajo, part Flathead, but most importantly, you are part me and everything. I am no longer me, and you are no longer you. We are *we*, as we have always been." She paused and smiled pensively before continuing. "We go far back in time together, way beyond Indians or white men. Your spirit must be dancing now."

"Yes, it is. I can feel it."

Back in the Hole

It's 8 PM, and I'm sitting here alone—again—in The Hole, and Kimimela has returned to her desert and her life alone in the wild.

The day was perfect. We laughed, we played, and we made love in many places. We talked about many things but mostly about art and what I will do with my life. I told her I didn't really know about my plans for the future. I'm young, and a lot can happen to change plans quickly, so it's foolish for me to set a course right now. I also told her that I'll never forget my time with her, regardless of what I do. That time contains an eternity of memories, ancestors, and things I have yet to figure out. The images I received on the Vision Rock included fleeting memories of a time long before those of the Indian village and Agate. They took place in a different setting, perhaps even another country. Kimi assured me that those experiences will be clarified as my life proceeds. I certainly hope so.

I have spent many hours alone here on my bed, but pulling away and disconnecting from Kimi has left me feeling disoriented and sad. To be sitting here on my bed without the naked body of Kimi clinging to me is the loneliest I have ever been. I would like to have stayed there with her on her land in the desert and never come back, but while we sat on the edge of the grotto overlooking the city of Riverside just before she left to go home, Kimi insisted that I had to live my life without her.

"You must gain knowledge of this world and its culture on your own," she explained. "That is the only way you will be able to retain what you learn and make use of it."

She went on to tell me that my journals would be a valuable resource one day. "The experiences recorded will find their way into the books you will write," she said.

When I laughed, she looked at me seriously and said, "Many people will read of your adventures, and it will all be to fulfill a purpose. Remember that just as those who paint for Wakan Tanka are priests, so too are writers who write for Wakan Tanka." Then she smiled and said, "But the true adventure of all time lies out there," pointing up at the stars.

What could be *out there* that would be an adventure for me? Somehow, I knew that what she had just said was more important than anything else I'd learned from her. I *felt*, deep down, that it was true.

That new sense that I can *feel* things is something that had returned with me from the desert. I've always been psychic, but something else happened on that desert hilltop that expanded my intuitive reach. Was it Kimi's blood? Was it our lovemaking on the Vision Rock? Was it my vision of the Indian woman, Agate, who is supposed to be very dear to me? Was it something from the long-distant past in a foreign land? Or was it all of the above? I suspect it was all of the above. During the unmeasurable time that Kimi and I laid on the Vision Rock with our mouths held tightly together, I *felt* something powerful that did not leave me when the vision was over, and I was back in the here and now. The power was now a permanent part of me.

I know I'm changed, but what have I become? I'll be going back to classes at RCC—I've actually missed a few to spend time in the desert, but I doubt anyone will notice. What's in store for me there? Will I hang out with the same old players, or will new ones come along in this game called My Life? I know I'll be cultivating my friendship with Frank Reed. Aside from all that I can learn from him, I genuinely like the guy, and he seems to take me seriously as both a friend and an artist. There are others I don't want to let go of, either: my best buddy Manny, Jack the sculptor, Wichahpi, of course—there's another relationship I need to think through. And Jenn, too. What do I do about Jenn?

And what about the person who is supposed to bring the Great New Mystery into my life? This person who, according to Kimi, will *be there and not be there*, and who is a part of both of us. What the heck does that mean? Who could that person be? I will be making many memories with many people, but I honestly believe that the memories of my time spent with Agate are enough to sustain me for at least two years, maybe a lifetime.

Whoa! Where did that come from? I just called Kimi, *Agate*. There is definitely more going on here than I can possibly understand. Where does reality stop, and memory, personal or ancestral, begin? Is the memory of an actual event any different from the memory of a dream or a vision?

How do I get on with my life knowing all I now know? How can I act normal around others when I know that nothing in this world is as it seems? How do I return to the life I knew just a few days ago? No matter what I do, I will be living a lie.

My only choice is to try to forget where I have been and what I have done. Forget Kimi—Agate—and my own ancient history. Forget it all and never think about it, talk about it, or mention it again. I will immerse myself in the routine of everyday life like everyone else does.

Still, this secret will always be with me, and it may want to burst out of me at any time. All I can do is control it as best I can, for as long as I can.

I'm not sure it can be controlled.

Made in the USA
Columbia, SC
20 May 2022